A BROTHER
TO DRAGONS

Also by Kent Harrington

THE GIFT OF A FALCON

A BROTHER TO DRAGONS

A NOVEL BY

KENT HARRINGTON

DONALD I. FINE, INC.

New York

Copyright © 1993 by Kent Harrington

All rights reserved, including the right of reproduction in whole or in part in
any form. Published in the United States of America by Donald I. Fine, Inc.
and in Canada by General Publishing Company Limited.

Library of Congress Cataloging-in-Publication Data
Harrington, Kent.
A brother to dragons / by Kent Harrington.
p. cm.
ISBN 1-55611-347-1
I. Title.
PS3558.A6294B76 1992
813'.54—dc20   92-54464
CIP

Manufactured in the United States of America

Designed by Irving Perkins Associates

10 9 8 7 6 5 4 3 2 1

To my parents Joe and Sally,
and again, to my wife, Toni

I went mourning without the sun.
I stood up and cried in the congregation.
I am a brother to dragons . . .

The Book of Job 30:28–29

CHAPTER

1

BLUNT FINGERS made a struggle of work in small places.

The night air had a pure mountain chill, steadily drawing warmth from bare skin. Under the car, Vito Rocchi blew on his hands, a vain therapy. He silently cursed the cold and the discomforts induced by his necessary contortion. On his back Rocchi reached up, feeling inside the fender to find the bottom edge. It was bent at a right angle, a tiny shelf created by the drop forge from the minor but necessary margin of steel sheet that had extended beyond the die for the rear body panel. Rocchi's fingers followed the sharp metal lip along the downslope of the wheelwell, then paused. He unrolled two wires from the spool in his pocket, fitting them into the convenient groove. Their insulation, tacky with mastic, bonded quickly to the tarry undercoating.

Rocchi slid forward, a childlike shimmy for a two hundred and twenty pound man. Searching, he discovered the heavy flange demarcating the end of the fender. He reached farther to explore the next body panel, a narrow strip beneath the passenger door. His hand played back and forth, fingers tapping. The hollow beat repeated arrhythmically, telegraphing his uncertainty.

A few feet away, under the engine block, Carlo Vitale froze at the sound. In the darkness, Rocchi appeared as a shape with animated appendages. "Hey," Vitale whispered.

The motion with accompaniment continued.

"Hey!" He whispered again, louder this time.

The drumming stopped.

"What's with the noise?" Vitale asked.

Rocchi muttered. "Fuckin' Japs."

"Huh?" Vitale craned his neck, as if a better view of Rocchi's supine hump would disclose the source of his prejudice.

"I said, fuckin' Japs."

1

"Whaddya talkin' about?" Vitale asked.

"Fuckin rocker panel, that's what!"

"For Chris' sake, keep it down, willya?" Vitale hissed.

Rocchi ignored him. "Ain't no lip on the fuckin' rocker! American cars, ya know what ya got, but this piece a shit? I mean what kinda rocker is this? Fuckin' thing's sealed up tight, front and back. You tell me. Where am I gonna put the wires?"

"What's this? You don' like the car, don' buy one. Jus' get me the leads. Wrap 'em around a hydraulic line or somethin'."

"Ya mean ya wan' me to pull all this out?" Half under the car, Rocchi tried to wave his arm and failed.

"Yeah," Vitale said.

"I mean, this ain't my fuckin' life's work."

"Jus' do it!"

Rocchi groaned. He squirmed on the concrete, edging back toward the rear of the car. He yanked on the wires, unsticking the pair as he moved. From the valley, a few morning sounds rose, transported by the night air in disembodied perfection. A truck laboring through its gears on the interstate expressway. More distant, an ambulance siren wavering in brief warning. Closer, a door slamming to record an early departure, a harbinger of the day.

Rocchi reached the rear of the car. He slid half his bulk underneath, his hand following the wires to the gas tank. Designed to allow for the rear suspension's knee action, the tank was oddly shaped. It hung between the axle and the floor of the trunk, fitted to the available space. Rocchi traced the twin wire strands into one of its indentations.

Even in the cold, the plastique was soft, a crumbly putty. It had molded easily, conforming to the niche in the fiberglass. The detonator, no bigger than a pencil stub, was buried a half thumb's depth inside. When the key turned, the first surge of current from the battery would produce incandescence, creating a small explosion, the necessary modicum of heat and pressure to ignite its host. A microsecond, quicker than the spark plugs would fire. That was all. No more.

Rocchi double-checked the detonator's leads. His yanking and tugging had not loosened them. He groped, this time finding the hydraulic lines from the rear brakes, and began again, using a long basting stitch to thread the wires around the steel tubing. In four minutes, grunting and squirming, he had retraced his path and was on his back head to head with Vitale, staring up at the engine.

"Hurry up, I'm freezin'." Rocchi thrust the wires toward Vitale, who ignored them.

A few inches above them, a bright dot danced erratically on the starter.

From the penlight clipped under the brim of his baseball cap, it identified the subject of Vitale's attention. Not unlike a surgeon, he had neatly arranged a small inventory of tools on a cloth beside him. Without turning his head, Vitale fingered the items, finding a knife. He gripped the starter's electrical cable and in a single stroke, slit the insulation on its underbelly. The incision exposed woven steel strands.

"Lesson number one. Never use the connectors. Starter, generator, nowhere. It's too easy. They always look there first," Vitale said. He put down the knife and ran a thumb along the cut in the insulation, opening it wider. "People are lazy, ya know? Maybe they open the hood, stare at the engine. Okay. But nobody looks underneath, crawls around, checks it out. Bobby Gambone in Seattle, remember him? He knew he had big trouble with Vegas. With Luigi Vario, my boss, ya know? I mean, when the contract went out on him, Gambone watched everything, what he ate, who he screwed, where he traveled. Never took a crap wit'out two other guys in the can, ya know what I mean? But get down on his knees in the driveway?" Vitale shook his head, contemplating the foibles of human behavior. "They don' wanna get their pants dirty."

"Get movin', willya? My ass is froze to the driveway." Rocchi's disinterest was palpable.

"What time is it?" Vitale asked.

"Whaddya gettin' paid by the hour?"

"I said, what time?"

Rocchi squinted at his watch. "Four-thirty, four-forty. Come on."

"Good. Nobody moves here till five." Vitale worked methodically. From his inventory, he picked up a small rubber ball. A shoemaker's needle, an inch and a half of tempered stainless steel, protruded. Threaded through the needle's eye, two bare wire strands stood erect like insect antennas, each canted at its own angle. Replicating the far-sighted's adjustment of object and eye, Vitale held the needle at half-arm's length and tipped his head, aiming his penlight. The small, bright circle homed on its target, illuminating a neatly soldered connection. He pulled at the wires and needle gently, testing its durability.

"Somethin' I don't understand," Vitale said.

"What's to understand?" Rocchi asked.

"I mean, your boss calls Vario for a special favor. I come all the way from Vegas. We could get this guy easy enough. What's his name? DiGenero?"

"Yeah."

"You found him, you cased him, you called me, we're in the driveway. So, why are we screwin' around with this job? Why not do him and get it over with?" Vitale asked.

"Cause that's not the way Johnny wants it."

"That don't answer my question."

"Scarlese wants to send him a message," Rocchi said.

"A message?" Vitale repeated the word skeptically. He took the pair of wires from Rocchi's hand and matched their bare ends with the needle's twin leads. "So you been lookin' to whack this guy for ten years. Finally, you find him, but Scarlese wants to send him a message?"

"What is this, twenty fuckin' questions? Jus' finish the job, alright?"

Vitale mated the wires with the needle's leads, twisting them together gently, a pair at a time. He rummaged in his jacket pocket, extracting two wirenuts, small black plastic dunce caps. He threaded each over the connections. Vitale focused the penlight, examining his work. He pulled gently, then smiled, satisfied. Vitale slipped his hands inside his jacket, warming them. "You hit even close to a FeeBee, they're gonna go crazy, you know that," he said. "I mean, if this is the guy that put away Scarlese's old man fifteen years ago, where do you think the FBI's gonna look first?"

"Johnny knows what he's doin'," Rocchi said.

"If you say so." Vitale extracted his hands and patted his jacket, finding the needle and wires where he had left them resting on his chest. The penlight's dot zigzagged on the engine's oil pan, then paused on the starter cable. Vitale slipped the needle into the cut, laying it lengthwise against the bare steel. He produced a small tube of epoxy, applying the glue fastidiously, then pressed the insulation closed, covering the needle. Only the two wire leads, the implant's umbilical, protruded. He curled the excess wire into concentric loops, securing them unobtrusively to the underside of the cable with a strip of electrician's tape, black on black.

Rocchi fidgeted. "Let's go."

The small white circle played back and forth from starter to cable to wires, highlighting the object of Vitale's concentration as he double-checked his handiwork.

"Come on." Impatient, Rocchi grunted, struggling from under the car.

Vitale collected his paraphernalia, pocketing his tools and folding the small cloth. He lay back for a moment as if contemplating additional finishing touches. "I don't know," he said.

Rocchi squatted, peasantlike, balancing with one hand on the car. He bent down, peering at Vitale's legs. "You don' know what?"

Vitale didn't answer.

A block distant, a dog barked tentatively, a morning inquiry seeking response, rather than a warning. Rocchi yanked on Vitale's pant cuff. "Come on."

Unperturbed, Vitale spoke. "The C4's okay, right? You double-checked the leads to the detonator like I told you?"

"Yeah."

"You sure?"

"Yeah, yeah."

Vitale's heels scraped on the concrete. He wiggled halfway out then paused, taking a final look. "I don't know."

"For Christ sake."

"It's jus' that I ain't never done a woman."

Rocchi rolled his eyes. "You stay there much longer, you ain't gonna do nobody. She's gonna run you fuckin' over."

Vitale emerged. He crouched, brushing off his pants and jacket. He glanced at the darkened house. "Well, one thing's for sure. With a half pound on the tank, she ain't gonna feel a thing."

As always, when she rose her sounds woke him. As always, he rolled to her side of the bed, into her warmth, and listened. As always, her sequence was unfailing, a ritual's certain routine. A few feet away, the rustle of a robe. A click, the bedroom door closing. Slippered steps, almost too soft for the hearing, then silence, the time of transit in the hall. Pipes banging hard, once, twice, then distant water running. A pause followed by a scrape, metal on metal, a full pot transferred to the stove. Silence again, this time broken by a whir, slow and droning to fast, high octave. Coffee grinding. Silence, slippers returning briefly. Another door opened and closed. A shower splashing. The coda.

DiGenero sat up. He'd been married once before. It had lasted three years, although it had actually been one, the last two the death watch and wake. It all happened at the beginning of the Scarlese undercover, when his second life became his first, a fictitious existence whose reality paradoxically guaranteed his survival. His second life, the one without her, inevitably became his only life, *the* only life. It killed their marriage as dead as if he'd cheated, wounding as mortally as any lie or infidelity, only surreptitiously, a slow poison destroying the nerves, then the muscles, then the vital organs, exterminating her fantasies, then her hopes, then finally, her desire, ending even the fact of their pairing. It killed them all, one by one, with each night he didn't come home. For them, there were no rituals, hers or his. The marriage didn't last long enough for either even to recognize the patterns. It was no secret. With the job, they never had a chance.

DiGenero rose and stretched. He found his tee shirt and jeans where he'd left them, draped over the chair. In the darkness, he scuffed bare-

footed into his loafers. After the divorce, the years were vacant, like a
control experiment in a laboratory, a generic existence. Work, eat, sleep,
constant components, albeit in varying proportions. Ten years he'd lived
alone. He'd woken often enough with women beside him, but most
times not. How many, he wondered. Twenty-five hundred, three thousand? Three thousand mornings alone, sufficient repetition to imprint an
image in the mind of even dumb animals, but since Erin he found he
couldn't picture it. He couldn't remember what it was like. What's more,
he didn't want to.

In the bathroom, the shower cascaded. DiGenero opened the door
and invaded the steam. He wiped the mirror's condensation and peered
at himself. There seemed more gray in his morning stubble. He preferred
a fogged image. Age showed least in its imprecision. He reached absentmindedly for the faucet and turned, instantly reminded of its effect on
the hot water pressure.

"Ow! You did that on purpose!" Erin's voice echoed against the tile.

He twisted the handle closed. Through the glass shower, she appeared
on tiptoes, trying to escape the suddenly cold spray. "Sorry. I forgot.
Cold feet on back on even days. Shot of cold water in shower on odd
days. Whips and chains in bed every third Thursday of the month."

"Very funny." The pebbled glass transformed her into an impressionist image. She turned profile. The water stopped. The shower door slid
open. When they first met, her hair had been long, accentuating her
height. It was shorter now, to the shoulders, but Erin was no less striking. The cold water had dimpled her breasts and erected her nipples.
"Give me a towel, will you?" She extended her hand.

DiGenero shook his head. "And let you hide that? Not on your life."

Her expression stalled between pleading and aggravation. He tossed
the bath towel. She caught it, exchanging a look of mock reproof. "And
how are you planning to spend your day? Pulling the wings off flies?"

"That's tomorrow," he said. DiGenero watched her dry. As she
leaned, her breasts swayed, full with a sculptor's lines. One foot advanced
to first position, she swept the towel down across her stomach to the soft
dark triangle demarcating the curves of her inner thighs. She straightened, vigorously rubbing her hair. Lithe, her body had improved rather
than softened with age, a shape in which strength, over time, defined
form.

"Coffee's made," she said. "Could you get me a cup? I've got to get
to the university early." In front of the mirror, she wrapped the towel
around her.

"Why?" he asked.

"New birds. Falcons. They're arriving from the breeding project in

Boise today. Want to come see?" The question betrayed a childlike enthusiasm.

He nodded. "Maybe I can stop by later. I'll get the coffee." DiGenero made his way to the kitchen. Odd for a city boy, but he knew falcons. In the mid-eighties, they had brought him west as head of an undercover operation to stop the trapping and trading in endangered species. He had met Erin in Montana. There, as here, the ornithology lab was her work, something she enjoyed. The falcons were more, of course. They were something she loved.

In the kitchen, he stood by the window and filled two coffee mugs. Even after his years in Salt Lake City, the mountains still awed him. They rose abruptly, an eastern wall cordoning the city as far as the eye could see. The kitchen's view faced southeast. Behind the serrated peaks, a blood red line outlined dawn.

DiGenero unlocked the kitchen door and stepped into the cold. On the small stoop, he sipped his coffee. Scarlese had let the contract from the federal pen in Atlanta, an open-ended offer, big bucks if someone would do the job. That was fifteen years ago. They had expected as much. The Bureau had moved him from job to job and city to city at least that many times, using half as many identities. Salt Lake was his longest stay.

It was a calculated risk. He knew that. Until a few years ago, he had checked every day and night, a habit, the house, the car, the windows, the doors. He still checked, although it was less often now. The Bureau still ran its trap lines, but there were no active cases where his name came up. No leads on the street. No word from electronic surveillance, the "wires," that they were looking for him. Nothing, as the Bureau put it, real time.

DiGenero carried Erin's coffee and his to the bedroom. He put the mug beside her and sat on the edge of the tub, elbows on knees, watching her blow dry her hair. She worked quickly, with no wasted motions, then combed. Finished, Erin sipped her coffee, a pause before the next phase. She turned, returning his stare. "You're certainly charging around all keyed up this morning. Big day?" she asked.

"I'm fighting the urge to rush in, prolonging the anticipation."

"How come?" Erin put down the mug. She studied herself in the mirror, then leaned forward, applying eye makeup. Her bath towel rode up, exposing the long firm line of her legs where it blended to the soft roll of bare cheeks.

"Performance reports. I've got ten to write. Tell me, what in the hell does this have to do with catching bad guys?"

"Poor baby. All those bright-eyed young FBI agents looking up to you for hope and guidance. Just like a mother hen and her brood. Cheer up. You're the special agent in charge. That's what you get the big bucks for."

He grimaced.

She put down a small brush and blinked, then reached for another from among her alchemist's array of mysterious utensils, cosmetics bottles, and jars. "Do you remember what I told you last week?" she asked.

"What?"

"The position at the law school is still open."

"Ah yes."

"I talked to the department head." She made the revelation matter-of-factly.

DiGenero looked up. "You did?"

She smiled. In any relationship of intimate familiarity, there was always satisfaction in provoking genuine surprise.

"He said someone with your background would be invaluable."

"Invaluable," he repeated.

"Yep." She nodded earnestly. Erin rubbed a powder of some sort into her cheeks. "That's what he said."

DiGenero finished his coffee before he spoke. "I can see the law school catalogue now. I'd be listed just below torts, contracts, civil procedure, litigation, and sexual deviancy law. Professor DiGenero's new course. Door Kicking 101. A survey of techniques and approaches to ballbusting, eyegouging, and headcracking, providing the theoretical framework for the real world, law enforcement *au naturel.*" He shook his head. "I don't know. Somehow I can't picture myself hanging around with all those buttoned-down types, you know what I mean?"

Irritated, she glanced sideways at DiGenero. "Frank, don't give me this dumb-cop routine. You've forgotten more about law, or law enforcement, or whatever you call it, than they ever knew. Besides, their biggest thrill is speeding through a school zone. Their tongues hang out when they talk to somebody like you." She found her lipstick and applied it, short quick strokes, the last step. She turned to face him. "Your problem isn't that you're a doorkicker. It's between your ears. You're tired of this, but you've got to make up your mind to do something else. You've got a pension and you've passed twenty years in the Bureau, so use it. We've got a house, I've got a job. This isn't a bad place to be. As far as I'm concerned, you can do whatever you want. I don't care if you teach, flip hamburgers, or catch dogs instead of crooks, for God's sake. I love you. I just want you to be happy. Do you understand?"

It was the conversation's hundredth iteration, with all the predictability of a morality play, scripted to touch the uplifting as well as the down-casting and, with Erin as author, to arrive inevitably at the climax, the unambiguously correct choice.

"You mean that?"

"What?" she asked.

"About not caring what I do as long as I'm happy."

Her voice softened. "Yes."

"Can I ask you just one question then?"

She nodded. "Sure."

"Is it tough to keep that towel up if your nipples aren't erect?"

She laughed. "DiGenero, you're a dumb shit."

He stood and took her in his arms. She pressed against him, hard between his legs, soft against his chest, warm on his neck. "Would you mind if we went back to bed and I checked your flavors from head to toe? Your franchise is supposed to have twenty-seven, but you can never be too sure." He tugged gently at the towel.

"I wouldn't mind," she whispered low, a prelude. Her lips brushed his cheek. She leaned back in his arms and smiled. "But you're not going to. Right now, I'm late." He dropped his embrace. She stepped into the closet and began to sort, examining her choices among the jumbled hangings.

DiGenero walked into the bedroom. He contemplated the rumpled sheets and blankets. Where they had risen, the sheets were turned back, two triangles of white. He straightened the bedclothes and pillows. Tomorrow, and the day after, and the day after that, the act would be the same, a simple preparation, renewing their place to be together again. It occurred to him that there was nowhere else in the world he wanted to be.

Behind him, Erin's heels clicked on the hardwood. She always dressed quickly. Today, a work uniform. Blue jeans, sweater, flat shoes. At her night table, she searched among jewelry for her watch.

"I'll give the law school a call," he said.

She looked up, eyes wide, her turn to be surprised. "You will?" She walked to DiGenero and circled his waist with her arms. "That's wonderful," she said.

"Only one condition," he said.

"What's that?"

"No tweeds. No pipes."

"Smack 'em with your nightstick if they even bring it up." She kissed him on the lips.

"Now about those twenty-seven flavors," he said.

She skipped back. "You're sneaky but I'm gone."

"Tonight," he said.

Disappearing, her voice came from the hall. "Tonight."

He stepped back into the bathroom and arranged his shaving cream and razor. The water steamed in the sink. Sunrise was minutes away. Through the window the dawn previewed an azure blue sky. DiGenero heard the front door open, but not close, breaking the normal sequence. He turned off the tap and listened.

In the entryway, Erin rummaged in her purse. No keys. "Frank," she called out, then retraced her steps. "Frank," she called again.

DiGenero looked into the hall. "What's wrong?"

"I must have left the car keys at the lab the other day. When you picked me up. Where are yours?"

"In the kitchen."

"Okay." She turned.

"You want to wait ten minutes and I'll drive you? I can pick you up later, when I come to see the new falcons."

"Can't wait," Erin called over her shoulder. "Besides, you're just trying to get me back into bed."

DiGenero heard the front door slam. "You're right," he said.

Erin hurried down the walk. The gravel crunched, an awakening sound. Heavy dew covered the car, including its blemishes. The moisture foretold the seasons. After the arid summer, it was a precursor. The westerlies crossed the Salt Lake, now warmer than the air, absorbing the evaporation. When the winds climbed the mountains, they chilled abruptly, dropping their burden. Powder. In a month, it would begin in earnest, producing hundreds of inches of snow, burying the peaks and high valleys.

She breathed deeply. Cold had aromas, telltale scents of time and place. This was November cold. Emptied of its moisture by dawn, it was dry and sharp at first light. For her, it also served as a reminder that they would ski soon, after Thanksgiving. The first weekend was always the best. The days outdoors together, dinner for two, then making love, aroused somehow by the exertion to explore each other's body for hours. It didn't make sense, but exhaustion produced passion. Perhaps it was a different biochemistry, tired synapses energized by new organic compounds, creations of fatigue. Or something genetic, like a woman's scent, an inherited characteristic, naturally selected, that ensured even species that exhausted themselves foraging, or hunting, or surviving were still driven to procreate.

She slipped the key into the lock, opened the car door, and threw her purse on the seat. Erin looked back at the house and hesitated. She pressed her thighs together. She was wet. Goddamn DiGenero. She smiled to herself. Whatever it was, she wanted him even now.

In front of the bathroom mirror, DiGenero waited. Their regular morning rhythm disrupted, it seemed important to hear it, the sound of the last event, an engine turning over. He stepped into the bedroom. Or was he just killing time, no more eager to prepare for work than to go to the office? Maybe it was just habit, the mind conditioned to expect an event and now seeking reassurance, repetition for its own sake. Maybe that was it. Razor in hand, he ambled toward the hall. Habits ordered existence. We were all their creatures.

Erin slid onto the seat. Frank wouldn't forget, but she'd call him later nonetheless and leave a message. Remember the twenty-seven flavors. Something like that. She slammed the door. Tonight. Soon enough. She inserted the key in the ignition. The windshield was opaque, a colorless gray that dimmed the interior despite the dawn. With the season, darkness came back earlier now. So would she. Night would come, she would return, they would be together. As always. She turned the key. As always.

Halfway down the hall, the crystals appeared like a fine snow. As planes of glass, even shards, the plate glass windows were gone, not broken or missing, but disintegrated, transformed. They sparkled, refracting the dawn in a million facets, as if proving for one irrefutable instant the particle theory of light. The shockwave spared DiGenero's eyes, blowing him backward, head over heels into the bedroom before the shower of glass caught up. He slammed into the floor and rolled half under the bed. The blast was feeling, not sound, encores reflected by the mountainside that shuddered through the neighborhood over and over again.

DiGenero rolled to his hands and knees, staring dumbly at the drops of blood collecting on the floor beneath him. Until he moved his head, they made four circles. Markers each of their source. Two ears, two nostrils. He spit more blood, obscuring their accounting for his orifices, rose unsteadily, fell, and rose again. His tee shirt was gone, torn off, revealing a pox of red dimples, an uneven pattern on his chest and side where the glass had abraded as he turned in the air.

He stumbled down the hall. Around him, firelight overwhelmed the dawn. The front wall of the foyer as well as the door were gone, replaced by splintered timbers, sagging roof, and rubble. With each step closer, warmth radiated from the inferno. Beyond the flames, he could see movement, people running, shielding their eyes, someone motioning. To him? A police car's lightbar turned, a kaleidoscope. Somewhere beyond the ringing and rushing in his ears, he heard sirens. Coming or going, he couldn't tell. He stood on the front step, lit by the fires, strangely comfortable in the cold air. The twisted shape lay on the lawn, on its side, although he couldn't be sure. All of it seemed to be burning, even the steel. A crater had replaced the driveway. Around it, flames consumed the shrubbery. A policeman in a windbreaker walked toward him, a blanket extended on his arm.

DiGenero waved him away. He didn't need more distractions. He had to concentrate, to understand. She had left. Now, where was she? Had he heard the engine start? Yes, he had, hadn't he? So, she'd driven away. That's right. She must have. Did she know what had happened? Had she heard the explosion? No, or she would have come back. He'd call and tell her. No. She'd be upset, worried about him. He'd wait, tell her later, when she came home. No. She'd see the house, the yard. He'd go in person. He'd find her at the lab. Tell her there. No. She had work to do, important things. Falcons coming today. He'd have to find her later. Yes, later, but where? Where would he find her? He'd wait in a place on her way home from work to intercept her. No. There were two or three ways she could come. He'd miss her. What day was it? Friday, Wednesday? Did she go to the supermarket? Could he find her there? The cleaners? He had to think, to find a place. To find her. Not here, not at the lab, not in between. Oh God, it was hard. Where could he find her? He had to talk. They had to talk. Where? Where could he ever find her again?

There were more lights and sirens, fire trucks now. One, two, three, many. Long yellow coats and medieval hats with peaks and face masks ran toward him. He waved again, back and forth hard, angry this time. The gesture unbalanced him. He tottered and fell to his knees. One of the yellow coats tried to approach him. He groped on all fours, finding a shattered two-by-four, a foot of broken timber. He threw it. It sailed, end over end. It was good. The yellow coat backed away. To his left, only yards distant, fire consumed the twisted thing. Black smoke billowed, adorning its gnarled red heart. No matter. Nothing about it mattered anymore.

Suddenly, he saw it all more clearly. On his knees, he rocked precariously. He steadied himself, one hand on the ground. They were at eye level now. All of them. The bushes. Burning. Not one, but all of them. Burning, closer and brighter. He would embrace them. Not one, but all of them. They were his, only his, meant for him. He crawled forward. From the closest, he could feel the heat. He reached for it. Hands stopped him. They shouldn't, couldn't. Yellow coats, a cop, two cops, three, four. He twisted and kicked. Somewhere, someone was screaming. He couldn't recognize the voice, but he felt it, inside him. Like the explosion, he couldn't hear, but only feel the words. Oh God, what had he done? What sin that was so wrong to take her? The bushes. The message. They were for him. His message. The bushes. Not one, but all of them. They were burning, every one telling him. God telling him. She was gone. It was his fault. It was his turn to die.

The first snow came that night. It arrived tentatively, transforming to rain in the valley, but falling as a powder, almost invisible higher up. On the Bench, the narrow plateau just above the city, once the shore of a great inland sea, now shopping strips and suburbs, it clung to the skirts of the mountains. The next morning with the sun, most was gone, although from his bed, DiGenero could see the remainder on the steep. In the war between the seasons, the first snow was a skirmish. A probe, then withdrawal. Nothing lasting, but a warning of what was to come.

Sometime in the small hours, the ringing in his ears had stopped. Despite the sedative, the silence woke him. The drug lingered, inhibiting any serious ambitions, and he lay in the dark, a passive observer. The room was small, with dresser, nightstand, chair, and an adjustable tray on wheels, the only furnishing clearly intended for the bedridden. He had tried to listen, to use the sense just regained, but the returns were limited. Once he heard voices outside his door. Women making small talk, one black, one white, a conversation about unfamiliar names and unknown events. Children, a good boy, but a problem for his mother, and someone else, a man, coming or going, no account, not doing right. A dissection of the trivial for its own sake. They drifted away and so did he, all marking time on the graveyard shift.

Shortly after sunrise, a nurse entered, cheerfully inquiring. He ignored her. Talking regardless, she busied herself with his vital signs, taking his temperature and pulse. Finished with him, she shuffled papers in a metal clamshell file, then, no less good humored, left. An aide of some sort came next, working quickly. A tuck to the sheets, a refilled water carafe, a quick inspection of the bathroom. Focusing on inanimate things, she complemented her predecessor's ministrations, a practical division of labor. His breakfast appeared. Uninvited, an orderly raised his bed, then cantilevered the adjustable tray over him, positioning the food an infantile equidistance between his nose and chest. Plastic, covering plastic, on plastic. He ignored it, too.

DiGenero looked out through the room's single window. Elevated to a new angle, his perspective had changed. He judged he was on the fourth or fifth floor. He could see the intersection that bordered the hospital compound. Arriving, the cars stretched bumper to taillight for several blocks. Each slowed at the corner with a tap on the brake, a perfunctory obeisance to the stop sign, before turning hard right. As they did, their windshields captured the sun, brief novas. One after another, slow, right turn, a flash of light. For each of them, a spark, for only an instant. He watched for several minutes, counting the cars deliberately, then, when his eyes started to fill, desperately, as if it mattered.

Benedetto entered the room. He stood just inside the door, hesitating awkwardly. Medium height but square, his bulk connoted brute strength, the build of a childhood bully grown into a man. His rumpled suit, an indeterminate gray, bore witness to cross-country confinement in an economy fare seat. His face was scraped and knicked, obviously shaved before an airplane's restroom mirror.

He stepped to the bedside and took DiGenero's hand, trying but failing to hold his eyes. "I'm sorry, Frank." Benedetto spoke quickly, as if there was more to say, although only silence followed.

DiGenero nodded.

Benedetto clasped his hands in front, a parishioner's pose. He tried again. "Everybody wanted me to tell you how sorry they are. They wanted me to tell you. Everybody."

"That's okay, Tony." DiGenero motioned to the chair. Benedetto pulled it to the bedside and sat. He surveyed the room. DiGenero knew the conclusion Benedetto would draw from his inventory even before he spoke.

"Like old times," Benedetto said, gesturing at the surroundings.

"Like old times," DiGenero repeated.

All told, they'd spent weeks, even months together in single rooms with beds and chairs, sometimes for only an hour, sometimes all morning or afternoon, sometimes late into the night. Apartments, hotels, flophouses, high rent and skid row. For five years, most of DiGenero's undercover in the Scarleses, Benedetto had been his case agent. When he was inside, Benedetto was his contact. His only contact. His outside guy.

The case agent. In *The FBI Manual on Clandestine Operations,* it appeared a bloodless task. "The case agent administers the undercover operation. He gives operational guidance; briefs and debriefs the penetration or agent/operative; conveys orders from higher authorities; provides necessary administrative support and counseling, including on personnel and personal affairs; and ensures that Bureau policy and procedures, including a regular and full accounting for time, financial and other resources, meet all administrative and legal requirements as stipulated in Headquarters and applicable field office regulations." The manual was nonsense, of course, a bureaucratic catechism from the Bureau's high priests of process, the prescribers, reviewers, and approvers. The monks sequestered from the streets in Headquarters' windowless rooms.

For DiGenero, Benedetto was more, much more. He was the critical link in the chain, a lifeline. They would talk for hours, about women, about friends, about work, about wiseguys, about the life inside the Scarleses that was then DiGenero's twenty-four hours a day. For DiGenero, Benedetto was his human connection, his way back, if only temporarily, to a reality left behind. To unwind, to explain, sometimes just to recall people whose very existence he purged from his mind when he was under in order to avoid a slip, the wrong word spoken, the wrong name remembered. In order to avoid mistakes. In order to stay alive.

"How long since we've seen each other?" DiGenero asked.

"How long?" Benedetto scratched his head. "Ten years, I guess, maybe eleven."

"Too long," DiGenero said.

"Yeah, too long."

Growing up, they had been passing acquaintances, part of the small world of Little Italy, Bensonhurst, and Howard Beach, the Italian havens surrounded by metropolitan terra incognita. Each had gone his own way and, unknown to the other, joined the Bureau. Benedetto first, DiGenero later, in 1974, the year the Scarlese operation was gearing up. Both were handpicked after a fashion, chosen from among the few then in the FBI whose names ended in vowels.

"Answer a question for me," DiGenero said. "As a friend. No bullshit. Okay?"

Benedetto looked down. "I know what you're gonna say."

"You do?"

Benedetto tensed, as if preparing to take a blow.

"How come?" DiGenero asked.

Benedetto shook his head.

"Tell me."

"It's complicated, Frank."

"Come on. You can tell me. How come they didn't know? How come they didn't warn me?"

"You gotta understand," Benedetto said. He shifted uncomfortably from cheek to cheek, oversized for the chair.

"Understand what?"

"It's complicated today."

"Complicated," DiGenero repeated the word neutrally. He rolled and unrolled the blanket, a weave of unnatural fibers. In his fists, the edge stiffened into a tube. "Tell me what's complicated, Tony."

"It's not the same, Frank, not like when you and I was together."

"Oh yeah?"

"The city's different, the family's different." Benedetto cleared his throat, as if reluctant to mention the name. "Scarlese's different. Junior ain't the same as his old man. He's not like the old dons who started the business or the wiseguys, the Gallos and the Gottis, the bozos who came up from the street. They were in the old rackets. Still are."

"He's not?" DiGenero asked.

"I didn't say that. But he's smarter. So help me God. His fingerprints are on nothing. Junior's a different breed. He don't hang around the neighborhood. I mean, he's got degrees, an office downtown. He moves with the big money, belongs to the right clubs, goes to the glitzy parties, gives to the gold-plated charities. What can I tell ya? We know the family's still his, but he's a toe dancer. He don't leave tracks. Not like the others."

"No tracks, huh?" Knuckles white, DiGenero had rolled the edge of the blanket as tight as a cable. He released it and leaned over, yanking angrily on the drawer of the night table. It stuck. The table danced before the drawer jerked open. DiGenero groped inside. He tossed a piece of paper at Benedetto, who caught it in the air.

Benedetto unfolded the sheet. He stared, then slowly straightened the crumpled edges. "This a copy?"

"Yeah," DiGenero answered, breathing hard.

Like a man handling a fragile object, Benedetto laid the paper carefully on the bed. An FBI evidence number was typed in the upper right hand corner. The only message, two words, all capital letters, was centered on the page.

YOU'RE NEXT

"Where'd they find this?" Benedetto asked.

"In the mailbox," DiGenero said. "Or maybe you need a return address to figure it out."

"Take it easy, Frank. We're gonna get 'em. I swear. But you gotta bear with it. This is gonna be my case. I asked for it. We'll do it, so help me, we'll get the bastard who did this, but I gotta tell ya, it's gonna take time," Benedetto said.

"Time?"

"Yeah."

"Because things are different?"

"That's right." Benedetto nodded earnestly.

"Because they're smarter than when you and I were working together?"

"Yeah." He nodded again, encouraging the apparent effort at understanding.

DiGenero couldn't control the trembling in his voice. "Well, tell me,

Tony, how come *we* ain't smarter? How come Scarlese's cornered the market on human knowledge in the last fifteen years? How come we can put taps on their phones, bugs on their cars, stick wires up their fuckin' asses, send 'em to the slammer for fifty years, and nobody in the Bureau can warn me that Scarlese gonna kill my wife?" DiGenero's voice echoed in the room. The door opened and a head appeared. DiGenero grabbed a plastic water bottle from the night table and threw it. Off target, it ricocheted on the doorjamb. The door swung closed. DiGenero glared at Benedetto. His breath came hard and fast, like a sprinter's at the end of a race. "My wife is dead and I asked you a question. How come? How come no warning? How come all of a sudden we're so fuckin stupid and they're so fuckin' smart?"

The door opened again, abruptly this time. A cop in uniform stepped inside. He eyed DiGenero warily. "What's the problem?" he asked.

Benedetto turned and waved him away. "Nothin'. It's under control."

The cop hesitated.

"Go on," Benedetto said.

He nodded and left.

"Who's that?" DiGenero asked.

"Your fastball almost brained one of Salt Lake City's finest. He's part of your security. We got 'em here and in the lobby. Just in case."

DiGenero sat back, trying to collect himself. "So, answer the question, Tony."

"Maybe you taught Junior some things," Benedetto said. He fished in his pocket, extracting a pack of cigarettes. He glanced around, searching for an ashtray, then frowned and put the pack away.

"What are you talkin about?" DiGenero asked.

"When you was in the family, I think Junior learned. From you. We're tryin', Frank, but he's not gonna make the same mistakes." Benedetto cleared his throat. He spoke quietly. "How old was he then, when you was on the inside?"

"Seventeen, eighteen years old," DiGenero said.

"He idolized you, remember?"

"Yeah."

"I mean, you weren't just another neighborhood type. You'd gone to college, joined the Air Force, been a fighter pilot, gone to Vietnam, finished law school. You had everything nobody else had. On top of that, his old man jumps you to the head of the line. He makes you family counselor, consigliere, years ahead of your time. Then what happens? You put the don away. Junior's world fell apart. He swore to kill you for what you did. Not just for what you did to the old man. For what you did to him. You know that? Love and hate." Benedetto sighed. "Who can tell the difference sometimes?"

DiGenero sat silently for several minutes. After the anger, he felt dull, as if his nerves had been severed. For an instant, but only an instant, he knew what it would be like when Erin would be only a memory, when he would think of her without the tears that suddenly streamed. He put his head in his hands. It took time, a long time, for the crying to stop.

Finally, when it was over he stood. Benedetto watched him. DiGenero wavered, unsteady, wiping his eyes. On his arms, the abrasions and cuts from the glass were nasty but minor, already healing. His shoulder and hip ached where he'd hit the floor and bed, tumbled by the blast. He stretched hard nonetheless, welcoming the physical sensation, a distraction. Open at the back, his gown gaped ludicrously. A hospital robe lay across the foot of the bed. He put it on, and stepped to the window, his back to Benedetto. Below, traffic had thinned. As usual, a gray haze had begun to accumulate over the city, as yet too thin to obscure the stark lines of the Bitterroot peaks to the west or the skyline's closer details. Behind him, DiGenero heard the chair scrape. He glanced over his shoulder. Benedetto was standing.

"Thanks for coming, Tony," DiGenero said.

"They're going to move you, Frank. The plan is a safehouse for a few days, somewhere other than Salt Lake. Then, they want you to go back east. But I'll keep you posted." Benedetto opened the door.

"You do that," DiGenero said.

"We'll get him. Just leave it to me."

DiGenero continued to stare out the window. He nodded without looking at Benedetto. "Soon, Tony."

"You bet. I'll be back in touch soon."

"No, Tony, you don't understand." DiGenero turned, facing Benedetto. "You get him soon."

"Frank, take it easy." Benedetto half waved, then was gone.

"Soon, Tony." DiGenero watched the door swing shut. He whispered, "Soon."

2

THE MAIN CORRIDOR was impressive, a thoroughfare of imperial proportions. It reminded DiGenero of the boulevards in Paris, conjoining aes-
thetics and utility, attractive vistas to reveal the city's grandeur and if
needed, ample fields of fire against the howling mob. In the case of the
J. Edgar Hoover Building, the design served its purposes equally well,
memorializing its namesake in halls of timeless marble while accommodating the activity of his professional progeny at their busiest hour.

On Friday at five-thirty, however, the legions were gone, impelled to
the suburbs earlier than usual by the weekend's centrifugal force. Driving
into the city, DiGenero had passed the outbound stream, long lines of
commuters crawling south, away from Washington on Interstate 95.
Alone behind the wheel or together, carpooled hip to hip, they comingled in the exodus. Justice, along with the other fields of governance,
receding in the rearview mirror.

DiGenero found an exit sign and pushed open the door, choosing the
stairs rather than the elevator. On the third floor, the progression of
office numbers confirmed his course.

He came so seldom to Headquarters that the experience never ade-
quately immunized him against its absurdities. When he asked for directions at the entrance, the receptionist had punctiliously rechecked his
identification, dubious that any *bona fide* agent would not know the way.
Aggravated, he had grabbed when she proffered his ID card, nearly taking her thumb. He apologized, but walking away he heard her compound epithet. An incestuous bodypart. Nonsensical but colorful. He
didn't look back.

At regular intervals the hallway grid branched left and right. Below the
office symbol for Organized Crime, an arrow pointed down an inner
corridor. Compared to the first floor's marble expanse, it seemed too
narrow, confining. The trail or a one-way trip into the maze? He paused

at a bulletin board, curious about the contents. Subdivided, one half
neatly arrayed the Bureau's official notices. A reminder about annual
physicals, a pistol range schedule (Thursday was ladies' day), a training
roster for a course in "forms management," whatever that was, even a
flyer with home safety tips. The unofficial half displayed a jumble of
three-by-five cards. Ads mostly, they offered used cars, apartments to
rent, washers for sale, a vacation condo to let, two shotguns, cheap. Yin
and yang. The penchant of organizations to impose their arbitrary disci-
plines juxtaposed to the evidence of life's randomness. Opposites creating the whole.

   The pressure to conform was strongest at Headquarters, like gravity's
strength, greatest at earth's core. For twenty years, DiGenero had made
a point of being somewhere else. His personal rule was simple. NIH.
Not In Headquarters. It hadn't hurt him. Carried by the momentum of
the Scarlese case, his celebrity status lasted for several years. They recognized his syndrome and played along, at first assigning him as an in-
house "consultant" touring field offices to proselytize undercover operations. They brought him down slowly and, over time, things worked out.
More undercover jobs and promotions in Miami, Atlanta, and finally,
Salt Lake. But not on the inside and not in Washington. Here, he was
still a stranger, an outsider, Headquarters still the black box. It hadn't
mattered then, when he wanted his distance. Now it did. The answers
were here. If he was going to get Scarlese, what choice did he have?

   Two weeks had passed since the bombing. The security team had kept
him moving, hotels for a few days in Dallas and Memphis, then almost a
week in a safehouse in Detroit. Finally, they reached Quantico. He asked
for New York, but Virginia was their choice. The FBI Academy was best,
they explained. Protection and room on the Marine base. A controlled-
access environment with maximum personal mobility, the security
specialist told him in his clinical jargon. They had even arranged an
assignment a month hence, teaching "Introduction to Undercover Operations" in the new agent course. Something useful, although on that
point nobody tried to be convincing.

   This was his second trip to Headquarters. The first, the day after he
arrived in Quantico, was their treat. They sent a car for him. They had
expected him to go up the line, to argue for a part in the case. Their
choreography was accommodating, but as standard as the script. They
kept him aloft, on the seventh floor, not once below the deputy assistant
director level and always in tow, never allowing him to find his own way.
At each station of the Bureau's cross, he'd been greeted with sympathy, a
pastoral hand-over-handshake, followed by the arm-on-shoulder treatment, ushering him to the sofa and coffee table in the corner of the

office. None of it mattered, of course, except the gesture, the institutional solicitude, for what it was worth. They all promised action and at the same time implied that if the investigation didn't produce, they would take a second look at giving him a part. When he got the same message for the third time, he remembered wondering if it was written down somewhere, or if those who rose in the firmament simply were the ones skilled enough to master the art of the gossamer promise, soothing but ambiguous, the bureaucrat's ultimate interpersonal technique.

In the end, when he pressed, the answer was always the same: no. They said he had every right to see the Director, but reminded him that the rules came straight from the top. They would find who did it, not him. The investigation couldn't be personal, for his sake and the Bureau's. You couldn't fault their consistency. It was what Benedetto had said, albeit less felicitously. After Salt Lake, he'd called once from New York, telling him to be patient. To sit tight.

At the end of the corridor, the small sign hung beside the door. OCD/NYO. Organized Crime Division/New York Operations. DiGenero entered. The secretary's desk was empty. On the telephone bank, only one light glowed. From behind the glass partition, the conversation was clipped, in its terminal phase. The receiver hit the cradle, louder than necessary.

He stepped to the cubicle's entrance. The desk and swivel chair occupied most of the space, a safe and straight-back chair the rest. Preoccupied, the agent didn't look up, continuing instead to scrawl a note. Before him, a computer screen glowed. The paperwork, strewn randomly, looked all too familiar. Files, evidence inventories, investigation sheets, cable forms. An inbox marked "Priority" balanced on the edge of the desk. DiGenero recognized the contents. Covered with a pink routing slip, each folder sported neat tabs. "Decision Memoranda." Peculiar Headquarters creations. They recorded the hierachy's official approval for a proposed FBI operation.

Like the arguments of Jesuitical scholars, Decision Memoranda demanded perfection in form, whatever their substantive merits. No paper out of place. No step in the sequence transgressed. On the left side of the folder, clipped and tabbed, they assembled the record in full detail: the plan of operation; status reports; evidence; legal opinions; accounting for resources; roster of assigned personnel. The heart of the matter was on the right: the case summary, succinctly put for senior readers; the decision paper, with "approve" and "disapprove" blocks; and the "Miscellaneous Issues," the innocuous tab always thumbed first. "Miscellaneous Issues" covered any bite-your-ass problems, whether, for instance, a decision to go ahead might net a congressman, a prominent cop, or one of the President's leading political donors. DiGenero counted the pink routing slips. Sixteen. Too many. A burden for even a disciplined Jesuit.

The agent finished writing and looked up. His expression was worn. "What can I do for you?"

"You run ops support for New York?" DiGenero asked.

"Yep," the agent said.

"How about the status of a case?"

"A case?"

DiGenero nodded.

He leaned back in his chair, its springs squealing a protest. He rubbed his face. Ten years younger than DiGenero, the agent examined him with tired eyes. "One case?"

"Yeah," DiGenero said.

He stretched and yawned. "How 'bout this? You get a case number and a 412, a file requisition form, okay? Put the number on the form. Put the form in distribution. When the form comes to me, the case file goes to you. Voilà."

"Voilà," DiGenero said accommodatingly.

"Monday soon enough?" He smiled, pleased with his own reasonableness.

DiGenero shook his head. "Nope."

"No?"

"Now," DiGenero said.

The smile disappeared. The agent righted himself slowly in the chair. He motioned toward the paper covering his desk. "Look, I got two hundred cases."

DiGenero nodded understandingly. "You got a hell of a job."

"What if one hundred and ninety-nine other guys came in on Friday afternoon and everybody wanted cases pulled? You can't wait till Monday?"

"I don't see one hundred and ninety-nine people in line behind me, do you?" DiGenero asked.

"You know what time I get outa this place at night?"

"A lot later than you need if you fuck around with everybody the way you're fuckin' around with me," DiGenero said. He leaned against the doorjamb and folded his arms.

The agent eyed him for several moments. A look of resignation supplanted his irritation. On Friday afternoon, obstructionism equally affected the actor and the acted upon. "You look like the type that isn't gonna get lost," he said.

DiGenero smiled benignly.

"Jesus," the agent sighed. "Which case?"

"DiGenero."

"DiGenero?" He stared blankly. "Don't remember that one. Who's he?"

"A murder two weeks ago. Scarlese's connected."

The agent muttered, "Ancient history." He squared himself before the computer and tapped the keyboard. The screen erased, flashed, and lit with a menu, white on black. He typed, then looked up. "And?"

"And what?" DiGenero asked.

"You got a case number? You got a file reference? How about 'em?" DiGenero shook his head. "Don't have."

"Great." He hit the keyboard, skipping over the entries. The computer's prompt, "Requester," appeared on the screen. "Your name?"

"DiGenero."

The clicking stopped. "What kinda games we playin'?" he asked.

"No games," DiGenero said coldly.

"Come on."

"She was my wife."

The agent's eyes widened. He hung his head. "Oh my God, I shoulda put two and two together." He rose sheepishly and took DiGenero's hand. "I'm sorry. It's been one of those days. New York's OC section has three hundred agents on the street. I've got five guys here to chase the paper. It's a losing fight."

"Don't worry about it." DiGenero motioned to the computer. "Whaddya got?"

The agent sat. "Lemme see." The keys rattled, followed by the computer's peremptory beep. He squinted at the screen. "That's funny. It's 'R and C.'" He looked at DiGenero. "You didn't know that?"

"Nope."

"Sorry."

"Whaddya mean, 'sorry?'" DiGenero asked. "You still can retrieve the file, can't you?"

"Yes and no. A 'Restricted and Controlled' file's not on the system. At least not on this system. It's 'need-to-know.' Special handling. I can't bring it up on the computer or get the hard copy without seventh floor approval."

"Special handling," DiGenero repeated sarcastically. "So goddamn special nobody's told me a word about it in two weeks?"

"I can call the deputy director's office. Maybe we can get it released."

"No," DiGenero interrupted. He already had the seventh floor's answer to that question. There was no point in bearing personal witness to his own disobedience, at least not yet. "Why's the case 'R and C'?" he asked.

"Don't know." The agent shrugged. "Let me try some key words and do a scan, you know, the other active cases where they may have cross-referenced the file. Sometimes we can get in that way. The back door. You can't get a complete 'R and C' case, but usually you can pull up some of the paper." He tapped the keys. DiGenero waited. A series of brightly colored screens appeared and vanished. The agent shook his head. "Funny. Not a trace. They've sucked up every scrap. The record shows there's an 'R and C' file here and one in New York. In the Field Office. Beside that, the only thing here is the name of the agent in charge. Benedetto."

DiGenero bent down, peering at the screen. "That's it?"

"Uh huh."

DiGenero straightened up. "How 'bout this?" He motioned toward the safe and the scattered papers. "You got a soft file?"

"I've got nothin'," the agent said. "If you want to call Benedetto, I'll get his extension."

"No." DiGenero shook his head.

"Maybe he could do something for you. Give him a ring," the agent suggested helpfully. "Wait a second." He worked the keyboard. The screen darkened, then transformed itself, a new color spectrum. A telephone listing appeared. The FBI's New York Field Office. "Here," he said. "I got it here." He read Benedetto's phone number aloud, but DiGenero had already closed the door behind him.

The notables looked down, an assembly of expressions alternately good humored and reserved. DiGenero examined the photographs, a Washington sampler. Among the vaguely familiar and the unknown, the stars hung randomly: a Massachusetts senator in earlier years, much thinner and younger; two powerful congressmen, hearty perennials; the former Speaker of the House, Texas suit and cowboy boots; a junior Supreme Court justice, a somber expression to match her new black frock. On the portraits, notes accompanied the signatures, lauding the recipient's virtues or cryptically recalling a personal moment. Altogether, the wall was a testimonial to McChesney Monroe's membership in the permanent government. Under the sediments that accumulated in two-, four- and six-year strata, he was part of the bedrock. A servant to the nation for the duration, acknowledged as such by the sojourners who came and went according to the transitory measures of political time.

The door to the inner office opened. Monroe emerged. He took DiGenero's hand. "Frank, I'm so glad you came." The welcoming smile faded followed by condolences, brief but sufficient.

Monroe stood to one side and beckoned. DiGenero led the way. The office, small for a seventh floor suite, personified the man. The antiques were eclectic, Shaker and Queen Anne, suggesting individual selection, rather than a decorator's choice. Pines and maples, they had mellowed to warm hues. Monroe motioned to a chair, one of two leather wingbacks. "Please, sit."

McChesney Monroe had seasoned, not aged. The ruddy complexion and lean build bespoke no change in his sailing and tennis. He was approaching sixty, but the only visible transformation was salt-and-pepper hair, at best an indeterminate indicator of maturity.

Twenty years before, when DiGenero was in the Scarleses, Monroe had run the Organized Crime Section in New York. Three layers above him on the inside, he was Benedetto's boss's boss. They talked occasionally on the phone, but DiGenero's security as well as Monroe's rank dictated the distance. When the Scarlese indictments came down, the case boosted both of them. They followed separate trajectories, but "their" success was a bond. DiGenero knew "Mac." More importantly, Mac knew him.

For a time, Monroe was fast rising. After New York, he moved up in Chicago and Los Angeles, the shark tanks where ambitions drove cases and cases made careers. He arabesqued to Headquarters in the mid-eighties, coincidentally just when the second administration suffered its seven-year-itch, the usual end-of-term, high-level departures. The changes opened fissures and Monroe found himself closer to the top, prudent stairsteps but noteworthy, marking him for bigger things.

Then, something happened, stopping the ascent. Not totally, of course, but a missed selection as chief of a premier division and an odd temporary assignment, task force chief on a second-rank problem, transformed his corridor reputation. He was no longer on the fast track, inevitably destined for one of the senior deputies' jobs. Rumor had it that he had erred politically, informally advising a presidential challenger whose fortunes had flagged in his race with the vice president to succeed the incumbent. Nothing was ever proven, but Monroe's friendship with the challenger—prep school, Princeton, Yale Law—was enough for the White House personnel minders, who verified the politics of all proposed deputy directors. After the inauguration, when Monroe's name came to them for the Bureau's number-three job, it languished. In a new administration struggling to fill three thousand political appointments, a delay for a career officer carried only one message: deadend.

His fortunes notwithstanding, the skills that had helped Monroe to the Division Chief level, a step below the political appointees, were deeply ingrained. He kept in touch with those who had worked for him.

If paths didn't cross, he sent a note at least once a year, not a holiday card, but a personal remembrance. For a select few, he phoned. Those who had done well, who "helped" as he put it, DiGenero included.

"What are you doing in the building at this hour?" Monroe asked.

"Looking for answers," DiGenero said.

"Ah yes," Monroe reacted knowingly. "You were here two weeks ago. You didn't stop in."

"Not my call."

"The treatment, eh?"

"All four deputies," DiGenero said.

"A four bagger? Congratulations. Home run." Monroe motioned, a jerk of the chin. "I seem to remember an undelivered Christmas present somewhere in my desk. Join me?"

"Why not?" DiGenero said.

Monroe bent down and opened a drawer. When he entered, DiGenero hadn't bothered to look at the office symbol beside the door. "What are you doing now?" he asked.

Monroe straightened, a bottle of scotch and two glasses in his hands. He put the glasses on the desk. "About what?"

"I mean, what's this job?"

He poured. "Liaison and public affairs."

"What's that in English?"

"I talk to Congress and the press." Monroe corked the scotch and returned with the drinks. He handed a glass to DiGenero and sat in the wingback beside him. "It's a priestly role. Part-time on the Hill, part-time with the fourth estate. The expiation of sins and the education of the innocent. Or dumb animals, as the case may be." He raised his glass. "To us."

"Yeah." DiGenero drank.

Monroe examined him with a fatherly expression. "Are you sure you should be here?"

"Where should I be?"

"The boat's still in the water," Monroe said.

"Annapolis?" DiGenero asked.

"Same spot. South River. Margery's in Connecticut this weekend, visiting the kids. We could go to St. Michael's. We'd have the Chesapeake to ourselves. They've hauled the stinkpots for the winter. Wouldn't be a powerboat in sight. The fall colors are gone, but the Bay is better in monochrome. Steel on steel."

"I wouldn't be good company."

"Nonsense. I'm going out anyway. How about it?"

DiGenero nodded noncommittally. "Why is Erin's case an 'R and C'?" he asked.

Monroe ignored DiGenero's rejection. He raised his eyebrows. "Who told you that?"

"The desk. New York ops."

Monroe cleared his throat politely. "You know the rules say you're not supposed to be involved in the investigation. Not unreasonable, I suppose. Lawyers don't represent themselves, doctors don't operate on their own family, that sort of thing."

"Fuck the rules," DiGenero said.

"I see." He smiled. "I take that to mean you're not interested in discussing the professional and philosophic rationale underlying FBI procedures."

"Correct."

He raised his glass, holding the scotch without drinking. The burned-oak aroma seemed to evoke his approval. "You realize I'm not in the loop. I can't give you answers because I simply don't know."

"You hear things," DiGenero said.

He sipped. "I hear all kinds of things. But not about this."

DiGenero stared. "In other words, you're telling me to buzz off."

"No. I'm being honest. I'm telling you I can give you an opinion. If you want it. But opinions are like assholes: everybody's got one. However much I'd like, I simply can't give you the facts."

"I'll settle for opinion."

"Just so you understand."

"I understand," DiGenero affirmed.

"What have they told you?" he asked.

"Not a goddamn thing," DiGenero said.

Monroe sat back, collecting his thoughts. He began like a storyteller, establishing the seemingly extraneous details of a scene before unfolding its central event. "In part, I suspect it's New York. Here, they'd call it a management problem. Too many cases, too many players, too many priorities. It's more, of course." He smiled wryly. "Much more. Decline and fall. It's difficult to comprehend."

"Decline and fall?" DiGenero asked. "Whose?"

Monroe spoke. "New York's. Ours. It's too obvious. The mind is overwhelmed, lost in the particulars. With the benefit of distance, it's always much clearer. After all, Rome's last days spanned quite some time. A hundred, two hundred years? Who couldn't be expected to make mistakes in interpreting the significance of events? To guess wrongly that one or another victory would change the course of the war? After all, year after year, the trends seem the same. Barbarians on all sides. The

Roman legions contending, fully engaged on the frontiers. To the north and west, the Vandals, the Saxons, the Goths hack away. To the south, the Christians subverting, boring from within. But in the capital? The scribes toil in their cubicles, writing reports to the Emperor, summaries of battles, recommendations, second guessing, rationalizing why it isn't so bad, disasters and all.

"New York's like that." The analogy seemed to please Monroe. "Decline and fall. One-stop shopping, all the country's problems on display in one place. Drugs, corruption, racial skirmishes, white-collar crime, gangs, the Colombians, the Jamaicans, the Chinese, the newcomers, and, of course the old guard, the mob. In some cases, diseases once thought fatal become chronic. We claim progress. In others? Cassandra cries out. A new life-threatening challenge arises to take their place. We go after that. We convince ourselves there are wins as well as losses, but we never add up the score. Better for a time, here or there, but overall, worse. Overall, losing, year after year."

Monroe swirled the contents of his glass, contemplating the currents. "The mob," he said. "We got the first generation with criminal statutes, then taxes. It took from the thirties to the sixties but it worked, finally. Hoover didn't want to acknowledge the bigger problem: when you cut off the head, the body doesn't die. But what the hell? Nothing is but thinking makes it so. For him—for us—until the seventies there was no 'organized crime.' He said so, right? I mean, Jesus, unless you wanted a field office of your very own in Messabie, Minnesota, who was going to argue?

"Hoover died in 1972 and it took a few years to regroup. It was 1980 before we figured out RICO—the Racketeer Influenced and Corrupt Organizations Act. New York was the big leagues, so that's where we used it. In the eighties, we told ourselves we did alright. We rolled up a bunch and their businesses. The Gambinos, the Geneveses, the Luccheses, the Colombos. Hard times for the second generation."

Monroe rose and walked to his desk, retrieving the bottle. He returned and topped up their glasses. "So, you might ask, what's the problem? A good job done by all. In this area at least progress, correct?"

DiGenero shrugged, "I guess."

"The problem—inevitably the problem—is that very fact," Monroe said. "The consequence of success."

"I don't follow," DiGenero said.

"Neither did the Romans. The barbarians learned from their mistakes. They learned from the victors. The point is they learned. Over a very long time, they got better and began to defeat the legions."

Monroe put the bottle on the small end table between them and sat.

"The same for the mob. Darwin, that's all. Second generations beget third. Saints be praised, most replicate themselves. Clever, vicious, stupid. But, a few, a precious few, the ones with a higher intelligence, do not. Quick of mind as well as of foot, they watch and learn. They get smarter and better. They evolve. They've got all the old skills and the street rat's morality, but they're put to new purpose. To be sure, there's only a few. But they're good. Very good, in fact." Monroe met DiGenero's eyes. "Very, very good."

"Junior," DiGenero said.

"Natural selection in the land of opportunity. After all, Joe Kennedy began as a bootlegger, his son became our president. The Harrimans helped give the railroad robber barons their name, Averell died a world statesman."

"And what's Junior?" DiGenero asked. "The next fucking secretary of state?"

Monroe shrugged. "Columbia undergraduate, master's degree in politics and economics from Tufts, the Fletcher School of Law and Diplomacy, a few years in banking overseas. Socializes with the foreign affairs types. A member of the right business and social clubs. He runs his own international investment company. An office on Park Avenue. A different breed."

"What's wrong with RICO?" DiGenero asked.

"You mean why can't we nail him with it?"

"Yes," DiGenero said.

"His assets are parked where RICO can't get them. After all, the mob didn't invent Euroyen and Eurodollar accounts, international mutual funds, or instantaneous electronic swaps and transfers. The art forms didn't even exist when they wrote the RICO statutes. But they do today. Evolution. Once upon a time, Junior's old man used to put money in an iron box and bury it in the garden. Junior understands international financial liberalization."

"Why not do something else to get to the cash?" DiGenero asked.

"You mean, extend the long arm of American law by, say, asking another government to seize his accounts?"

"Yeah."

"Good question. But here's another one. When the world's biggest debtor begs the Japanese, the Europeans, and everyone else to lend us enough to pay the bills, do you think the Department of Justice is going to waltz over to Treasury and ask for a ruling that would make the deep pockets nervous? More to the point, do you really think Treasury would agree to do anything, if they did?"

DiGenero stood and walked to the window. Rain fell. Traffic below had thinned. The headlights shone feebly. Taillights glowed, pinpoints of red lost in matte black. "So the message is Washington doesn't give a shit," he said.

Monroe shook his head. "Ah, but you see they do."

DiGenero turned. "Wait a minute. Are you telling me Scarlese's not to be touched?"

"No. He's just, well, not easy. Not an unambiguous target, shall we say. And meanwhile, the legions battle on the frontiers. Rome is preoccupied with new barbarians." Monroe sighed. "And that's not all. Scarlese's not the only thing that's changed."

"Now you're going to cheer me up."

"We've changed."

DiGenero snorted. "Tell me about it."

"Frank, your operation was our first real push to get inside the families after Hoover. He was the kiss of death on undercovers. But even after Hoover died, when anyone mentioned the word 'undercover,' his clones, the blue suits and white shirts, ran away. With you, we were alone, feeling our way, but at least there was no competition. We had the field to ourselves. Now?"

"You need a scorecard to tell the players," DiGenero said.

"At least in New York," Monroe agreed. "The United States Attorneys, the New York District Attorneys, the Organized Crime Strike Force, the cops, the Bureau. They've all got a dog in the race. Most of the time they cooperate. But most of the time isn't all of the time, is it? Lets face it. Turf will out."

"You're saying there are things going on with Scarlese that the Bureau doesn't want to show? Rocks they don't want to turn over?" DiGenero asked.

"Maybe. I don't know."

"For Christ's sake!" DiGenero's anger flared. "Drop the 'I don't know' horseshit, Mac. I only get one message from you. Scarlese killed my wife and the Bureau doesn't give a damn. They know who did it. They know goddamn well who did it. But they're going to look the other way."

"Calm down." Monroe shifted in the chair, as if physically discomforted by the outburst. He spoke, enunciating precisely. "I don't know that. I don't know the facts. I've given you my opinion. That's all. Now, let me give you some advice. The worst thing you can do is push. They don't like that here"—he gestured toward the surrounding executive suites—"they don't like that at all. If they discover a zealot, someone who's running with a case, its quite easy to take care of him. The word goes out that the seventh floor would like to be kept 'aware.' 'Aware.'

Do you know what that means? It means everyone involved in the case looks harder, longer, closer at all the details. When in doubt they write another memo, seeking 'guidance.' They meet more frequently, just to keep people abreast. They make more phone calls, checking and double-checking. And they drop in on their superiors, more 'heads up,' the kind that begin, 'I just thought you should be aware.' No one says, 'lay off.' Or 'drop it.' Heavens forbid. No such fingerprints. The giant mill continues to turn, but more slowly, much more slowly. It grinds, but o' so fine." Monroe looked down, fastidiously straightening his tie. "In a word, don't push. You need to understand that pursuing this case isn't a simple matter. Scarlese's changed. Times have changed. We've all changed."

"No. What's changed is that my wife's dead."

Monroe was silent for several moments. "You don't get it, do you?"

"I guess not," DiGenero said.

Monroe finished his scotch. "Don't do anything rash, Frank."

DiGenero put his glass on the desk. In the wingchair, Monroe sat unmoving, as if posed. Tweed jacket, soft rolled collar, subdued tie, dark flannels. Among the old furnishings, he seemed perfectly suited for the present and the future as well as the past. An appropriate addition to the traditional decor. Someone who understood how things fit in.

"You're right," DiGenero said.

"What's that?"

"I shouldn't be here."

"Sailing is still open," Monroe said, but there was no invitation in his voice.

DiGenero walked to the door. He thrust his hands into his pockets. "I should know more about the Romans. I mean, an Italian from New York, that's my roots, right?"

Monroe didn't reply.

DiGenero continued. "Actually, when I was a kid, I was interested in the gladiators. I read all I could find. I was fascinated. What a job. They were rewarded, honored, heroes as long as they fought. But nobody could retire. Lousy pension program. No annuities. The only way out was to lose. To die. So it was up to them. Each one. On his own. They had to fight to stay alive." He paused at the door. "We've come a long way since then, haven't we?"

Monroe frowned reprovingly. "Don't be melodramatic, Frank."

"Right. I don't know the facts, do I? But, you see, that's only my opinion."

CHAPTER

3

AT THE SOUND of the bell, the chef cursed the world that made him work during a Sicilian's hour of rest. He pushed aside the plastic curtain, a reclaimed, red and white checked tablecloth. The kitchen's small serving window framed a customer, who stood just inside the door, surveying the empty tables. He shuffled his feet on the welcome mat, instigating the off-tempo chiming.

The chef let the curtain fall. "Why do I do this? To serve an antipasto and supper, that's one thing. But dinner? Minga! It's a man's time for himself."

The trattoria's kitchen was narrow, its single aisle overhung, jungle-like, with pots, pans, whisks, ladles, and strainers.

"Lunch," the chef spit out the English word like an epithet. He squeezed by his wife. Bent over a steaming kettle, the heavyset woman poked with a calloused finger at the slow rolling pasta, testing its texture, seemingly oblivious to her husband as well as the boiling water.

He paused at a second stove and stirred the contents of an oversized saucepan, then brandished the spoon, scattering fragments of tomato flecked with basil, onion, and garlic, the basic ingredients of the *sugo di pesce*.

"Who goes out for lunch? Who, I ask you? Nobody, that's who. Civilized men go home. They rest. They eat. They talk. They sleep. They don't have 'lunch.' They have a time of peace. An hour, two hours. Is that too much to ask?"

His wife straightened and wiped her hands on her apron, two movements that habit long ago had fused into one. She stared at her husband, head lowered slightly to peer beneath the uneven edge of steel, cast iron, and copper stalactites between them.

"Too much?" she asked. "No, that's not too much, as long as you don't wan' no business." Her shoulders humped, an exaggerated shrug.

"You come to America to find 'peace'? Okay, that's what you did just fine in Paterno. Sit on your ass at the taverna and watch the goats shit in the square. You had plenty of peace, you and your goombata, your 'friends.' That's good, eh? In Sicily, you didn't have no two hours a day to be a civilized man. You had twenty-four."

"Whadda you know?" The chef tossed the spoon in the saucepan. The thickening tomatoes, rich and deep red as they gave up their moisture, enveloped it without a splash. "Peace, that's all." He raised both hands, palms up, and stepped toward the dining room. "Just a time of peace in my day."

Moments before, the trattoria's first and only customer of the afternoon also had bestirred himself at the sound of the door. Seated in his usual corner, Vito Rocchi had shifted his two hundred and twenty-pound bulk to examine the newcomer. Rocchi turned back to his antipasto and racing form. He couldn't place the face, but with the flood tide of outsiders that was not unusual. Little Italy was not what it used to be. He tore off a piece of fresh bread and glanced over his shoulder. By the door, the man eyeing him looked away.

Rocchi shook his head. Whaddaya gonna do? East Harlem, Bushwick, Bensonhurst. Once they had all been Italian. Now? In Brooklyn and Queens, they still had their neighborhoods, but Little Italy was a shadow of itself. Only Mulberry Street was left. For forty-one years, Rocchi had never lived anywhere else. His father and mother were still here, in the shotgun walkup, five rooms in a row, front-to-back, above the shoe shop. His brothers and sisters had moved to Long Island with the rest, but not him. Not Vito. Little Italy was home, his home. Anybody who mattered knew Vito Rocchi. Anybody who didn't? Rocchi reached for his last piece of bread. Well, that was their fuckin' problem.

"*Buongiorno.*" The chef's smile froze as he entered the room.

The newcomer had moved toward Rocchi with an arm extended as if in greeting, or for an instant it seemed so. In his chair, Rocchi jerked in time with popping sounds before he suddenly slumped. The man stepped forward and put something to his ear. Rocchi's head snapped right, tipping his bulk into an uncomfortable repose, wedged between the table and wall.

"*Prego,* no, please," the chef moaned as the man turned. His lips moved, but the words were useless. He was alien, with an alien's eyes, windows on a heart that pleas could not soften. The automatic with silencer protruded from his fist.

The blows struck the chef like a hammer. His legs slid from under him. He fell back and rolled on his side. The doorbell chimed, followed by tires squealing.

The chef tried to raise his head, to call out, but it was hard, too hard. He closed his eyes. No matter. There was no pain and he was no longer in the trattoria, but in his straight-back chair, tipped against the familiar stuccoed wall, his usual spot at the taverna on the square in Paterno. In the Sicilian sunshine, all was quiet. He felt the calm. Paterno was at peace. It was the time of rest. All was as it should be, although for reasons he could not explain, the midday light was fading fast to the pitch of night and his wife was screaming, close by, but also far, far away.

The dining room was filled with a mixture of plainclothes detectives and uniformed patrolmen, each wearing surgical gloves and carrying pens and notebooks, antiseptic students of mayhem in a badly contaminated world.

Three had gathered around Vito Rocchi, who remained where the final shot had impelled him, bent forward in a poor-postured slouch. Two more blue suits and a police photographer stood by the chef. Tipped on his side, knees drawn up, he seemed to have found a comfortable, fetal recumbency. A photographer, in his ponytail, jungle fatigue jacket, and jeans, was finishing. The chef demanded attention from several different angles to complete the official record of the scene. Nuzzling his camera, the photographer circled, his strobe lighting the room, flashes in quick succession.

The front door opened and closed, admitting a middle-aged man. Heavyset, in a cheap, black raincoat, he removed his hat and gloves. He stood, arms clasped in front, with the stolid posture of assumed authority. Several officers looked up, offering glances that conveyed a recognition without welcome.

From the rear of the dining room, Harold Shaeffer stepped forward. Tanned, with razor-cut silver hair, his only discordant adornment was the shield of the New York Police Department dangling from the breast pocket of his well-tailored suit.

Shaeffer spoke with a salesman's forced conviviality. "Good to see you, Tony."

Tony Benedetto shook hands diffidently. "What happened?"

Shaeffer motioned. A squat detective in a rumpled carcoat detached himself from the trio examining Rocchi.

"Give him a rundown." Shaeffer continued to smile. Detective Arnold Silverstein thumbed to the front of his notebook and began to recite in a thick Brooklyn accent. "For Rocchi, eight shots in the back, then one in the head. In one ear and straight out the other." He grinned. "The headshot ain't nothin'. Vito could always clean both ears from either side." He pointed at the chef. "Three in the chest."

"Weapons?" Benedetto asked.

"No piece so far. Maybe Vito's is out there." Silverstein nodded toward the street. "That's his Oldsmobile. We ain't gone through it yet. Motor was still warm when we got here, so he musta just sat down to eat."

Outside, the gray November morning had become a leaden afternoon. Beyond the Day-Glo orange bunting that marked the police boundary of the crime scene, a cluster of the curious had gathered. Two television vans had parked, half on the curb. Their protruding portable satellite dishes, extended on stalks, waved off tempo in the gusts from the northwest. The temperature and biting wind kept the spectators down, but the numbers wouldn't get much bigger. Even in good weather, hits in Little Italy didn't draw crowds.

"Why him?" Benedetto pointed at the chef.

Silverstein shrugged. "Looks like he picked the wrong time to walk out and ask, 'How's the soup?' I doubt he was part of it. If the shooter had wanted to whack 'em all, he woulda got the wife."

"Where was she?" Benedetto asked.

"In the kitchen."

"Did the shooter know?"

"Did he know?" Silverstein's eyes opened wide. "It took a horse needle fulla Demerol to shut her up. The precinct's five blocks away. I could hear her wit'out the telephone."

In the kitchen, a door slammed, followed by sound of heavy objects being dragged across the floor. The trio turned in unison. The fingerprint technician dropped two metal suitcases at the dining room's threshold. Overweight, he caught his breath as he surveyed the surroundings, calculating where to begin.

Benedetto spoke, "Call 'em off."

The trace of Shaeffer's smile disappeared. "What?"

"We'll take it from here."

"Whaddya mean?" Shaeffer asked.

"I mean Rocchi's ours. He belongs to the Bureau. I don't want anybody fuckin' up the evidence. Call your boys off. My squad's on the way."

Silverstein's eyes shifted from one man to the other.

"Come on, Tony." Shaeffer struggled at diplomacy. "You know what the memo says. The Scarleses are a joint operation. We do this together. Bureau and NYPD. All the way."

"The memo says we got the lead, you support. That's all it says. It's our call. I say we work up the scene, process the evidence, and handle the investigation. And, I say you pack it in."

Shaeffer stepped closer to the FBI agent. He lowered his voice, "That's bullshit and you know it. This is my precinct." Shaeffer glanced around. A few, who were watching, looked away. "I gotta position here, you know what I mean?"

Benedetto stared, expressionless. "Call 'em off."

Shaeffer sighed imperceptibly. By rights, the initial investigation belonged to the precinct, but for reasons it had not deigned to reveal to the New York Police Department, the Federal Bureau of Investigation, in the person of Special Agent Anthony Benedetto, was asserting its claim on the Scarlese family, right down to the murder of one of its foot soldiers. Shaeffer knew he could stall, pitch a fit, call in his superiors and, if need be, string out the contest with a paper war, a blitz of memos and meetings among the highly paid help. But with one hundred and twenty-four unsolved murders in the precinct, an organized crime squad that was already five officers undermanned, and reservations on a cruise ship leaving Miami in forty-eight hours, made by a wife who had talked non-stop about six days in a deck chair rather than another week of a grimy New York fall, he also knew the budding conflict fell into the category of things simply not worth the fight.

One of the policemen searching Rocchi's pockets interrupted, "Hey, you wanna see this?" He held up a wallet for Shaeffer's perusal.

"Call 'em off," Benedetto repeated.

"Hey, Silverstein," Shaeffer began, but the detective had already turned to take the offering.

Silverstein opened Rocchi's wallet. He glanced at the contents before spotting the slip of paper tucked behind the cash, an American Express receipt.

"Lemme have it," the FBI agent said, extending his hand, palm up. Silverstein ignored him. He unfolded the receipt, looked through the wallet again, then at Shaeffer. "Rocchi don't have no American Express card," Silverstein said.

Benedetto's hand was still outstretched.

"And funny thing," Silverstein added, digging in the wallet and removing a driver's license, "the receipt ain't got Vito's name neither."

Silverstein held the license and the slip of paper side by side. On the receipt, the signature of "Andrew Markham" was scrawled in the same childlike strokes and miscellaneous angles as Rocchi's own.

Shaeffer motioned. Silverstein handed both to Benedetto. The FBI agent compared the license and slip of paper. "Rocchi used a boosted card, then tossed it. Not a big surprise."

"Maybe." Silverstein lit a cigarette. "But why charge with hot plastic, throw the card away, and keep the receipt? A brilliant operator Rocchi was not, but that's too stupid, even for Vito."

Silverstein plucked the receipt from Benedetto's hand and squinted at its details. The FBI agent glared at Shaeffer, seeking the appropriate imposition of discipline. "Let's wrap it up, Hal."

Ostensibly distracted, Shaeffer read over Silverstein's shoulder.

"Lemme have that back." Benedetto snapped his fingers.

"I think Vito's been traveling," Silverstein said. "Look at this." He handed the receipt to Shaeffer.

The embossing stamp, imprinting the merchant's name, address, and account number, was blurred but legible. Shaeffer read aloud, "The Mourning Dove Bed and Breakfast, Dundalk. So?"

"Look at the charges," Silverstein said.

Shaeffer read aloud again, "Thirty-two dollars and fifty cents."

"That ain't no dollar sign. It's thirty-two pounds, fifty pence."

Shaeffer eyed the receipt. "Silverstein, we got Vietnamese, Guatemalans, Pakistanis, Iranians, and God-knows-what-other Third Worlders running cash registers all over this country. You telling me they all gonna have perfect penmanship? Pounds, schmounds, gimme a break."

Benedetto grabbed the receipt, "I said, wrap it up."

"Lieutenant," the cop searching Rocchi's body spoke again, this time to Shaeffer. "You might wanna look at this."

Shaeffer glanced at what was being extended, then nodded at Silverstein, who took the passport. The detective opened it. The feel was supple, not new. Inside the cover, opposite the secretary of state's formal salutation and request to grant the bearer unhindered passage, Vito Rocchi's face stared back, accompanied under the tamper-proof plastic laminate by the name, date, and place of birth of "Andrew Markham."

"Whaddyaknow." Silverstein thumbed to the back of the passport. It was nearly filled with entry and exit stamps. "Vito Rocchi, alias Andrew Markham, was a real traveler," Silverstein said, flipping through the pages, "but Vito's been in a rut. The stamps are all for Shannon. Looks like he went there four, five times a year." He furrowed his brow. "That's an airport in Ireland, right?"

"Gimme the passport," Benedetto said. He stepped toward Silverstein, but Shaeffer was in the way.

"Ireland," Shaeffer said the word quizzically. "Anywhere else?" he asked.

Silverstein shook his head. For the first time, he looked at Benedetto and smiled. "I don't get it. What's a dago making five trips a year to Ireland for?"

Benedetto shouldered past Shaeffer. "Hand it over."

Silverstein stood unmoving until Shaeffer spoke. "Go ahead."

Benedetto grabbed the passport, stuffing it into his pocket. Behind them, the front door opened. Queued on the sidewalk, six men, some with briefcases and cameras, filed inside. Dressed alike, they wore blue windbreakers with "FBI" stenciled in yellow on the back.

"America's team." Silverstein nodded at the squad. Two cops nearby laughed.

"It explains Dundalk," Shaeffer said.

"Huh?" Silverstein raised his eyebrows.

"The place on the receipt. I shoulda remembered. Dundalk's in Ireland."

"How do you know?"

"A priest in my neighborhood parish—the one I grew up in—came from there."

"Around Shannon?" Silverstein asked.

"No, near Ulster."

"What's that?"

Benedetto had half turned toward the newcomers, but stopped. He stared intently at Shaeffer.

"Northern Ireland," Shaeffer said. "Dundalk's on the border with Ulster, just south of the Northern Ireland line."

C H A P T E R

4

EXCEPT FOR THE polite formalities, the conversations were curt. "United 3770, New York Center."

"3770." The pilot acknowledged the air traffic control center's call, repeating his flight's number.

"Cleared for 27,000. Contact Washington Center on 134.2." The controller spoke, a monotone.

"Roger. Out of 21 for 27. Washington Center on 134.2. United 3770. Good day."

Somewhere above the overcast, Flight 3770 was ascending, slipping into its place among the aircraft in the southbound air corridor. Bell-flower looked at the clock. 4:20 P.M. Time to kill. Bellflower thumbed through the airline guide, finding the entry.

UA 3770. 1600 SPR 1725 DCA 0 B727.

Twenty minutes before, United 3770, a Boeing 727, had taken off from Springfield, Massachusetts, a nonstop for Washington, D.C.'s National Airport. In New York's regional air traffic control center, the controller had just radioed the flight, clearing the pilot to climb to his assigned cruising altitude. The controller also had "handed off" UA 3770, providing the flight's new radio frequency and passing responsibility to Washington Center, the regional control facility outside Leesburg, Virginia. Two hundred and fifty miles away, another voice would guide UA 3770 for almost an hour until handing it off again, this time to an approach controller at National Airport.

Bellflower tapped the scanner's keypad, selecting the new frequency. The pilot was already on the air.

"Washington Center, United 3770 is with you at 25, heading for 27. What you got for weather down there?" he asked.

"United 3770, Washington Center. Last I heard National is 600 and a quarter mile, winds 5 at 180. Should be GCA all the way."

"Roger, thank you. United 3770." The pilot signed off.

This day in Washington, with a 600 foot ceiling and a quarter mile visibility in rain and fog, UA 3770 would approach from the north. The controller would direct the aircraft through a twisting descent over the Maryland and Virginia suburbs. The radioed instructions would point the pilot down the Potomac River at the heart of the city. Then, after a whippoorwill's turn around the Rosslyn, Virginia, highrises, he would flash below the overcast, lined up for the usual tub-thumping landing on National's brutally short main runway.

Bellflower glanced out. From the penthouse office, the clouds had closed over the East River and to the west, Central Park, obscuring even the brilliant red beacons ornamenting the heights of the General Motors Building. The cold front had spread a shroud over New York's Indian summer. Conditions had unfolded as planned. The forecasters had determined the optimum week, although not the day. That was Bellflower's choice.

It was 4:30 P.M. The time had come. A touch on the keypad reprogrammed the scanner. New York Center's radio transmissions tumbled over each other. As each controller spoke, the constant staccato of voices in the background testified to the nonstop activity. It was the hour of European arrivals. If it was on schedule, the flight would be near Montauk, probably forty or fifty miles from the eastern tip of Long Island. At that point, it would still belong to New York Center, ten minutes or more from hand-off to Kennedy's approach control. Even so, Bellflower needed forewarning. The window was small. Above the North Atlantic, November was the cusp of the season and the jet stream was fickle. Its shift in the stratosphere by only a few degrees could prematurely transform the always difficult westerlies into winter's battering headwinds, producing delays and sometimes diversions. On rare occasions, it could also free westbound arrivals from the struggle, allowing early arrivals.

The scanner came alive. One after another, the daily flights from Paris, Frankfurt, Geneva, Rome, Gatwick, and Heathrow checked in. It was usually seventh or eighth in the five o'clock bloc, mingled among the regulars from TWA, United, Air France, Lufthansa, El Al, Delta, Continental.

A crisply British voice cut through the polyglot of accents. "Good afternoon, New York Center, this is BA 121 Heavy, with you at 35."

Beside the scanner, the computer screen glowed.

"BA 121 Heavy, New York Center. Descend to 27 and hold 240," the controller responded with initial instructions.

"To 27,000 and heading 240. BA 121 Heavy," the pilot confirmed.

Bellflower worked quickly, inserting a small data disc and pressing several keys. Normally, it took only a few seconds to link the computer via its internal modum and the telephone lines to other systems, even those half a world away. In this case, the instructions on the disc required four minutes to execute.

Bellflower had written and rewritten the software to minimize the delay, but only so much could be done. Time was a measure of complexity. The program was one of a kind and its thousands of lines of code did more than unlock doors. They camouflaged themselves even as they worked, removing the electronic footprints that could be followed to their source. The result not only provided access to the FAA's air traffic control computers, but also deceived its sophisticated security system into believing the user was not miles away, but on the inside, working at New York Center.

"BA 121 Heavy, New York Center. Descend to 15,000. Turn right to 260." The controller spoke, obviously busy.

"To 15. Right to 260. BA 121 Heavy."

The computer screen bloomed and darkened, flashing colored codes and logos as Bellflower's program slipped past barrier after barrier into the air traffic network's electronic inner sanctum.

"BA 121 Heavy, New York Center. Descend to 12,000. Keep it at 320 knots and hold 260. We're going to move you right along. Now handing you over to TRACON for your Cat 3 approach," the air traffic controller said.

"Out of 15 for 12. Speed 320. Hold heading 260. Thank you. BA 121 Heavy."

Bellflower eyed the clock. The flight would make only a few more turns. The final vector would come in minutes. No more.

The screen lit with a brilliant blue background, then the words.

THIS IS THE NEW YORK CENTER'S TRACON IV AIR TRAFFIC CONTROL SYSTEM. YOU NOW HAVE ACCESS TO THE ON-LINE, REAL-TIME FLIGHT MANAGEMENT FUNCTION. SPECIFY FLIGHT CALLSIGN FOR ENTRY OF COMMANDS TO CONTROL AIRCRAFT.

ENTER CALLSIGN:

Bellflower moved the cursor on the screen and typed:

BA 121 HEAVY.

TRACON IV responded instantly:

BA 121 HEAVY. STATUS: APPROACHING FINAL VECTOR, JFK RUNWAY
13L. BA 121 HEAVY FLIGHT PROGRAMMING NOW UNDER YOUR COM-
MAND.

Bellflower worked quickly. The keys rattled. Fifty-eight seconds later,
the last strokes erased the screen. Its colors blossomed and died. Bellflower turned off the computer. Beside the blank screen, the scanner
emitted fragments of dialogue. Outside, a squall passed the windows,
replaced by a steady rain. Bellflower silenced the radio. There was no
longer reason to listen. It was done.

Descending, the darkness surrounded them, creating a mirror from the
windscreen that moments before had revealed the coverlet of clouds
stretching unbroken to the horizon. On the thick glass, three faces appeared, dull etched against a soft velvet background.

"Pea soup, eh?" Seated at the instrument console behind the captain
and first officer, the flight engineer looked up from his logbook. He
stared past them at the blackness.

"Right to the ground." In the left seat, the captain spoke. "Well
below minimums in the old days."

The captain studied his own image on the windscreen. His expression
seemed confident or, he thought, perhaps disengaged, depending on
one's interpretation. A cultivated self-control after thirty-five years of
practice. Unflappable, designed to inspire confidence. Suited to a senior
British Airways captain with twenty thousand hours in command of a
Boeing 747 bearing four hundred souls across the Atlantic.

"BA 121 Heavy, turn right to 260. Descend to 9,000." The radio
transmission from New York Center cut through the cockpit's temporary
silence.

"Right turn to 260. Leaving 12,000 for 9. BA 121 Heavy." The first
officer repeated the new compass heading and altitude as well as their
callsign, acknowledging the instructions. A native of Birmingham, he
spoke with the flat Midlands accent of England's industrial heartland, a
contrast to the American tones of the computer-generated voice from
New York Center.

"Nothing makes me feel quite so foolish as talking to a computer.
Sounds real enough. Even gets rather nasty if you don't reply," the first
officer said. He shook his head, "I suppose there's a human being down
there, somewhere."

The captain watched the flight controls. His wheel turned, rolling the

747 gently to the right as the yoke—the control column—moved forward, pitching the nose down.

Mounted between the captain and the first officer, the throttles eased back, then up slightly in unison, adjusting their rate of descent. The roar of the four Rolls Royce engines modulated, reflecting the new setting.

"We have 220 knots on the mark. Now out of 10 for 9." The first officer confirmed their airspeed and altitude for no one in particular. The twin control columns moved toward them, raising the nose a few degrees to settle the 747 gently into its newly assigned altitude.

The intercom from the passenger cabin chirped in their earphones. The first officer answered. "Yes?"

"Ready for final check?" It was the purser's voice.

The captain nodded at the first officer, who replied, "Right. Button them up, if you will."

Behind and below the cockpit, the fourteen stewards and flight attendants were tidying up the last of the paraphernalia that had fed, entertained, and comforted their travelers. Most passengers assumed the maneuvers transforming their flight from its level, eight-hour-long trajectory across the Atlantic into a banking and turning descent to Long Island were a product of the captain's hand. They were not. In fact, neither the captain nor the first officer moved the controls or adjusted the throttles. Despite the clouds, rain, and fog that had closed airports from Providence to Baltimore, BA 121 was descending toward John F. Kennedy International Airport through the afternoon murk on a Category 3 approach. Like the other airports, JFK was "zero-zero," no visibility and no ceiling, but the 747 would fly to the outer marker, the radio beacon for its assigned runway, make its final approach, land, and brake to a stop automatically. The airliner would be guided by signals transmitted directly to its onboard instrument landing and autopilot systems from TRACON IV, the Federal Aviation Administration's new, state-of-the-art air traffic control computer.

A Category 3 approach. A landing with no ceiling, no visibility, and now, the captain thought, no controller. It still made him wonder. Until six months ago, when the FAA had inaugurated TRACON IV, an air traffic controller had always been part of the chain of command. To be sure, the controllers were still there, inside New York Center, monitoring "the system," as the Americans liked to call it. But monitoring was all they did. Now, it was hands off at both ends. The controllers and the pilots only watched. TRACON IV did the work, flying as well as guiding the aircraft to the final touchdown. It was quite an innovation, allowing one controller to oversee five times as many incoming flights, even in the worst conditions.

The captain examined the instruments, habitually checking. All was well. Still, even after thousands of instrument landings, relinquishing all his decisions to a machine felt odd.

He glanced at the first officer. His hands rested on the wheel. Most were like that, maintaining the fiction. Atavistic, really. A throwback, like silk scarves and goggles. The software engineers had even tried to salve their egos. On the radio, TRACON IV's computer-generated voice wasn't actually relaying instructions—the data transmissions from the control center to the 747's computers took care of that. Rather, the radioed commands simply advised them what the machinery was up to, reassuring that they hadn't been forgotten. The requirement to respond —to answer the computer—was for safety's sake, making sure they weren't nodding off.

The message was clear, he thought. There, there, be good boys, sit still, and let the black boxes do the work. What was the joke the American who briefed them on the new system had told? Because of TRACON IV, the airlines were cutting back. The new cockpit crews would consist of a pilot and a dog. The pilot was supposed to sit quietly and mind his own business. The dog was trained to bite him in the ass if he tried to touch the controls.

The captain folded his arms. Of course, they weren't helpless. The button was there. If something went wrong, you could disengage the autopilot and take over. But that would simply mean an aborted approach. With no visibility and no ceiling, your only choice would be to land somewhere else. Oh well, hats off to the wizards with their integrated circuits, video displays, and miraculous software. If it wasn't for them, he'd be humoring four hundred irate passengers, explaining why he was delivering the lot to a bus ride home from Philadelphia, or Boston, or wherever the airports were open, rather than to the arms of their loved ones in New York.

"BA 121 Heavy, turn right to heading 310 and descend to 5,000," the computer's voice said.

"Right turn to 310. Leaving 9 for 5, BA 121 Heavy." The first officer repeated the instructions, then returned to the landing checklist, his question-and-answer catechism with the flight engineer.

The 747 began a gentle roll and descent. Miracle of modern technology or not, the captain thought, it was mildly depressing. For thirty years, whatever the engineers had devised, takeoffs and landings had always been his. Now, he was reduced to pulling two levers. Setting the flaps and putting down the gear. Galling. Never mind that the airplane could land itself more smoothly than he could. To add insult to injury, he couldn't under these conditions manage what the bloody system was

"Do you, Mr. Falcone-McGuire?" She smiled, acknowledging the compliment.

He stood. "You know my life story and I don't even know your name."

"Easily remedied." She dug into her purse, producing a business card.

He read aloud. "Jilian McCray, Correspondent, Dublin *Register.*" He looked up, puzzled. "You said London. I thought you were English."

"A grievous mistake," she said solemnly. "The newspaper's international bureau is in London. That's where I work. Home base, as it were. As to your other assumption, actually I'm Irish. Or Irish-English. If that's a matter of any interest, it will take time to explain. After all, seventy years of Falcone-McGuire union is hard enough to fathom, but seven hundred years of my family ties could prove impossible to sort out." She paused. "At least in one sitting."

She glanced outside. "Is it still raining?"

He looked through the window. "Yeah."

"And I don't have an umbrella."

"Take mine." He reached down and placed it on the bar. "I'm catching a cab anyway."

"I must return this. Where are you staying?" she asked.

"Don't worry." He slipped her card into his pocket. "I'll find you."

This time she extended her hand. "I hope so. It's been a pleasure, Mr. Falcone-McGuire."

"Frank."

"Frank," she repeated.

He held her hand a moment longer than necessary, then stepped away to retrieve his raincoat.

She watched him until the door closed. She motioned to the bartender. "Do you have a plastic bag? I've got a few things I'm afraid will get soaked."

The bartender rummaged under the counter. "Here."

When he turned away, she grasped the fabric of the umbrella, slipping the bag over the handle, then bent down, replacing the umbrella on the floor.

"Mr. Ferringa's late," the bartender said.

She started. Concentrating, she hadn't heard him return to refill her wine glass.

"So he is." She brushed back her hair with an unconscious motion. "No matter. It's the weather. Whenever it rains, you simply can't count on plans working out."

The bartender nodded perfunctorily.

doing at all. He couldn't even put his own aircraft where it was supposed to go on the ground.

"BA 121 Heavy, maintain 310 and descend to 2,000. You are cleared for a zero-zero Cat 3 approach to Runway 13 Left. Advise when over outer marker."

The captain glanced out. They were deep in the murk, embedded in blackness. The rain swept across the glass, a changing pattern of veins and veneers. The altimeter unwound as the wings leveled.

"Flaps 40, gear down," he spoke.

The first officer set the flaps at 40 degrees and lowered the gear. The shudder of the airstream coursing over reshaped wings and around the massive struts and tires slowed them momentarily before the autopilot adjusted the throttles, adding power.

The captain eyed the flap indicator and landing gear lights.

"Flaps 40. Gear down and locked," the first officer said.

The catechism was complete. On the navigational video display, the needle of the radio direction finder swung through its arc, indicating they had passed over the transmitter beacon.

The captain spoke, "Outer marker."

The first officer reached for his microphone, "New York Center, over outer marker, BA 121 Heavy."

"BA 121 Heavy, cleared to land on 13 Left. Contact tower on 119.1 before departing the active. Ground radar will direct to the taxiway and your pier."

"Roger. Cleared to land on 13 Left. Contact tower before departing the active runway, BA 121 Heavy," the first officer said.

The blaze of their landing lights captured a vision of motion and space, an abstract of grays, torn streamers of cloud, sheets of rain. Night and fog, the captain thought. His public school German came back to him. *Nacht und Nebel.* The words sounded right, better than the English for what surrounded them. Their descent became steeper.

"I have the runway lights. Wait a minute. Where the hell are they? I . . ." The first officer's voice trailed away uncertainly.

The captain's hands moved automatically to the controls. The throttles inched back, allowing the airspeed to bleed away as the nose of the 747 rose. The autopilot was preparing them to flare, to settle on the runway. They were still flying but approaching the transition when for an instant they would hang suspended, balanced between two states of being, a creation meant for the air but at that speck in time, one bound to the earth as well.

Beneath them, a stain of light suddenly spread across the blackness, then disappeared.

"What was that?" The first officer, straight in his seat, scanned the onrushing darkness.

"A go-round?" The flight engineer leaned forward.

The captain shook his head. "No reason." Before him, on the instrument landing system's video display, TRACON showed they were perfectly positioned. On glide path, on glide slope, about to touch down. He had flown the Kennedy approach hundreds of times, hands on. With even a little visibility, they should see the strobe, maybe even a hint of the runway's centerline lights.

"There," the captain spoke, motioning. Ahead and to the left, a rich green reflected through the mist. "Taxiway markers."

The clouds parted. Suddenly, the green changed. To yellow, then red.

"It can't be," the first officer whispered, disbelieving.

The bank of traffic signals, indelible spots of color against the sky's monochrome gray, hung across a six-lane highway. On either side of the 747, where JFK's taxiways should have been, a grid of neighborhood streets organized the clutter of bungalows, apartments, and stores.

"Max power! Now!" the captain shouted. The first officer shoved the throttles forward. Behind them, they could hear the banshee wail of the engines responding, spooling up.

"It's a go-round!" The captain had barely spoken when they felt the first sickening yaw. At one hundred feet, the 747 pulled right as the eight massive tires of the rear main landing gear, trailing at treetop level, tore the roof from the three-story duplex on Island View Lane.

The captain jammed his foot on the rudder pedal, correcting reflexively. The airliner slewed left, straightening its course.

The engine's muffled roar and shudder surrounded them, but the sinking sensation told him their power was rising toward its crescendo too slowly. Even with fuel spilling into their hot sections, the giant turbofans needed five or six seconds to build full thrust. Too long to hold their altitude. Too little to pull them away from the edge. Too late to end their purgatory. To avoid the moment of judgment.

There was only one choice. Airspeed. He shoved the control column forward.

"Come on!" The first officer's voice was guttural, willing them into the air. The nose leveled. For a moment, the three men sat transfixed. A quarter mile distant, rushing toward them, the line of cars snaked bumper to bumper from the parking lot to the supermarket entrance. They could see the drivers. Turned up, their faces made pale ovals, like those clustered on the sidewalk, the bagboys and customers who had stepped from under the store's awning into the rain to stare incredulously at the seven hundred thousand pounds of 747, engines screaming, descending on the Bayshore Boulevard Shopping Center.

"Christ, get up!" The flight engineer's plea was hopeless. The landing gear raked across the roof of a warehouse. The right wing dipped, jerked from below by the torn power and telephone lines, splintered rafters and tangled debris.

The captain wrenched desperately on the wheel and yoke, but it was not enough. Struggling like a beast trapped and condemned, the 747 wallowed and stalled, losing the last of its lift as he drove the left wing low.

Two hundred and thirty feet behind the flight deck, the underbelly of the tail struck first, surgically bisecting a row of parked cars. For an instant, the cockpit and most of the fuselage remained in the air, but they were nothing now, not an aircraft under control or even a body in flight, only a hurdling mass, sparks, and tortured metal, irredeemably lost for reasons that none in the cockpit could discern, much less understand.

It was then the captain saw her. Locked in their queue, the cars and their drivers were frozen in life as soon they would be in death, but on the sidewalk, people were moving, some backing away, some running, others holding up their arms as if to ward off a blow. Only she was standing, alone and unmoving, as if waiting for him to arrive. She was the same height as his wife, with the same dark hair, even the same manner, head turned slightly, seeming to favor a certain perspective that would allow her more easily to pick a known face from the crowd. He knew it wasn't her. But in that instant before the left wingtip caught the macadam and they began their fiery cartwheel he spoke with a terrible sad helplessness. "I'm sorry, I'm sorry."

Ten miles away, in a spartan office on the second floor of the windowless building outside Westbury, Long Island, the red light flashed on the computer monitor just as the phone began to ring.

The area manager read the message printing across the video display screen: "Aircraft Lost By Cat 3 System Control. 2114 Hours Zulu. Final/ Kennedy/ 13 Left."

He lifted the phone. The voice of the approach control section supervisor was taut, "A British Air 747 is off the scope on final to JFK. The system was normal when she disappeared. We got a confirmed crash from Disaster Control."

"Where?"

"Valley Stream. A shopping center."

The supervisor felt the knot tighten in his stomach. "You're holding and diverting?"

The crash would occupy them for months of investigations and postmortems, but at this moment the scores of flights converging on New York's three major airports were his only worry.

"All Cat 3's in the sequence are holding. We're passing word to the Center to begin diverting the en routes."

It was the right answer. They would stack the aircraft that already had been handed off to them for landing at Kennedy until they could sort out who could go to LaGuardia, Newark, or elsewhere. The flights still on the way to New York were the responsibility of the FAA regional throughflight facility, "New York Center," in Islip, Long Island. It controlled the air traffic between Boston and Washington and would send Kennedy's inbound aircraft somewhere else.

"What about the REACT net?"

"We've pushed all the buttons. Fire, police, hospitals, FBI, Safety, British Air, British consulate," the supervisor answered.

"Okay, I'm coming downstairs." The area manager hung up. Through his picture window, he could see them all, a story below. On the second floor, he overlooked "the platform," the heart of the New York Terminal Radar Control Center. TRACON. It seemed almost normal. The evening shift controllers were moving in their usual pattern, some standing, some sitting before the banks of green screens, video displays, and radio transceivers, connected by their headsets to the scores of aircrews above New York, and the hundreds of controllers from Massachusetts to Virginia. Like the others, this shift handled the flights approaching or departing Kennedy, LaGuardia, and Newark. Five years ago, they needed two hundred qualified controllers. Because of TRACON IV, today they had half that many. TRACON IV's supercomputer did the calculating, arranging, guiding, and flying. Half as many people to control twice as many flights.

He rose from his desk. Even if you didn't know the controller responsible, you could tell. He had seen it before. Not often, but more times than he wanted to remember. The first reaction never varied. They stood, fixed in place, always a few steps back from the screen, staring but keeping a distance from the horror each one feared but never believed would happen to him. Only a few broke down, instantly bereft of the confidence that let them compose their intricate, invisible patterns from the changing shards of time and motion, maneuvering thousands of lives through a three-dimensional maze overhead. Most wouldn't let go, wouldn't relinquish control. They fought, argued, protested, swore, held their ground. As if by staying they could change fate. As if they could bring Lazarus back from the dead.

He stepped through the doorway, crossed the hall in a single stride, and descended the stairs two at a time, pausing briefly on the platform.

On the opposite side of the dimly lit room, under the white-on-black lettered sign, "JFK Approach," a small semicircle had formed. He strode ahead, his pace deliberate. It was important to show urgency, not haste. The small group was growing by ones and twos. Some put a comforting hand on the approach controller's shoulder. Others seemed only to stare silently. The area manager frowned. What's to see? He needed the shift, all the shift, on the job. This wasn't the time for another accident.

"Pardon me, pardon me." He pressed into the gathering. "Okay people, let's get back to work."

The group parted and reformed behind him. He stopped beside the approach section supervisor. Like the others, he was staring at the display screens.

The area manager kept his voice low, although there was no mistaking his irritation, "Come on, we've got aircraft up there. Let's get organized."

"Look." The section supervisor pointed at the Kennedy approach controller's console. On it, three radar screens glowed. Two displayed electronic maps. One, on the left, showed Kennedy's immediate airspace. Another, on the right, outlined western Long Island. The third, in the center, provided a schematic diagram of a glide slope, the final approach to JFK's Runway 13 Left. The bright white line depicted the correct descent from the outer marker to the end of the runway. Halfway down its length, a small red blip flashed, accompanied by the green lettering, "BA 121."

The approach controller's face was ashen. "It was on the slope and the path. The system said nothing was wrong. Nothing at all. Then this. Then this." His voice trailed away.

The area manager touched his arm. "You can't do anything more. The plane's down."

"Look!" Agitated, the section supervisor pointed again at the console.

"At what, for Christ's sake?" the area manager asked, aggravated. Then, he saw it. At first, he had noticed only the red blip, BA 121's last position in the air, its electronic epitaph. The message was printed lower, at the bottom of the center radar screen.

He read it over and over until his lips moved, unconsciously forming the words. They were words he had never seen before. Words that had never appeared before. Words that made him stand in silence like the others, in a room that had suddenly become very still and very, very cold.

BA 121 IS THE FIRST. FREE NORTHERN IRELAND OR OTHERS WILL DIE.

CHAPTER

5

THE TELEPHONE RANG only once before he cuffed it into silence. Dislodged, the receiver eluded him, slipping off the table to hit the floor with the crack of cheap plastic. He leaned down, groping until he found it, then lay back for a moment, listening. From the earpiece, a voice called his name. Outside, water struck leaves unevenly, an indeterminate sign, rain ending or beginning.

He raised the receiver. Plaid shadows, the creation of a forgotten porchlight, decorated the bedroom and hall.

"Frank?" Silverstein was shouting his name.

"Yeah."

DiGenero could hear a diesel's heavy idle, accompanied by the flat bleat of taxicab horns. He pictured Silverstein. He would stand with his back to the street, facing the sidewalk to watch New York's one A.M. flotsam. DiGenero knew the pose. Leaning against the phone booth, cigarette-in-mouth, receiver-wedged-between-ear-and-shoulder, arms-up-to-elbows in the terminally bagging pockets of his mauve-grime carcoat, the only one he ever wore.

They'd met on a cold March night in 1977. Two city detectives had stopped DiGenero and another wiseguy driving to Queens. The cops knew DiGenero only as the Scarlese's consigliere and put both of them against the wall. The roust was routine, but he was wearing a wire. If they exposed it, the undercover was dead. Assigned to DiGenero's operation a few weeks before as one of NYPD's loaners, a foot soldier who worked the streets as his countersurveillance, Silverstein was following a block behind. He ran a red light, broadsided the unmarked car, did a stumbling-drunk routine, and started a fight. By the time the detectives had Silverstein down, DiGenero and the wiseguy were gone.

DiGenero held the phone, waiting for the traffic noise to subside. After seeing Monroe, he had called Benedetto four days running. Ask-

50

ing, questioning, finally, drunk, badgering. Pressing for something, anything. Proof, however small, that Monroe was wrong. Benedetto had no answers and finally, no sympathy. It was then he'd called Silverstein.

The rumble of the diesel deepened to a roar as the bus pulled away. The phone was suddenly quiet. Silverstein spoke. "Rocchi's dead."

"What?" DiGenero sat up.

"Professional job. At lunch. They took out the poor *telenner* who owned the restaurant, too. But that was only 'cause he got in the way. No question Vito was the hit."

"How come?"

"Don't know," Silverstein said.

"What do you think?"

"Who's paid to think? I'm a detective second grade, remember?"

"You got the case?" DiGenero asked.

"Nope. Shaeffer."

"What's he doing?"

"Whaddya expect? He's too close to a pension. Everything is heavy lifting." Silverstein began a Yiddish singsong. "If it's drugs, it's a pain in the ass. You gotta see DEA, the narc squad, the Mayor's special coordinator, Mother Teresa, the whole shmegeggie. If it's a hit, it's a pain in the ass. Then, it's the FBI, the Strike Force, the Justice Department, the United States Attorney, the District Attorney, everybody's putzin' around. If it's just a murder, it's a pain in the ass. I mean, you gotta go to the supply cabinet, get a manila folder, type a name on the top, open your desk drawer, make some room in the pile, put it in. Oy vey, what a job!

"Better Vito should have gotten run over by a garbage truck. Much simpler. Go to the Sanitation Department, put five points on the driver's license, that's that. Next case."

DiGenero recognized the metallic click as Silverstein flipped open his old Zippo lighter. A squeal of brakes preceded another bus to the curb. Pneumatic doors hissed.

"There's something else," Silverstein said.

Shouts and laughter rose as the bus passengers disembarked. Black banter and the unintelligibly amplified lyrics of boombox rap overwhelmed Silverstein's voice.

DiGenero spoke louder, "What?"

"Rocchi had a passport on him. His picture, Andrew Markham's name."

DiGenero switched on the light. He pushed his wallet, change, and pistol into a jumble, making room on the night table to slide the phone closer.

"Vito'd been traveling," Silverstein said. "According to the stamps in the back, he went five, six times to Ireland last year. This year maybe more."

"Ireland?"

"You tell me what that's all about," Silverstein said.

"You got the passport?" DiGenero asked.

"I got nothin'. The FeeBees are checkin' it out. They was at the restaurant. One of them's got a major interest in Vito. I tried to stiff him. You know, to get my hands on Vito's stuff. It was no good. Shaeffer would let the fuckin' Girl Scouts take over the case if it meant less work."

"Who was it?"

"Didn't recognize 'em. Shaeffer called him Benedetto, I think." Silverstein coughed, a smoker's rasp.

"Heavyset, almost bald, late forties?" DiGenero described Benedetto.

"Somethin' like that. Friend of yours?"

DiGenero ignored the question. He held the phone without speaking. The decision came easily, without hesitation, although until this moment, he had thought it would be days, perhaps even weeks away.

"Arnie, I need some ID. Driver's license, credit cards. I'll Fedex pictures for the license in the morning. Then make me a reservation, a Manhattan hotel, someplace out of the way. Cheap but not too cheap, you know what I mean? Check-in day after tomorrow."

"Frank," Silverstein drew out his name. "This is not a good idea. Better you should stay put. Let me do some more legwork. Maybe Vito wasn't the only one. Maybe there was two. He coulda got help from the Varios, from Las Vegas, you know? Salt Lake's in their territory. They're tight with Scarlese. Maybe they was in on it. I can find out. Maybe . . ."

DiGenero cut him off, "I'll call you day after tomorrow."

"Frank . . ."

"Go home, Arnie, it's late."

DiGenero hung up. He pushed the phone away. The night table wobbled. Like the double bed, dresser, and chair, it was new, government-issue, a cheap Danish modern that testified to the enduring affection of procurement clerks for the style of the 1950s motel.

A tremor passed through him. He turned on the lamp and put his head in his hands. There was no reason for everything to come back, but it did. At that moment, at every moment he opened his eyes in darkness. Erin rising. The front door closing. The explosion. A seer's vision. A malevolent surf suddenly risen on a quiet sea. Nothing ever woke him that didn't make him remember.

On the night table, the glass was empty but not the bottle of cheap cabernet. He poured the remainder and drank half, a swallow of thin Romanian red. The envelope with Silverstein's return address was propped against the lamp. DiGenero reached for it and shook the contents onto the bed. It had come yesterday morning. From the time he called Silverstein to ask for the favor, it took him three days to make the connection between Rocchi and Salt Lake City. DiGenero had phoned Benedetto again, yesterday afternoon, but he was out. At Rocchi's murder no doubt. His office took the message. Benedetto hadn't returned the call.

The computer printout, faint but readable, recorded an airline reservation from New York to Salt Lake City for "Markham, A." The black-and-white telephoto, a surveillance shot, was typically grainy. DiGenero tilted the lamp shade, casting light across the late Vito Rocchi. Bearlike, with a prematurely middle-aged pear shape, Rocchi was bent forward, locking a late model Oldsmobile. In the corner of the photo, the New York Police Department's developing lab had printed the place, date, and time beside its logo.

"LaGuardia, Parking Lot C, 8 Oct, 6:50 A.M."

An hour before Andrew Markham's New York to Salt Lake City flight.

It wasn't so much that Silverstein had known what to look for, but where to look. For thirty years, NYPD had "temporarily" housed its Organized Crime Intelligence Section behind two steel doors with combination locks in Murray Street's decrepit precinct house. Decorated with coffee stains and heel scuffs halfway up its hospital green walls, the warren of cubicles and file rooms shared the top floor with the chickenwire cage protecting Manhattan's trove of derelict umbrellas, broken suitcases, and other nondescript paraphernalia, the borough's official "lost and found."

The surveillance photos were arranged in randomly sized cartons by subjects, dates, and times. Silverstein had searched the Scarlese family pictures. A routine stakeout had recorded Vito at LaGuardia a week before the bombing. Once Silverstein had found him, he checked the airlines. No one named Rocchi had flown to Salt Lake that day, but it didn't matter. As usual, Vito hadn't gotten the details quite right. When he'd reserved "Andrew Markham's" seat, Rocchi had given the sales agent the number of his own home phone.

DiGenero replaced the papers and photograph in the envelope. The memory of fishing with his father came back. He was a quiet man of simple words, who solved problems, such as undoing the terrible tangles only small boys could put in fishing lines, by a careful, slow unraveling. DiGenero remembered standing on the dock, pestering him to cut out the knots. He never did, and when DiGenero waited and whined, his father would only say the same line that had been neatly wound on the reel was there, with its beginning, middle, and end. You simply had to be patient to find them. Rocchi and Benedetto were the same as his father had said about the fishing line. The beginning, middle, and end were there, somewhere. Only he was still his father's son, without patience or now, even faith that good men could find truth given time.

DiGenero reached for the phone. He dialed long distance information and waited. They'd received a few Christmas cards from Benedetto, maybe three or four over the years. DiGenero remembered a Staten Island return address. Benedetto had homesteaded, choosing to stay in the Bureau's New York Field Office, risking a top-out as a Grade 13 street agent, rather than transfer, chasing promotions and the step to management, the proverbial brass ring.

For most who weren't New Yorkers, the city was best avoided, expensive, hard on families and, with a two-thousand-man field office, cursed with headquarters-class paper shuffling on top of long days on the street. For a native, other things compensated. New York was a known commodity, not culture shock, and it was comfortable combat, offering a twenty-five percent cost-of-living differential and company car. But it was more than home with perks. The city was The City, a magnet for the helicopter cadre, the aspiring assistant special agents in charge, and the Southern Federal District's prosecutors-on-the-make. Their targets had names and they got priorities, running money-is-no-object operations and front-page cases, not the trash that came with bottom feeding in Boise or Dubuque.

New York. Big time. Addictive. The Apple. Impossible to love. Harder to leave.

The operator came on the line. Nine Tony Benedettos lived on Staten Island. Irritated, she read seven listings until DiGenero recognized the street. He remembered a pastel permastone duplex, divided from its clone by contrasting siding. One Christmas card had a picture of the decorated house. A chain link fence had corraled Santa and his sleigh in Benedetto's half of the front yard.

He dialed again. Once they'd had things in common, working together when DiGenero was inside the Scarleses. It had made them close. Once. A long time ago.

The ringing stopped.

"Hello." Benedetto's voice was thick with sleep.

"Get a grip on yourself, Tony. I don't want you to have a heart attack. It's Frank again."

"Frank?" Benedetto repeated the name uncertainly before it registered. "DiGenero? What time is it?"

"You don't want to know."

"I got your message," Benedetto said preemptively. "Look, I was goin' to call you back. So help me."

"Not necessary," DiGenero said. "I'm going to be in the city."

"In the city?" Benedetto sounded puzzled.

"Yeah. I need to see you."

"Yeah, sure." Benedetto paused uncertainly. "I thought they wanted you to stay out of circulation for a while."

"There's something we gotta talk about," DiGenero said.

"What is it?"

"Vito Rocchi."

"Rocchi's dead." Benedetto spoke quickly, then hesitated. "How'd you find out?"

"I heard about it."

"I'm surprised it made the news where you are. Must have been a slow day." He chuckled mirthlessly.

DiGenero waited.

Benedetto cleared his throat, "Another squad, somebody else is handling that, Frank, not me."

"Come on, Tony."

"Come on where? What can I tell ya?"

"About Vito." DiGenero spoke matter-of-factly.

"Like I said, I'm not working Rocchi's case."

"How about Andrew Markham's?"

The silence was longer this time. DiGenero heard bedsprings creak. In the background, a woman's voice asked who was on the phone. Benedetto's hand cupped the mouthpiece, muffling the reply.

"What do you know?" Benedetto asked, professionally inquiring.

"Exactly my question."

"I can't do much for you, Frank."

DiGenero interrupted, "Don't bullshit me. This is just between you and me. Tomorrow night, seven o'clock, your place. And Tony, I don't want anybody else to know I'm there."

Benedetto sighed. "You're puttin' me on the spot."

"Hey," DiGenero said. "What are friends for?"

From the ferry, the city seemed smaller. Edged by the steel and concrete seawall at the tip of Manhattan, Battery Park suggested New York had an end, a boundary where it stopped and could spread no farther. Or perhaps, it was the illusion of the skyline receding, at once showing its expanse but also diminishing in detail, first to a postcard image, then as the darkness erased all but the lights, to an illuminated sketch of itself, an outline in two dimensions.

Rush hour was almost over and in the cabin, the benches were half full. A panhandler glanced up, for a moment appraising DiGenero. Otherwise, no one took notice. He walked forward. The currents of the harbor revealed themselves in the ferry's undulation. At Quantico, he'd left a message on the shrink's answering machine. He had to get away for a few days. To think, he said. Security would raise hell, but she'd quiet them down. He hadn't asked, but the Bureau had assigned him to counseling anyway. The psychologist, thirty-something, had an aerobics instructor's body. Today, her socially redeeming value would be to rationalize his absence with feeling and her professional credentials.

The propellers reversed. Like a beast bearing an impossible load, the ferry shuddered and rebounded against battered pilings. Chains rasped medievally. The gangway lowered, mating with the terminal ramp. DiGenero walked quickly, in step in the phalanx. Outside the Staten Island terminal, he queued for a cab. An old Lincoln, a limousine fallen from grace, pulled to the curb. He gave the address. A series of religious amulets and a pinetree-shaped deodorizer hung from the visors and rearview mirror, divine and temporal adornments. The cabbie, an elderly Indian or Pakistani, drove with a teenager's one-handed grip.

DiGenero stopped him a block from Benedetto's house and crossed the street to the alley. The rear porch jutted behind the row of duplexes. Closed in twenty years before with jalousied windows, it was now the breakfast nook. Inside, a man moved back and forth. He paused and peered out, motionless. Benedetto was alone, waiting.

The metal screen door rattled open with DiGenero's first tread on the stairs. Benedetto waved him inside.

They stood awkwardly for a moment, exchanging rote greetings.

"Beer?" Benedetto asked. He opened the refrigerator and reached in.

"What else?" DiGenero took the bottle. The kitchen was less than three paces across, bringing them closer than they might have been otherwise.

Benedetto opened one for himself. DiGenero's gaze wandered. Even the clock and crucifix hung where he remembered. The dinette set, pastel appliances, and formica counters had the dull patina of diligent cleaning. Unchanged 1960s decor and compulsively spotless, cared for in the way only an old-world mother could inculcate in her female offspring.

They sat at the kitchen table. Benedetto's neckline had softened along with his stomach.

DiGenero tilted the bottle in toast. "Where's Rosemary?"

"Her sister's. I told her we were going to talk. She says hello."

"Sorry I missed her. You're lucky, Rosemary putting up with you all these years."

The compliment was obligatory, but Benedetto smiled anyway. DiGenero remembered Rosemary then, a random giggle, giant tits, pedal pushers, teased hair, and a cosmology that put Brooklyn at the center of the universe. Today, he knew, she would be somewhere beyond size 16, with a camouflaging wardrobe to match.

"How's the kids?" DiGenero asked.

"Angela's married. Lives in Trenton." Benedetto sipped his beer. "Tom's in his last year at Rutgers. Wants to go to law school." He burped. "I told him to get an honest job."

"How about you?"

"Stayin' out of trouble. I got my own squad."

DiGenero offered a congratulatory nod.

"We've made a few cases. Not bad, but no celebrities, not like you rolled up," Benedetto said.

DiGenero picked at the label on his bottle, then drained the contents. "Spare me the celebrities."

Benedetto stood and walked to the refrigerator. He removed two more beers, put them on the table, and settled back in the chair. "You know they still talk about you."

"Who?" DiGenero asked.

"The crews. I hear things. Now and then. In the wires. After a bust. When they call each other and they're worried we got somebody inside. They say, 'Hey, we don' want no Frank the Brain. Check 'em out that he ain't no Frank, got that?' " Benedetto laughed softly. "Frank 'the Brain' DiGenero, the Scarlese's youngest consigliere. Four years you were in their pants."

Next door, voices intruded. A woman's, imperative and climbing the scale, and a teenager's, defiantly hitting an even higher octave. The libretto abruptly stopped. A door slammed. Footfalls pounded on steps, followed by sudden quiet.

"The Abbruzzis," Benedetto said, gesturing toward the commotion. "Mama's worried little Angelica's goin' to get knocked up. Little Angelica's been gettin' laid since she was ten. She's already forgotten more positions than Mama knows."

"Remember Teresa? What was her last name? Montefiore?" DiGenero asked.

"Teresa?" Benedetto scratched his head, pondering. "Oh yeah! The Bushwick Avenue Teresa. Saint Teresa of the Instantaneous Penetration. The one who used to climb in the backseat and spread her legs even when she was driving. She didn't have no trouble until the day her mother figured out why she had so many car emblems on her charm bracelet."

"A real shame." DiGenero chuckled.

Benedetto sipped his beer. "Growin' up. When was that? Two, three hundred years ago?"

"At least."

Benedetto was quiet for a moment. "I used to envy you."

DiGenero examined him. "Whatsamatter, you fall down and hit your head?"

"I mean it. I couldn't believe you pulled it off."

"Pulled what off?"

"The undercover."

"Showtime." DiGenero shrugged. "That's all."

"No," Benedetto said. "Not that. I mean the whole thing. Kids pretend, you remember? We was always pretendin' to be wiseguys. Tough motherfuckers, huh? But you did one better. You got to be one of them, what we wanted to be once upon a time. You had it made and you got away with it. The money, the trips to Florida, to the islands, the broads, the clubs, the parties. Then, on top of that, you got the megabust. The big one. I mean, you played both games. You won 'em both."

Benedetto smiled. "I remember watchin' you on TV, beside Rosenthal, the District Attorney. It was on the steps of the Federal Courthouse, right after the indictments. When was that? Seventy-eight? Rosenthal was jumpin' around like he had ants up his ass, tryin' to get in front of the camera, but the reporters was only talkin' to you. You was the star."

"The class picture," DiGenero said. "When the lights go on, everybody wants in."

Benedetto finished his beer. He stared at the kitchen windows, seeming to study his own reflection in the glass. "Still, I used to envy you," he said.

"You envy me now, Tony?"

Benedetto didn't answer.

"Who wasted Vito?"

Benedetto stared in silence, then turned away. DiGenero stood and walked to the counter. Arms folded, he positioned himself before Benedetto, a presence that couldn't be ignored.

"I can't help you," Benedetto said.

"Is that a philosophical statement or an answer to the question?"

"I told you before, it ain't my case," Benedetto shot back.

"And I told you, don't bullshit me. I want Johnny Scarlese."

Benedetto looked down. His voice softened. "I know." He picked absentmindedly at a button on his shirt. "Junior's put the family back together, piece by piece. But he's not the same as the old man. He's out there." He gestured toward Manhattan as if indicating a distant star. "He's a different breed. Smarter and meaner." Benedetto looked up. "When you were inside the family, Junior was just a kid. He idolized you. Now, he's grown up and he's sworn to kill you for what you did. He wants your ass. Everybody knows that. Believe me, we'll get Johnny. But you gotta give it time."

"Time?" DiGenero asked sarcastically. "I didn't have to break a sweat to find out Rocchi flew to Salt Lake and back from LaGuardia the week Erin died. You tellin' me the Bureau couldn't have done that? Somehow, I don't think time's the problem."

Surprise registered clearly on Benedetto's face. "So what is?" He tried unsuccessfully to reclaim the initiative. Uncrossing his legs, Benedetto inadvertently assumed the posture of a man under interrogation.

"Rocchi's story." DiGenero paused. "Or Andrew Markham's."

"I wish I could help you."

"Oh yeah? Everybody may wish you could've helped me if you don't and I do what comes next."

"Like what?" Benedetto asked.

"Like taking advantage of a world-class inferiority complex."

"Huh?"

"Between the Mississippi River and the California border." DiGenero smiled. "You live out there and you learn things. Like everybody believes the cityslickers think they just don't quite measure up. State after state, it's the same story. What can I tell ya? They all think they're below average and the rest of the country knows it." DiGenero shook his head, "It's a tragedy. A massive mental problem. A country fulla head cases dying to prove how wrong it is that people in New York and Los Angeles are looking down their noses at them."

"What the hell are you talkin' about?" Benedetto shifted uncomfortably.

"Human beings. They just want a chance to get even. My guess is, it would only take a phone call. Say, to the Salt Lake *News,* describing how the Federal Bureau of Investigation in New York City is fucking up the only major murder case in their very own town. I mean, overlooking obvious evidence, right under the FBI's nose, like one dead slimeball named Vito Rocchi. No guarantees, but I bet they'd trip over themselves running to put it all over the front page."

"You'd do that?" Benedetto's eyes widened.

"Without a second thought."

"Jesus Christ." Benedetto leaned forward, elbows on knees. His head hung as if pulled down by the gravity of his considerations.

DiGenero opened the refrigerator. The beer was gone. He explored the cabinets. The bottle and tumblers occupied the same shelf. Removing two glasses, he poured an inch of Canadian whiskey in each and set one next to Benedetto, then resumed his position beside the counter.

The color had left Benedetto's face. He spoke to the floor. "The Bureau would shitcan you. No job, no pay, no protection."

"Then you can save me from myself," DiGenero said.

"If they found out, they'd shitcan me."

"Uh huh."

Benedetto looked up, "So help me God, Frank . . ."

"So, consider this a nonconversation."

"If you . . ."

DiGenero interrupted. "I said, this never happened."

Benedetto stared, mouth open like a small child, a portrait of vulnerability. Finally, he took a long, deep breath. Beside the table, Rosemary had bundled several days' worth of newspapers. He reached down and snapped the twine. He sorted through the latest edition, retrieving the first section and opening it on the kitchen table.

The headline ran above two pictures. One recorded a scene of wartime devastation. The blackened shell of a supermarket cradled a smoldering skeleton, barely recognizable as an aircraft fuselage. The other, an aerial panorama, showed the destructive path of the 747's final landing.

DiGenero stared. "I heard about it on the radio this morning. First time I've seen the pictures."

"You know all about airplanes, right?" Benedetto asked.

"I don't know everything, but I flew two thousand hours and never did that."

DiGenero leaned over, reading aloud. "The FAA says their preliminary investigation is underway. Blah, blah. Informed sources suggest a computer malfunction in the new, state-of-the-art automatic landing system at Kennedy may have guided the British airliner into the ground two miles short of the runway."

"That's about half right," Benedetto said.

"Oh?"

"It's a cover. For as long as it lasts, anyway."

"How do you know?" DiGenero straightened up.

"I know."

"Your case?"

Benedetto nodded.

"And?"

"Sabotage."

"Who?" DiGenero asked.

"The IRA."

"The Irish Republican Army?" It was DiGenero's turn to appear puzzled.

"Yeah."

"You mean in London, right? They put a bomb on board before the flight took off?"

"No." Benedetto shook his head. "The Brits say they had security screwed down tight at that end. They knew something might go down. They say whatever happened, happened here."

DiGenero bent over the newspaper again. He looked sideways at Benedetto. "You believe that? I mean raising money from the Sons of Kilarney and buying guns in Boston, okay. But for this? The IRA needs more than a tin cup and a panel truck. They gotta have support."

Benedetto nodded.

"So how?"

Benedetto squirmed. "Jesus, Frank."

"Come on."

"They got a connection. At least they had one." Benedetto paused. "Past tense."

DiGenero straightened up. He stepped to the counter and leaned back. "Rocchi."

Benedetto took a swallow of his whiskey. "The Brits say the IRA contacted him here. Probably true. Vito hung out sometimes in one of the bars in Hell's Kitchen, or what's left of it. Went out with some broad over there. Maybe she was the honeypot. Maybe not. Anyway, she's gone."

Hell's Kitchen. Until the Manhattan real estate market soured, the metastasizing growth of new offices and condominiums had all but eliminated the midtown immigrant enclave on the far West side, where the turn-of-the-century tenements had once been an Irish stronghold. In the 1970s, the "Westies," a murderous remnant of the Irish mob, even had intimidated the city's Mafia families into giving them a share of the local turf.

"Vito wasn't exactly Harvard material. Point man on an operation like this would be a big step," DiGenero said. He picked up his glass and studied it. "As I recall, the closest he ever got to a piece of the action at Kennedy was boosting airfreight and shakin' down the Jamaica Teamsters. Am I right?"

Benedetto shrugged. "I don't think Vito did much. He was probably a cutout, somebody who helped them set up. Safehouses, equipment, maybe casing the job, that kinda thing. I mean, they only pitched him a few months ago. How much could he do?"

"A few months ago?" DiGenero raised his eyebrows.

"Yeah. Three, four months ago. That's all. He made one trip over there, to Ireland, as Andrew Markham. That's it."

"One trip?" DiGenero asked.

"Yeah."

"Anybody else involved? Up the line in the Scarleses?"

"Don't know. Anyway, we got nothin' else," Benedetto said.

DiGenero poured another finger of whiskey and swirled the glass. "Who shot him?"

"Somebody who didn' wanna do it a second time. First class. Flow-through ventilation." Benedetto sighed. "The answer is, I don't know that either. Best guess is IRA, tying up loose ends." He extended his glass. DiGenero poured another inch. "By the way, who told you I was workin' Vito's murder?"

"A couple old buddies." DiGenero swallowed the last of his whiskey. He put the glass on the counter. "Nobody you know. You didn't exactly take a low profile on Mulberry Street. Word gets around when you bodyblock the cops off a case."

Benedetto stood. "Frank, my squad's secret, you know what I mean? We're working with the Brits. Nobody's supposed to know they're operatin' here. Understand? It's hot. If the papers or the IRA's local political sweethearts find out, there'll be hell to pay. That means the cops can't know. It means the prosecutors are cut out. It means the rest of the Field Office is, too. You understand?"

"Sure."

"Nobody knows you're here, right?"

"Nobody," DiGenero said.

"And this is between us?"

"Between us."

Benedetto put his hand on DiGenero's shoulder. "I'm worried about you, Frank. New York ain't good for your health. And, I'm so sorry about Erin. So help me, we'll get Johnny Scarlese."

"Yeah?"

Benedetto gripped his arm. "Go back to Washington."

"Sure, Tony." DiGenero stepped to the door. "By the way, how did they bring down the 747? A missile, or what?"

"I said the story was half right."

"Which half?"

"The part about the computer failure."

DiGenero turned back toward Benedetto. "You mean it was an inside job? They got inside the FAA?"

"Possible. We don't know yet."

"Jesus." DiGenero whistled softly. "In that case, I think I'm taking the train."

CHAPTER

6

DIGENERO COULDN'T MISS the naked woman on all fours. He stared through the open apartment door as two men appeared, also naked. One knelt before her, the other at the rear. They coupled, then synchronized, finding their rhythm. The woman moaned encouraging obscenities, implausibly articulate for someone already engaged in another form of oral expression.

Silverstein didn't seem surprised to see him. He beckoned impatiently. "Come in, already."

DiGenero stepped inside. The door closed behind him.

"I didn't know you liked PBS," DiGenero said.

"When you gotta improve your education, you do what you can." Silverstein pointed the remote control. The VCR clicked. On the television screen, the *ménage à trois* froze, one member inserted, another extracted. The glare from white flesh and bedsheets radiated, lighting the living room.

"A 1982 classic. *Bonnie Blows Baltimore,* or somethin' like that. You wanna beer?" Silverstein asked.

"No."

"I don't believe it." He disappeared into the kitchen.

DiGenero sat on the couch. Opposite, in front of the sexual still life, a lounge chair canted in a permanently reclined position. The apartment was adorned only by its accumulations. In one corner, an ironing board, its cover torn, rested against a bicycle with two flat tires. In another, newspapers lay in yellowing strata. Along the walls, stacks of books and magazines leaned precariously. Where their balance had failed, they formed foothills of mixed media, sloping upward to the still standing peaks. Otherwise, there was only Silverstein's once gold shag rug, its worn paths recording his countless migrations.

Silverstein had lived in the same building for twenty years; the remaining tenant guaranteed the right to his nine hundred square feet at five hundred dollars per month in perpetuity by the city's Byzantine rent control laws. To the landlord, who had all but completed the building's renovation, he was like an inoperable disfigurement, something that could neither be removed nor cosmetically hidden. With little interest in worldly possessions, Silverstein had ignored proffered bribes as well as threats. A block from the 86th Street subway stop and the express to the precinct in lower Manhattan, he was perfectly content. His struggle with the owner, a little man who phoned periodically from Great Neck to berate him, also had become an almost welcome diversion, for a solitary bachelor, the kind of intimate antagonism usually reserved for married couples. Silverstein, of course, continued to live in prime squalor, suffering the telephone harassment along with unanswered maintenance calls. But on balance, he was satisfied with his condition as well as comforted by the knowledge he could impede the building's sale as a condominium, and its owner's retirement to Palm Beach, for life.

Silverstein emerged from the kitchen with two beers. He handed one to DiGenero. "I thought you was gonna call tomorrow."

"I missed you so much I couldn't wait."

"I booked the hotel, like you said. It's under the funny name you gave me. Gramercy Park. One hundred and ten a night, okay?" Silverstein asked.

"Yeah."

Silverstein switched on an ancient floor lamp. He bent down beside the reclining chair, digging through an assortment of junk mail and half completed police department paperwork. "Here's your ID." He tossed a manila envelope to DiGenero.

"Who did it?"

"Manny."

"Manny the printer?" DiGenero sounded surprised.

"Yeah."

"Is he still working in Long Island City?"

"Twenty years in the same location. When he saw your picture, he said you looked like a wiseguy who made good." Silverstein's laugh was phlegmy.

"Play the part long enough you don't need the makeup. Life imitates art."

"I dunno. I always thought all you dagos looked alike." Silverstein sat down. He wiggled as he put his feet up, settling into the worn contours of the reclining chair. Without heels and toes, his socks appeared part of a derelict dancer's attire. "I told Manny you was one of my old snitches, who needed some help. You owe me a hundred for the ID."

DiGenero took out his wallet and handed over a bill. He opened the envelope. A New York driver's license and two credit cards spilled out. He held up the license. Silverstein had copied his handwriting to create a reasonable replica of his signature in alias. "Not bad."

"Details." Silverstein nodded condescendingly. "Ya gotta watch the details."

DiGenero smiled. Silverstein was the best kind, a cop with a street degree who had learned the lessons that mattered.

Silverstein scratched himself through a hole in his tee shirt. Short and wiry, his body had melded into the chair, assuming the two-dimensional form of a recumbent cat. "Wit'out Vito, whaddya gonna do?" he asked.

"Vito had a crew boss, right?"

"Everybody's got to have somebody."

"Who?" DiGenero asked.

"Sallie Ferringa." Silverstein's *r*'s came out as *w*'s.

DiGenero raised his eyebrows. "Sallie was a wild man. I never thought he'd live long enough to get promoted."

"He calmed down. It was after you left town, 1980 or 1981, I think. Scarlese was dividin' up the pie, tryin' to keep the family together from inside the slammer. He gave everybody somethin'. Sallie got a piece of the fish market. He became a genuine serious person. Amazing what a little prosperity can do for your outlook on life."

The fish market. It was part of the empire. From the beginning, the Scarleses had clearly identified the virtue of associating themselves with the hierarchy of human needs. Food, shelter, self-esteem. It was an elementary strategy, powerful because it was simple and simple because it applied everywhere, whether on the docks of Palermo or the streets of Manhattan. The wholesale restaurant business, the building trades, and the protection racket. Johnny Scarlese, Sr., built the triad into an empire, underpinning the family's profits for a generation.

In New York, the Scarleses had controlled the meat and produce wholesalers for forty years. To be sure, theirs had become a specialized role. In the West side poultry warehouses, for example, they ensured the compressors chilling the trailer vans of fresh chicken never failed in the small hours of the night. Those who chose not to retain the services of Scarlese Refrigeration always realized the error of their ways. One Monday, they would discover the chillers had mysteriously quit over the weekend, leaving sixty thousand pounds of putrifying breasts and drumsticks for the morning shift.

Fulton Street was a different line. There, Scarlese Transport hauled from the stalls to the trucks. At thirty-eight dollars an hour for a porter and dolly, the cost of moving one hundred pounds of salmon across

South Street raised the wholesale price of a filet from three to nine dollars a pound. DiGenero knew the math. The porter took eighteen an hour and paid the Scarleses twenty for the privilege of getting the work.

"What's Sallie got?" DiGenero asked.

"At the market? About a third of the action. It wasn't nothin' to sneeze at ten years ago, but now the fuckin' Japanese is here. They eat things I don' even wanna know is under water. Sallie's making money hand-over-fist. He moves the fish right to the sushi shops. It's like takin' candy from a baby. I don't think he even hadta beat up one Jap."

"Is he still living in Queens?"

"You kiddin'? He's got a penthouse across the bridge in Jersey." Silverstein motioned westward with a bob of the head.

"Where?" DiGenero asked.

"Fort Lee," Silverstein said, bemused. "The best view Sallie ever had before looked out on an airshaft. He used to think that pigeons could only fly straight up. Now the son of a bitch can see all the way to Connecticut."

"What's his address?"

Silverstein eyed DiGenero suspiciously.

"What is it?"

Silverstein waved his beer bottle, warding him off, "Don't ask."

"Come on."

"You got a hole in the head? Sallie ain't lookin' for no reunion with the guy that put his capo away."

DiGenero interrupted. "Vito was a spear carrier. Somebody had to tell him to make the hit. Junior wouldn't do it face to face, you know that. Junior wouldn't give Vito the time of day. If Sallie was Vito's crew boss, the order had to come through him."

"Sallie ain't the only one livin' in Fort Lee," Silverstein said. "There's two or three others from the family in the same building. You just can't go waltzin' in. Somebody's gonna make you. Then whaddya got? Junior'll know you're nosin' around. He puts the word out to watch for DiGenero. Once that happens, phony ID won't do you no good. You either gotta stay where you are at Quantico, safe and sound in jarhead heaven, or come to the city and take a chance they'll blow you away. That's a wonderful fuckin' choice."

DiGenero's silence acknowledged the logic.

Silverstein leaned forward. He picked unconsciously at a ragged toenail. "Like I said before, lemme work on it a little longer. I can turn something up."

DiGenero listened, noncommittal. "What else does Sallie do?"

"Whadda they all do?"

"I mean, how does he spend his time these days?"

"Like always, go to work, hang out wit' the boys, see his dollies," Silverstein said.

"The same places?"

"Yeah."

DiGenero remembered the routine, as predictable as any corporate treadmill. Six days a week, Scarlese's crews would gather, a few by nine or ten, most by late morning. Whether in Bensonhurst or on Mulberry Street, the social clubs and storefront shops never varied, facades with a few tables and chairs, a pinball machine and pool table, or a dusty counter and depleted racks of candies and magazines. The neighborhood knew. Only the occasional stranger or tourist would venture in, almost always leaving moments later, expelled by the palpable hostility.

Inside, when they were together, the talk never stopped. It was the feedstock, the source of their manna. The conversations were cryptic but clear, a perpetual scheming. There was always action: a scam with counterfeit credit cards, to be used in a larcenous hopscotch from cash machine to department store to designer shop; boosted jewelry or furs from the airfreight terminals at Newark or Kennedy, to be fenced at thirty cents on the dollar or delivered to Manhattan's better showrooms at seventy percent wholesale, no questions asked; negotiable paper from Wall Street's back offices, to be recorded as phony receivables, discounted, and swapped for cash by friendly retail factors; cars stolen on order, to be stripped for parts and trucked to waiting auto supply warehouses out of state; loans laid out on the street, small and big time, to be repaid or else at five points a week. And the drugs. Horse, coke, weed, sometimes to be moved in quantity from Miami, sometimes to be cut and distributed on the East side or in the South Bronx. For each deal that went down, five fell through, although that didn't matter. The talk went on because ultimately it always produced, yielding the ten percent cuts, the five points off the top, the fifty-fifty splits, the five-hundred-a-week "guaranteed." The parts of the whole that added up to a livelihood. The take-home of a wiseguy.

By one or two, DiGenero remembered, most were gone. The afternoon was the time for business, for making calls, the circuit of collections or contacts or casing jobs. Around six, when they returned, they came together to eat and drink. Afterward, a few went home to stay, but they were the exceptions. Most spent an hour or two with their wives and children, then went out again. Like the other families, Scarlese's code was clear: for a made man, the wives of the others were off limits, on pain of death. But wiseguys were expected to have women and, whether bought or attracted, they were easy to find. Some came from the old neighborhoods, seeking escape from two-bedroom walkups and the drudgery of caring for the consequences of perpetual pregnancies on truck driver salaries. Others, from the East side bars, were part of the inventory of high-priced hookers who preferred a regular stipend to one-night stands. A few, from uptown, came looking for them. The wives of doctors, or lawyers, or investment bankers, they trolled the clubs, searching for excitement beyond the run-of-the-mill affair. They were trophies, drawn by the aphrodisiac of brute power and willing to pay by giving pleasure and allowing themselves to be kept.

"Who's he playing around with?" DiGenero asked.

"The usual bimbos. Nobody to write home about, except one. On the West side. They meet in a bar on Tenth Avenue. Tenth and 45th, I think."

"Hell's Kitchen?"

"Yeah." Silverstein was oblivious to DiGenero's stare. "He sees her on weekends. She comes at five or five-thirty, on Friday and Saturday. Sallie shows up around six-thirty, sometimes later. They have a drink, then leave for dinner. After that, they go to a hotel."

"How long have they been an item?"

Silverstein scratched his head. "Sallie started goin' to the bar a year and a half, maybe two years ago. I remember seein' her in the surveillance shots, when I was lookin' for Vito's pictures. Knock your socks off. Tall, maybe a head taller than Sallie. Must be able to wrap her legs around him two, three times."

"Sallie got a piece of the place?"

"Don't think so. It's an Irish joint." Silverstein paused abruptly. His eyes, small and dark, flicked back and forth, activated by his concentration. He looked at DiGenero. "Vito used to hang out there. I remember a couple of pictures in the file, him in front of the place."

"Lately?" DiGenero asked.

"Nah. I don't know when he stopped goin', but the last shots was taken maybe two years ago."

"About the time Vito started traveling to Ireland."

"Yeah. After that, nothin'."

"What's the name of the bar?"

"The Old Sod," Silverstein said.

"Anybody else from the Scarleses show up there?"

"Besides Sallie? Not that I seen."

DiGenero stood. He looked at his watch. It was past midnight. "You haven't told me yet how much you want to talk to Sallie, have you?"

Silverstein's brow furrowed. "Whaddya mean? It ain't our case any more. Your buddies wit' the wingtips and the buttoned-down underwear took it over, remember?"

"Hey, does Sallie know that? Besides, it wouldn't be good manners if you didn't give him your condolences about Vito. Tomorrow's Friday. I don't think you should miss the chance to see him, do you? Say, in the afternoon, around five or six."

"In other words, you want me to keep Sallie busy," Silverstein said.

DiGenero nodded. "For an hour or so. That's all."

Silverstein stared. "You ain't goin' home, are you?"

The literal meaning of the question struck him. Erin's voice came back. Every night, when he opened the front door, she would greet him. Even when he knew she would be late, the quiet made the house seem vacant, a discarded shell on an empty beach. Now there would be no sound, save for his own inanimate echo. He looked away and shook his head.

"The FeeBees find out I'm talkin' to Sallie, I'm in deep shit, you know that?" Silverstein said.

"How they gonna find out?" DiGenero lifted the remote control and pointed. On the screen the undulations of the naked trio resumed, as did the soundtrack's sensual moaning. "In the meantime, do me a favor." He tossed the remote control to Silverstein and walked to the door. "Leave the broad's picture at the hotel desk in the morning. I need something to decorate my dresser."

The rain had hopelessly snarled Manhattan's Friday afternoon traffic. In each intersection, the lines of cars, buses, and trucks meshed at right angles, nose to door, then as each maneuvered for advantage and escape, in a random weave. Finally, from Greenwich Village to Midtown, they knotted. At first, only horns blared, but as the predicament sunk in, the collective cry rose. One by one, windows rolled down. Fists and solitary fingers emerged, shaking and jabbing, physical punctuation for the shouted profanities. Patience as well as reason, it seemed, were water soluble.

DiGenero abandoned the cab at 42nd Street and Broadway and walked north. The steady drizzle had soaked the neon colors from Times Square. In the window of a variety store, a "Going Out Of Business" banner, soiled with age, proclaimed its perennial come-on. He ducked inside. By the door, a cardboard box held an assortment of cheap umbrellas. He selected one and glanced around, searching for the cash register amidst the jumble of gaudy jewelry, tasteless souvenirs, and Asian electronics. Behind an elevated counter, a lone clerk beckoned, staring down from the parapet with the suspicion of a sentry eying an intruder. DiGenero raised up a ten dollar bill and waited. His change came back, accompanied by wordless indifference.

Outside, he turned west on 45th Street. Twilight and rain had emptied the sidewalks. Behind the umbrella, DiGenero bent into the wind, lengthening his stride. From entryways, a few gray shapes leaned out, muttering supplications. It was too early for the theater crowd. Like the marquees, the panhandlers attracted no one's attention.

Leaving the theater district, the long crosstown blocks held only vestiges of the past. The occasional tenement, now a co-op apartment or office, had been refurbished to a polished shine unknown when it was new and immigrants fresh off the boat crammed its airless cubicles, ten to a room. Otherwise, history was gone, replaced by blank-sided warehouses and parking garages, the city's industrial epidermis, and its newest additions, hermaphrodite office–shopping mall–sports club–apartments. Chrome and steel wombs offering all the necessities, designed to ensure their inhabitants need not emerge to confront urban life's ever-present dangers.

DiGenero stopped at Tenth Avenue. Across the six lanes of traffic, he saw the border. Compared to the encroaching highrises, the buildings on the opposite side of the street were old and low, as if worn down by an invisible glaciation. Their mismatched facades advertised produce, liquor, shoe repair, bakery goods, plumbing. Mom-and-pop operations interleaved with a nondescript office, a lawyer or doctor, here and there. Down the street, bare awning poles and a brightly lit greenhouse window marked a new, trendy restaurant. It was an evolutionary sign, the beginning of the end. The spoor of the next generation.

The bar commanded the opposite corner like a fortified outpost, a single smoked glass window and solid wood door penetrating its brick walls. Under the second-floor eave, the sign, protected with wire mesh, shone a predictable kelly green.

DiGenero looked at his watch. Five-thirty. He crossed with the light, pulled open the door, and walked inside.

The room was almost empty. She had glanced up and then away. Even seated on the barstool, she seemed tall enough to look him directly in the eye. Her dress, a soft wool, accentuated her height. Its rich brown blended into the tones of her hair. Framed by a long wave that fell to her shoulders, her profile was strong, a beauty that could be sketched in a single line.

"This taken?" DiGenero pointed at the adjoining stool. He propped the umbrella behind the brass footrail.

"Not yet."

The bartender raised his chin, inquiring.

"McCredens," DiGenero said. "No ice."

"A single-malt neat? Very good." Her gaze, self-assured and direct, captured his. "Someone who's obviously risen above the American affliction with scotch on the rocks." Her voice was low with an accent neither English nor Irish, but something in-between.

"Glad you approve." DiGenero extended his hand. "My name's Frank Falcone."

"Falcone is it?" She smiled, eyes wide, politely mocking. She grasped his hand firmly. "Sounds as if you might be more at home with a Grappa at this hour."

"My mother's maiden name was McGuire." He settled onto the stool. The bartender placed the glass before him. "Immigrants in New York came and went seventy years ago, but parish boundaries didn't. The last Irish out of a neighborhood sometimes got mixed up with the first Italians in. It made for some hellacious fights, but some wonderful hybrid combinations."

"I see. I assume you're a product of the latter."

DiGenero laughed. "In the wilder days of my youth, my parents weren't always sure."

"Is that behind you?" she asked.

"Which? My youth or my wilder days?"

"Both."

"One is," he said.

It was her turn to laugh.

DiGenero raised his glass. "Cheers." He sipped the single-malt. After the chilling rain, it offered a lubricating warmth.

"I don't detect a New York accent," DiGenero said.

"They're very difficult to acquire in London. You'd truly have to work at it."

"London? Is that home?"

"For now."

"What part?" he asked.

She parried the question. "Why? Have you been there often?"

"Now and again."

"I see. And is New York home for you, Mr. Falcone-McGuire?"

"A long time ago. I've been overseas for a while." DiGenero had remembered the alias and the cover story. Five years before, the Bureau had asked him to come east for a few days to advise on an operation, a penetration of one of the Connecticut families. Some time afterward, it had gone bad. The agent had worked his way inside as "Frank Falcone," but was pulled out when the underboss ordered him to make a hit.

There was no going back. "Frank Falcone" disappeared, letting it be known on the street he'd been tipped to a drug bust that was going to take him down. Later, the Bureau tidied up, putting out the word he'd left the country.

"What brings you back to the city? Business or pleasure?"

"Neither. A friend of mine died," he said.

"I'm sorry." Her sympathy sounded genuine. "Had he been ill?"

"Killed. The story was in the papers the other day."

"Oh? An accident?"

He shook his head. "Murder."

She fell silent, obviously taken aback. "It must be a shock. When it's someone you know, that is."

"Some things can be more shocking than others."

She hesitated, for the first time seeming uncertain about her reply. "Did he live"—she searched for the right word—"dangerously?"

He swirled the whiskey gently. "We grew up in the same neighborhood. I moved to Connecticut and went into business. He stayed here. He did alright for a guy who barely finished high school, but Vito wasn't exactly affiliated with a Fortune 500 Company."

Her hand, stroking the stem of her wineglass, stopped. "Vito?"

"Yeah. Vito Rocchi." He smiled slightly. "That may give you a clue."

Her stare was steady, appraising.

DiGenero paused, as if considering whether to continue. He spoke matter-of-factly. "For some, it's fated, like predestination. If you're Vito, with nowhere to go, sooner or later you're going to be part of it."

"Why?"

"Because they're your kind. You know them, their fathers, their mothers, their grandfathers. Maybe you all came from the same village. Maybe you've lived together in the same apartment or on the same block your whole life. Maybe your brother married one of their sisters. Maybe they're just your friends. It doesn't matter really. One way or another, you're involved, whether you want to be or not.

"And?" She encouraged him to continue.

"Something happens. Who knows? You need a favor. Sometimes important, sometimes not. A little money. Help with the rent. Or maybe it's just a word, say, with a cop who caused you trouble. If you're part of the neighborhood, it's taken care of. Whatever it is, you get it, no questions asked. You might even forget you asked until one day the telephone rings. This time, they ask *you* for a favor. It could be nothing. To deliver a package, or pass a message, or drive a car. What can you say? 'Of course.' After that, one thing leads to another." He shrugged. "A few volunteer. They got an uncle, a cousin, or a buddy who's already part of it. They want in. But for others, it's different." DiGenero met her eyes directly. "So, what's wrong with that? If you're Vito, what are your choices?"

He finished his drink. "Vito told me a few things. He was small-time, strictly a helper, you know what I mean? Not an operator. Just small-time."

"And Vito was your . . ." she hesitated.

"Compari? 'My friend?' " He finished her question.

"Yes."

"Not that way. In our case, it was the dictionary definition. Nothing else." He waved. The bartender reached for the bottle and poured another drink.

"But you must have been close. It's a long way to come, back to New York I mean, to pay your respects to someone you haven't seen in years."

"Oh, we've seen each other. Once in a while, when I'm traveling. I'm in the wholesale tour business."

"Wholesale? I'm afraid I'm not familiar with that," she said.

"Packaging and booking. When the dollar went through the floor in the eighties, the good ole' United States turned into a bargain. So, I said to myself, why not bring over the folks from the old country. With my background, I specialize. The Falcone family tree got me started in Italy. My maternal connections set me up in Ireland." He lifted his glass. "Minga John and Faith and Begorrah! What a stroke o' genius! The wops and the micks are comin' in droves."

"And Vito?" she asked.

"Oh yeah. I saw Vito from time to time over there."

"Over there? In Italy you mean."

"No." He shook his head. "In Ireland."

Her brow furrowed. "Ireland? Was he . . ."

"Half Irish, like me?"

She nodded.

"No. Vito traveled. We bumped into each other by accident, the first time in Shannon two years ago. We talked, got loaded, had a hell of a time. After that, we made a point of meeting when he came over."

"I can understand a Falcone-McGuire visiting Ireland, but a Vito Rocchi?"

"Business," he said.

"I see. Something like yours?"

"Not really. Sometimes I could help him out. That's all. You know, for old times' sake." He glanced at his watch. "I've got to go, but I wish I didn't."

"No," she said, this time more quietly, "sometimes, you simply can't count on plans working out at all."

The Japanese clumped, a quiet flock occupying the minimum space. The Germans spread out, a picket line of ample bodies, garrulous, expansive. Between them, Americans wandered in singles and pairs creating their own itinerant territory.

Johnny Scarlese, Jr.'s address was a name not a number, one of the venerated buildings on Fifth Avenue along Central Park. The duplex took up two-thirds of the thirtieth and thirty-first floors. Its tiled foyer funneled the guests, first to the bar, then the dining room. Across from the tiers of sushi and *pâté*, a trio of electronic synthesizers, black, white and Asian, emitted new-age sounds.

Drinks in hand, the newcomers circulated slowly between the windows and the long living room wall, passing the art. A faux marble pillar divided masters and moderns. From above, cylinders of light seemed to hold both in invisible traction. Opposite, on the rain-blackened glass, the images of the Monets and Warhols also hung, suspended in double exposure.

One foot on the low sill, Scarlese faced the floor-to-ceiling windows, gesturing at the unseen. A rotund German and a diminutive Japanese bracketed him. On both sides, heads bobbed. "Take the city," he said. "New York. It's a microcosm of the country, always reinventing itself. For the Dutch, New Amsterdam. For the British, New York."

"But you forgot the Indians? After all, what was new for them?" The German laughed, pleased with his own wit.

Scarlese smiled coldly. "Glass beads." He turned, bestowing his intimacy on the Japanese. "And for us?" Scarlese asked rhetorically.

"For us?" the Japanese repeated, struggling to follow.

"For us," Scarlese said, as if including the Tokyo banker in his category, "the smart money today is out there." He pointed.

"The Japanese beamed. *"New* Jersey."

"Not quite." Scarlese pointed again, down this time. "Here."

"Ah," the Japanese said.

"Exactly." Scarlese touched his elbow, as if acknowledging a brilliant insight. "The city." He turned back, deigning to include the German once again. "Times have been tough but we're leaner, meaner. This is still the place to invest. Think about it."

From behind Scarlese, a dark suit interrupted. He whispered, then disappeared. Scarlese excused himself. Moving against the flow of guests, he walked purposefully, acknowledging greetings but dissuading conversation.

At the far end of the living room, the polished brass staircase spiraled to the bedroom level, secluded space within already private quarters. His footfalls rang on the treads. A floor above, he entered the library. The room was small, three walls of shelves, the fourth mahogany paneled. A man waited. Medium height and blunt cut, he idly spun an antique globe. Sallie Ferringa's heavy shape was wrapped in an expensive double-breasted suit. Strength gone to seed. In the warren of books, he was the picture of alienation.

Scarlese ignored Ferringa's greeting. He crossed the room and sat behind a finely shaped writing desk, burled wood, an Italian antique. On the leather inlay, a folio and papers lay neatly arranged. He leaned forward, elbows on desk, and steepled his fingers. "Well?"

"Nothin'." Ferringa shook his head.

Scarlese stared. "What do you mean, 'nothing'?"

"I gotta tell ya, Johnny, we looked."

"I assumed that much," he said coldly.

Like a conductor, Ferringa performed with both hands. "We checked everything you said. I went up and down the street myself, every foot. I mean me, personally, so help me. Nobody seen nothin'. What can I tell ya?"

"And?"

Ferringa took a deep breath. "Then, I checked the job. You know, to see if maybe Vito pissed somebody off. All he did for us was collections, but who knows? Maybe he used a little too much muscle on somebody. The straw that broke the horse's back, you know what I mean?"

"Camel," Scarlese said.

"Huh?" Ferringa paused.

"The straw that broke the camel's back," Scarlese enunciated deliberately.

"Yeah, right." Ferringa shrugged. "Nothin'."

"Finally, I checked the other crews. Usually you hear, you know, if somethin' ain't right between people. I didn't hear nothin', but Vito coulda caused some aggravation, Somethin' personal." Ferringa raised his hands, palms up. "I mean, you don't like to go lookin' for people to speak ill of the dead, but everybody says the same thing. Vito ain't got any problems."

"Women?" Scarlese asked.

Ferringa's brow furrowed. "You think a broad shot him?"

Scarlese frowned, irritated. "The question is: was he involved with a woman?"

"Vito? Involved?" Ferringa snorted. "He don't even know how to use the part that talks. I mean, Vito gets laid, but it's biff, bam, you know what I mean?" Ferringa fished in his back pocket. He wiped his neck with a handkerchief. "I know this guy. He's one of mine. But I swear, Johnny, I don't know what's goin' down."

Scarlese leaned back, contemplating in silence.

"I can't figure, I just can't figure," Ferringa said.

Scarlese rose and walked to a bookshelf. Ferringa shifted uncomfortably, trying to wiggle his toes. His search for Vito's killer had taken half the week, most of it walking. His feet felt like sausages. High blood pressure and low circulation, the doctor had told him. He'd cut back on salt but thrown away the antihypertension pills when he couldn't get an erection. Fuck it if he couldn't fuck it, he told the doctor. He eyed Scarlese's chair longingly, but thought better of it.

Hands clasped behind him, Scarlese stood at the bookshelves. He scanned the selection. Ferringa had read a few titles while he was waiting. Nothing he could recognize. Some he couldn't pronounce. *Power, Politics, and the International System. A Cost/Benefit Analysis of Investment in Third World Agriculture. Econometric Modeling: Alternative Theories. Interfirm Trade and National Borders: A Review of Balance of Payments Implications. Technology Transfer and Aerospace Joint Ventures in Japan —A Case Study.*

Scarlese removed a book, examining the cover. He spoke with his back to Ferringa. "Do you know who's downstairs?"

"You're havin' a cocktail party or somethin'. For the Germans and the Japs. Eddie told me at the service door, where I came in," Ferringa said.

Scarlese nodded. "They're our bankers. The ones who move the money." He replaced the volume on the shelf and removed another, resuming his casual perusal. "Our two most important partners took me aside tonight. Their regulators are looking at them and they're nervous."

"Regulators?" Ferringa asked. "Who's that?"

"Who? In this case, the German Finance Ministry and the Bundesbank."

"The Bundeswhat?"

Scarlese glanced over his shoulder at Ferringa. "The German central bank, Sallie. The law."

Ferringa's eyes narrowed. "Whatsamatter? You think these guys are gonna roll over? Rat us out?"

Scarlese closed the book and replaced it on the shelf. "No." He resumed scanning the titles. "At least not yet."

"Why not?" Ferringa asked.

Scarlese turned and walked back to the desk. He sat, crossing his legs carefully. "Very simple. They need us. All the banks are operating under new international rules that require them to keep more money on hand. Bigger reserves. You understand?"

Ferringa nodded uncertainly.

Scarlese continued. "But capital's tight. Scarce. There isn't enough to go around." He smiled. "That's why I approached them three years ago, when the new rules first went into effect. I offered a simple proposition. We needed them. They needed us. No more client who pays twenty points off the top to wash the cash. Now we're a partner. Our cash deposit goes into the bank's house account, in their name, recorded as, say, "profits" from foreign exchange trading. They move the money offshore and park it in another branch. A few days later, we walk in—in Frankfurt, Luxembourg, or Tokyo—and borrow against it. We take the loan in deutschmarks, francs, yen, whatever."

"Whatever," Ferringa repeated ambiguously.

"Everybody wins. For the bank, it shows up twice on the balance sheet. Double the money. On the books, our cash looks like theirs and the loan is recorded as an asset. Bingo. A million turns into two. Ten million into twenty."

"What about us?" Ferringa asked.

"Us?" At first, Scarlese failed to realize how far he had traveled without Ferringa.

"Yeah, what do we get outa the deal?"

He sighed. "We walk away with clean money. One hundred percent laundered, banked in Europe where RICO can't get it, at no cost." Scarlese contemplated his manicured nails. "No. The pig won't take his snout out of this trough until the butcher comes."

"I don't get it," Ferringa said.

"Don't get what?" he looked up.

"The problem. I mean if this is workin' okay and those guys ain't gonna roll over, what are we worried about?"

Scarlese examined Ferringa with the expression of a teacher attempting to come to terms with a hopeless pupil. "For Christ's sake, just what I said!"

"What's that?" Ferringa asked.

"Greed," Scarlese said, exasperated. "Look, do you think they're only playing games with us? If the regulators are investigating, who's to say what they'll find? Who's to know what these bastards have fixed up with somebody else? Suppose they stumble across some half-assed setup. What are they going to do?"

"I dunno."

"You don't know? What the hell does the law always do? They

squeeze," Scarlese said. "They're going to squeeze whoever they got." He motioned toward the cocktail party a floor below. "Who knows? Maybe one of them. If that happens, we've got no control over what the bankers put on the table to save their own ass. Including us."

Ferringa nodded vigorously. "That's a problem."

Scarlese rose and buttoned his suitcoat, fastidiously smoothing the dark gray flannel. He stepped toward Ferringa and paused, face to face. Scarlese straightened Ferringa's tie. "But, truth be told, what the bankers do is only *a* problem. It's not *the* problem. *The* problem is that times change. The bankers served us well, but we've got to look ahead. After all, we've done it before. Once upon a time, the families controlled neighborhoods. Then, we grew. It was the cities. Then, we got together. We divided up the country." Scarlese stepped back, brushing Ferringa's lapel. "Now? When you can move money from one country to another by pushing a computer button, tell me, why should we stop at the border?" He smiled. "It's a new world, Sallie. We're multinational and we need to recognize the fact. We need to be in Europe on our own." He removed an invisible speck from Ferringa's suitcoat. "And, we will be, won't we?"

"You bet, Johnny."

"That's right." He patted Ferringa's cheek. "So don't disappoint me, Sallie." Scarlese's smile disappeared. "We're almost there. Don't fuck up. Find who killed Vito. Now."

C H A P T E R

7

A THOUSAND HANDS had polished the bannister to a velvet sheen. DiGenero climbed the stairs slowly, his fingers trailing along the smooth oak. His memories came back as they would to a child who could describe but not explain, a catalogue of the senses. Around him, echoes and aromas melded, the hollow striking of leather heels on wood treads and the lingering redolence of garlic and tomatoes permeating the hallway. Once they had been Sunday afternoon's harbingers, the product of new shoes worn only for mass, and the prelude to supper, *pasta alla Bolognese* and, for a boy, a single glass of deep, red wine.

He paused midway on the landing. The windowless stairwell formed a column of darkness. The building was small, two stories, a duplex with four apartments. On each side, there was one flat up, another down. Ninety years before, the hallway sconce lights had been converted from gas to electric. On the walls, behind their translucent oyster-shell shades, the bulbs still burned dim, but there was no need for more illumination. The shadows hid nothing. The last flight led to a solitary door and he knew the way as well as if he had come only yesterday.

At the top of the climb, DiGenero stood for a moment. In the silence, the sound of his own breathing seemed intrusive. He thought of waiting and returning later, but dismissed it. It had already been too long. He knocked. Steps approached slowly, followed by the deliberate turning of the lock.

The old man appraised him. "I knew one day it would be you."

"Hello, grandfather."

DiGenero felt familiar hands on his shoulders. Their grip belied the assumed frailty of age. He was still a big man, but his clothes hung loose, only suggesting the once powerful form. He turned and walked to the parlor. DiGenero followed.

The apartment's front room overlooked Bushwick Avenue. The windows, shut against the fall chill, were curtained for the night. In the stale air it was obvious they'd been closed for some time. DiGenero remembered when it had been otherwise. As a boy, he had passed hours, his arms resting on the sill, leaning out to watch the street. In the 1950s, Bushwick Avenue had been a parade, alive with Italy's offspring, the first generation, products of towns and villages from the Piedmont to Calabria, as well as their sons and daughters. His grandmother beside him, he would observe them, strolling, gesturing, flirting, arguing, a once geographically pedigreed society that had transplanted, hybridized, taken root. Now, the street belonged to others. Most recently, the Asians had arrived, joining the blacks and Latinos, who had come earlier to follow the Italians, who had long before displaced the Irish and the Jews. Today, the nationalities and races rarely mixed, but moved in wary eddies, each creating its own world.

The old man paused to switch on two ancient table lamps. He reached carefully under the small floral shades that perched precariously on their ornately painted china bodies. Like the heavy furnishings, embroidered cushions, and tinted family photographs, the tight circles of light seemed vestiges of the past.

"Your grandmother is at the church. Every Friday evening, it's the same. First mass, then her meeting. The Society of the Virgin Mary."

"I know," DiGenero said.

His grandfather continued. "Most of her friends have passed now, but she goes nonetheless. The father of the priest who gives instruction wasn't even born when she first came through the church door." The old man stepped deliberately as he spoke, maneuvering around the obstacles created by too many objects in too little space. "I know the Bible says a child shall lead you, but at my age it's not easy to accept. This priest is a nice boy. When bingo is over, he brings her home in the car. These days in this neighborhood, even four blocks is too far to walk at night."

The decanter was centered on the sideboard. His grandfather lifted the stopper and poured slowly, a ritual motion. DiGenero took the glass. The marsala, Palermo's finest, had aged from amber to brown. The wine emitted a sweet bouquet.

The old man eased into his chair, unconsciously straightening the antimacassars on the armrests. DiGenero saw the tremor in his hands. He motioned to the sofa. DiGenero sat.

"How long has it been?" his grandfather asked.

"Since when?"

"Since you left New York?"

"Almost ten years," DiGenero answered.

"And now you've returned?"

"Temporarily."

"Temporarily?" his grandfather repeated.

"Yes."

He contemplated DiGenero's confirmation. "Your grandmother would give the world to see you."

"I know."

"But you came on Friday night."

"Yes," DiGenero said.

His grandmother's routine followed the certain pattern of a peasant's life, despite her seventy years in the city. She rose before the sun, prayed, and passed the day tending to her home and the cares of her husband. The details of her existence were immutable. Friday night mass and the meeting of her devotional society afterward were fixtures in time, assuring DiGenero he would find only his grandfather at home.

"After all these years, she still looks for your letters," the old man said. "When the holidays arrive, if you've not called, she waits until the last moment to leave for church. On those days, she never lingers after the service. She wants to come home in case the telephone rings." He paused. "You knew I couldn't speak with you?"

"Yes," DiGenero answered.

"You knew I couldn't even ask her whether it was you?"

"I knew."

"Good." Vincenzo DiGenero seemed satisfied. "I'm glad you knew." He examined his grandson for several moments in silence. "I see your father in you. In your eyes. Youth hides the details. Age reveals."

The old man leaned back, resting his head against the chair, a posture suited to reflection. "Even as a boy in our village, I studied the people around me. In Alcamo it was easy to understand where you came from and where you belonged. Each day, the fathers and sons, the grandfathers and great-grandfathers walked, arm in arm, making the late afternoon stroll. As they went by, you could see the present, the future, and the past. I remember watching them and thinking that God must have created the village like the vineyard. Each family had its arbor. Some years the vines were full and thick, others not. But no matter. When the season was finished and the leaves fell away, the original roots and trunk always were clear." He straightened. "Your father was younger than you are now when he died, wasn't he?"

"A few years," DiGenero said.

"Yes, a few years." He nodded, agreeing with the approximation. "His tracings are in your face, but I wonder what it means. Is the son becoming the father, or is the father revealing himself in the son? That's a question of philosophy not anatomy, is it not?"

"I suppose."

"For you, it's difficult to answer. We can only wonder what would have been if death had not interrupted." His brow furrowed in an effort to remember. "Your father's heart attack—when was it?" his grandfather asked.

"1973."

"It was summer," the old man said.

"That's right. Just after I came back from Vietnam," DiGenero confirmed.

"Yes, from the war. And before you joined them."

"Them?" DiGenero asked.

"The FBI."

"That's right." DiGenero took a deep breath, anticipating what was coming next.

"If he had lived, would you have stayed with him?"

"Here? In New York?"

"Yes." The old man said.

"And become the grocer's son?" DiGenero shook his head. "I don't think so."

His grandfather stiffened. "Why not? Was that something beneath you?"

"No. I couldn't have inherited his past any more than he could have inherited yours."

"For him, it wasn't a choice."

DiGenero shrugged. "Too much had changed. That's all."

"So much that you'd turn against your own kind?" The question had a cutting edge. It had been waiting for him for a decade, honed sharp by time.

DiGenero sipped his wine. "When you came to America from Alcamo, you told me that to exist here was a matter of survival. It was no easier to be the last off the boat than it was to be the first. To live was hard and you did what you had to. But you said when you had a choice, you took it. When the time came, you put it behind you. You left the Mafia. You walked away from the life. Forty years ago, you broke with Johnny Scarlese because he knew right from wrong, but still chose the life. He and the others, the ones who stayed, had become men without honor, you said." He met his grandfather's gaze. "To me, that doesn't make the Scarleses my kind."

"I'm not speaking of the Scarleses, Francesco." For the first time, his grandfather slipped from English into Sicilian. His was the old language, not the bastardized argot of second- or third-generation Italian-Americans, but the communication of conspiracy, the product of an island people, born of centuries of secrecy under successions of oppressors, the clipped intonation as well as the dialect of a coded tongue. "When I left Alcamo, Alcamo didn't leave me. I knew our values. They were inside me, like my blood, like the air we breathe. Yes, I met my obligations. Yes, I quit the life. But I didn't leave it. I didn't run away. I stayed here, among them. I waited for them to come. I gave them their chance to judge me and, if they were man enough, to act. To take their retribution, if they chose. I lived by the rules. I still do. To this day."

"Your rules, grandfather, not mine," DiGenero said.

"Not yours?" The old man's eyes widened. "You think so?"

"Yes," DiGenero said.

"Even now, with what has happened, you think so?"

DiGenero stood and walked to the window. He parted the curtains. The rain had stopped, but not the wind. Against the streetlights, the bare branches of the old oaks, too thick to bend, jerked in crude animation. Traffic was light and the sidewalks were empty. He turned to face his questioner. "I didn't come here to explain myself. My life had its reasons, just as yours does. What's done is done."

"Then why did you come?"

"To see you," DiGenero said.

"After all these years?"

He nodded. "And to ask advice."

DiGenero waited. He wanted the old man to reach out, to beckon him closer, but his grandfather stared impassively. A reunion and a request. Was that why he'd come? Was that all? His grandfather was the only one left, all he had. But the old man was more than that. He was the only one who knew DiGenero's past—what he once was, what he had risked, what he had lost. The only one who could understand, who could see the right and wrong of it. The only one living who knew him and could forgive.

"You know what has happened," DiGenero said.

"I know what you did. I know what they did to you," he said.

The words struck DiGenero like a slap, stinging because of their diffidence rather than their strength. "Do you?" He walked to the couch and sat. "I betrayed them. That's a fact. I took the oath with my blood on the picture of the saint and the gun in my hand, and I repeated the words as they burned the picture in my palm. I wanted to get inside and I succeeded. I spent five years as their consigliere and when it was over I put Johnny Scarlese away. I did it, no one else. For that I'm responsible."

DiGenero leaned forward. "Do you know how hard they looked, grandfather?"

The old man didn't answer.

DiGenero continued. "They looked for me under every rock. We knew. The Tattaglias, the Varios, the families on the East Coast and the West Coast, they all helped. We knew that, too. And finally, after almost ten years, what did they do when they found me? What was their retribution?" DiGenero twisted the word contemptuously. His voice wavered. "They killed my wife."

DiGenero turned away, struggling to control himself. Tears blinded him. He spoke facing the window, as if addressing an audience that was waiting in the darkness outside for the curtains to part. "Rules. You talk of rules, grandfather. Alright, but what are they? What do they say? I know. They violated their own code. Whatever my betrayal, theirs was the cardinal sin. They murdered the innocent, not the one who had broken the oath."

DiGenero wiped his eyes. When he looked up, his grandfather was watching. "The rules make no exceptions," DiGenero said. "You know that. Never the innocent. Never."

His grandfather spoke slowly, not without kindness. "You live in two worlds, Francesco. In one, to be sure, you are the hunted. You've made that so. But in the other, you are still the hunter. As one of the FBI, you have the power of the government. Can it not give you justice?"

"Justice? I'd settle for a telephone call. For two weeks I've waited for something, anything. Word of a lead, a hint they were working."

"And?" his grandfather asked.

"Nothing."

"Why? Surely they know they must do something, for the sake of the others who risk themselves. You're one of their kind."

"Am I?" DiGenero sat back against the sofa. He closed his eyes momentarily. In the last two weeks sleep had become only an unconsciousness interlude, never rest. He heard the fatigue in his own voice, the sound of someone speaking from very far away. "Do you know where Erin is, grandfather? In a folder, somewhere. She's been around. From the Salt Lake City field office, to undercover operations staff, to organized crime division, to the deputy director's office. From inbox to inbox and back again. She's a tough case. The wife of an agent, murdered by somebody from one of her husband's past operations in a town where he's undercover again. Tangled and messy. That's how they look at it. Start pulling on the threads and the whole fabric can unravel. Who knows what you'll find?"

DiGenero smiled sardonically. "You say I'm 'one of them.' Maybe it looks that way, but I don't think so. To them, even the best undercovers are a little seamy, not to be trusted, no matter how good they are. I can hear them now. 'DiGenero did alright work, but who knows what he was really into? Who knows what he really did when he was out on the end of the string? Who knows why they really want to kill him? Who knows why his wife got hit? Lie down with the dogs and you can't help gettin' fleas, right?' "

"Is that the way they think?" his grandfather asked.

DiGenero shrugged. "Oh, they worry about the case, even the highly paid help. They've put it in a special category. In Washington, I discovered that much."

"A special category?" his grandfather asked. "What does that mean?"

"It means they hold meetings. They pass the file back and forth across big mahogany tables. They talk, write memos, talk some more. 'Not something you'd like on the front page, is it? Not one to ask the local cops about either. Embarrassing if it gets out that we haven't gotten a piece of the guys who blew her up. We got to do something. Bad for morale if we put it in the "too-hard pile" too soon. But we've got to take it a step at a time. What to do? What to do?' " DiGenero put his head in his hands. "They don't give a shit about Erin. Why should they? She's paper. A case, that's all. To them, she's just a messy, fuckin' case." He looked up, his eyes wet again. "But she's not. God knows, she's not."

His grandfather sat, silent.

DiGenero spoke deliberately, for the first time in Sicilian. "I'm not going to wait for them. I'm not going to wait for them to decide what to do."

The old man examined him for several moments, his expression opaque. Finally, he spoke. "Is this why you come? Is this the advice you want? How I can help you kill the young Scarlese?"

DiGenero didn't reply.

"Answer me. Is this why you come? After ten years. Is this why you're here?" His grandfather rose from his chair. His hands balled into fists. The anger was sudden, a vessel cracked, its molten contents revealed. "Listen, Francesco, and listen to me well. I care nothing for Scarlese the father, or Scarlese the son. They have no place among those who matter to me. But when I left the life, I kept my oath, whatever the evil of those to whom it was pledged. I stayed here and waited like a man to be judged. Why? Because it was my oath. My word. The word of our family." The old man looked away. "And you? What did you do?"

"I only want Scarlese," DiGenero said quietly. "This isn't a matter for anyone else. There'll be no policemen, or lawyers, or courts, or judges."

"Is that so?"

DiGenero nodded. "In this I'm alone, grandfather."

The old man stared, his eyes slate hard. "You should leave now. Before your grandmother arrives."

DiGenero rose.

His grandfather picked up their glasses and turned away. He walked slowly into the dining room, then deeper into the darkness of the pantry hall. DiGenero looked around him. Nothing had changed. There was no trace of his presence, no sign that after ten years he had come again to call.

DiGenero stepped to the edge of the dining room and spoke. "I'll see you again."

The hinge on the kitchen door squeaked, followed by the sound of water splashing in the sink. A tap turned. Glass scraped on porcelain, then silence. No one returned.

He spoke again. "Good night, grandfather." No reply.

DiGenero stood on the threshhold, hoping. He walked to the door and let himself out. Alone.

"So whaddya suppose this kike cop finally says to me?" Fork in one hand, spoon in the other, Sallie Ferringa worked ambidextrously, carving at his veal piccata as he dredged his soupbowl for the remains of his minestrone.

"What was that?" Jilian McCray leaned back in her chair. Busy, Ferringa failed to notice her distraction.

She glanced at the street. The rain had stopped. Ferringa had called the bar, explaining he'd been held up. She'd taken a cab to the restaurant. On her plate, the fettucine remained, half eaten. The conversation with Frank Falcone replayed itself, preoccupying her with the task of arranging and rearranging its few details into notional configurations of coincidence or conspiracy.

Ferringa spoke, his mouth full. "He smiles and says, 'I jus' come to pay my respects for Vito.' After two hours of chickenshit questions! How goddamn stupid do they think I am? They think I'm goin' to say somethin'?"

His voice was loud, but seated in the restaurant's window alcove, a half step down from the sidewalk level, the small space enclosed them. The table was permanently reserved for whenever they arrived on Friday nights. Despite the crowd lingering because of the rain, the maître d' never lost sight of Ferringa's progress through the antipasto, bread, wine, soup and entrée.

"Does the name Frank Falcone mean anything to you?" Jilian asked.

"Nah. Why?" He lifted his glass, draining the last of the Chianti. The waiter appeared instantly. He poured more wine, then slid away.

"I met someone at the bar tonight by that name," Jilian said.

"So?" Ferringa worked both utensils.

"He said he knew Vito."

Ferringa paused, mouth open. He put down the knife and fork, groped for the napkin tucked under his chin, and blotted. "Whaddya mean, 'knew Vito?' "

"He said he was an old friend from Connecticut. In the travel business."

"Connecticut? Vito couldn't find the fuckin' Bronx if somebody didn't take him there. How's he gonna have friends in Connecticut? What else this guy say?" Ferringa asked.

"Nothing, really."

"You sure?"

Jilian nodded.

Ferringa's pupils had contracted to punctuation marks, a predator's stare. "You ever seen him before?"

"No."

"He smell like a cop?"

"I don't think so. I just thought you might know him." she said.

"Frank Falcone?"

She nodded again perfunctorily.

"That's it?" Ferringa asked.

"Yes."

"I'll check 'em out," he said. Ferringa resumed sawing at the veal. "I wish I knew who did Vito. We ain't gettin' no heat from anybody else, so it can't be somethin' to do with the family. Vito didn't have nothin' goin' on the side, so it couldn'a been personal. And our connection with you is clean." He skewered three pieces of meat along with a tangle of pasta, filling his mouth before glancing up. "Right?"

Jilian returned her gaze from the window to Ferringa. "Right."

"I mean, I been beatin' the fuckin' bushes." He chewed and sighed. "Johnny ain't happy we ain't found out nothin'."

"Well, that's too bad." Jilian leaned forward. "But why don't you tell me about that later?"

He grunted.

Beneath the table, she slid her hand up Ferringa's thigh. She stroked the soft bulge in his crotch. "You see, I've found something that I know will make me very happy."

Ferringa stopped chewing.

"When we get done you can tell me all about Johnny's problems, alright?" she asked.

He nodded obediently.

Jilian smiled. "That's for later. Right now, I don't think we should worry about anything else tonight."

CHAPTER

8

LOUIE VERGILIO WALKED purposefully in the morning darkness. At Water and John Streets, the wind buffeted him. Vergilio was a small man, but gloved, hatted, shod in galoshes, and wrapped in an overcoat, his protection nearly doubled his size. As always, he was nothing, if not prepared. He had risen two hours earlier, bathed and shaved twice, and reread the newspaper's roadwork-in-progress column, ensuring he had two routes to Manhattan in case traffic blocked one. In fact, Vergilio did everything twice. For a certified public accountant, it was a professional as well as personal habit, including keeping two sets of books for Scarlese Transport's office at the Fulton Street fish market.

Just beyond the intersection with Fulton Street, a small sign marked the building's entrance. Vergilio stood on the threshold. He inserted one key. Fumbling with the second lock, his concentration was so complete that he failed to hear the footsteps behind him or even utter a cry when DiGenero's body block tumbled him onto the office floor the instant he had opened his door.

Face down, Vergilio gasped and wiggled under DiGenero's weight. His arms and legs flailed pathetically, the protest of the congenitally defenseless.

DiGenero lifted him to his feet. "Relax, Louie, you'll live." He dusted off Vergilio's overcoat solicitously, smoothing the collar.

Goggle-eyed, Vergilio opened and closed his mouth like a landed fish, emulating nature's most perfect portrait of mute surprise. "You!" The little man exhaled the word, gulping more air.

"Precisely." DiGenero smiled. "Take off your coat."

Like a schoolboy, Vergilio obeyed, handing the coat to DiGenero, who hung it behind the door.

"What do you want?" Vergilio's voice quavered.

"Sit down, Louie." Vergilio sat. DiGenero felt a brief sympathy as well as a passing sense of guilt for what he was about to do.

91

The chain of relationships that bound the Scarleses together also separated the family and its enterprises. Each was its own organization, insulated from one another by design as well as by the best security known, the inherent rivalry of men driven by greed. DiGenero knew the family's moneymaking could begin and lead anywhere. Years before, he had watched from the inside with a sense of awe as well as the depressing feeling that even close attention to the details would never provide the full picture. It hadn't, of course, but even an organization meant to obscure was not without patterns. At the end of the day, someone had to do the numbers, to be trusted to add up the columns, to figure the percentages. For Johnny Scarlese, Jr., as for his father, DiGenero knew, Louie the bookkeeper was that someone.

DiGenero dragged a chair in front of Vergilio and straddled it backward. His proximity made the small man hunch like an animal trying to secrete itself from an imminent danger.

"You shouldn't have pushed me down like that." Vergilio snuffled.

DiGenero took a Kleenex box from the accountant's desk and offered it. Vergilio extracted a tissue and blew his nose hard. He wiped and looked up. "What do you want?"

"Answers to a couple questions."

"I could get hurt bad talking to you. Johnny goes crazy when somebody mentions your name." Vergilio's hands trembled.

"Okay, let's not waste time. How come Vito did all that traveling?" DiGenero asked.

"I don't know what you're talking about." Vergilio replied too quickly to be convincing.

"Come on, Louie, don't shit me." DiGenero leaned forward, putting his hand on the accountant's knee. Vergilio shrunk back, seeming to become physically smaller. He spoke. "Louie, there are certain eternal verities. The *capo di tutti capi* sets a certain standard, you know what I mean?"

Despite the cold room, small rivulets of sweat coursed down Vergilio's neck, absorbed by his collar. His complexion, moments before mottled from unexpected exertion and fear, had turned chameleonlike to a dead gray pallor.

DiGenero continued. "We both know how things work. The don makes the rules. The capos and the crew chiefs enforce them. The soldiers, like Vito, live by the word. Am I right?"

"Uh huh."

DiGenero pointed. "That's Sallie Ferringa's desk, right?"

Vergilio's eyes darted from DiGenero's outstretched finger to the desk and back again, as if scrutinizing the gesture for some revealed meaning. "Uh huh."

"Sallie's alright," DiGenero said. "He always took care of his friends. I gotta believe he takes care of his crew."

"Uh huh."

DiGenero tipped his chair forward, leaning within inches of Vergilio's face. "But his crew's gotta take care of him. They gotta live by the rules. And you know what they are. Sallie's gotta be there when the don calls. That means they gotta be there when Sallie calls. Whenever he calls. Twenty-four-hours-a-day, seven-days-a-week. No excuses."

DiGenero smiled. "Sallie's a lucky guy to have you keeping his books. The don trusted you. I gotta believe Johnny Junior trusts you. I mean, when Sallie got a piece of the fish market, he got you. He doesn't even have to add or subtract. Whenever money comes in or goes out, you're on top of it."

DiGenero's smile disappeared. "The bottom line is, Vito can't go anywhere or spend a fuckin' dime without Sallie knowing it. So, tell me what the books say about Vito's traveling."

In the quiet, Vergilio's respiration came in small darting gasps. "I don't know anything. So help me God."

"Louie."

His voice broke, verging on a sob. "They don't tell me. They just say, 'Deposit the money. Write the check. Gimme the cash.' That's all, Frank, that's all."

"Not fucking good enough, Louie." DiGenero leaned closer. Vergilio had contorted himself to one side, trying to turn away.

"Please." He took a deep, shuddering breath.

"Who's 'they?' "

" 'They?' " Damp-eyed, Vergilio was a picture of fright compounded by confusion.

"Who tells you to deposit the money? Who says, 'write the checks?' " DiGenero asked with deliberate patience.

"First it was Vito, now it's Sallie," Vergilio said. "When Vito started doin' the traveling two years ago, Sallie took over."

"Took over what?"

"The details. Vito made the trips, but Sallie managed things. You know, the arrangements, like collecting the payments. That's all I know, so help me."

DiGenero put a steadying hand on Vergilio's shoulder and squeezed. In his grip, the bony frame felt fragile, birdlike. "Not fucking good enough, Louie."

"Oh mother of God, don't hurt me."

"I'm not going to hurt you, Louie." DiGenero squeezed harder, contradicting the assurance. "But I'm the least of your problems if word gets out we had a conversation."

Vergilio moaned.

He relaxed his grip. "Who wrote the checks?"

"Nobody."

"Nobody?"

"I mean, I don't know. They're cashier's checks. That's what Sallie always gives me."

"Always?" DiGenero asked.

"Always."

"All from the same bank, different banks, what?"

"From the same bank," Vergilio said.

"Which one?"

"Credit International."

"What's the money for?" DiGenero asked.

Vergilio shook his head with a small child's sincere exaggeration, emphasizing his ignorance. "So help me, I don't know."

"What does Sallie tell you?"

"Nothing. He just says it's for expenses. That's all. Expenses. I put it on the books that way every month."

"So Vito traveled and they covered him, pay-as-you-go?" DiGenero asked.

"No, no. Vito went maybe four, five times a year at the outside. We always got more than he spent."

"Oh? How much more?"

Vergilio closed his eyes, mentally calculating. Concentrating on debits and credits, the accountant's familiar abstractions, the task seemed to calm him. "Vito's trips were $2,000, maybe $2,500 each. We normally got $20,000 a month. So that's 240 minus twelve-and-a-half. I'd say we'd average $227,000 difference each year."

"What did you do with it?"

"Wash it, like everything. You know, move it into other accounts."

"Then what?" DiGenero pressed.

"Then Sallie asks for cash and I give it to him."

"Cash?"

"Uh huh." Vergilio sounded childlike.

"For what?"

"I don't know. He doesn't tell me. Once a month I give him $5,000. It's always the same. Then, every other month or so, I give him $15,000, sometimes a little more."

"Only Sallie?"

Vergilio nodded.

"Who else is involved?"

"Nobody."

"Nobody?" DiGenero asked with obvious sarcasm. He stared. In the silence, Vergilio looked left and right, trying unsuccessfully to focus somewhere that could provide an alternative to DiGenero, to discover something that was still intact and could offer even for a moment a visual tether to what remained of his small safehaven, the world of numbers, ledgers, and spreadsheets that his own words were eroding away.

DiGenero answered for him. "Johnny Junior."

Vergilio made an indeterminate sound, a whimper in minor key.

"Does Johnny draw from the kitty?" DiGenero asked.

Vergilio's nose was running. The trembling had begun again. DiGenero waited, then took a deep breath, as if concluding his inquiry. "Let me guess. Johnny doesn't draw from you, does he?"

Vergilio sat still for several moments. The motion was barely apparent when he finally shook his head.

"Sallie gives him the money after he makes the draw," DiGenero said. This time a nod.

"Which draw, the big or the little, the $5,000 or the $15,000?"

Vergilio's lips moved, but no sound came out.

"Which?" DiGenero asked, this time more loudly.

"The big," Vergilio whispered.

DiGenero sat back and smiled. Vergilio looked exhausted. He reached out, patting Vergilio's cheek. "That's good, Louie, very good. You've been a real help."

"What are you going to do?" He examined DiGenero with a doe's vulnerable eyes.

"Nothing, Louie. Nothing at all." DiGenero stood. "Consider this just catching up on old times."

"Don't get me involved. Please. They'll kill me."

DiGenero managed a sympathetic expression. He buttoned his coat. Vergilio watched him in silence.

"It was a real shame about Vito," DiGenero said. He finished buttoning and looked up. "By the way, when Vito went out west two weeks ago, did he get his cash from you, or did Sallie pick it up for him?"

Vergilio looked puzzled. "Out west?"

"You didn't know about the trip?"

"No. When was it?"

"Two weeks ago."

"Two weeks?" He thought for a moment. "Middle of the week?"

DiGenero nodded indefinitely.

Vergilio furrowed his brow. "Sallie, I think. Why?"

DiGenero shook his head. "No reason." He stepped toward Vergilio and extended his hand. "Gimme your wallet."

Vergilio drew back.

"Gimme." DiGenero snapped his fingers.

Reluctantly, he withdrew his wallet from his trousers and handed it over.

DiGenero opened the folio, found the driver's license, and removed it. He tossed the wallet into Vergilio's lap and walked to the timeclock.

"Whaddya doing?"

DiGenero ignored the question. The laminated rectangle with Vergilio's picture, name, and address slipped easily into the timecard slot. DiGenero pushed it down against the trigger. Inside the clock, the printer banged, accompanied by the flat ring of a bell. He extracted the license and examined it. The ink had smeared on the plastic, but the words and numbers were legible. "Scarlese Transport," followed by the date and time. "6:55 A.M."

He held the license for Vergilio to see. "Here's the deal. You don't say a word about our talk and this stays lost. You open your mouth, it gets found." DiGenero paused. "With a love note from me. In Johnny Junior's mailbox."

DiGenero slipped the license into his pocket. He walked to the door and opened it. A taxi passed by slowly, the only traffic. The overcast gave the morning a flat, colorless light, without tones or brightness. He turned for a final time toward the seated man. "Nice to see you, Louie."

Vergilio said nothing, but only stared back with the dazed look of an accident victim as DiGenero closed the door.

CHAPTER

9

DiGenero took the stairs from the subway platform to the street in two-step strides. The sky had bowed low, threatening rain. He crossed Third, then Second Avenue against the lights. Leaving Vergilio in lower Manhattan, he had walked west, finding the Lexington Avenue line. The express took fifteen minutes to reach 125th Street. Harlem. The only white face on the platform, he'd waited until another train passed. Most ignored him, although a few had watched him pace, their glares illuminating his alien presence. Satisfied no one had followed, he had boarded a southbound local for 86th Street.

He double-timed, tacking back and forth against the sidewalk's opposing current. Transformed from workday to weekend, the street reflected the signature of life in the city. A few wholesale delivery vans, scarred denizens of the night, remained humped over the curb, but most were gone, as were the ubiquitous wanderers, the lost souls who owned the empty darkness just before morning light. In their place, dressed in expensive casualness, singles and couples emerged from the highrises and brownstones, the latest cohort of the young, upwardly mobile inhabiting Yorkville's waystations to the suburbs. Some, attentive to their offspring, pushed strollers or held small hands. They moved toward the supermarkets or the park on the river with grocery lists or the accoutrements of a child's play as the destination demanded.

DiGenero glanced at his watch. Nearly eight. Benedetto would be waiting. He passed a bus stop. Liberated for the weekend, the maids and nannies queued. Dark-eyed Latins and ample black women, they straddled their worn shopping bags and overnight cases with a practiced defensiveness, waiting for the crosstown to the West side or farther still, the Bronx, their weekly transit from less to more congenial ghettos.

At First Avenue, DiGenero made out the taxis a block ahead. Bumper to bumper, they created a cordon surrounding the corner, a train of battered wagons circled for the defense. The Mansion. York and 86th. The diner was incontestably theirs. Hackers' territory. Only two blocks from the mayor's residence, the name was meant to be a locator, a practical lesson learned by an owner who survived in a city where originality always died the death of instant replication. The diner was a magnet for generations of cabbies, the regular stop for a three-dollar breakfast, lunch, dinner, or whatever passed for a meal in the small hours of the night.

DiGenero pushed open the door. A single row of booths paralleled the long counter. At the far end, Benedetto slouched, an arm's length from the kitchen door.

Despite a beckoning wave, Benedetto didn't seem happy to see him. "Why you tryin' to convince me you're not too bright?"

"Well, good morning to you." DiGenero ignored the illhumor. He slid onto the bench seat. The waitress, a brittle blonde, paused, an eyebrow raised in wordless query. He ordered coffee and reached for the laminated menu. She reappeared with a full mug and the pot.

DiGenero looked up. "Eggs over easy, bacon, toast."

Benedetto pushed his mug across the table. The refill came with a practiced flourish. As quickly, she was gone.

DiGenero sipped the steaming coffee. He glanced over his shoulder. No one glanced back. Nothing had changed, including the customers. At the counter, the stools were full, a tableau of figures hunched in stylized concentration. They were dressed in different versions of the same nondescript uniform. Wool shirts or sweaters, poplin or leather jackets, and cotton pants, permanently faded, wrinkled, or worn shiny. The faces were all white, additions to the old stock, East Europeans, Italians, Irish, and Russians. The others who piloted the city's cabs, Latinos, Vietnamese, and Indians, chose places more welcoming to their kind. Conditioned as front-seat interlocutors, the cabbies talked without making eye contact. Mouths full, they gossiped, argued or declaimed, reciting views gleaned from the Daily *News,* radio stories repeated on the hour, and the occasional snatches of conversation with passengers, then mulled during solitary interludes, internalized as opinion, and finally stated as fact.

"I haven't been here since you left town," Benedetto said.

When DiGenero was inside the Scarleses, it had been one of their meeting places. Always busy, the diner trafficked in anonymity. There were too many comings and goings to allow any one to be remembered as more than a first name, even at three in the morning.

He looked at Benedetto. "Come to the big city and you learn the damnedest things."

"Whaddya talkin' about?" Benedetto drank and grimaced. "Too hot."

DiGenero started to answer but a crash in the kitchen interrupted. The drone of voices abated as a fountain of Spanish epithets spewed from behind the swinging door. One of the cabbies said something. Several laughed. The waitress rolled her eyes.

"My old buddy, Sallie Ferringa."

Benedetto looked puzzled. "Since when was that moron your 'old buddy'?"

"Since he done good. Sallie's got a piece of Fulton Street, hasn't he?"

"For the past ten years, yeah. So?" Benedetto said.

"So success changes your lifestyle, right?"

"What's the point?" Benedetto asked.

"Tell me something about him," DiGenero said.

"Such as?"

"Like does he travel?"

"Whaddya talkin' about?" Benedetto's irritation was obvious.

"To Ireland. Like Vito traveled."

Benedetto put down his coffee. In the unforgiving fluorescent light, his skin showed a fine checking not unlike the pattern on the diner's mugs, the vulnerable epidermis of an otherwise impervious glaze. He studied DiGenero before he spoke. "How much time you spent inside?"

The question caught DiGenero off-guard. "Inside what?"

"The Bureau," Benedetto said.

"Oh." DiGenero looked up, remembering. "When the Scarlese case wrapped up here, a little in Atlanta. Then, back undercover in Miami. After that, Salt Lake. Same thing. You know that. I'm an outside guy."

"An outside guy?" Benedetto said.

DiGenero heard the sarcasm. He nodded.

"Then you don't know a fuckin' thing about what you're askin', do you?"

He started to reply, but Benedetto didn't give him time. "I told you more than I shoulda the other night. If anybody finds out, it's gonna cost me my ass. But that's okay. People talk. I mean, let's not get hung up with this 'need-to-know' horseshit. You and me, we're real, not some buttoned-up bastards from Headquarters with rule books and big desks. It was my call. I didn't have to say nothin' if I didn't want to, right?"

DiGenero didn't answer.

Benedetto leaned forward, claiming the space between them. "Right?" he repeated, louder this time.

DiGenero nodded, assenting.

Benedetto straightened, opening his arms expansively. "Besides, you said it. You're an outside guy. You know what I'm talkin' about. You're no virgin." He smiled. "I trust you. You trust me. That's the way the world works. We know how it really is, right?"

Benedetto's neck had thickened with age. DiGenero could see the color rising, mottling the folds of skin above his collar. The smile disappeared as anger burned through. "Wrong! You don't know nothin'." He reached across the table, jabbing his finger into DiGenero's chest. "You come to my house and think you can have whatever you want. You're even goin' to bust my balls to get it. I tell you for your own good to get outa town. Scarlese finds you and you're dead meat. But whaddyado? You come lookin' for me again. Jus' like the old days. Jus' like when you was on the outside and I was on the inside. Your inside guy. 'Meet me here. Go there. Do this. Do that.' Whatever you want, old Tony's goin' to do. Jus' like your whole fuckin' career. You're a one-man band and everybody's there jus' to help you play the tune."

"Wait a minute." DiGenero flushed.

Benedetto interrupted. "Whaddya gonna say? Whaddya gonna tell me? You're out there, all by yourself? You take chances? You take the big risks? Maybe things go wrong? What's that? Maybe a one-out-of-a-thousand shot and you get waxed? Well, rest in fuckin' peace! But what about the rest of the time? You think you're some kinda movie star. You think you can have anything you want by snappin' your fingers. Well, you don't know shit about how the other half lives. You don't understand a thing about what I put up with to do my job. You ain't got the faintest notion what it takes. I mean, I'm sorry they killed your wife. I truly am. But you don't have one fuckin' idea what you're askin' me to do."

Benedetto was breathing hard. DiGenero leaned back against the booth. "All I got is a simple question," he said quietly.

"That's the point. Nothin's simple."

"What's the problem, Tony?"

"You don't understand, do you? You really don't understand." Benedetto started to speak again, but the waitress reappeared. They fell silent.

DiGenero salted and peppered his eggs. He slid the side order of toast to the center of the table, a peace offering.

Benedetto took a slice, then sighed, apparently spent. He spoke more quietly. "Like I told you the other night, I got a squad. We're working with the Brits on the IRA. It's a compartmented operation, sealed up tight. That means nobody knows. Nobody. We get our orders from the intelligence side of the Bureau, direct from Washington. Everybody else is outa the loop. No 'ifs, ands, or buts.' "

DiGenero ate slowly, listening, mindful that even the wrong gesture could snap the thin tether between them.

"About six months ago, maybe a little less, the Brits come to us. They got a source. On the inside. I don't know where, here or over there. The source tells 'em there's somethin' goin' down in the States. It's big time, not nickel-and-dime shit like gunrunning. Unfortunately, the Brits tell us, they don't know what it is. Or at least they won't say. Naturally, Washington goes bananas. They get excited and start wavin' their arms. They got visions of the crazies highjackin' the Empire State Building or blowin' up Central Park. So we go all out. We work the West side, the docks, the clubs, the churches, the snitches in the Sons of Hibernia. You name it. I mean, I'm turnin' over rocks, readin' the backs of old bubblegum wrappers, doin' whatever I can, but we still get nothin.' Then, one day, the phone rings."

Benedetto paused.

DiGenero looked up. "And?"

"The Brits got a name."

"Vito," DiGenero said.

"It don't make sense, I tell 'em. I mean where does Vito come off mixin' it up with the IRA. The only micks he knew were his punchin' bags after grammar school. Besides, he's a street guy. A soldier. Strictly penny-ante. That don't matter, they say. They spotted him in Dublin travelin' in alias, and traced the connection. They found out he was recruited on the West side. A broad, like I told you the other night." Benedetto shrugged. "So, we watch him. Where he goes. Who he sees. What he does. He hangs out with the usual crowd. Runs the usual two-bit shakedowns. Meets the usual bimbos."

"And?" DiGenero asked.

No broad, no action, no Irish connection. A big zero. Until two things happen."

"The plane goes down and Vito's dead."

Benedetto nodded. "Now, whadda we got? You believe the Brits, Vito's involved. You look at the timing—they blow Vito away on the day the plane crashes—Vito's involved. You think about the circumstances. Scarlese's into the rackets at Kennedy. The freight handlers, the ground service contracts, ya know? That gives 'em access. The plane's bound for Kennedy. Add up two and two. Vito's involved." Benedetto took a deep breath. "But involved in what, I ask ya? Put it all together and whaddya got? Look for the evidence and it ain't there."

"What about OC?" DiGenero asked.

"The Organized Crime Squad?"

"Yeah."

"What about it?" Benedetto asked warily.

"I mean, the New York Field Office has an army to watch the families, Scarlese's included. Maybe the squad saw something you didn't. Maybe there's something on file about Vito you could use."

Benedetto shook his head. "Can't."

"Why not?"

"First, I can't talk to them. Nobody's supposed to know we exist," Benedetto said.

"What? You couldn't clear somebody on the squad? A contact for your operation?"

"Headquarters won't. Besides, that ain't all. Between me and organized crime there's a Chinese wall. I got my investigation and they got theirs. Mine's counterterrorism, theirs is the rackets. What you learn on one side of the wall, you can't pass to the other."

"That's nuts," DiGenero said.

Benedetto shrugged. "I don't make the rules. What can I say? Washington already is scared shitless that we'll actually make a case against the IRA and all political hell will break loose. They don't want any slipups. No tainted evidence, no civil liberties suits, no senators from Massachusetts taking the skin off the Bureau's ass strip by strip, you know what I mean?" Benedetto leaned forward, putting his hand on DiGenero's arm. "That's why they didn't run down Vito's trip to Salt Lake, Frank. They're frightened. It's not that they don't want to get Scarlese for what they did to your wife. We'll get him. Believe me. It's just that we gotta be careful."

"We gotta be careful?"

"Yeah," Benedetto said.

"Is that right?" DiGenero asked.

Benedetto nodded vigorously. "Believe me."

"All of a sudden it's *we?*"

The nodding stopped, like mechanical animation slowing down. Benedetto stared without speaking.

"No, Tony, *you* gotta be careful," DiGenero said. He felt the hand slip from his arm. Benedetto leaned back slowly.

DiGenero crushed his napkin. He tossed the ball on the table. "You watched Vito pretty close over the last couple months?"

"Yeah," Benedetto said. "I told you. We covered his ass wherever he went."

"Day and night."

"Day and night."

"Then tell me something." For an instant, DiGenero hated with every fiber. He wanted to grab Benedetto by the neck, to choke him, to smash his face into the table, to exact all the retribution that was due for the stupidity that had snuffed out the single flame lighting the darkness of his life.

"What?" Benedetto asked stolidly.

"How come nobody called me when he got on the plane to Salt Lake?"

Benedetto opened and closed his mouth without speaking. He looked away, his expression quick frozen. "Take my advice. Don't get involved."

"That's a little difficult at this point, don't you think?" DiGenero said.

"Like I told you the other night. Go back to Washington. Vito doesn't make any difference. Neither does Sallie Ferringa."

DiGenero nodded ambiguously. He stood. "You know how the system works as well as I do. Vito didn't wake up one morning and decide to kill me. Scarlese put out the contract. Somebody, maybe Sallie, laid it on." DiGenero put his hands on the table and leaned down. "Don't get me wrong. I'm not gonna make anybody do a lot of paperwork. I don't want to arrest them. I don't want to see them on trial. I don't even want them to go to jail. I did that once. There's no reason to do it again. This time, I want them dead. Especially Junior."

Benedetto's voice was flat, without emotion. "You don't have to believe me. Maybe OC's got something on Ferringa, maybe they don't. The point is, I can't help you."

DiGenero straightened. "Can't or won't?"

"You want me to say it again? I can't help you."

DiGenero tossed a five-dollar bill on the table. "I don't remember hearing that from you before."

"Like I said, Frank, you just don't understand."

Ian Barry hated the bubble. No bigger than a closet and curtained on all four walls, it reminded him of a coffin. An unambiguously unpleasant object, unsuccessfully disguised.

Its Plexiglas walls formed a chamber on rubber and phenolic mounts, a room within a room. Inside, two could sit at a small café table, but any attempt to stretch or move, much less add a third person was out of the question. With the inner door dogged shut, it was impervious to penetration, protecting the conversation of its inhabitants from eavesdropping or interception. Or so its manufacturers said.

He turned on the lights and air conditioning. Blowers whined. Bernoulli's principle applied, speeding the draft through the small space. The chill came with a rush.

Barry returned to the hall and shut the outer door. In a few short years, empires had fallen, armies demobilized, rallying cries against evil and for God and country muted, even disappeared. But for M15, Britain's internal security service, rules were rules. The bubble lived on, a talisman against once and future threats.

Barry well remembered the day he had stepped from the tube at Marylebone, the Bakerloo line's stop and the namesake for M15's London headquarters. Fresh off the overnight flight from New York, blueprints in hand, he had come straight from Heathrow to the meeting. They were waiting. Whenever M15 invested any part of its steadily diminishing annual appropriation in a new office, the administrative chieftains required a secure conference facility. He had argued that his one-man shop should have an exception. The ludicrous size of the available space only encouraged the two bespectacled clerks who heard his case. Talmudic debate over administrative scriptures, honed fine in civil-service college and ministerial halls, was not a street man's skill. Not only was a bubble necessary as regulations required, they said smugly, but as his plans plainly showed, it could be done on the cheap. Barry lost in five minutes, just as their morning tea came to a brew. One saw him out while the other filled their mugs. Point, set, match.

He walked past the communications room. Another closet, it housed his high-frequency radio, fax, and encryption gear. The buzzer sounded over the rear exit. Two shorts and a long. He deactivated the alarm and opened the fire door. The odor of damp concrete permeated the stairwell.

"Morning," Barry said. "Seven A.M. on the dot, no less."

Jilian McCray stepped inside. "Hello."

He locked the door. "When the phone rang at six I knew it was either you or word the Queen was dead. What an ungodly hour."

"At least I'm thought of in good company. Sorry for the wake-up, but I need some help," she said.

"A welcome admission. Anyone downstairs?" he asked. Their offices were on separate floors—his with the Northern Ireland Economic Development Council on the tenth, hers with the newspaper a floor below. Trade and journalism. As covers, they were shopworn but comfortable creations, used often enough over the years to be replicated plausibly even by an unimaginative bureaucracy.

"Reporters at work on Saturday morning? Hardly." Jilian handed him DiGenero's umbrella. "Something for you."

He took it, avoiding the plastic-wrapped handle. "Expecting rain?"

"No. Prints and a name trace." She raised an eyebrow. "Could you have it by tonight?"

"Tonight? You realize what you're asking? The Americans invented the weekend."

"Ah, but your colleagues are ever vigilant, Saturday football notwithstanding. Fidelity, Bravery, Integrity. Isn't that what FBI stands for?"

"They'll be pissed."

She patted his shoulder. "You're a dear. When do you think I can get it?"

Barry sighed. "Can't be sure exactly. Not before five. I'll put the report in your desk."

"False bottom in the left-hand drawer, okay?" Jilian said.

"Right."

"Thanks much." Jilian turned to go.

"Is that all?" Barry asked.

"All what?"

"I mean, you get me out of bed at six in the morning to do prints and a name trace. A little explanation would be nice," Barry said.

"Is this purient interest or official consultations?"

"I'm doing the bloody work for you. Let's be civil about it. In the first place, when I ring up the Bureau, they're going to ask what I'm up to. Why I want the prints run. After all, they're cops and this is their country. It would be useful to have something halfway plausible from you to help me lie."

"That's never seemed to be an impediment before," Jilian said icily.

Barry ignored the cut. "Look, We've both got an interest in making sure we don't stumble over each other. The concept isn't entirely new, you know. I'll scratch your back, you scratch mine kind of thing. You don't need my permission to run your op, but I don't need any trouble either, especially if we can avoid it by just talking. Let's call it professional courtesy. If something blows, you'll just get on the plane and disappear, won't you? I'll be the one that stands up, salutes, and takes the pie in the face."

Jilian thrust her hands into her coat pockets. Her silence acknowledged the point.

"What say?" Barry had the look of a man trying to be reasonable.

"Alright," she said reluctantly. "Bubble ready?"

"After you." Barry motioned with exaggerated gallantry. He followed her into the chamber, closing the first door, then the second.

Jilian began to take off her coat, then thought better of it, rewrapping herself against the chill. For an instant, Barry caught her scent, clean hair and a hint of cologne. It reminded him of a woman he'd slept with years before, a labor federation leftie. Marylebone wanted her as an informant on a third secretary in the Soviet Embassy, one of its cohort of spy trainees. He'd struck up an acquaintance and taken her to Brighton for the weekend. Her aroma was the same. Early morning before the sun. A detail remembered but unrecorded on his contact report.

"Any traffic for me?" she asked.

He feigned indignation. "You want me to power up just to print off your paystub from Stormont? Could I get your tea and muffins as well, mum?"

"Never mind." Jilian dismissed her own inquiry. "Just a question." Belfast was five hours ahead and Stormont rarely transmitted after its close of business, midday, Friday, New York time. She had emergency instructions in case she needed to make contact by phone, but otherwise her cabled messages came and went on a civil-servant's schedule, Monday through Friday.

Stormont, the Castle, was the seat of London's Northern Ireland Office. Like the occupants' political writ, it stood distinctly above Belfast, Ulster's capital. After three years of bombings and killings, Parliament assumed direct rule over Northern Ireland's six counties in 1972. Technically speaking, Stormont was not a colonial administration, at least not in the nineteenth-century sense. As a succession of British officials repeatedly explained, London encouraged local participation. The Northern Ireland Office was quite clear on that fact, if indefinite on its particulars. Stormont, they said, joined in governance with Ulster's elected assembly, which "undertook important consultative functions in matters concerning Northern Ireland affairs." But London's infrequent public attention to Stormont's powers was not unlike that given Britain's formal name—the United Kingdom of Britain and Northern Ireland. Both the Castle's commanding position above Belfast and the United Kingdom's full title usually went unmentioned. Better that way. Simpler if certain things were left unsaid.

"Any cables yesterday?" Jilian asked.

"No," Barry said as he bent down to dog the bubble's door. "Only routine stuff. It's all in your folder."

"Wait a minute. Let me get it." She stood and squeezed by him. "I can browse through while we talk." Jilian went out.

Barry waited. His mailman's role rankled. Marylebone had told him about her before he left for New York and he had pushed hard for control, very hard. Marylebone commiserated, of course, but said that the terms of her assignment were out of their hands. It was a Home Office affair, one of those decisions among the rat's nest of arrangements involving the score of agencies, each with their piece of the problem. She was to operate via her own chain of command. Heads shook knowingly.

Worrisome flap potential, as were all such officers who worked on one's turf.

But, they said encouragingly, Barry was a street man, creative, and he did have certain powers. For instance, under Whitehall's standing directive on interagency cooperation, M15 was obligated for the sake of economy to provide services of common concern for others posted abroad in its territory. Administrative and logistical support—heat, light, water, that sort of thing. Most important in this case, they noted with a smile, her communications to Belfast. For her part, she was obligated to "coordinate." As M15's senior liaison in New York with the FBI, Barry was to be advised of any plans that might go awry, operations with the potential to cause London problems. Marylebone was confident, of course, that he could handle things "at his level." But if differences between them arose and his best efforts failed, copies of her relevant messages could be transmitted to London to enable them to pursue the matter higher up. So much better than one of those "I said, she said" cables, they explained. In cases that could flap and cause problems, so much more effective to have the facts in black and white, on the responsible agency's letterhead. One had to be judicious with that kind of intervention, they cautioned, and Marylebone, too, could only influence, not command. But London was London and Belfast was Belfast, and in relations between M15 and her employer, the Royal Ulster Constabulary's Special Branch, the intelligence-gathering arm of Northern Ireland's police, Marylebone had certain advantages. If events required, he should be aware, they were quite prepared to make the forty-minute flight to Belfast for private consultations, reminding the RUC—and, if needs be, Stormont —of the risks, including those for 10 Downing Street, if the Americans discovered an undeclared RUC officer operating on their soil.

Jilian returned and sat. She spoke, flipping through the messages accumulated in the manila folder. "What can I tell you?"

Barry crouched to dog the door. "Spare me the parlor games. It's freezing in here. What are the prints all about?" He sat. Arms folded, he listened in silence as she described the meeting in the bar the night before. When Jilian finished he spoke. "It's not implausible I suppose."

"What's that?" she asked.

"A coincidence. Your meeting a friend of Vito Rocchi's. Especially in a bar he used."

"Do you think so?" she asked.

He was silent for a moment. "No."

"Neither do I," she said.

A smile crossed his face. "It's what we would do. A test. Running someone up against you to see what you might say. How much you like to talk."

Jilian shrugged skeptically. "Why now? After all these months?"

"If Scarlese's as exercised as your 'friend' says—what's his name?"

"Sallie," she said. "Sallie Ferringa."

"Yes. Sounds charming. If Scarlese's as exercised as Sallie says about finding whoever shot Rocchi, perhaps he's the suspicious one."

"I don't think so."

"You sure?"

"Yes," she said.

"Is that because of a professional inquiry or woman's intuition?" he asked.

"Don't be cute, Ian. It doesn't become you."

"Pardon me. But you do sound a tad defensive," he said. "It's an honest question. What have you checked up on lately?"

"What do you mean, 'checked up on'?" Jilian repeated sarcastically.

"I mean, done any countersurveillance to see if you're being followed? Taken new routes home? Used a switchback routine? Front door, back door, you know. How about tried a tech kit to sweep your place and do a phone check? I don't remember you asking for one. I assume you're doing the little things, examining your mail for tampering, toting up your wrong numbers, inquiring at your bank from time to time about any credit checks to find out if anyone's been asking about you." He smiled benignly. "All I'm asking is if you've done any of that, well, recently?"

"Are you?" she asked sharply. "Tell me, who do you suppose works for me? A bloody station house full of police?"

"No." He shook his head. "I know you're all alone." He looked down, as if embarrassed. "I'm not trying to intrude, just to be helpful."

Jilian caught herself, stifling another retort. For an instant, Barry seemed genuinely hurt. She was tired, tense, still angry after seeing Ferringa. She'd left him asleep in the hotel before dawn, gone to her apartment and showered, trying as always to scrub away the feeling of him along with the scent. No matter how she rationalized it—that it was the best way, the only way, her only option to move things ahead—to have him on top of her, inside her, made her hate. The choice, the anticipation, herself. She scrubbed sometimes until her skin was raw, until she hurt, turning up the water until it was too hot to stand, until the pain supplanted the loathing. She took a deep breath. "I'm sorry, Ian. I'm wound up. That's all."

He nodded. "I understand." He sat back, quiet for a moment. "What if it's the PIRAs?" he asked. He spoke the acronym as if it was a word. Pierah.

"What if? There is no 'if' in this case. If they suspected me, I'd be dead," she said categorically.

"Are you sure?" He persisted. "Perhaps the PIRAs are running one of Scarlese's types up against you. Or perhaps they have one of their own. How do you know they're not doing the testing?"

She shook her head. "No. My cover's good. I'm confident of that."

"Hmmm." Barry sat back. "I remember my first case that really worked. A Bulgarian code clerk. It was 1966 and 1967. I recruited him and ran him for eighteen months. He was quite a character. He recruited himself actually. I just happened to be the straight man asking the right questions. He was confident. Confident he could work well with me. Confident about not being found out. When they caught him, we knew from other sources that he was even confident he could talk his way out of trouble. Can you imagine thinking that in some cell in Sofia? He was extraordinary. I suspect he was confident they wouldn't shoot him right up to the moment they put him against the wall." Barry shivered. hunching his shoulders and folding his arms more tightly. "This business is like learning to ride a bicycle, isn't it? It's not enough to be confident you can get up and going. You also have to know you can keep your balance when you slow down or stop to get off."

"Don't patronize me, Ian." Jilian watched him, expressionless.

He ignored the warning. "All I'm asking is whether you've thought about downshifting, just for a while. Since 121 crashed, the pressure's been on all of us, God knows. But now's not the time to push too hard. Am I right?"

Jilian looked away. What was the time? Now, later, never? For so long, her job had been nothing but patience. A slow patient burrowing. From the very beginning, it had been all preparation, laying the groundwork, one day at a time. Even before the operation, at the Defense Ministry in London. There, she had volunteered, passed the interviews, and waited. That took a year. Finally, the call came. Defense Ministry staff special branch had approved her selection as an operations officer. Then the training, another nine months, followed by seconding to the Home Office and more waiting. Then, the word. It was on. She moved, disappeared, then reappeared again as Jilian McCray.

Dublin was more and less than she expected. At first, the work was interesting, then not. A year's apprenticeship at the newspaper, writing and reporting. Town council meetings, graduations, marriages, fires, shootings, dog and cat stories, the trivial realities of a city beat. At night, she began to open the door. As the plan called for, she attended their meetings, sporadically at first as if unable to spare the time, but often enough to be noticed, speaking up in question periods, even debating, a thinker who wasn't afraid to doubt. She knew she was noticed, watched by the handful who didn't have titles but wielded the power. The ones who were always there and when they weren't, returned later, sometimes days, sometimes weeks, with no explanation but only the occasional comment over coffee or after the speeches about Londonderry, or Belfast. No news, just the passing hint where they'd been.

After six months, the committee chairman asked for her help. Sinn Fein, the political party—the legitimate movement for a free Ulster—needed writers, people who knew the story of Northern Ireland and could tell it well. She refused. Writing, she said, was not a reporter's avocation after a six-day week. Enough was enough. They persisted and as intended, finally she gave in. Six months later, they knew her sympathies from the long conversations, evenings that made clear she no longer believed nonviolence would work. At the end of the year, she passed word to RUC Special Branch, Belfast. She had done all she could. It was time.

Like her employment at the newspaper in Dublin, the assignment in New York was engineered via a chain of relationships almost biologic in its complexity. The Dublin paper was one of several owned by a British conglomerate. Its managing director was an alumni of a Lancaster Royal Army regiment. So was the RUC's chief constable, a Home Office mandarin who had chosen to meld his military training with the diversity—not to mention political opportunity—offered by a civil service career as leader of police. Appointed by London, the position of RUC chief constable was his penultimate step, the last on his perfectly crafted professional ladder before his arabesque to the final plateau in London again. There, the Home Affairs minister himself had told him before his departure for Belfast, the position of Home Office permanent secretary, the senior-most career post, awaited. In short, for the managing director, the RUC chief constable's very private approach was far more than an old friend's request for help on a sensitive matter. It was an investment that would appreciate over time. A favor done now by the managing director would generate a favor due, one that appreciated as the chief constable rose. Money in the bank to be drawn on later.

Six months before Jilian had even been selected, the two sealed the arrangement over brandy and cigars, an hour's conversation in their favorite corner of the Athenian Club's second-floor library overlooking Pall Mall. First, an officer's employment at the newspaper in Dublin. Then, when the time was right, the holding company would direct the paper to create a new overseas posting—a position for a syndicated reporter employed by the Dublin newspaper but serving the entire chain. The officer's application would find favor at the holding company, producing ultimately selection as the syndicated correspondent in New York.

When Jilian told Sinn Fein about her good fortune, the phone call came two days later. They picked her up after dinner on a Friday night and drove northwest, back roads after the first forty miles, barely two lanes without shoulders. The hills rolled ahead of them, parting frequently to reveal the hiding places for a myriad of lakes. They stopped after midnight another sixty miles farther on the Atlantic coast, a small town just off Sligo Bay. The PIRA brigade commander waited behind the dark windows of a one-story bar. He had come south by boat and would return when the meeting was over.

He was matter-of-fact. America was the lifeline and she had been chosen to help them. If she agreed. She would not have traveled this far, Jilian said, if the answer wasn't yes. Instructions would come before she departed, the commander told her, but he could say this much. She would be part of the most critical phase of their struggle. For the first time, they would strike the British in America. She listened without reaction as he explained the target. The operation, he said, was self-contained, already underway. Timing was yet to be decided. If all went well, she would not be needed. If it didn't, she was the back-up link from the central command to their penetration of the American air traffic control system. For now, she had no need to know any details. If and when she did, they would fully apprise her. She was to associate with no one from the movement, save for those who might cross her path as a reporter. Even then, any contact was to be professional. Nothing more. No socializing that could draw the Brits' or the Americans' attention. Nothing that could raise suspicions or taint her. She was, in short, their sleeper. An insurance policy. Put in place. In case. To guarantee their success.

"Well?" Barry asked.

"I don't know," she said.

"Believe me, taking care doesn't mean giving up."

Jilian looked at Barry. "I'll think about it."

Above the bubble's Plexiglas ceiling a small red light flashed.

"Who's that?" she asked.

"Barry looked up at the flashing light. "That's the doorbell. Chris is ringing." Barry said. "She's got the American disease—works on Saturday. Her office is just down the way. She always goes in at sparrow's fart. I see her so seldom these days, after you called I rang her up to suggest an early breakfast."

Jilian smiled courteously. "Is that all you want to know?"

Barry stood, undogging the door. "Let her in the office for me while I secure things here, will you? I'll have the name trace later today. As soon as I can."

"Thanks." She stood and walked out. Barry's front office, the home of the Northern Ireland Economic Development Council, was small: two desks, file cabinets, a copier, assorted chairs, boxes of government literature on trade and investment opportunities. A shoestring effort to project an image of opportunity. Optimism against all odds.

Jilian unlocked the front door. Chris Barry had a child's beauty. Her eyes widened in pleased surprise. "Fancy meeting you here!" She put her hands on her hips. "Wait a minute! Just what do you have going with my father, anyway?" She laughed.

"Please! Don't breathe a word!" Jilian joined her laughter. They embraced. "How are you?" she asked.

"As well as can be expected given seventy-hour weeks. It's been nonstop at the office." Chris stepped inside.

Jilian twirled her finger, a silent instruction for a pirouette. Chris turned in dramatic flourish. In black from head to toe, her red hair fell over a full-cut leather jacket. Jilian stepped back, ostentatiously examining her. "I believe New York's yuppies have taken another prisoner. What happened to the demure young Englishwoman I once knew? Practical shoes, tweeds, and woolens, hair done up in a bun. Body parts never visible, even to the owner."

"Irish, if you please." Chris rolled her eyes, a mocking beseechment. "England is his cross to bear." She gestured toward her father, who had waved from the hall. "I identify with mum."

"Ah yes," Jilian said. "I forgot. A mixed marriage. Father, loyal subject of the Crown. Mother, citizen of the Irish Republic."

Chris dropped her bag on a chair. She sat, straddling the edge of a desk. "Actually, I think I'm going to apply for American citizenship. The green card's fine, but I've all but decided I'm here to stay."

"Really? After only two years? Things must be going well?"

"Well enough, but the point is, what's back there? The Yanks recruited me—no one in Ireland or England did that when I finished school. I've got my own place, not a cold-water flat in some nineteenth-century tenement in Dublin or London. Rooms with heat, plumbing, a view. Pay's good, spectacular by UK standards, in fact. And, I'm not caught up in the eight-hundred-years' war. I mean, the Brits raped the Republic before they set it free seventy years ago and now they're fully prepared to fight to the last Irishman for the miserable counties they have left."

"This isn't nirvana either, is it? Crime, murder, mayhem," Jilian said.

"New York's no picnic, but at least the Americans are inventive. They find a new social problem to riot over every twenty years or so, rather than hanging on to the old ones, gumming them to death." She leaned toward Jilian and whispered conspiratorily, "You know the reason, don't you?"

Jilian leaned, too, and whispered, "What's that?"

"The Brits' gene pool's too small. Great, great, great granddaddy Sir Clifford Crifford, or whatever, pissed on the Irish like his father before him, and great, great, great, great grandson Sir Clifford Crifford automatically unzips his fly and walks around with his thing in his hand looking for a mick to do the same. Poor sod. He's simply incapable of doing anything else. They should be put out of their misery. Or maybe they could be mixed. With a few Puerto Ricans or Vietnamese. Improve the breed, don't you think?"

"I admit I've never thought of it quite that way," Jilian said.

Chris stood. "The thing is, I've had enough. I'm not the only one, you know. I mean, I've spent time living with mummy while Ian was posted abroad. We did live in London quite a long time, but I knew Irish my age, even before university in Dublin. Ireland's educating an entire generation that's getting on the plane for the States. There's nothing, no future there, south or north. The British stole that a century ago, along with everything else. Why bother? Ireland's history."

"That's a profound conclusion, if I ever heard one," Barry said. "I'm not sure I want to hear the preamble." He stood, coat over his arm. "Ready?"

Chris stepped to him and kissed his cheek. "The only Englishman I'd save from the litter." She gestured at Jilian. "Why in the world are you two here, jawing at this hour?"

"Just bumped into each other on the way into the building. I kept talking in the elevator right past my floor," Jilian said.

"Yes," Barry confirmed. "Join us for breakfast?" he asked Jilian.

"No, I must be going." She nodded at Chris, then opened the door and looked at Barry. "I've got to come back to do some reading later on."

CHAPTER

10

AT FIRST AVENUE and 46th Street she turned south, walking with a man's determination. DiGenero was able to follow her even as she overtook a clutch of pedestrians. Her stride, long and smooth, was athletic, distinctive in an otherwise commonplace current. He stepped to the curb. A tall black man in technicolor tribal robes and topcoat, a diplomat of some sort, glanced at him. DiGenero tried to cross against the light, but a bus bore down, horn blaring. He cursed and drew back. The African gathered his skirts and moved sideways, conspicuously ignoring the outburst.

He'd almost given up. The voice on the answering machine at her apartment was more businesslike than he remembered. She wasn't home. He called her office. Whoever picked up told him she was out but might return. He decided to chance it. He waited across First Avenue, the barred gates of the United Nations rising at his back, protecting his rear as well as the East side's extraterritorial enclave. Their suspicion tempered by boredom, the guards had peered from behind the fence, pacing nearby for a moment, then ignored him. The evening had turned cold and the sky was spitting, but he had decided against looking for cover on her side of First. Just in case she returned with Ferringa. It wasn't the time or place to find him, or to be found. Not now. Not here.

The light changed. He hurried into the crosswalk, weaving among the recalcitrant taxis. She reached the entrance where the revolving doors culled her from the passing flow. In the lobby, she disappeared into a waiting elevator. DiGenero looked up and down the street, checking. No one waited or watched. At the threshold of the building, the concrete sidewalk gave way to a quarried stone step bordered by a miniature oriental garden and a facsimile of a natural pool. East River Zen. He entered. The doorman's stool was empty. The overheated lobby felt luxurious after the chilling wind. He found her name on the building directory and took the elevator. Inside, quilted pads covered the walls, prefiguring the tenants' comings and goings.

The elevator rose with a tired heave. DiGenero had wanted to be better prepared for their encounter, to know more about Ferringa. To have another card to play. For almost two hours that evening, Silverstein had wheedled and flattered his favorite file clerk at police headquarters. Finally, she queried the computer for Ferringa's FBI file. Nothing worked. The gates were locked, tight. Ferringa's file required a special password. DiGenero had hacked with his own access code from Salt Lake, but the screen only lit once with an electronic admission: NYFO/CI/2 had the file. New York Field Office Counterintelligence Squad 2. Tony Benedetto's squad.

The doors opened on the ninth floor. The bay, an expanse of worn linoleum, was bounded by plate glass. The New York bureau of the Dublin *Register* nested in a corner, one cubicle among several, each labeled with its own sign. "Irish Newsline." "Europress." "Business Continentale Wire." One-man shops and small-time trade journals. A few papers, but mostly boutique news services and the occasional stringer well enough off to rent floor space. Cheap dividers and modular furniture substituted for real walls and more substantial desks. An architectural recognition of the modern concept of labor. The provision of a "workspace," rather than an office. Here today, reconfigured tomorrow. For those who toil, no fixed address, only temporary territory, underscoring their purgatory as forever transient economic beings.

Bent over her desk, Jilian McCray held the telephone, transcribing as she listened. Her back was toward him. In a long plaid skirt and boots, she was dressed for day, not evening. Pulled back with severity, her hair suggested a woman of serious purpose. Her coat, still damp at the collar, hung from an old-fashioned tree.

She put down the phone. Before her, DiGenero's life-sized reflection loomed, as if he had levitated nine floors to wait, suspended in the night. She gasped and spun to face him. "It's you!"

The apology tripped over his greeting. "I'm sorry. I mean, hello. I didn't mean to frighten you."

"My fault, really." Her hands fluttered momentarily with uncharacteristic vulnerability. She smiled, embarrassed as well as relieved. "When I concentrate, I block out everything. A bomb could go off under my chair and I wouldn't notice."

"Jilian! Are you alright?" The voice was taut and menacing. DiGenero looked around. The man was tall and bearded. Despite his size, DiGenero judged he could move quickly.

"Oh yes. I'm fine, Ian, thank you."

"I thought I heard you cry out."

She shook her head. "No, just surprised. This is Mr. Falcone. Frank Falcone. Ian Barry."

"Hello." Barry nodded without extending a hand.

DiGenero recognized the stare. Professionally inquisitive, it amounted to a stocktaking.

"Ian runs the Information Bureau for the Northern Ireland Economic Development Council. Upstairs." Jilian pointed.

"You've got your work cut out for you," DiGenero said.

He shrugged. "We all have our crosses to bear."

Barry didn't act like a public relations man. For a moment, DiGenero wondered whether there was something else, another explanation accounting for the diffident behavior. Perhaps, he had walked into the invisible force field of a relationship? But what were the poles? Attracting or repelling? Positive or negative? In love? Out of love? Sleeping together? Past or present tense? It was hard to say, although Barry's wrinkled shirt, hopelessly knotted knit tie, and corduroys seemed anything but a complement to the elegance he'd found the other night.

"You're a reporter?" DiGenero asked.

"Might say." He held an envelope. Like his build, Barry's hands looked powerful, large with blunt, utilitarian fingers.

"Been in the States long?" He tried again.

"A while."

"A while?"

"Uh huh."

"That long?" DiGenero returned the stare. Barry obviously wasn't inclined to reciprocate the polite inquiries. Perhaps, DiGenero thought, he already knew all the answers.

Jilian stepped between them. She patted Barry's arm but looked at DiGenero. "Ian fancies himself a once and future journalist. Now, he has a cause. We never let him forget he's a card-carrying flak." She forced a laugh.

"I come to save a damsel in distress and all I get for my chivalry is abuse." He smiled without the pretense of humor. He handed Jilian the envelope. "I brought this down. Just received. You might want to have a look." He nodded at DiGenero and walked away.

"Well, to what do I owe this honor?" Jilian asked quickly, foreclosing any impending questions. She snapped her fingers. "Of course! The umbrella!" She searched behind her desk. "I left it in my apartment. I'll bring it back. I promise."

"To think that the only thing I impressed you with the other night was my umbrella fetish."

She laughed, genuinely this time. "I have much more interesting recollections than that."

"Then you must remember I'm a native. You couldn't do better than to let me take you to dinner at a restaurant of choice."

"Couldn't I?"

For a second time, her reaction flustered him. He felt a genuine pang of disappointment. "Don't tell me you have other plans."

"An aging matron alone in her office at eight on Saturday night? How credible do you suppose that would be? Hand me my coat, would you?" DiGenero turned to reach for her raincoat.

When he turned back, Jilian was rummaging in her bag. She withdrew a mirror and began to repair her lipstick. She wore little makeup. With the color of the cold still on her face, even small touches had a dramatic effect. She tilted the mirror, carefully examining the results. "Did you go to your friend's funeral?"

"I paid my respects."

She tucked away the lipstick and mirror, as if finding their proper place was an act that deserved concentration. "Then, the sad part of your visit is over."

He nodded.

"Good. This evening we can talk of happier things."

DiGenero began to drape the coat over her shoulders.

"Damn," she said. "I just remembered some odds and ends. Tell you what. I'll meet you in the lobby. Five minutes, I promise. I need to tidy up a few things."

"Okay, five minutes. Meet you downstairs," DiGenero said.

Jilian waited until she heard the elevator's chime. When its doors closed, she opened the envelope and read.

The cab took them south on Second Avenue, then west on 21st Street. The rain had stopped. They got out at Fifth Avenue and walked the last few blocks. After his years away, DiGenero remarked on the changes. Manhattan was constantly reinventing itself. Too expensive to knock down and too potentially profitable to pass up, block after block had been gentrified by the developers, producing gilt-edged iterations of the city's history labeled as new. North of Union Square, along lower Broadway and Fifth, the wholesalers and jobbers who had subdivided the long-abandoned department stores and shops into cheap offices and storage lofts were gone. The restorations were everywhere, from entire buildings to co-op apartments, galleries, and homes. They had a scientific perfection, a museumlike quality, reproduced to be uniformly worn, but without the lived-in look. Among those who could afford them, they were ideal, a three-dimension collectible for a generation that wanted to enjoy the past, but also when the time came, to discard it for whatever was trendy and new.

The small French restaurant on West 19th occupied the basement of a Japanese clothing designer's turn-of-the-century brass and oak front salon. With luck and a twenty-dollar bill, they found a table just inside the door.

To begin, he ordered the wine, a rich, almost chewable Sirah. They shared half the bottle with small talk, then studied the menu and chose. The first question came with the soup.

"Forgive me, but I can't disguise my curiosity."

"What's that?" DiGenero had been waiting.

Her spoon displaced a mussel shell from the shallots and stock. Jilian expertly extracted the contents. "Why did you and your friend, what was his name?" She looked up.

"Vito?" DiGenero asked.

"Vito." She nodded. "Why did the two of you ever meet in Ireland? It seems so," she paused, "well, so odd."

"Does it?"

"Yes."

He stirred his soup, examining the ingredients as they surfaced and disappeared. He knew she was watching. "Tell me, who wants to know?"

"Who? I do," she said.

"No, which one of you?"

"What do you mean?"

"The reporter or the beautiful woman with a passionate interest in my life story?" He smiled.

She stiffened. "Do you think I came to dinner with you for a story? If I was working right now, you'd know it. That's a shitty thing to say."

The pique seemed genuine. He shrugged. "But not an unreasonable question."

"Like hell." She looked down. The conversation around them camouflaged their silence. DiGenero refilled her wine glass. She ate, ignoring him. There was a certainty to her, he thought, a sense of self-possession that permeated, making even her small motions seem totally assured. He guessed she was thirty-five, maybe a year or two more. It was the time when women became interesting, the point when accumulated experience began to tip the scales, counterbalancing the pipedreams and fantasies. His wife had been the same age when they met, although from the first, Erin had been easier, more relaxed, someone who didn't snap at the first provocation, who knew strength came in bending. Jilian was different. The fiber was obvious. DiGenero wondered whether he could discover the soft core, or for that matter, if it even was there.

Jilian dissected the last mussel in the bowl. The envelope from Barry held several pages and she'd only had time to skim them. The synopsis of DiGenero's background raised more questions than it answered. At one level of surmise, she thought, it was simple enough. An FBI agent. A career undercover against the Mafia. A wife murdered by Scarlese. A man seeking revenge. Whatever the danger DiGenero might represent to Scarlese, he was not, on the face of it, a threat to her, save as an interloper, an accidental intrusion who might draw unwanted attention. A manageable risk. Someone she could handle by playing along. She swirled the wine, releasing the bouquet, and sipped, all the while examining him. But was it that simple? Had all this begun with the death of DiGenero's wife? Or was there another thread? Was DiGenero a singleton or part of something more? An FBI operation that had come across Scarlese's IRA tie, but then gone badly wrong? The question was—what did the Bureau know? What was cause and what was effect?

The smile began first in her eyes. She spoke. "Your question."

DiGenero looked up. "Yes?"

"Consider it the woman. But edit out the 'passionate.' "

He grunted as if he had taken a body blow.

She laughed. "The truth always hurts, doesn't it? Well?" she asked. "Why Ireland?"

"Off the record," he said.

"Oh?" She feigned surprise. "You even know the reporter's jargon, do you?"

"Yep."

"And to think I believed you were a simple travel agent."

"Agreed?" he asked.

"Agreed."

"Permanently?"

She sighed in mock exasperation. "This will be deep background only." She extended her hand. "You have my word."

They shook. Her hand was warm. She gripped his like a man, completely.

The waiter reappeared, ostentatiously clearing their table. DiGenero ordered another bottle of wine. They both had chosen salmon with capers. It arrived atop a two-tone oriental rendering, yin and yang in cream sauce. He gingerly traced his fork through the chef's artistic statement, wondering if he was supposed to disturb it.

Jilian ignored her plate. She interlaced her fingers prayerfully under her chin. "Come on. Don't put me off."

"Travel's a funny business," DiGenero began.

"How so?"

"You see all kinds," he said. "For the ones who can afford it, it's strictly pleasure—business or holiday, it doesn't make any difference. First-class this, four-star that, only the best, you know what I mean. For others, at the other end of the spectrum, it's a different story. Where things are tough, it's escape, pure and simple, a way out. They don't care if they're in a seat, or a ship's hold, or a box. They only want to go. To a better life. Sicily is like that. There, I get all kinds of business." She listened intently. "Including one-way trips."

Jilian eased back into her chair, contemplating the revelation.

"Don't get me wrong," he continued. "It's not my stock in trade."

"Of course not." She nodded credulously.

"But occasionally you do favors, like I told you the other night."

"Is it difficult?" she asked.

"What?"

"The favors. Arranging the one-way trips."

"Not if you know what you're doing," he said.

"And you do?"

DiGenero nodded. "Canada's best. From Rome to Shannon. Shannon to Montreal. For a few hundred bucks plus the price of an airline ticket and twelve hours of flying, you're a hop, skip, and jump from the world's longest unguarded border."

"Then?" she asked.

"You wait where you're told until somebody comes." He took a bite of salmon. The capers were pleasantly tart. The cream sauce had become a mess. "Sometimes they've got papers. Who knows? For enough money, you can get a driver's license and a social security card. If you're traveling on a shoestring, the trip's the thing. You just curl up in the trunk of a car. In an hour or two you're in the States."

DiGenero smiled. "Or so they say. That's not my end of the deal. I book them on the charter flights. That's the way the Europeans like to travel. It's best around the holidays, when everybody wants to be with their families. Easier, that is. I mean, picture the airport. You got a jumbo jet full of bleary-eyed paisans babbling in Sicilian to some Canuck at the immigration counter. Arms waving. Babies crying. Olive oil all over the floor. What's he gonna do? Play twenty questions? Nine times out of ten, he lets them all through."

"Vito handled the rest?" she asked.

"Vito? He had nothing to do with it," DiGenero said.

She looked confused.

"Actually, I helped Vito."

"I don't understand."

"From time to time, Vito bumped into people in Ireland who wanted to get to the States. In the worst way," he said.

"And?"

"From time to time, I happened to have an extra seat and a passport. When a charter flight landed at Shannon to refuel, all they needed was a picture and a little iron-on plastic. Simple."

"Who were they?" She picked at her filet.

"I can tell you they weren't dagos who took a wrong turn." The waiter leaned over the table, checking their progress. DiGenero waved him away.

"But you must have known something about them," she said.

He shrugged. "Not really."

Jilian toyed with the salmon. She looked up, her tone curious. "What if they were terrorists? Say, IRA."

"What if?" DiGenero repeated, questioning the question.

"You must have been suspicious."

He didn't answer.

"Or did you know?" She persisted.

"And if I did?" he asked.

"What do you mean?"

"I mean, are you going to kiss me on both cheeks or break the wine bottle over my head?" He smiled.

"No." She shook her head. "It doesn't matter."

"Maybe if you're Lithuanian or from New Guinea. But you're Irish-English. So when I answer the question, what's it gonna be? The lady or the tiger?"

"That's not it at all." She spoke quickly, as if trying to clear up an obvious point unexpectedly confused. "I mean, I'm not some bleeding-heart partisan. I don't like the army shooting Irishmen in the street any more than I like the Provos bombing pubs in London, but what can I do about it? Besides, it's more than that. I'm interested in you." She flushed, embarrassed by the choice of words. "After all, I'm a reporter."

"Oh? I didn't think I was talking to a reporter. I thought I was talking to a woman with an interest . . ."

"Touché." She laughed softly. "A *passionate* interest in your life story."

DiGenero put down his knife and fork. "Look, Vito and I had an understanding," he said. "We knew each other. Trusted each other. So I'd help. It was between him and me. For old time's sake."

"I see."

"And for future considerations," he added.

"Future considerations?"

"Uh huh." He drank his wine.

"You mean money," she probed.

"Not really. Vito had a connection. An important connection."

"To?"

"He told me why he took his trips." DiGenero refilled his glass. "And about the operation."

"The operation?" Jilian listened intently, like someone about to receive complicated directions. The thread led on, she thought. But where? And how far?

DiGenero spoke barely above a whisper. "Let me put it to you straight. Vito's gone. I'm not. I'm prepared to pick up where he left off. The travel. The payments. But I need to get to the right people, to let them know."

"And who are the right people?" she asked.

"I thought you could help me with that."

"Me? What gave you that idea?"

"Sallie Ferringa," he said.

She stared, contemplating what he had said. "If that's what this is all about, why didn't you wait for him the other night? At the bar."

"It doesn't work that way. Maybe Sallie knows my name, maybe not, but he isn't going to have a sitdown with me because I ask. I need an introduction. Somebody who'll vouch. You understand?"

Jilian sat back slowly. Her mind raced. The thread had become an entanglement, a snare. She feigned anger. A woman used. "Oh, I understand, you son of a bitch. Now, you understand. Find someone else." She rose.

"Please." DiGenero took her wrist.

"Let go of me!" He felt her strength as she tried to pull away. On either side of their table, heads turned and then turned back, the prurient curiosity of the public place, in the case of New Yorkers, easily sated.

"Before you leave, think of something. Not what I just said. But what I know."

For a moment she remained poised, as if about to take flight. DiGenero felt the tension in her arm relax. She settled back into the chair. He released her wrist.

He spoke slowly to underscore his candor. "I'm sorry, but I came to you because Vito told me about you, a long time ago. He told me where he'd met you. I knew it was only an outside chance. I didn't go to anyone else. You can walk away from me. That's your choice. But then, where do I go? Who do I talk to? Money isn't the only reason I got involved with Vito. It's easy to make money. Relationships are harder to get, especially with the people he worked for." He paused. "And with you."

Jilian studied him with a clinical detachment. DiGenero poured the last of the wine in her glass. "I'm offering help on the same terms I helped Vito. In exchange for future considerations."

She held the glass but didn't drink. "I can't promise what he'll say." "I know."

"If," she repeated, *"if* Sallie will meet you, I'll call."

"Okay. But it has to be soon. Sallie has to be alone. I pick the place."

"Really? Is that the way you create a 'relationship'?" The sarcasm was obvious.

He ignored it. "With Sallie, yes. But not with you."

"Oh? You think you're safe with me?" she asked.

"I think so," he said.

DiGenero signaled the waiter for the check. When he turned back, she was watching him again, this time with a worried expression he hadn't seen before. For an instant, before he dismissed the notion, it seemed to be for him.

"I trust you," he said.

"Do you?"

The check came. He paid, then stood, beckoning her. "Besides," he smiled, "I picked this place, too."

They walked upstairs and paused on the sidewalk. The line of would-be diners was gone and the street was empty.

"Let me get a cab—" DiGenero intended to complete the sentence, but the arm that encircled his neck choked away the sound along with his air.

The mind was a repository of experience and instinct. The new-agent's class. Gym mats, sweat suits, locker-room smell. The crewcut instructor. Accountants, lawyers, college jocks, city cops, now trainees wrestling, jabbing, shoving, muscling each other to the floor. The garroting attack had been repeated again and again, Pavlovian imprinting to evoke a reflex, rather than panic. DiGenero jammed his elbow back, looking for anything soft and vulnerable. No good. He twisted and tried to drop low, snaking out of the grasp, but the biceps tightened around his neck. His throat collapsed. Other hands pinned his arms. No air. He flushed, eyes swollen like melons, gasping, spine arched. He was lifted. The bum's rush. They were over the curb and into the street. His toes and heels hit pavement in a cartoon dance, spastic and desperate.

The car squealed to a stop, doors open, headlights suddenly on. In the rear, a man leaned out as if about to greet him. DiGenero couldn't see the face. His forehead slammed against the roof. The blood flowed. It was a diversion, for a moment shock, then pain that obscured the choking. Hands jammed his head down, forcing him to bend double.

"Fuckin' blood's all over me! Get in the car, asshole!" There were at least two behind him. They shoved.

He fell onto the front seat. Someone jerked him upright, then jammed in beside him. DiGenero realized the arm around his throat was gone. He tried to take a deep breath.

"Go! For Christ's sake, get outa here!" The one beside him ordered. The doors slammed shut.

The engine roared and the car lept. At the corner, the driver hit the brakes. DiGenero pitched forward, smashing into the dash. Fingers entwined in his hair, yanking him back. Something mottled the leather, just above the radio. His blood on the pebbled grain made an abstract pattern. An apostrophe surrounded by dappling. A wave breaking on the beach. Modern impressionist or Rorschach? The car turned hard right, running the light. Angry horns sounded. They accelerated, hitting passing gear, then turned right again, fishtailing around a corner.

The voice came from the backseat. "Nobody's followin'. Slow the fuckin' thing down! We don' want no tickets."

His neck and back began to throb. It was like an awakening, consciousness dawning after a violent dream, first the images, then the sensations. He tried to move. His arms were free, but there was something new, a muzzle intruding below his ribs.

"Don't even think about fuckin' around, asshole."

He didn't know the face, but recognized the type. Long hair, razor cut and oiled back, a leather jacket, bluejeans, Cuban boots. He was from the corner, any corner. A Tony, a Vinnie, a Donny, a Louie. He wanted to move inside, to join the club. The expression was familiar. Malevolent, ignorant, staring. Sympathy was implausible. Empathy out of the question. "I was just checking to see if my seatbelt was fastened," DiGenero said.

"Which way?" the driver asked.

"Take First to 47th, then up the FDR." From the backseat, the voice sounded accustomed to giving orders.

DiGenero spoke, "Hello, Sallie."

"How are ya, Frank?"

"Couldn't be better." The words made his throat spasm. He coughed convulsively.

"Long time," Sallie said affably.

"Not long enough."

Ferringa chuckled. "Be nice, goombah. You gonna hurt my feelings." In the rearview mirror, he had the posture of a man accustomed to being chauffeured. His arm, draped casually over the seatback, extended behind Jilian. She sat, expressionless, a small space between them, eyes fixed straight ahead. Ferringa's face, creased but full, was marked by the contradictions of a prosperous middle age. DiGenero could make out a dark, double-breasted suit and expensive tie. Not a workman's outfit. Tonight someone else would do the heavy lifting.

"Hey, Sallie. Explain to this cutie that if he aims real good he can probably hit me without having to poke his gun halfway to my kidneys."

Ferringa nodded. "Relax."

DiGenero felt the pressure of the muzzle ease.

"Here." Ferringa leaned forward. A handkerchief appeared in DiGenero's peripheral vision. "Let him take it."

DiGenero reached for the folded square. Silk. He made a ball and wiped his forehead and cheek, then pressed the handkerchief against the gash. The bleeding had slowed. In a moment it stopped altogether. They turned north on First Avenue, accelerating again.

"You look like a real *macher*, Sallie. The fish business must be good," he said.

Ferringa smiled. "Can't complain. You like the suit?"

"Beautiful. Where'd you get it? The trucks, the ragmen, what?"

"Nah. Jilian, she picked it out. She knows what's good. The best English wool. Number-one English tailor. Over on East 59th. Measured me six times. Everything. I mean, you wouldn't believe it. I'm in there one day and the guy asks me, 'How do you dress?' I say, 'What the fuck you talkin' about? I put my shirt and pants on like everybody else.' He says, 'No, no, not that.' You know what? He wants to measure for my balls. He wants to know where they hang. Right or left. So he can cut the pants good. Whaddya think about that?"

DiGenero glanced at Jilian in the rearview mirror. She was staring out the window. He followed her gaze. The traffic had slowed them in front of the New York Medical Center. A police car sat at the curb. The two blue suits were finishing hamburgers and paperwork.

Ferringa saw that the cops had caught DiGenero's attention. "They ain't gonna help you, Frank."

"Why do I need help when I got friends like you?"

"That's right," Ferringa agreed.

"But tell me something," DiGenero said.

"What's that?"

"Didn't all the plastic surgery hurt?"

"What plastic surgery?"

"The one that made your lips a perfect fit for Junior's ass."

The driver chortled.

"Shut up!" Ferringa snapped. The silence lasted half a block. "Seriously," DiGenero said. He saw that Ferringa was scowling. "What's it like working for Junior? The don treated you like a son. He knew the street. He knew who was good and who was bad. He was real people. But Junior? All those fancy schools and college degrees. It's okay with him if you keep the piece of Fulton Street the don gave you. Junior thinks that's small change. But Sallie, you're the kinda guy that doesn't come in the parlor. You open doors and take out the trash."

"Don't piss me off!" Sallie's temper was legendary, a catalyst for all manner of imprudence.

"What? Then I'm in real trouble? You never gonna speak to me again?" Beside him, DiGenero could feel the driver shaking, trying to suppress a laugh. On his right, his minder sat slackjawed, watching, struggling to comprehend.

They reached 42nd Street. The UN, half lit, loomed. They passed Jilian's office, where he had begun a few hours before. The beginning of the end, DiGenero thought, although he didn't know it then. He felt suddenly dizzy, a vertigo of the spirit as if something deep inside sensed, even before his mind consciously accepted, that the vortex yawned. Was Erin watching? Clancy, his backseater in Vietnam, the one whose chute streamed? His father? His mother? They were gone, but were they waiting? Did they know he was coming? Or was there no one? Nothing? Nowhere? Only the black and emptiness. No one home. He was slipping, losing control. DiGenero shut his eyes hard. His head ached. He tried to focus. The code was simple. You went without pleading. There was no point, no ambiguity, no mercy, no hope. He concentrated on Sallie.

The on-ramp snaked upward from 47th Street to the FDR. They pounded through its potholes and merged into the northbound traffic on the expressway. Steel mesh netting blanketed the concrete guard rails and retaining walls, surgical dressing that held back the city's decay. The East River was their border, a dark glass pane reflecting the lights of Roosevelt Island.

They accelerated behind a garish white stretch limousine. Around them cars jockeyed, yellow cabs and gypsies, mongrels with stenciled signs and no fenders undented. In all aspects, New York traffic was an experience of extremes. Block after block of hard won, yard-by-yard gains, punctuated by bursts of high-velocity, broken-field running. Its constituent elements were the same, a combination of unblemished, six-figure, custom-made creations surrounded by battered wrecks without cosmetic pretensions.

"Hey, Sallie," DiGenero said.

Ferringa didn't answer, his reservoir of good humor exhausted. "Was killing my wife Junior's idea, or did you dream that up all by yourself?"

"It was nobody's idea," Ferringa said.

Jilian stared across the river, expressionless.

"A no-brainer? No wonder Junior picked you and Vito," DiGenero said.

Hatred disfigured Ferringa's face. "Keep talkin'. I guarantee it's only gonna get worse for you."

"You know my buddies will roll you up, Sallie. For what you did."

"Vito's dead and you're history. Ain't nobody gonna care."

"Which reminds me," DiGenero said. "After you're gone, whose going to take over?"

"Whaddya talkin' about?"

DiGenero ignored the question. "I suppose anybody can make Vito's trips. But who you got to make the payments?"

Ferringa's eyes darted toward Jilian. She ignored him. They were moving faster now. The bilious glow of sodium vapor bathed them as the highway disappeared undercover, a story below street level. They sped beneath the fashionable river-view apartments of Manhattan's East End. In confinement, the road noise reverberated.

DiGenero raised his voice. He spoke solicitously, like someone trying to help solve an unexpected problem. "Maybe Junior can do it himself. After all, he's already got half the action."

Ferringa stared out the window, malevolently addressing his own reflection. "You don't have one fuckin' idea what you're talkin' about."

"The Bureau's been pleased you're so regular, you and Junior," DiGenero continued. "Our green-eyeshade guys wanted me to pass along their thanks. Your dumbshit operation's so easy to trace they've been going home early."

Ferringa made a guttural sound, an animal warning needing no words. He reached forward. DiGenero's head slammed back. Fingers tightened in his hair. Ferringa pulled. His back arched even in the cramped confines of the front seat. Upside down in the rear window, he saw the three of them, Ferringa, Jilian, and his own reflection. Lit by the sodium vapor, they were yellow, a trio of sulfur-stained voyagers descending into an imminent hell.

"I don't have to wait till we get where we're goin' to cut your fuckin' eyes out. Whaddya you know?" Ferringa's breath was the essence of whiskey.

His neck vertebrae compressed, DiGenero felt a pulsing ache. The gash on his forehead opened again. Flowing with gravity's guide, the blood warmed his temple. "It's not what I know. It's what they know. How many more airliners do you think they'll let you bring down?"

"What he knows doesn't matter," Jilian said. "Believe me. Let go of him." She put her hand on Ferringa's arm.

"What's he talkin' airliners?" The minder on DiGenero's right swiveled in the seat, obviously confused. "I thought 'dis was the guy we was gonna whack 'cause he gave up the don."

"Will you shut up?" In one motion, Ferringa released his grip and smacked DiGenero's seatmate. "Turn around!"

DiGenero straightened his neck slowly. He wiped away the blood with the handkerchief. In the rearview mirror, he could see that Jilian had turned toward Ferringa. Her voice sounded almost motherly. "If they know, now so do we. We can make other arrangements."

Ferringa was breathing hard. "Jesus Christ! Johnny's gonna be pissed. I mean, it's him and me. We're the ones in charge."

"Sallie, wheredaya wanna go?" the driver asked.

"Take the ramp from the Triborough."

The FDR was behind them. They were climbing, looping east toward the Triborough Bridge, Queens, and Long Island. High over the river, the taillights in a steady eight-lane stream melded and diverged, a random interweaving like seagrass in a current. The suburban traffic leaving the city. Home in an hour, bed, a good night's sleep, then a Sunday paper, maybe TV and a Giants game in the afternoon. At the end of their road, another day, another week, another lifetime. At the end of their road.

Behind him, DiGenero could hear Jilian, but not her words. She seemed to be soothing Ferringa. The driver slowed. He pitched his toll into the booth's waiting receptacle, then accelerated into the center lane. He hit the brakes and, without signaling, slipped onto a narrow access ramp, two car widths and bracketed by heavy steel. It was more like a chute than an off-ramp. Suddenly the bridge was beside them, then above, a scaffolding of girders, monumental in its ugliness. They dipped and wound downward.

DiGenero felt the muzzle poking his ribs. His minder's leg jiggled. He fidgeted, picking at something on his face. A case of nerves. Maybe this was his chance to be made. A made man. Who knows? DiGenero closed his eyes and tried to pray. No words came. The car bottomed hard. They were down, off the ramp at river level. They accelerated again. A nondescript campus of brick buildings behind wire fencing passed on the right. MPC. The Manhattan Psychiatric Center. Now he knew. MPC, a park, the sewage plant. Ward's Island, the smaller of the rocky outcroppings that bisected the East River, ending where the channels merged at 96th Street.

"Go to the plant. Gate's open," Ferringa said.

At the end of the Psychiatric Center compound, they bore left, hugging the river's east channel. DiGenero tried again to remember. His rosary, the Lord's prayer, a dinner blessing, the 23rd Psalm. Nothing came back. Maybe the asylum had an aura. Like sunspots, electromagnetic energy that made static out of radio transmissions ninety-three million miles away. From behind the fence, all the scrambled minds in the nut house were emitting, jamming his brainwaves. If you had to die somewhere, maybe this should be it. Maybe Sallie had an innate sense of order. A place for everything and everything in its place. Insanity outside as well as inside the fence. DiGenero concentrated on the lights along the far shore. Each a candle, lit for a soul. Which one burned for him? Which candle on the river? Which candle in Queens? Soldiers, sailors, sealing waxes, cabbages, and Queens. He couldn't help the tears. Nothing made sense. His mind wasn't working.

"Here!" Ferringa said.

They swung off the paved road. The gravel ground beneath the tires. The open gate beckoned through a chain link fence. Even with the windows closed, the odor of sewage enveloped them. The driver killed the lights. DiGenero could see the silhouettes of the settling tanks and the piping. On the left, several sheds and trailers, outlines against the night, perched along the island's eastern shore. They turned again and slowed. Ahead, he could make out the seawall. It was chest height. He couldn't see beyond, but he knew what was there. The confluence of the river's two channels around the island. Hell Gate.

They stopped where the gravel ended, a car length from the seawall.

"You got anything you wanna say, asshole?" Ferringa asked. DiGenero was afraid to speak, afraid he would lose control. He shook his head. The hand closed on his arm.

"Get rid of him," Ferringa said.

The snap of the doorlatch broke the silence. DiGenero felt the tug as his minder moved, pulling him out.

Inside the car the gunshot was a sensation, not a sound, shocking to the core of his being. His paralysis shattered. Why were they killing him here? Now? Wedged in the front seat? For the love of God, at least give him thirty seconds more! A walk to the seawall! A last minute alone in his final night! At least let him stand up to die! A man screamed. No! For an instant, he didn't recognize the voice. He twisted, searching for his benefactor. Then, he realized the cry was his.

Beside him, his minder seemed oblivious. His face contorted in terror, he was trying to raise his pistol above the seatback. Confused, DiGenero leaned away, politely making room. Suddenly, in their small shared space, the man seemed to do the impossible. He rose from the seat and threw himself against the windshield before folding, arms disarrayed, into the footwell.

Dazed by the second shot, DiGenero shook his head, trying to clear the ringing. The smell, smoke and blood, overwhelmed him. The third explosion spun him to his left as well as deafened him. The other door was open. The driver had fallen forward as he hurried to climb out of the car. On his knees, he was leaning on the door, pulling himself erect. Two bursts of incandescence lit the interior. Spots danced. His ear burned. The driver gave up. Arms extended to support himself on the doorframe, he slipped again to his knees, rocking for a moment in time to some unheard music, then relinquished his grip. He fell, rolled on his face, and lay still.

Alone in the front seat, DiGenero turned around. Sallie Ferringa sat cattycorner, staring back. His expression seemed more expectant than surprised, as if still awaiting DiGenero's answer to his parting question. Ferringa's head rested comfortably against the seatback. Only the gaping red hole between his ear and temple marred an otherwise natural pose.

Jilian had opened the right rear door and backed out of the car. She was crouched, the automatic extended in both hands. It was leveled at him.

"Get them over the seawall!" Her voice was tinny, not at all what he remembered.

"What?" He held his hand to his ear, signaling he couldn't hear. Where he touched, his skin felt raw. Powder burns. The cacophony, roaring, rushing, whirring, squealing, high pitches and low, confused him.

Her lips moved. DiGenero concentrated. "Get them over the seawall!"

He nodded like a slow learner suddenly apprehending a difficult lesson. DiGenero slid across the seat and out the driver's door. His knees buckled. He steadied himself against the car.

"Go 'round the front." She motioned with the automatic. With an instant realization of his inanity, he waved and smiled.

The muzzle followed him. He walked slowly, keeping one hand on the hood. He opened the passenger door. DiGenero tugged on his minder's arms. He was heavy, but balled into a child's tumbling pose, the moment of his roll carried the body from the footwell to the ground. He dragged him to the seawall by the ankles. Half zipped, the leather jacket rolled back, decorously covering his deathmask. He boosted the body up, and laid it gently on the concrete. The man slid, rather than fell over the side and disappeared into the current.

He returned for the other two. Jilian had jerked Ferringa from the rear seat. Arms and legs oddly bent, he lay on the gravel, the midnight blue wool of his English suit marred by great patches of gray dust. Jilian leaned inside, wiping the rear window with her scarf. Her gun was missing. She ignored him. He dragged Sallie to the seawall. Ferringa rolled over the edge, departing with a graceless splash. The driver was a struggle, not the heaviest, but DiGenero's strength was gone. He rested the body on the seawall before the final push. The face looked vaguely familiar. A relative of the don's? One of Sallie's buddies? For some reason, it seemed important to remember. He stared, but couldn't. He shoved and leaned against the concrete, head down, hearing but not seeing the splash and breathing hard. They would float for a time, in their dark clothes invisible in the night, then sink, and finally rise. Depending on a body's size and the current, the trip to the river bottom and back could take several days. Separated by Hell Gate's cauldron and the tide, each would make his own course. Eventually, they would be found, here and there. By Roosevelt Island, splayed on the riprap. Curled around the piling of a Brooklyn dock. Maybe as far as the lower harbor, drifting leisurely toward Gravesend Bay. Gone fishin', the don used to say. DiGenero tried to straighten. His head spun. He threw up.

The car started. Jilian beckoned from the driver's seat. He turned and walked slowly toward her, knowing he would stumble and fall if he even let his eyes drift.

She motioned. "Get in."

The words sounded muffled, far away. He sat beside her, hands in his lap, waiting for his next instruction. Jilian reached across him and gently closed the door. She looked pale, but composed, not unlike someone who had prepared herself for a sad and serious task and remained burdened by the weight of it even after it was done.

She said something. He nodded without intending. He knew the trembling meant shock was setting in. He felt cold and sweaty. Her coat was between them. She spread it over him.

"I don't understand," he said.

"What's that?" She put the car in gear.

"I don't understand."

They were moving. Although her eyes were on the road, she seemed ready to explain. DiGenero leaned toward her. He wanted to hear her answer, but it didn't come in time before he passed out.

CHAPTER

11

THEY LAY LIKE SPOONS in a drawer. From behind him, she stroked gently, as if she had no intention to arouse, but only to soothe, to induce a deeper, more pleasurable sleep. Curled on his side, he reached back, brushing his hand along her leg, then higher over the contour of her cheeks into the sanctum of her thighs. Her mound pressed against him, encouraging. He turned toward her, but she moved, just beyond his fingertips. He wanted her, needed her. It had been too long. If it took words, they were easy. He'd spoken them a thousand times. They absolved his sins. Others were good at forgiving, he at being forgiven. Why not here? Why not now? He reached out, groping, but touched no one. She seemed indistinct, shrouded somehow, like the light in her eyes, fading and distant. He reached again. The covers slipped away and the cold washed over him. A window shade flapped as if recording a hurried departure.

DiGenero woke, instantly across the edge of consciousness. The pillow exuded the sour odor of night sweat. Someone had braided the bedclothes, sheets over blankets. The darkness yielded no suspects. His heart pounded. Erin hadn't come to him in days, but it was still the same. No matter how he tried, he couldn't reach her even in dreams.

Outside the door, voices intruded. How long had he slept? An hour? Ten hours? A few feet away, the window framed a gray rectangle. An airshaft. No help in determining night or day. He switched on the light and propped himself on his elbows. On the bedside table, a woman's things, a purse and cosmetics, mingled with a package of gauze, a bottle of antiseptic lotion, and bandage tape. A television-desk-dresser combination, hotel modern, filled the far wall. Through the open bathroom door, he could see a stainless steel rack filled with towels. He examined the furnishings a second time. There was nothing personal, only the usual hotel decor. A fifty-dollar landscape, simulated wood-grain veneers and cheap carpet.

132

The face of the clock radio glowed. Seven-ten. But was it A.M. or P.M.? DiGenero swung his feet to the floor. His pulse kept time with the snap of the clock's second hand. He touched his forehead and winced. Under the dressing, the lump seemed disproportionately small for the accompanying pain. He poked gingerly, attempting a self-diagnosis. Last night's dizziness and vomiting meant it was more than a headache and contusion. Probably a mild concussion.

He rose like an old man, prudently testing his capabilities. His clothes draped over a chair. He dressed, minimizing unnecessary motion. The shirt wasn't his. Two sizes too large, it hung like a smock. His suit jacket also was gone, another casualty of Sallie's hurried invitation. Outside the door, the voices continued. He couldn't make out the words but their tempo rose and fell in the meter of argument. He pulled on his pants and shuffled to the bathroom. At the sink, he leaned forward, bracing himself with both hands. In the mirror, his reflection looked better and worse than he expected. Where he'd hit the dashboard, his forehead glowed a livid black and blue. The muzzle flash had seared his left ear. On the nape of his neck, Sallie's wrenching had installed a mellow bruise deep in his muscle. He opened the medicine cabinet and rummaged. Toothpaste, deodorant, shaving cream, throw-away razors, but no liniment. Dislodged, a plastic bottle of mouthwash rebounded in the sink. The voices stopped. He leaned into the bedroom, listening. A door opened and closed, then silence. A departure, not an arrival.

Last night came back as film clips, amateur rather than avant-garde. It was not what he remembered from flying in Vietnam, the fast forward of combat, of speed and surviving, but the slow motion of a failed execution, a deliverance via reprieve, not salvation. There was nothing redeeming in the memory. It was utilitarian. A reminder. It still waits.

He'd passed out twice. The first time he woke, they were on the Cross Bronx Expressway. He'd babbled, barely coherent. The route had confused him until they reached the George Washington Bridge. Then, heading west to New Jersey, he'd figured it out. She drove to Ferringa's apartment and parked in his spot. It was smart, the right place. The cops wouldn't look in the car even if it sat for a month. When Sallie didn't show, his crew might, but not right away. For a few days at least, anyone who knew about the hit would figure Ferringa was lying low. As for others, family values worked in their favor. Wiseguys didn't put a premium on intellectual curiosity. The rule was simple: if it ain't your business, don't ask.

For the return to Manhattan, they took two cabs, first to the Port Authority Bus Terminal on the West side, then to Grand Central. They walked crosstown, then south, four blocks, maybe five, although by then he was fading and couldn't be sure. He remembered an alley, a rear entrance, and a freight elevator. A pill and the scotch had put him out the second time. The rest was a blur. She must have undressed him and put him to bed. He slept, dead to the world.

DiGenero stepped to the bedroom door and tried the handle. It was locked. He heard someone approaching, then a click. Jilian opened the door. Wrapped in a bathrobe, she faced him, her expression both wary and caring. "How do you feel?"

"I haven't been locked in my room since I threw my sister's cat out the third-floor window. Don't give me any hints. You sent me to bed without supper, right?"

She smiled. "I'm sorry. With the blow to your head, I couldn't be sure what would happen when you came 'round." She cradled his elbow and guided him to the sofa. At one end, pillows and blankets lay jumbled. The overstuffed cushions still held her impression.

"You slept here last night? It is morning, isn't it?"

"Almost seven-thirty."

"I heard voices. Who just left?" he asked.

Jilian ignored the question. She eased him to a seat. "Coffee?"

He nodded and grimaced. The headache lurked.

"This your place?" he asked.

She stepped away, speaking over her shoulder. "Temporarily. It's let monthly."

The Pullman kitchen, barely an alcove, made a right angle with the living-dining room. She busied herself, reaching into the cupboard to remove two ceramic mugs and a painted pitcher. On a tray, she carefully fitted a placemat, red like the pitcher, then opened a drawer, collecting two spoons and two napkins. Unlike the bedroom, there were a few personal touches. They reminded him of Erin's kitchen, overflowing with the small things she had chosen to create her own world. Nothing and everything matched. Pans, pottery, wooden spoons in an empty crock, coasters and chopping blocks, grinders, mixers, odd silverware. It was all still there, just as she'd left it. He struggled, trying to think of something else. His eyes filled and he looked away. A pot scraped and a refrigerator door opened and closed. He wiped his hand over his face, feigning a slow awakening, hoping there'd been no notice. His expression betrayed him.

"Are you alright?" Jilian stood before him.

He contrived a smile. "Wonderful."

"I see." She occupied herself with arranging the tray on an end table, a sign that for the moment there would be no prying. He took the full mug. She sat in the armchair opposite, legs curled beneath her. Even bundled in terrycloth, she had looks other women envied, a beauty enhanced all the more when adornments were taken away.

DiGenero glanced at the floor. The *Times* and two tabloids were scattered, obviously read. Jilian answered his question before he asked. "Nothing. Nor on television or radio."

"Did I say thank you?" he asked.

"Several times."

"I hope your feelings won't be hurt if I don't send something more formal. Under the circumstances, it's so hard to find the right card."

"I understand," she said. "Under the circumstances."

"Are you alright?" he asked.

"Quite." The question obviously displeased her.

"I mean, last night was . . ."

She cut him off. "I'm fine. Thank you," she said sharply.

The words disciplined him. They sat in silence for several moments. Car horns intruded, muffled but angry. The volume told him they were on a lower floor, close to the street. DiGenero listened to the music. It was atonal, a cab and a car playing in minor key. Or did the counterpoint have too much bass? A cab and a limo? The duet faded as the performers drove down the block. Music? Was he coming unwrapped? What was it? The concussion, an epiphany, or both? His mind wandered, an excursion from right to left brain, traversing from intuition to analysis. Suddenly, he understood. Sounds, sights, touch, today, now, this instant, he was here and they weren't. After last night, he'd woken up, they hadn't. No good or bad, right or wrong. Others had found the oblivion meant for him. That was that. He looked up, smiling despite himself.

Jilian examined him over the rim of her coffee mug. "What do you want from me?" she asked.

"I'm sorry?" The question caught him off guard.

"Last night you wanted an introduction to Ferringa," she said.

"Uh huh."

"Now?" she asked.

"Nothing."

"Nothing?" She eyed him skeptically.

"Right."

"Do you expect me to believe that?"

He shrugged. "You don't?"

"No," she said.

"Okay. You saved my life yesterday, but what have you done for me lately?"

She seemed about to retort, then to reconsider. DiGenero watched, tracing the inner debate in her changing expression. When she spoke, her voice was softer. "You pose something of a problem for me." The prop-osition—resolved: to relent—had carried.

"Based on what I saw last night, nothing you can't handle," he said.

"That's not what I mean."

"Thank goodness."

She spoke casually, but her thoughts seemed nonetheless prepared, gone over and ordered in logical sequence. "The FBI is looking for you. Here, in New York."

"I'm not surprised."

"When they discover Ferringa and the others, they'll search harder. And, when they find you . . ."

He jumped to her apparent conclusion. "I'll give you up. Is that what's bothering you?"

"No." She shook her head. Loose, her hair rearranged itself on her shoulders. "When the time is right, your 'giving me up,' as you put it, won't matter."

"Of course. How silly of me. After all, most people do overreact to the prospect of being arrested for murder."

She continued, businesslike. "I have only a few days to find someone. Perhaps less. Until last night, Sallie Ferringa was the means to that end."

"Sallie? Then why did you kill him?"

"Why?" The question seemed one that hadn't occurred.

"If you don't mind me asking," he said.

"I had no choice."

"You mean if you had one, you wouldn't have?" he asked.

Jilian appeared to weigh the merits of candor. "It was part reflex, I suppose. Something you've trained for, but never believed you'd do. Like what happened to you."

It was DiGenero's turn to be puzzled. "What do you mean?"

"In Montana. In 1985. When you shot the Iranian, the one who murdered your friend."

His surprise clearly registered.

"Or so your file said." His reaction made her smile.

"How did you get that?" He blurted the question guilelessly.

"You don't know?"

The realization dawned. "The umbrella," DiGenero said.

"Very good."

"You lifted the prints." He examined her from a different perspective.

"When we first met in the bar, I had to know who you were. If someone sent you. You played the part very well," she said.

"Practice," DiGenero said.

"So I learned. I gather it's rare to find an FBI agent with your experience. Undercover, that is. An entire career. I didn't expect the Bureau to be so forthcoming with your background, but they are anxious to get hold of you."

"You've said." DiGenero settled into the cushions. He stretched his arm along the sofa, hoping to claim the initiative as easily as he had just claimed the territory. "I don't want you to take this the wrong way."

"Please." She nodded politely, inviting him to proceed.

"You don't make any sense," he said.

"Really?" Jilian's eyes widened, mirrors of innocence. "How so?"

"How? If you're working with the Bureau, why am I here, talking with you?"

"I don't understand."

"You said it yourself. They want me. So how come I'm not downtown in the field office with a guy holding each wrist, waiting for a ride back to Washington?"

"Ah, I see." Jilian nodded slowly.

"More to the point, we dumped Sallie and his buddies in the river? Even in New York this is not standard police procedure."

"True," she said.

"Why?"

"Why, indeed." Her self-possession was unnerving. She unlimbered her legs and crossed them demurely. "Why do you suppose?"

"What is this, a test?" DiGenero silently rebuked himself for fencing. It was the mistake of novice interrogators. His head hurt and he felt clumsy, like a dancing bear following its lithesome trainer across the circus ring. A pirouette and she was gone, leaving him to trundle after.

"If you like," she said encouragingly. "Think about it."

She was off again, an arabesque this time. He lumbered after. Think about what? The little she'd told him, or the logic of it all? For some reason, his first jigsaw puzzle, a Christmas gift, came to mind. He had opened the package upside down, spilling one thousand pieces on the floor. With its mountain peaks, meadows, villages, and shepherds, the alpine scene on the boxtop seemed to mock him even as he whittled away at the pile. It had taught him two things. He hated jigsaw puzzles and the big picture was always obscure if you only concentrated on the details.

"Because you're not working with the Bureau," he said.

"Very good again," she said encouragingly.

"But somebody is." DiGenero pressed.

Jilian motioned toward the tray. "More coffee?"

"Somebody passed my prints to the Bureau. Somebody picked up my file. Who?"

She proffered the pot.

"Scotland Yard?" He extended his mug automatically. Its earth brown glaze was embossed with a single Chinese character. What did it mean? Who knew? One man's language, another's decoration.

She poured, leaning forward. Her robe bowed, exposing the soft swell of her breasts and at the end of a thin gold chain, a crucifix. Between her contours, the body of Christ lay comfortably at rest.

"Intelligence?" he asked.

She replaced the pot.

"MI5? MI6?" DiGenero persisted.

Jilian held her coffee mug as if warming both hands.

"Wrong? Okay. Sergeant Preston of the Yukon sent you."

"I beg your pardon," she said.

"Let's cut the crap. Who are you?"

"Does it matter?" She blew across the mug.

"Yeah. At some point, we've got to start out even. Why not with that?"

" 'Even?' This must be the American sense of fair play one hears so much about."

"Whatever you want to call it." DiGenero's pulse drummed anew in his temples. Caffeine aside, his patience was corroding.

"Someone did help with the file, of course," she said, admitting nothing, albeit matter-of-factly. She studied him as if the time had come for a determination, a judgment about how to proceed. "Do you know Coventry?" she asked.

"In England? The Cathedral?"

"Well, yes, but it's a town, north of London."

"So?"

"Ten years ago, the IRA bombed an officers' mess there. I think you call them clubs. Officers' Clubs. Do I have that right?" she asked.

DiGenero nodded.

"It was on a Royal Army post, a small one. A training command. Nothing operational. No commandos or SAS or intelligence. Administrative officers and clerks. Just paper and procedures. Nothing to do with Northern Ireland at all. Vulnerable for that reason, I suppose. No one went out of their way to enforce security. It wasn't very important or high priority in a place like that."

Jilian continued. "My fiancé was having lunch. He'd just popped in for something quick. He'd been assigned there for a year or so, right out of university. That's where we'd met. I was working at the Defense Ministry in London then and he was coming down to meet me. He was leaving Coventry actually, car packed, orders in hand. We were getting married a week hence. After the wedding we were going to Hong Kong. A four-year assignment. I heard about the bombing on the radio in the office, but didn't even listen closely enough to notice the name of the place. I was thinking of the mysteries of the Orient, the trip, a flat on the Peak overlooking the harbor, shopping, babies. All the things that seem important when nothing terrible has ever touched your life. I waited that night, getting madder and madder at him for being late until the telephone rang. It was his mother. They'd rung her up first. 'I have something I must tell you,' she said. It was just like a movie, except I didn't hear a word after that. It didn't matter. From the first, I knew. I remembered the radio news report and I knew." Jilian sipped her coffee. "The IRA claimed credit. It turned out to be the beginning of one of their periodic bombing spasms in England. Pubs, military bases, department stores. A strike against the occupiers, they said. A blow against British oppression, that sort of thing. I remember reading the newspapers and magazines for months afterward, searching for some connection between the act and the cause. I'd never paid much attention to the Irish business before that. Close to none at all. But I needed to make sense out of what happened. I wanted to know there was a reason, a reason he died, even if it was malevolent. It didn't matter that it might be hateful. I just wanted something that would help me understand why."

"And what did you find?" DiGenero asked.

She shook her head. "Nothing, of course. And that is the reason, isn't it? It's Zen. There is none. The acts are vessels, just like the words that justify them. You fill them with whatever meaning you want. They do it. We do it. Everyone does it. Ever after, words like 'oppression,' 'justice,' 'liberation,' 'law and order' have sounded evil to me. They justify the ultimate theft, not only taking your life, but even your reason for being. Someone else making you part of their idea of history. Instead of an obituary that records you, the small scratches you've carved in the rock —raised roses, taught school, had children, made money, whatever— you're forever theirs, their victim, a casualty in their mindless struggle." Jilian looked away, as if something in the distance had caught her attention. "He was a wonderful man. He might have done wonderful things. But even if he hadn't, I would have loved him. It was a senseless death, like all deaths for causes. It shouldn't have happened. Nothing served. No one changed."

"Except you," DiGenero said.

She looked back. "Except me," Jilian repeated. Silence surrounded them. "I'm sorry about Erin," she said. His wife's name surprised him. Incarnated by Jilian's accent, the sound hung in the air like a physical presence. "Revenge can't bring anyone back. It can only consume you."

"As long as it consumes Johnny Scarlese I'll be happy," DiGenero said.

"Will you be happy if four hundred innocent people also die?" she asked quietly.

He remembered the newspaper Benedetto unfolded, the photos of the wreckage filling the front page. Vito Rocchi's and Ferringa's connection to the Irish Republican Army still seemed incredible, like rats and scorpions plotting, characters that only made sense together as cartoons on the big screen.

"Let me put it this way," he said. "If you can bring peace in our time, more power to you. I'm not that ambitious."

"They're going to do it again unless we can stop them."

"Do what?" he asked.

"Sabotage another plane. We know that."

"That's too bad, but it's not my problem," DiGenero said.

"I don't believe you mean that."

"You should."

"She shook her head. "You don't realize."

"Realize what?" he asked.

"The stakes."

"You mean God, country, and all that? I thought you just told me that kind of cheerleading didn't matter?"

Jilian spoke, contempt glittering. "It doesn't. But four hundred people do, for Christ's sake. The killing is its own end now. You must understand that. You can't be that cynical."

He shrugged. "I know what the stakes are."

"You think so?"

"For people like you and me, yeah. The stakes are what you say they are."

"How succinct. Ethics in a sentence. The one-minute moralist. Very American," she said, cutting him with her condescension.

"I've been there," he shot back.

"And where, pray tell, is that?"

"For you right now?" He let the question hang momentarily between them. "On the edge. Wondering if you can still make everything come together. All the pieces—the time you've spent, the planning you've done, the chances you've taken, the lies you've told, the fear you've felt—everything you've invested to make this operation go. It's all on your back. Just like last night. You knew then you'd come too far to let Sallie blow it away. That's why you pulled the trigger. Not because of anything else. And not because of me."

"My, my. Don't we sound so sure of things." Her voice was flat, without affect.

"It isn't all that hard to figure out," he said. "My guess is you've been at this a long time, a year, two years, maybe more. First, to get inside the IRA's organization, then Scarlese's, right?" DiGenero looked up.

Jilian didn't answer. She returned his stare cooly like a clinician, an observer not a judge.

He leaned forward, elbows on knees. "Let me try to put the pieces together. Somebody spotted Vito on his trips to Ireland, assessed him, and made the right call: vulnerable and not too bright. Courier, bagman, important as a money mule, but no mover and shaker. You got the orders. Make the play and score. You did. Vito got you going, gave you access, a way inside. He was the beginning, not the end. That was the plan. You established yourself with Vito, then went up the food chain. Maybe you had others in mind, I don't know, but you knew you had to go farther. And you did. You got to Sallie and wonder of wonders, he bit. After all, with you, who wouldn't?" DiGenero paused. She didn't react. "The next move was simple," he said. "You shucked Vito—what's he gonna say? Sallie's his boss. Ferringa was who you wanted, someone in the chain of command, closer to your target. But how close? That was the question. It still is, isn't it?"

This time he waited longer for a reply, but Jilian didn't answer. He continued. "At any rate, you were on the trail, right? Sallie talked and you listened. Maybe he told you things, maybe just hinted. Maybe it was what he didn't say, the questions he wouldn't answer." He raised his eyebrows. "What do I know? Maybe he told you he was the paymaster." On her lap, Jilian's fingers stopped tracing small figure eights in the fabric of her robe. "How much was it?" DiGenero looked at the ceiling, as if calculating. "Ten, twenty thousand a month? Who knows? Anyway, you were moving." He sunk back into the sofa, resuming a comfortable slouch. "Until last week. Then, the surprises. Right?"

This time Jilian nodded.

"On the same day, Vito gets whacked and the plane goes down. What a coincidence," DiGenero said. "What do you do? You start thinking backward, right? Like a mechanic fixing a car, trying to remember what happened last, what button you pushed just before it broke. First, you run down the simple questions. Who did you talk to? What did you do? Where did you go? Then, come the hard ones, the application of industrial strength professional paranoia. Are you next? Is somebody going to roll you up? Should you fold up the operation or wait? Go now, or hang around, play it by ear? You rack your brains. Maybe you had an answer. Maybe not. But then what happens? Surprise number three."

"You," she said.

"Correct. Me." He smiled. "Bottom line?"

"Please," she said politely.

"If they'd killed me last night, you knew the consequences. The feds would have been all the place and your bosses would have pulled you out. The operation would have been finished. Everything you worked for. But with Sallie and the other two shot instead, who knows? After all, wiseguys get hit all the time and if that's the way it looks, even for a few days, the ball's still in play. Am I right?"

Jilian finished her coffee.

"It's simpler now. For both of us," he said.

"Is it?"

"Vito's dead. So's Ferringa. That leaves Scarlese. Sallie said as much in the car."

"So he did." She agreed.

"We both want the same man." He sounded as cooperative as possible.

"But for different reasons," Jilian said.

He saw the pistol. She had removed it from between the cushion and chair. Palm-sized, it lay in her lap, pointed toward him. The silencer doubled the length of the compact barrel. Her finger curled around the trigger. Jilian's eyes held his, gauging his reaction before she spoke again. "I don't care about Scarlese the way you do. I don't care if he lives or dies. I'm after someone else. Somewhere in your air traffic control system there's a member of the IRA. Until two years ago, we had intelligence—leads, you'd call them. With that sort of information, we usually do quite well. We can penetrate their network. In this case, we couldn't. The trail ran cold. No one knew a thing. None of our sources could help. Then, we discovered why."

"The IRA isn't running the show," he said.

She nodded. "Ingenious really. The Mafia as a subcontractor. Who would bother to pay attention here? And on your territory, how would we discover them? Transparent to you and opaque to us."

"But why not go to the Bureau and bring them in? They work terrorism as well as organized crime."

"We have," she said.

"And?"

"Nothing."

"I don't understand," DiGenero said.

"Nor do we." Neither the pistol nor Jilian's finger on the trigger had moved.

"Look," he said, "I don't care what you're running or whether you're working with the Bureau or not."

She shook her head. "I know you don't, but I can't take the chance. You're marked. Scarlese wants you. The Bureau wants you. You make me too vulnerable."

"I make you vulnerable?" DiGenero laughed. "You don't expect to get close to Scarlese after they find Sallie, do you? Maybe you conned Ferringa, but Scarlese won't have idea number one which side you're on."

"Perhaps."

"No perhaps about it."

"We'll see what he does with my message," Jilian said.

"What message?"

"About last night," she said. "You should be flattered. You were really quite formidable. You had a gun concealed somewhere. After you killed them, you put me out of the car and sped off."

"Why in the hell do you think he'll believe that?"

"Because it's the story he'll read in the newspapers."

"What are you talking about?" DiGenero asked warily.

"Being part of the fourth estate does confer some advantages."

"You called," he said.

"I'm afraid so. There's going to be some speculation about you in the press. Given your motives, I can't imagine there won't be great sympathy."

DiGenero rolled his eyes.

Jilian continued. "It would be good if you stayed out of sight for the time being. For you and for me. I have someone coming to see to it. As for the newspapers, truth will out. It shouldn't be long."

Choices that had saved or condemned him had rarely come rationally, nor necessarily after due deliberation. Twenty years before, when he was first inside the Scarlese family, his outside handler had told him the sum of all wisdom regarding decisions that mattered: go with your gut.

DiGenero stood unsteadily. His head pounded. "Thanks for everything."

Jilian gestured with the gun. "Sit down!"

"No thank you." He walked to the door, put one hand on the knob, and threw the deadbolt with the other. Behind him, the automatic's action snapped metallically. When he turned, Jilian was standing, arms outstretched in a shooter's two-handed grip. Nothing in her eyes betrayed indecision.

DiGenero held the knob, hoping he'd stopped swaying. "You're right, you know. After a while, the words don't matter. I don't know from oppression, liberation, legal, illegal, right, wrong. But I do know what I do—what you do—is its own world. You live it, twenty-four hours a day, seven days a week. It's not a job. It's personal. It changes you. You can ignore that until you stop and think about it. But when that happens, what you do has got to make sense, on your terms. Not for anybody else, but for yourself. You've got to have a reason for the lying and the cheating"—he held her stare—"and the killing. You've got to have a reason that you can live with."

"And you think I won't?" Her eyes flashed, suddenly challenging.

"I sincerely hope not." He swung open the door. The hallway was empty. "Is this where I'm supposed to say 'Cheerio'?"

"You ungrateful bastard," she spat the words. The automatic wavered.

DiGenero stepped outside. When he looked back, Jilian had lowered her hands. He closed the door and stood for several minutes until the trembling stopped. Then he crossed the landing to the stairway, and went down.

CHAPTER
12

SILVERSTEIN DROVE like he walked, charging his putative opposition with a fullback's finesse. One arm wrapped around the wheel, he hunched forward, poised, more than prepared, even welcoming a collision.

"I can't figure you out." The symphony of rattles from the unmarked sedan drowned Silverstein's muttering.

DiGenero glanced up. Newspapers covered his lap, Monday's early editions. Eighth Avenue was deserted. A block away at 31st Street, the light prepared to change. Crossing their path, a lone truck attempted to slip through the yellow. Silverstein bore down unforgivingly. The truck lurched in low gear and accelerated, emulating an animal's spastic fright. The car barely missed the tailgate, bottoming hard in the swale of the intersection.

"I mean, wanderin' around on the street all day. Whaddya gonna accomplish?"

Braced against the passenger door, DiGenero folded a tabloid lengthwise, a subway rider's crease. "I got 'em on the run. They don't know where I'm going to strike next."

"You know what?" Silverstein asked.

"What?"

"Last night I think you hit your fuckin' head a little too hard."

DiGenero waved toward the street. Silverstein looked out. They swerved left. A derelict breaking a trail in the gutter jumped right. The bundle of oversized army jacket and stocking cap stumbled over the curb. Dislodged from an already tenuous grip, a wine bottle skittered across the sidewalk.

"When I heard about Ferringa, I figured you was history," Silverstein said. "How come you didn't call?"

"I needed some time to think." DiGenero turned the page. "Here it is," he said. He angled the paper, trapping the dome light's dim illumination.

"Whatsitsay?" Silverstein leaned toward him. He squinted at the headline. The car drifted across the lanes. Behind them, a taxi horn blared.

"Watch the goddamn road!" DiGenero pushed him away. "I got enough trouble already. I don't need you trying to kill me."

Silverstein straightened up, pouting. He corrected course, then accelerated, registering his pique.

The story filled a column beneath a headline, Sallie's epitaph, "Alleged Mob Lieutenant Murdered." A photograph captured a police launch, stern-on. The boat was listing under the weight of three officers, who were bent at the rail, sliding a body over the gunnel. DiGenero scanned down several paragraphs of ostensible fact followed by several more of comingled background and speculation.

They'd found Ferringa on Sunday afternoon, wedged between the seawall and a storm drain on the west side of Roosevelt Island. It was just as Jilian had said. His name appeared halfway down the page.

"So?" Silverstein turned his head back and forth, birdlike, eyeing the street, then the paper.

DiGenero read aloud.

According to sources close to the investigation, Frank DiGenero, an FBI agent who infiltrated the Scarlese crime family in the 1970s, is wanted for questioning in the murder. Because of DiGenero's five years undercover, the longest-running penetration of a Mafia family by the federal force, Johnny Scarlese, Sr., was convicted in 1979 for racketeering, extortion, and other crimes. FBI sources have confirmed that a contract on DiGenero's life remains active. Two weeks ago, a car bomb killed DiGenero's wife in Salt Lake City, where he had been assigned. An FBI spokesman acknowledged that DiGenero's whereabouts are unknown.

"Sounds like I'm a celebrity." DiGenero put down the paper.

"Oh yeah? Sounds like you're up the fuckin' creek to me." They stopped at a light. "Tell, me somethin'," Silverstein said. "What the hell she do that for?"

"Do what?" DiGenero asked, distracted. He turned the page looking for more. There was none.

"Whaddya think? Give you up to the newspapers. I mean, she blows away Ferringa and these other two geeks and then turns in the only witness. It don't make sense." The light changed. Silverstein accelerated, steering into the left lane. In the street, illuminated by portable floodlights, temporary fencing protected an open manhole. A head with hardhat peered out, watching them approach, then disappeared suddenly, gopherlike, as Silverstein narrowly missed the flimsy barrier.

"This is a woman with a purpose in life," DiGenero answered. He opened the *Times* and scanned. "I gotta give her that. She's doing what she can to keep her operation alive."

"Well more power to her, but hanging a murder rap on somebody else is sure as shit one hardball game."

DiGenero slouched in the seat. "There's something that still isn't right, though."

"What?" Silverstein glanced over.

"She ran prints to get my background information, from the Bureau. That means she's hooked up, right? Working with a contact, or somebody on the inside."

"So?" Silverstein asked.

"So how come the Bureau didn't come looking for me? Why did they turn over the file without following up?"

Silverstein broke in. "Maybe she didn't go through the Bureau. She coulda gone through NYPD. You got all kinds of cops in the city. French, Italians, Germans, who knows who else. They all got somebody at their consulates or at the UN. She's English, right? They gotta have 'em, too. I mean, maybe that's who she used. Then, that guy goes to the PD. The PD asks the Bureau. Back comes the info. We even got our very own 'dip dicks' to do that kinda thing."

"Your very own what?" DiGenero asked.

" 'Dip dicks.' You know. Mosta the time they're parkin' ticket rippers. The ones who tear up the meter maid citations when the dips leave their limos on the sidewalk. Must cost the city a million fuckin' bucks a year." Silverstein scratched his head. The car meandered. "Whaddatheycallit?" He thought out loud. "Dip section? Dip squad? Diplomatic somethin'-or-other. They're at headquarters. Mosta them retire on disability. Piles and too many paper cuts." Silverstein gave up. "Can't remember. Maybe that's how she made you, got your file, you know what I mean?"

"I don't think so," DiGenero said.

Silverstein looked disappointed. "Why not?"

"The Bureau doesn't give out what she had. They don't hand over 201s," he said.

"You mean background files?"

"Yeah," DiGenero answered. "Not on agents. They'll confirm whether you're on the rolls or not, but that's it. She had more than that. A hell of a lot more."

Silverstein had slowed to a few miles an hour. They coasted over bumps, wallowing in the right lane. A car sped by on their left, the driver offering a single-fingered salute. Absorbed, Silverstein ignored the gesture. "So what's goin' on?" he asked.

"I'm not sure. Obviously, she's got somebody doing favors for her, or for whoever's her inside contact. Somebody who's willing to give more than the rules allow." DiGenero smiled. "I mean, that's no big deal. After all, you're not signed out to help a fugitive FBI agent, are you?" DiGenero put his foot on the dash and rested his head on the seatback. "As a matter of fact, where's the PD think you are anyway?"

"Me?" Silverstein asked innocently. "I'm scopin' out new safehouses and surveillance sites in the boroughs. That's good for a few days."

DiGenero played with the police radio. He turned up the volume. There were no voices, only static. Close to shift change, the dispatcher and patrol units were keeping their own counsel, not anxious to handle calls that would produce overtime, prolonging a dull Sunday night. He turned off the radio. "That leaves a couple possibilities," DiGenero said.

"Such as?"

"Such as she's involved in a special op, where the rules don't apply. In that case, whoever got the prints and the trace request for her had authorization to turn over the file. That simple."

"You think so?" Silverstein asked.

"It's possible, I suppose. It's also possible the Bureau doesn't know anything about the request. A make on prints, a file search, a printout of the records, everything's done electronically. Untouched by human hands. All you need is somebody on the inside with the authorization to punch the keys, rip, and read. Maybe the Bureau doesn't know anything about her, or even about the fact she's wired into the system. It could be that whoever's doing the asking—her contact with the Bureau—is a cutout. Maybe as far as the Bureau guy knows—the one who's doing the button pushing—her contact wanted the make on me. Maybe no one in the Bureau knows about her at all. At least that possibility's a little more comforting."

"Comforting? Whaddyamean?"

"What do I mean? Jesus, I'd like to think the Bureau didn't give her the nod to put my name in the newspaper as the murder suspect *du jour* so that every fuckin' shooter in New York with a badge can go looking for me. Somehow it doesn't seem like the best way to build closer employer-employee relations."

Silverstein shrugged. "I dunno. Sounds like PD policy on a good day to me."

The car humped and thudded across steel plates and shoring timbers, the scabs on the city's perpetual digging, underground surgery to forestall the collapse of New York's antiquated water and sewer systems. Silverstein hit passing gear for no discernible reason. Atop the construction barricades, the yellow strobes captured whirling eddies of trash in freeze frame. DiGenero contemplated the darkened stores. They seemed abandoned, their signs in Spanish, English, or both the only evidence of what sheltered behind the heavy steel curtains drawn against the night. New York, the modern urban archetype, was evolving again, this time in an ironic revival. Instead of walls to stop invaders, the city was fortified against itself, the design of the middle ages turned inside out.

Silverstein braked and turned right, heading east. Except for the odd taxi, the cross street was vacant and under the sodium lights, cold.

DiGenero's head began to throb. The painkillers Silverstein had given him were wearing off. After leaving Jilian, he'd made an attempt to sort out his choices. With Silverstein's help, he could still try to get to Scarlese, but every day made him more vulnerable. Not only to the cops, but to Scarlese as well. Junior had a hundred wiseguys. Another thousand "associates" worked for them. Each had family and friends. A hundred who were made, plus a thousand more on the streets, plus another ten thousand who could be contacted in the neighborhoods. He knew what Scarlese would do. The word would go out. Look for DiGenero. It would be worth the effort. Five thousand dollars, twenty thousand, fifty thousand. Who knew how much would be offered? New York was no different than a Sicilian village. A whisper would spread, transforming normal suspicion into vigilance. Even big cities were only a collection of villages with their own blocks and streets where everyone knew who belonged and who didn't. Each day he persisted, he would be drawn deeper into them, deeper into their web. Time turned predators into prey, one and the same.

Silverstein spoke. "Just one thing. No more wanderin' the streets. You're goin' to my place. You got it?"

"I know, but you'll protect me, officer." DiGenero patted Silverstein's cheek.

Silverstein rolled his eyes. "Fuck."

CHAPTER
13

THE COOKWARE HUNG randomly above the stove, pots and pans, eclectic in type and implications. The cast iron, fire blackened, was well seasoned, suggesting knowledgeable use. On the aluminum, the same effect raised questions.

At the stove, Silverstein stirred a potage of pasta, ground beef, and tomatoes. The exhaust fan whined, struggling against its near impenetrable accumulations.

DiGenero sipped a beer, watching skeptically. He had slept until noon, risen, soaked in a bath, and slept again. When he awoke the second time, his headache finally was gone.

Silverstein laid down a cutting board, opened the refrigerator, and rummaged. He piled onions, carrots, and green peppers on the counter and reached for a knife. His habits were careful, the practices of someone who used tasks to do time, rather than vice versa. He peeled, then chopped, dicing the onions in a fine hatchwork and slicing the carrots lengthwise, julienne-style.

"What do you call it?" DiGenero asked.

Silverstein looked up. "Call what?"

"The dish," DiGenero said, clarifying.

"Kosher chili." Silverstein bisected a carrot. An end skittered across the counter, disappearing over the edge. He pushed the remainder aside and reached for an onion.

DiGenero finished his beer. "This isn't a subtle way to make me turn myself in, is it?"

"Very funny." Silverstein sliced. The onion's pungent aroma filled the small alcove. He wiped his eyes. "I was gonna do Mexican kishka, but the butcher was all outa intestine." Silverstein sniffled and diced. "In cookin', ya gotta know what's good. Any shmuck can read a book. But talent? That's in the genes." He put down the knife and reopened the refrigerator, handing DiGenero a fresh beer and taking one for himself. Silverstein popped the top with his thumb, drank, and belched before resuming. "In my case, it's my uncle Manny. From Chicago. He gets laid off and comes to New York in the sixties. He needs a job, right? Manny don't even have a high school diploma, but chutzpa? This he's got, industrial size."

"What did he do?" DiGenero asked.

"He goes to work in a restaurant, an Italian joint over on the West side. He's there for a few months and starts to look around. What's he see? A little dough, a little cheese, some sauce, *telenners* bumpin' into each other and makin' money. So he says to himself, 'Why not me?' " Silverstein looked up, visualizing. He raised both hands, framing an imaginary sign. " 'Manny's' In the history of the race, this is a first."

"I don't get it." DiGenero looked puzzled. "A restaurant's a first?"

"I'm not talkin' restaurant. I'm talkin' Jewish pizzeria."

"Oh."

Silverstein smiled. "Whaddaguy. I remember the first time when he brought one home. My grandmother, this little two-hundred-year-old babushka, comes outa her room, takes a look in the box, and says in Yiddish, 'What's this? A paving stone?' Believe me, it wasn't easy." He diced the onion. "Now, ya gotta understand, Manny's not expert on Italians. Whadda they eat, what's good, what's bad? Who knows?" Silverstein turned, waggling the knife at DiGenero for emphasis. "But about Jews? This, Manny knows."

"Knows what?" DiGenero asked, warily this time.

"Silverstein looked at DiGenero as if somehow, incredibly, he had failed to apprehend the obvious. "Whaddyamean 'what'? Why did Moses and the Jews wander around for forty years?"

"I can't imagine," DiGenero said.

"Nobody could agree which way to go. Five thousand years later, what's new? It don't make no difference. Whatever it is, everybody wants it their own way. So? Manny don't sell one kinda pizza, or two kindsa pizzas, or ten kindsa pizzas. That won't work. Some guy's gonna walk in and want number eleven, which you don't got. Instead, Manny sells pizza by the pound. You make it. You want a pound of sauce and no cheese? Fine. You want a pound a cheese and no sauce? Fine. You want a pound of onions and peppers, hold the crust, sauce, cheese. Fine. That's it. No fights, no arguments, none of this, 'Whaddya chargin' me the same as him? I didn't get no pepperoni? Ya think I'm gonna pay for what I don't get?' Everybody loves it. And whaddyathink?"

"What?"

"God smiles. It's 1967. The Six-Day War. Manny comes up with a

new product line. 'The Sinai Special.' 'The Moshe Dayan Delight.' "
Silverstein sighed. "Whaddaguy."

"Pure genius," DiGenero said. "Manny still in business?"

"Nah."

"What happened?"

Silverstein scooped up the onions and carrots and dropped them in the
pot. "Occupational hazard. Ate his own cookin', gained two hundred
pounds, had a heart attack, and died."

The telephone rang.

"I'll get it," Silverstein said. He wiped his hands on a towel and
pointed at the pot. "Watch this stuff. You see any flames, it's gone toxic.
Pull the alarm and run like hell." Silverstein disappeared into the bedroom.

DiGenero turned down the burner and wandered into the living
room. The television flickered. The local evening news filled the screen,
three figures perched between a futuristic console and an ersatz New
York skyline. He adjusted the sound, amplifying their strained camarade-
rie. The five o'clock segment was ending, one said. Six o'clock was next.
The two men bantered, while the woman laughed humorlessly. They
were clones, identical from coast to coast. Pretty faces with permanent
smiles describing lost puppies and natural disasters in the same homoge-
nized tones. Sports scores, suicides, scandals, secrets of sexually transmitted diseases, equally ballasted with all the substance sixty-seconds-a-piece
allowed.

A new square-jawed-and-blown-dry cast began the second hour. The
first story covered the President's speech, an obligatory lead despite the
vacuous contents. His was number two in the lineup, a longer "live"
report. They had extracted the maximum titillation from the story's
three-minute running time. Renegade FBI agent killing mobsters in revenge. The right concept, but one off on the details. More at eleven, the
anchorman said, but now a first look at this startling case that has
shocked New York.

A videotape rolled. The voice-over described Ferringa's background
and those of the other two as the medical examiners' crew unloaded a
bodybag from the police launch. History followed, a few seconds of file
footage from the Scarlese trial, fifteen-year-old film of the federal courthouse lobby in lower Manhattan. DiGenero almost didn't recognize
himself in the crowd of wide lapels and long hair.

They cut to a live segment from Salt Lake City. Two hours earlier than
New York, the late afternoon sun was slipping low. Its azimuth mellowed
the light, burnishing the mountains in soft reflection. The local reporter,
one of the state's nordic blonde legion, glanced off-camera for her cue.

The investigation, she said to her microphone, was continuing. He recognized the Bureau's familiar public relations prose, spoon-fed and duti-
fully repeated. "The FBI is pursuing several leads and is notifying its
offices across the country to concentrate their resources in exploiting all
possible information on this case."

As she elaborated on the obvious, DiGenero no longer heard her
words but only saw the house just over her shoulder. Scarred and broken, it looked violated, abandoned. The front door and windows were
boarded with plywood. He watched until the camera began to pan across
the yard, then turned away. His eyes filled. DiGenero put one hand on
the back of the worn recliner, steadying himself. Silverstein's voice carried from the bedroom. He was talking louder and faster, up-tempo,
seeming to end the conversation.

The remote control lay on the recliner's cushion. He picked it up and
pressed a button. The television screen flashed. Wheels and lights appeared. A host strutted across a carnival set. He waved and danced,
motioning to the contestants to follow. Two middle-aged matrons complied, jumping up and down obligingly. One of them spun a giant rou-
lette wheel and spoke. The camera cut to a blonde in a black sheath
standing before a giant upright checkerboard. She turned four squares.
The same letter appeared on each, evoking manic jubilation. DiGenero
stared. He felt suddenly alien, like someone who had found a primitive
tribe performing peculiar mating rights. Where was he? Who was he? He
tried to think of Erin. For a moment, he could neither picture her nor
feel his emptiness. Instead, there was only Sallie Ferringa's face, and the
pleasure of remembering his final, quizzical stare.

Silverstein returned. He saw the screen. "Yo, Vanna! Nobody oughta
be allowed to have a body like that."

The other contestant leaned over and spun the wheel. The audience
clapped and waved, collectively hyperactive.

"A unit," Silverstein said over the sound of laughter and shouts.

"What?" DiGenero asked.

"A unit. A hundred thousand bucks. That's what Junior's gonna pay
to anybody who makes you dead."

The contestant spoke. A buzzer sounded. No blocks turned. Silverstein shook his head. "Dumbshit. You gotta pick vowels first off."

DiGenero motioned toward the bedroom. "Who was that?"

"The call? One of my snitches. Don't worry. He don't know from
nothin'. The other day I asked him to check around. For that kinda
change I don't think the new price on your contract is gonna be a secret
too long."

DiGenero sat on the sofa.

"Come on, let's eat," Silverstein said.

"I'm not hungry," he said.

"Don't hurt my feelings." Silverstein turned off the television. "Look at it this way. Everybody wants to be rich and famous. You just got the order screwed up. Come on." He motioned as he walked away.

DiGenero rose. The dining room was an alcove, barely enough to accommodate the card table. Silverstein had cleared two spaces among the magazines and bills for the paper plates and mismatched silverware. Between them, an economy-sized ketchup bottle and a roll of paper towels provided the centerpiece.

Cupboards banged and the refrigerator door opened and closed. Silverstein carried two more beers to the table, then returned to the kitchen and brought out the pot. Balanced on a dented bottom, it rocked precariously as he spooned. He heaped DiGenero's plate, sat, and repeated the task, filling his own. He ate silently with a steady shoveling, then rested and drank his beer. "We gotta regroup and think this through."

"Great idea." DiGenero toyed with his food.

Silverstein took another mouthful and spoke. "The problem's not the wiseguys or the wanna-be's, you know what I mean? A hundred thousand's gonna mean alot of talk, but mosta these assholes couldn't shoot somebody if their life depended on it. Besides, they're not gonna know where to look." He drank and burped. "Even if they found you, my guess is they'd run the other way. Just like Fat Eddy Artola. You remember him?"

DiGenero thought for a moment. "The Tattaglia family? From New Jersey. Right?"

"The same," Silverstein said. "One of Tattaglia's crew chiefs. They had a contract on Fat Eddy for five years. I swear to God. What was it? Twenty-five, thirty thousand dollars? The old man found out he was suckin' money from the freight handler's pension fund. Pissed him off. It was supposed to go straight to Tattaglia, do not pass go, do not skim two hundred dollars. He kept askin' the morons that worked for him when they was gonna shoot Fat Eddy. They kept sayin' they couldn't find him, but they was workin' on it. Couldn't find him? Shit! Fat Eddy weighed four hundred and fifty pounds. All ya needed to do was follow the vibrations when he walked. They knew where he was at, but every time they got close they'd hear a siren someplace in Pennsylvania, or see a guy puttin' out the trash and wet their pants. Point is, ninety percent of these punks got no balls. They ain't shooters."

"I'm not worried about the ninety percent," DiGenero said. "I want

Junior. The contract makes it harder to get at him. That's all." He pushed the plate away. "How did Scarlese find out I was in the city?"

"How?" Silverstein balanced his beer on the edge of the table. "You want a guess?"

"Sure."

"The Irish broad."

"You think she set me up?"

Silverstein nodded. "Uh huh."

"Then why didn't she let them shoot?" DiGenero asked.

Silverstein peered into the pot. The goulash had solidified. He poked with his fork, retrieved a carrot, and bit off half. "Who knows? She coulda had a deal with Ferringa—finger you and walk away—and they double-crossed her." He munched. "Maybe it wasn't supposed to go down with her in the backseat. So, she thinks, 'oh-oh.'" Silverstein raised his fist, pointing his finger like a gun. The fork protruded, an oversized hammer. He pulled the trigger. "Bang." He put down the imaginary weapon. "Maybe she didn't have a deal, but when she saw what was happenin', she figured they was gonna do her next. So? She reaches the same conclusion. Bang." He probed inside the pot without looking this time. "What do I know? Maybe she changed her mind at the last minute and did the right thing. You know. Bad guy goes straight. Whore with the heart of gold. Happens all the time in the movies."

"I don't think she set me up," DiGenero said.

"Oh yeah? You still on the lookout for the Easter bunny and the tooth fairy, too, huh?"

"It doesn't fit otherwise."

"What doesn't?" Silverstein asked.

"The fact that she didn't know when or where I'd get back in touch. After we met in the bar. There's only one explanation. Ferringa had her followed."

"Or you," Silverstein interjected.

DiGenero nodded. "I can't take Scarlese head-on, Arnie. It's too hard. But neither can she."

"Whaddya talkin' about?" Silverstein asked.

"I mean, she's a way to get to Scarlese. A way he's not going to expect."

Silverstein examined DiGenero. "You're kiddin'."

"No," he said.

Silverstein sat back slowly. He smacked his forehead with his palm. "Now I get it! How could I be such a dummy? She's on our side, right? Why didn't I think of that? Let's see. What did I miss? Her boyfriend Sallie just happens to find you with her and you almost get whacked. She frames you for killin' him. That gets every cop in the city, not to mention the FBI after your ass and doubles the contract on your head, makin' you part of the Mafia's mileage-plus program. Then, she takes you home, tucks you in bed, pulls a gun on you. But you got it figured. That all adds up and now she's gonna help you out." Silverstein shook his head. "This is the kinda logic they teach in law school?"

"Somehow, I get the impression you don't fully share my view," DiGenero said.

"I mean, you got part of this right. There's no way you're gonna get in Scarlese's face. It just ain't possible to do it with all the heat." Silverstein tipped the pot on its side and spooned another helping onto his plate. "I don't know from nothin' about the IRA—I mean, blowin' up airplanes and all that. I also gotta admit we stumbled across some weird shit. Vito travelin' outa the country. Sallie hangin' around with this Irish honey, with some kinda FBI connection no less. What can I say? I'm only a dumb cop and this is tough enough to figure. But Scarlese and IRA types? And inside the FAA? With Rocchi and Ferringa as 007 and 008? If you think that makes sense, okay. But I gotta tell ya, I got big-time doubts."

"So what are my choices?" DiGenero asked.

Silverstein shrugged. "Ferringa's gone, so's Rocchi. Maybe there's somebody else out there who knows. But you ain't gonna have a lot of witnesses to tell the jury that Scarlese personally ordered 'em to kill your wife." He speared a macaroni. "Frank, you blow Junior away and you're gonna get all kindsa sympathy. But you're also gonna do twenty-to-life. My goulash won't keep so good on the train up to Attica."

DiGenero stood.

Silverstein looked surprised. "Where you goin'?"

"Back to the hotel."

"Not too smart. Why don't you stay here?"

DiGenero pointed at his plate. "I want to be closer to medical help."

"That's gratitude."

"I need some clothes."

For the first time, Silverstein seemed genuinely concerned. "You oughta think about the fact that all your FeeBee buddies are lookin' for you. It's a long shot, but one of these days they might get lucky."

"Tomorrow morning I may want you to rent a car for me," DiGenero said.

Silverstein eyed him skeptically.

"If I do, I'll call you later tonight and tell you when to bring it to the hotel." DiGenero walked to the door.

"You want me to go someplace with you?" Silverstein's eyes betrayed him. They followed DiGenero as a mother's would a child.

"No," DiGenero said.

"Whaddya gonna do?"

"Relax, Arnie. I think maybe I'll just take a drive in the country."

CHAPTER
14

DiGenero spotted the water tower as he passed the laboring tractor trailer and crested the hill. It stood at the far north end of the valley, the widest part, where a plane could line up for its final approach to the runway with room to spare. Once a landmark for pilots who flew in open cockpits, the checkerboard paint remained an airport adornment. Like red fire engines and yellow rain slickers, an historical artifact.

He stopped at Treadwell's first traffic light. Affixed to its pole, an aircraft silhouette pointed straight ahead. He looked at his watch. Nearly eleven A.M. He was two hours late. Silverstein had delivered the rental car to the hotel a little before seven. Once out of Manhattan, the traffic had moved quickly. Past Yonkers and Scarsdale, he had headed west on the Tappan Zee Bridge. Across the Hudson, the worn foothills previewed the Catskills. DiGenero had let his speed climb, cruising close to seventy until just west of Bear Mountain Park when three state police cars overtook him. Minutes later, he spotted the fourth idling in a rest area. At the next exit, he had abandoned the pace and the route for a two-lane road.

The tractor trailer he'd passed on the hill idled behind him, filling his rearview mirror. The signal light changed. DiGenero pulled away. Treadwell had two main streets sporting new architecture at their intersection. What remained of the old was at either end, houses set close to the road. Greek revival with elegant proportions and fine touches, wood turned gracefully in front-porch pillars and dentil under the eaves.

His call had surprised Darden the night before. Despite the late hour, he had been eager to talk. The airport had just celebrated its golden anniversary, Darden told him spontaneously, fifty years since the Army Air Corps had arrived in 1942 to create a runway, parking apron, shops, and barracks. Treadwell Field. The state's National Guard took over in the fifties. After they left, the county began to pay the bills. Treadwell

158

was too small for the Federal Aviation Administration to worry about, so they contracted with Darden's employer, a California company, for maintenance, housekeeping, and air traffic control. A twice-daily flight arrived from Newark, a twenty-seat commuter disingenuously bearing a major airline's logo. Beyond that, only the gaggle of Cessnas and Pipers occupied the tarmac. General aviation, it was called. The euphemism for everything else.

At the matched set of gas stations on Treadwell's northern boundary, DiGenero accelerated, then swung into the airport. The road ran straight toward two humped-back hangers and the operations-building-turned-terminal. Beyond, the tower protruded, five stories, a glass top, and antennas. Darden would be there.

No one challenged him as he crossed the parking apron. The door to the tower was propped open. DiGenero entered the stairwell and climbed. Midway, a window, dirty glass framed in rusted casement, looked north. In the distant field, a section of steel fence stood on either side of a closed gate, all that was left of the once guarded perimeter. A memorial to fifty years of threats, real and alleged.

Darden sat in a swivel chair reading a magazine, his back to the door. He had put on weight. In the Air Force, he was barely one hundred and thirty pounds, at the end of a parachute slightly more than the radio, navigation beacon, portable generator, M-16, ammunition, poncho, flares, and other supplies packed on his back when he jumped as a forward air controller. They'd met first in 1967 at the club in Nha Trang, then again four years later in Korat. On his second tour, the last, DiGenero spent more and more time away from the squadron, bored with the new faces, their predictable conversation, and the perpetual immaturity. Darden usually claimed the same barstool wherever he became a regular and DiGenero made a point of looking for him. He found him on the air sometimes as well. Near the end, there were only a handful of Air Force forward air controllers with ARVN. They worked with the Vietnamese FACs most of the time they laid down ordnance, but he always looked for the American voices.

He knocked on the doorframe. "Bobby?"

Darden swiveled. Cherubic, he popped up, obviously glad to see DiGenero. "Hey, buddy!" They shook hands and embraced. "For a guy in deep shit, you look great!" Darden beamed. He bounced on the balls of his feet, as in the past, DiGenero remembered, never still.

"Just the second half of that sentence would've been plenty," DiGenero said. He gestured at the surroundings. "So this is your empire."

"Far as the eye can see. I'm not usually this busy, but the mail just came. I gotta read the seed catalogues before spring."

"No kidding?" DiGenero said. "Look, if you're tied up, I can go away and come back later."

"Nah. I'll risk this year's crop and squeeze you into the schedule. Sit down! Sit down!" Darden pushed DiGenero toward the couch, then sat again in his swivel chair. The tower was small but well equipped. Two banks of radios, a weather radar, direct lines to the rescue squad, fire, police, a public address amplifier, walkie-talkie and cellular phone planted in chargers, binoculars, signal lamp. The usual paraphernalia. DiGenero glanced at the status board. The morning and afternoon commuter flights were the only entries, neatly penned grease pencil notations in the arrival and departure columns, the solitary smudge on the far left where Darden changed the date.

Darden rocked back and forth rapidly, toes barely touching the floor. "So how the hell are ya?"

"Other than being wanted for murder, I'm doing great."

"Don't sweat the small stuff." Darden waved dismissively. He rocked faster, dissipating kinetic energy.

"Right." DiGenero smiled politely.

Darden examined him, concerned. "You okay? You sure?"

"I'm fine."

"You know, we gotta cabin up in the hills. Nice little place. You wanna hang around, take a little time away, I'll give you the key. It's all yours. As long as you want."

"Thanks, Bobby." DiGenero shook his head. "I don't want to get you in trouble."

"Bullshit, bullshit." Darden swiveled back and forth as he rocked, creating a new vector. "You tell me. Whatever I can do. You got that? Whatever."

DiGenero changed the subject. "You're doing okay?"

"I'm okay, I'm okay." Darden looked around as if checking his point of reference. "You may have noticed world class this ain't, but what can I say? I'm warm and dry. They pay me." His laugh was staccato, humorless. "I'm not selling cars, right?"

DiGenero nodded.

"It's okay. It's okay," Darden repeated.

"You ever think of going back?" DiGenero asked.

"Goin' back? To the FAA?" Darden looked as if he'd been struck. "Fuck 'em!"

"Absolutely," DiGenero said. Ten years after the fact, the wound was still raw.

The rocking accelerated, increasing Darden's range of motion. "I wouldn't go back if they begged me. Not if the sons of bitches got on their knees. They can go to hell, along with that fuckin' pusshead actor."

In 1981, when the strike came, Darden had six years with the Air Force and five with the FAA. When the President stood in the rose garden and dismissed eleven thousand four hundred air traffic controllers, none of them believed it. No way, they all had said. No way. Hot air from the White House. Simpleminded, just like Hollywood. Darden had walked the picket line at LaGuardia for five months, watching the passengers come and go, hearing the aircrews offer commiseration as well as encouragement. Hang in there, they told him. The union met once a week. Not possible for FAA to hold out, the shop steward reassured. No way they'll shitcan the entire FAA work force. They can't keep things together with the paper pushers manning the scopes. They're baling wire and rubber bands. Planes are going to crash, the system's going to shut down. Congress is going to raise hell. Listen to the pilots, hear what they're saying on the talk shows. Watch the commentators, the news on TV. It can't happen. A year later, the union was dead, their jobs were gone, they were blacklisted, forever. The strike was over. So was Darden's career.

"Answer a question for me," DiGenero said.

"Sure."

"If I wanted to get into the FAA's system, the air traffic control network, how could I do it?"

Darden looked momentarily puzzled. "Whaddyamean, 'get into?' "

"For instance, I want to send commands to an aircraft. Broadcast on the air traffic control frequency and vector the airplane."

"You mean, screw around with a voice vector?" Darden asked.

"Yeah."

"You can't. Whereyabeen? You're a flyer. You know that. Whoever's on the screen—whoever's working the aircraft at the air traffic control center—is gonna hear you. The same way the pilot does. He'll just tell him to disregard."

"That's all there is to it?" DiGenero asked.

"Hell no," Darden said. "They'll go out and grab your ass. They got a constant security scan. They sweep the frequencies to make sure nobody's even thinking about coming up on the circuit. When you key your microphone, even before you speak, you put out a carrier signal. Your transmitter is already sending."

"I know," DiGenero said.

"They got scanners tuned in to pick these up. They know where their own transmitters are. So they orient the scanning antennas to cover everything else. Every other place on the compass a signal could come from. They even go after transmissions that interfere by mistake. Sometimes some jerk's pushing a lot of watts—you know, a high-powered ham radio operator or something. He'll get into a transmit mode just a few points off the FAA frequency range and spill over into the controllers. They got RDF software—computer programs that do RDF. Radio direction finding. If this guy's signal is even near FAA frequencies, the software activates the RDF as soon as anybody keys a mike. All it takes is a minute to triangulate. They find out where he is. Then, this guy's got the cops knockin' at the door. For the ones that actually try voice vectors, it's a one-time thrill. After that, the only radio they got plays the top forty in the slammer."

DiGenero nodded. "What about GCA?"

"Ground Controlled Approach? You mean TRACON?" Darden asked.

"Yeah."

"What about it?"

"Could you break into that? Let's say you've got an aircraft coming in on a Cat 3 approach. It's landing and the TRACON system is doing the whole job, bringing the plane down by itself. In the cockpit, it's no hands. Could somebody get into the system and send out the wrong signals, vector it the wrong way?"

"Same-o, same-o," Darden said. His rocking had slowed, replaced by toe tapping in four-four time. "I mean, I don't think you can get past the security software that protects the system, okay? But let's say for the sake of discussion, you got a hacker, somebody who knows computers and can do it. Let's say he gets inside. He's still gotta transmit. He's gotta get on the air with a signal. The problem's no different. It's gonna be picked up by the scanners and triangulated."

"Unless," DiGenero said.

"Unless what?"

"Unless you can find a way to transmit where they're not scanning, like from right next to the FAA transmitter."

"Gimme a break." Darden rocked faster again. "You seen our"—he paused—"their transmitter sites. I mean, the goddamn things are block houses. They're inside the airport's security. They got three fences on top of that, plus guards and alarms. Who's gonna get inside one of those to stick up another antenna. And even if its possible to get close enough —say within a few hundred feet—whose gonna put up an antenna that somebody isn't gonna see?"

DiGenero shrugged.

Darden put a toe on the floor and shoved off, twirling slowly around. "Hmmm," he said. He twirled a second time.

" 'Hmmm,' what?" DiGenero asked.

He stopped for a moment, then began to twist back and forth, one toe anchored, like a child. "I suppose if you got into the software you could transmit using the system itself."

"Whaddyamean?" DiGenero asked.

"Okay, think about this," Darden said. "Where's the controller? Any controller?"

"At TRACON. At the air traffic control center," DiGenero answered.

"Right. He's not at the antenna. Neither is the TRACON computer. It's just like the controller. The computer's someplace else. So, if you got on line somehow—mind you, this is theoretical—you could send a signal to the same antenna the computer does, the one that transmits the real McCoy. I mean, all the TRACON computer does is figure out what the plane's supposed to do and send out a shot of electrons. They go to the antenna and get transmitted to the airplane as a command to its onboard computer. In fact, if you could get into the system, you could do that from anyplace."

"Anywhere?" DiGenero asked.

"Sure. Right now, you could have controllers in Bangor working airplanes over Kennedy as long as they had the lines in place. With modern commo—radios, telephone microwave relays, fiber optics—it doesn't matter where the TRACON facility is. You can send the radar signals from the airport's ILS—its instrument landing system—to a controller on the other side of the country. The controller gets them on the screen. He sends his instructions back the same way. So could TRACON."

"And so could a hacker who broke into the system," DiGenero said. Darden nodded.

"So if a bad guy could get through the system's security and plugged into the TRACON computer, he could control an airplane from anywhere in the country," DiGenero confirmed.

Darden held up a cautionary finger. "But not to crash."

"Why not?"

Darden flew one hand like an airplane nosing into a dive. "I think somebody's gonna notice, don't you? Besides, getting into the system and sending the wrong signal is only one problem. There's others."

"Such as?" DiGenero asked.

"Such as TRACON is still sending the right signal. Even if you're on a Cat 3 approach—with TRACON flying the plane—you still got the pilot and the controller. They're going to notice some awful funny things. For instance, let's say the bad guy gives the command, 'Descend from 5,000 to 4,000.' The plane does it. Radar sees the blip descend and tells the TRACON computer about it. TRACON's computer says, 'What the shit?' It sends a message to the aircraft autopilot, 'Climb from 4,000 to 5,000.' " Darden resumed flying his hand, porpoising this time. "You know what I mean?"

DiGenero nodded. "So it cancels out."

"Right." Darden was rocking fast again. "Unless."

"Unless what?" This time it was DiGenero's turn to ask.

"Unless you fooled TRACON."

"But you just said . . ." DiGenero began to repeat Darden's argument.

"I know, I know," Darden interrupted. "But TRACON is a closed system. The radars, the computer, the commo. They're all integrated. It watches itself. Nobody else watches it. There's all kinds of fail-safe, but the fact is the system's a closed loop. So, if somehow you could get its computer to think that the airplane was doing the right thing, theoretically, just theoretically, you might be able to screw things up."

"How?" DiGenero asked.

"For example, when TRACON sends a signal—say, tells an aircraft to turn to *xyz* heading and descend to such-and-such altitude—the autopilot on the airplane executes. Then, it transmits a radio signal back to TRACON that says, electronically speaking, 'I did it.' If that signal doesn't come back, TRACON checks with its own radar. If the TRACON radar says, 'It's okay, the plane did what it was supposed to,' everything's hunky-dory. The approach continues. If it doesn't, the computer says, 'Oh-oh.' Then, the computer either runs through a quick diagnostic program—a self-checkup—and discovers the problem, or it rings the alarm and human beings take over. But, let's say the bad guy can introduce his signal just ahead of TRACON's. Figuring out when you had to do that wouldn't be too tough. Each runway's got a standard approach pattern. You descend to a certain level, hold and fly, turn and descend to a new altitude, hold and fly. It's all setpiece, all the way to the ground." Darden was rocking faster, accelerating with his own logic. "Let's say you could get into the system with a program that knew when TRACON was going to transmit each 'turn and descend' command. And let's say the bad guy could transmit his instructions a microsecond before TRACON sent the real instructions along with a bogus response that makes TRACON's computer think the airplane had just executed what TRACON had sent. If you did that just before each real TRACON command went out, you just might be able to fox the computer."

"But what about the radars that are tracking the aircraft?" DiGenero asked. "They've got a blip that's going off the flight path no matter what the TRACON computer thinks, right?"

Darden smiled. "Nope. At least not until it's too late."

"I don't get it," DiGenero said.

Darden explained. "TRACON's radars are going to work on tolerances. I mean, a hundred feet or so either way. That means, as long as the airplane has got enough altitude, even if it's coming in shallow, below glide slope, the radar isn't going to blow the whistle. TRACON's computer is going to get a message from the radar that says, 'This guy's a little low.' But as long as the autopilot on the aircraft has acknowledged that it has complied with TRACON's command, the computer is going to tell the radar, 'Okay, let it ride.' Why? Because the radar is programmed to let the plane fly above and below the standard glide slope. Makes sense, huh? After all, what if it's bumpin' around up there? Rough air. You got 747s that's gonna move a hundred feet or so one way or the other on a bad night. You can't have the radar ringing the bell every time one of these mothers bounces, right?"

"Right," DiGenero said.

"So, this bad guy brings a plane in, foolin' the autopilot onboard and foolin' TRACON until the last minute. Then, maybe a mile out—who knows, even a couple miles—he sends the command to land."

"Wait a minute," DiGenero broke in. "At that point the radar's gotta get wise."

"Absolutely," Darden said. "But so what? By the time the radar tells the TRACON computer, 'Holy shit, you got a problem on your hands,' there's only sixty seconds to play with, maybe ninety at the outside. By the time things get figured out, the autopilot has started to flare the aircraft, the mother is sinking like a stone, the pilot's thinking about which one of the twenty flight attendants he wants to boff that night, and smacko! They're landing in somebody's backyard."

"So, it can be done," DiGenero said.

Darden shrugged. "Theoretically." He spun around in the chair slowly, a victory lap, obviously pleased with himself. "But not in real life."

DiGenero rolled his eyes. "Whaddyamean?"

It's brilliant, but . . ." Darden paused.

"But what?"

"How you going to get the airplane to cooperate?"

"Who?" DiGenero asked. "The pilot?"

"No, no." Darden shook his head. "He's pickin' his teeth and scratchin' his ass the whole way down no matter what."

"Your respect for the profession remains intact, I see," DiGenero said.

"I mean the aircraft's onboard software, the ILS and autopilot."

"Aah, I see," DiGenero said. "It's still sending out its own signals."

"You do have a future, DiGenero, but only if you study very, very hard," Darden said solicitously.

"So what you're telling me is that the bad guy—theoretically—could put commands into the TRACON system that told the plane what to do and fooled the TRACON computer into believing that the aircraft had complied with the right instruction. But the plane's onboard computer would still be sending its own signal back to TRACON acknowledging what it had done."

"Right. That's a problem. A real problem," Darden said.

DiGenero sat back on the couch. "Couldn't pull it off, huh?"

"Nope." Darden was rocking again. He stopped moving for a moment and stared at the ceiling. "Unless."

"Now what?" DiGenero watched the oddly immobile figure.

"Unless you could get to the software on the airplane," Darden said. "Unless you could program the onboard computer to send back the compliance message you wanted—the signal that goes to TRACON telling it the command has been executed. In that case there would only be one signal coming back to TRACON's computer. It would still be bogus, but it would be coming from the aircraft itself."

"You're telling me somebody would have to fix the aircraft's computer to accept one instruction, but reply that it had executed another. To send back a message that it had complied with whatever the real TRACON instruction was."

"Exactly," Darden said.

"Sounds complicated," DiGenero said."

"Nah. All it would take is fiddling—essentially telling the airplane's onboard computer to act on the first message, then disregard the real one, although saying it hadn't."

"Hard to do?"

Darden shook his head. "For a good hacker, piece of cake."

DiGenero stood. To the northwest, the clouds had broken. A shaft of sunlight moved apace with the opening across the far hills.

"Now let me ask you a question," Darden said.

"Sure."

"BA 121, right?"

DiGenero looked at Darden. "You don't want me to tell you," he said.

"Not necessary." Darden began rocking again and smiled. "I may be little but I'm smart."

CHAPTER
15

DUNE ROAD WAS dangerous when storms rose. Barely two lanes, it rolled unevenly, fifteen miles of blacktop on the sliver of sand separating the Atlantic from the quiet bays of Long Island's south shore. On either shoulder, the barrier dunes were at best a few hundred yards wide. At high tide, a modest southwester drove breakers across their narrower waists. In a hurricane, the sea breached even man-made rock and concrete defenses with the ease of a bully backhanding a child.

On the road's leeward, less-sought-after side, a few old cottages looked north, fronting Moriches and Shinnecock Bays. A half century before, they had been the first built for the summer people, boxes on stilts with only the rudiments scattered among the local fishermen's shacks. Weathered and lacking right angles, the survivors still sheltered behind natural berms, albeit with sagging rooflines and patchwork facades, clear evidence of the shifting sands and the inevitable price of the storms.

Opposite, facing south, the new houses confronted the ocean. From close by the deadend at Shinnecock Inlet, they crowded together, the creations of eager developers who encouraged the maximum investment on the minimum plot. Ostentatiously oversized replicas of turn-of-the-century gingerbread abutted stressed concrete engineering: Victorians, modern Cape Cods, and contemporaries with cantilevered decks and two-story glass, side-by-side. Perched on deep-driven pilings, they stretched from Tiana to Westhampton Beach where the ersatz skyline gradually fell away. The last house in the file, opposite Remsenburg, was empty, abandoned by the owners. Shored and braced, it waited for the inevitable. Beneath, the sea had eaten away, transporting the sand west with wave action. From each according to his vulnerability. A redistribution of wealth according to natural law.

In the backseat, Jilian felt the wind's buffeting as the limousine mounted the bridge. They crossed the narrow span between the town and beach. She could see the bay. Distant whitecaps raced toward her. In the channel below, the seawalls narrowed the competition. The waves converged, an angry chop subsiding finally against the piers, a finish line of gray foam.

She settled back. The driver slowed, careful to avoid bottoming the outsized creation where the bridge's ramp again met road level. Parked close to the tracks, the limousine had been waiting when she arrived. In her few short steps from the train to its door, the station and the bordering trees had broken the gusts, although their strength still surprised her. A steady rain had discolored the city, the product of a front arriving from the northwest to merge with a late-season disturbance skirting the coast. Despite its grime and tint, the coach window had afforded a glimpse of Long Island's bays, albeit too briefly to tell much of the storm. The weather was moving due east. Through the windshield, she could see the rollers slashing the shore, a flanking rather than frontal attack.

A sign pointed left. Westhampton Beach. The limousine obeyed. They turned, running before the wind. Scarlese had called early that morning, a brief, businesslike conversation. He told her to come alone after midday. She had phoned for a rental car, then canceled the reservation. The train was better. Time to concentrate, to practice her lines.

The limousine slowed. On the ocean side, a fortress of stuccoed walls rose between vacant lots. An automatic gate opened inward revealing a stark white facade trimmed with tile, a spare Mediterranean modern. They waited. Two men emerged. Leather coats and blue jeans. Each stepped into the road and looked both ways. Satisfied, one beckoned. The driver pulled ahead and parked as the gate closed behind them.

One of the pair who had scouted the road opened the rear door. She got out.

"This way." He motioned unceremoniously and walked toward the house. Jilian followed. Security cameras and floodlights stared down from the second-story heights. The surf pounded, a steady powerful beat. She had rehearsed like a schoolgirl preparing for the class play. But what if the words failed to come? She leaned into the wind. A gust suddenly struck, for a moment unsteadying.

The door opened at her approach. The man didn't follow. The first-floor foyer was skylit and spacious, if spare, a two-story atrium with a marble floor and stairs that seemed to float upward. A maid greeted her, an attractive Latina with unquestioning eyes. She took Jilian's coat and led her to the second level, then disappeared.

Jilian stood at the top of the stairs. The room was empty, save for a large oriental carpet, two director's chairs, and the ocean. A painting in motion, the Atlantic stretched from end to end. The horizon undulated, previewing the middle distance and the foreground, building rollers that crested before crashing soundlessly a story below. The effect was mesmerizing, as if the sea somehow had become a possession, captured and silenced behind wall-to-wall glass.

"Striking, wouldn't you say?"

Jilian started. The voice she'd heard on the telephone sounded younger in person. Scarlese stood in the shadows behind her. She wondered for an instant who else was there. "Extraordinary view. I've never seen anything quite like it," she said.

"I'm sure you haven't." He walked past her to the window. His smile was preformed. He dressed casually. Corduroys, button-down shirt, sweater, loafers. "I built it. My own design." He looked out at the ocean. "I wanted to capture space in space, like the concept of a cathedral. Something that inspires awe. In this case, without the divine connotations." He gestured toward the vaulted ceiling. "As you'll note, I spared the seraphim and cherubim."

Jilian looked up. "There is room for an archangel or two if you change your mind," she said.

He stood, silhouetted against the glass. The ocean surrounded him. "When it was finished, I bought the houses on either side and tore them down. To ensure nothing intruded." With the backlighting, it was hard to make out Scarlese's expression, although no illumination was needed to discern his self-satisfaction. "The room has never been furnished. It never will be. Nothing could do it justice."

The maid appeared.

"Something to drink?" he asked.

"Sparkling water," Jilian answered.

"That's right. You said this was business, didn't you?" He nodded and the maid retreated.

"You studied architecture?" she asked.

"Architecture? No. What you see is an avocation. Combined, of course, with pure talent."

"A man of parts," she said.

"An infinite variety."

The maid returned, this time carrying a tray. Scarlese directed her to Jilian. She offered a glass, then approached him with deference. He dismissed her with a nod.

"I must admit, you're not what what I anticipated," Jilian said.

"You expected what? A shirt open to the naval and gold chains?"

"A bit out of season, don't you think? Actually, I wasn't sure."

"You're not exactly what I had in mind either," he said.

Scarlese was trim, in condition. She guessed he was in his mid-thirties, although the obvious care with his appearance suggested the affectations of an older man intent on preserving his youth.

"I can see there was a good deal Sallie didn't tell me about you," Jilian said.

"Sallie? I imagine so." Scarlese paused, as if the name had prompted a recollection. "Poor Sallie. Loyal, trustworthy, brave, industrious, kind to children and small animals. And stupid to a fault."

"I thought he was one of your principal lieutenants," Jilian said.

"Who told you that?" he asked.

"He did."

"Is that so?" Scarlese laughed. "I suppose he was. In my position, some people you chose, others you inherit. Sallie was part of the legacy." He turned toward the window. "Sallie was fond of you," he observed.

" 'Fond?' Somehow, I don't think that's how he would have put it."

"Don't you?" He glanced over his shoulder at her. The contradiction seemed to challenge him. He mimicked Jilian. "Tell me, how do you think he would have *put it?*"

She ignored the sarcasm. "I don't know. You knew him a great deal better than I. It's just that 'fond' isn't a word I associate with his vocabulary."

His smile was rock hard. "You're right. Actually, I was trying to be polite. The truth is, the only thing Sallie ever said was that you were a good lay."

She recognized Scarlese's scrutiny. He watched, gauging her reaction. She approached the window. Six feet, a width of glass, separated them. Jilian looked down. The house hung on the last line of dunes. Just beyond, the beach fell away steeply. One after another, the breakers attacked the slope, then subsided. One of the leather jackets passed beneath the window. Patrolling, he plodded awkwardly through the sand, collar up against the cold.

Scarlese's tone softened. "It's a shame we haven't met earlier. Under pleasanter circumstances."

"Isn't it." Jilian spoke noncommittally. "I'm sure you're a busy man."

"As a rule I don't socialize with my subordinates," he said.

"I see."

"For obvious reasons."

"For obvious reasons," she repeated politely.

Scarlese circled behind her. "Had I known about you, of course, there would have been ample room for an exception."

"I'm flattered."

"But that does raise a question. These unfortunate circumstances have finally brought us together and as I said, Sallie did mention your name. But what *do* I know about you?"

"What you should, I trust."

" 'What I should, you trust'? Oh my. That has a nineteenth-century ring. But you are British, aren't you?"

"Irish," Jilian said quietly.

"Or in our modern age of ego *über alles,* do I hear the voice of sweet modesty?"

"Not at all," she said. She turned slowly, following his progress.

"Oh? Then why such mystery?"

"Because those are my orders."

Scarlese continued to amble slowly, keeping his distance. "Orders?"

"That's right," she answered.

"And who gives you orders?"

"The command," Jilian said.

Across the room, Scarlese stopped. He stood, half in shadow, where he had first spoken to her when she entered the room. Where they had begun. "The what?" He asked the question like someone who already knew its answer.

"To put it precisely, the general command of the Provisional Irish Republican Army."

The silence lasted several moments. "I'm afraid I don't know what you're talking about."

"I think you do," she said quietly.

Scarlese stepped into the light. They were the same height. He raised his chin as if seeking an advantage. "Look, sweetheart . . . ,"

Jilian interrupted. "Let's not play games. We have a problem on our hands. Our relationship with you supports our most important operation. At the moment, it's in jeopardy. That warrants some discussion and, I daresay, some decisions. We can fence about who I am all day, but I'd rather not waste time. Yours. Or mine. My purpose here is to make certain nothing"—she paused—"nothing further, that is, goes awry."

"Fascinating," Scarlese said. He regarded her impersonally. "Tell me what happened to Sallie."

Jilian recounted her meetings with DiGenero, their last dinner, the drive to Ward's Island, and the preliminaries with accuracy before describing his surprise. Ferringa's pair had frisked him, but DiGenero had hidden a pistol. In the backseat, she couldn't tell where. The two in front died first, then Sallie, who wasn't carrying a gun. DiGenero had forced her to drive to Ferringa's apartment in New Jersey, then disappeared. She had made her way home and called, leaving the message for Scarlese.

He listened without comment. He began to stroll again, putting more room between them before he spoke. "Why didn't DiGenero kill you?"

"Why? I'm not certain. At the restaurant, they bundled me into the car, too. I didn't say anything on the way. I can only assume he wasn't sure if I was involved."

"You didn't try to get away."

"When?" she asked.

"After the shooting," he clarified.

"That's right," Jilian said.

"Why not?"

"On Ward's Island? You're not serious."

"But I am," he said.

Jilian looked at him incredulously. "What would you have had me do? Drop in at the insane asylum? That would have been inconspicuous, wouldn't it?" She laughed, a short humorless burst.

"How did the newspapers find out?"

"Find out what?" Jilian asked uncertainly.

"About DiGenero. How did they make the connection with Ferringa?"

"I don't know," she said.

"Guess."

Jilian shrugged. "I shouldn't think it would be too hard. Not for a reporter with a source in the FBI. All one needs to do is put two and two together."

"What 'two and two'?"

"The bombing in Salt Lake City and Sallie's death. Hardly unrelated phenomena for the cognoscenti who follow your family's affairs. Then a telephone call to the Bureau. That's all."

"That simple," he said.

"You asked me to guess, didn't you? The point is, I don't know."

Centered in the room, the director's chairs were paired at an angle. Scarlese walked toward them. He sat without inviting Jilian to join him. "Now guess at something else for me. How did DiGenero find you to begin with?"

"No need for guessing on that. It's obvious."

"Oh?" Scarlese steepled his fingers.

"He knew where Sallie and I met," she said.

Scarlese raised his eyebrows. "He knew?"

"Of course."

"How extraordinary. Out of all the places in New York. All the people. All the possibilities." He smiled briefly. "All the pieces of ass that

Sallie laid. DiGenero happened to know the right bar, walk in at the right time, and strike up the right conversation."

"Are you always this charming?"

"Occasionally even more so. Answer the question."

"Because of you," Jilian said coldly.

"What are you talking about?"

She walked slowly along the windows. Scarlese's eyes followed her. "DiGenero knows," she said.

"Knows what?"

"About Vito Rocchi."

"What about Rocchi?" The question came back too quickly, like the sound of stumbling, the odd rhythm of someone momentarily off stride.

"He also knows about Rocchi's trips," Jilian said.

"Where?"

She stopped abruptly and turned, meeting Scarlese's gaze. "For Christ's sake, let's drop the pretenses, shall we? Where do you think? To Ireland and to Salt Lake City. Sending Rocchi to kill DiGenero's wife was a mistake. A stupid mistake."

Scarlese's color rose. "Don't push your luck."

"My job is to ensure we don't have another."

"*Your* job? Who in the fuck are you?"

Jilian spoke quietly, with deliberate self-control. "I want to be perfectly clear. We need to fix things. Fast. The facts are these. Since the crash, they've been looking for us. Hard. In London and here. They know this isn't like before, ambushes in Armaugh or bombs in Whitehall. Nothing so pedestrian. We're not out to embarrass the prime minister. Or to put pressure on the poor Cabinet Office sods with the Northern Ireland account. Or even to avenge the work of the SAS and the other murdering bastards they put in our midst. This time we're out to bring them down. Right here. Before their bosom friends. In the lap of their special relationship. Where the world will see it. They don't know who or how, but it's quite clear to them this isn't a fluke. We're inside the air traffic control system and they know we can do it again." Jilian paused. "Unfortunately, your little vendetta has made us vulnerable. We can take care of that, but it means we've got to rethink things. On that, I'm instructed to tell you, the two of us will work together."

The sky was darkening. The storm's outriders had passed. The main body, its strength, had arrived. In the glass, Scarlese's reflection watched her. Jilian remembered the ride to Ward's Island, DiGenero's provocation, Ferringa's reaction: only two of them—Sallie and Scarlese—knew. She strove for a reasonable tone. "Now that Rocchi and Ferringa are gone, that leaves only you to handle our friend. I'm sure you'll agree that poses a problem."

"What problem?" Scarlese asked.

"DiGenero."

"Bullshit."

"He intends to kill you."

Scarlese snorted. "I think you've got it backward."

"You don't seem to understand. Whether he can is beside the point. He's a wild card. Unpredictable. Something we can't control. At this juncture, we can't tolerate the risk."

"In other words?" he asked.

"In other words, we can't chance having you as our only link. My orders are to take over the management of our connection."

"I see." Scarlese looked away.

Jilian spoke, conciliating. "I'm sure you can understand our position. Given what's happened, the danger that something could happen to you —and, therefore, to us—is simply too great."

"Because of DiGenero," Scarlese confirmed.

She nodded.

He motioned to the chair beside him. "Please."

Jilian sat.

"I appreciate your frankness. It's refreshing. Now I hope you'll appreciate mine." Scarlese leaned forward and took her hand. His touch was warm. "You tell the 'command' "—he spoke the word contemptuously —"that a deal is a deal. Our arrangement was signed and sealed a long time ago. I handle Bellflower here. You provide the access we agreed on in Europe when the time comes. No amendments, addenda, revisions, footnotes. No loopholes when I get ready to collect. No one taking over. Not you. Not anyone else. Period." She tried to withdraw her hand, but his grip tightened. "I think English is your native tongue. Do I make myself clear?"

Jilian stared without speaking.

Scarlese relinquished her hand and sat back. The aroma of his cologne lingered. "That's point one. Point two: DiGenero is something we can fix." He smiled. "Together."

"What do you mean?"

"Obvious, isn't it? He found you once. He'll find you again. Therein lies the solution."

"It's not possible," Jilian said. "We can't wait."

"Of course you can. You don't have any choice."

She shook her head. "Look. My orders are . . ."

Scarlese interrupted. "Fuck your orders! I said I'd worry about Bellflower. I don't care what you report to Dublin, or Belfast, or wherever your 'command' is. Be creative. Tell them you've worked things out. Tell them I stood up and saluted. Tell them whatever you want. Even the truth. That we're going to cooperate." He paused. "We are, aren't we?"

Jilian didn't reply.

"Aren't we?" Scarlese repeated.

"It would appear so."

"Good." He looked at his watch. "I'm afraid you'll have to excuse me." Scarlese rose. "I hate to leave such a beautiful woman, but I've a dinner engagement."

Jilian stood. Sheets of rain suddenly rattled against the glass, one after another. The water ran down, obscuring their images.

"The car will take you back to the city," Scarlese said.

"I can take the train."

"I wouldn't think of it on a night like this." He clapped once. The Latina appeared. "The maid will show you out." Jilian descended to the foyer. Its brightness was gone. Scarlese's voice followed behind her. "I'll be in touch."

She put on her coat while the maid opened the door and peered out. Jilian heard a car start, then tires on gravel. The limousine waited. The maid handed her an umbrella and bowed as she stepped outside. The door closed quickly behind her. In the limousine's headlights, the rain came in sheets, flashing planes of horizonal and diagonal motion. Jilian stood for a moment under the portico, then leaned the umbrella against the wall, and stepped into the rain. There was no point. Captured by Scarlese's walls, the storm swirled in all directions.

The first-floor office was small and windowless. Scarlese watched the security camera's monitor as he dialed. On the television screen, the limousine's taillights receded into the darkness. He waited.

The phone rang four times, then clicked, the sound of the switch activating an answering machine. Scarlese cursed.

The recording began. "Hello. I'm not available right now, but if you'll leave your name, number, and message I'll call back as soon as I can. You can begin at the sound of the tone." The tape scratched and hummed followed by a peremptory beep.

Scarlese spoke without identifying himself. "I had a visitor this afternoon. I want you to . . ."

A switch clicked again. The answering machine snapped off, followed by the same voice, this time in person. "I'm here. I just walked in."

"Good," Scarlese said. He began again. "As I was saying to your goddamn machine, I had a visitor this afternoon."

"Oh?"

"The one with Sallie," Scarlese elaborated.

There was a pause. "The other night?"

"That's right."

"What does she know?"

Scarlese ignored the question. "I want you to find out about her."

"Like what?"

"Like everything."

"That's not easy."

"Easy or hard is not an issue," Scarlese said. "She says she's one of you and that she's been ordered to take over."

"I see."

Scarlese spoke. "I want an answer. Now. Is she or isn't she?"

"Alright. What do you need to know?"

"Very simple," Scarlese said. "Who is Jilian McCray?"

C H A P T E R
16

THE MASSIVE DOORS gaped open. Silverstein stood inside, dripping. The rain had marbled his carcoat. Kennedy's Hanger Four was cavernous, but the skeleton filled it, stretching the length and height. It was like a child's toy, a three-dimensional lattice. Aluminum tubes mounted on casters with brackets that allowed its bones to be moved and manipulated. The tubing was stenciled at regular intervals—numbers from nose to tail, letters from belly to crown. Two coordinates identified any point on the framework. An alpha-numeric guide to creation.

The epidermis and organs surrounded the incomplete body. They lay on the floor or rested on open shelves, catalogued with identical stick-on labels and depending on their type, one of a rainbow of colors. Even the empty squares and bins were carefully marked, reminders that like an anthropologist's discovery of ancient remains, the investigators' puzzle included parts that would never be found.

Silverstein walked tentatively toward the reconstruction, awed by its size. Work had started with the largest pieces. Suspended under the hanger's fluorescent lights, the 747's vertical stabilizer hung down. The crash had torn off the rudder, leaving the tail wounded, a jagged L-shape. Not quite halfway to the nose, a framework of tubing cradled what remained of the fuselage. The charred belly curved like a carcass with ribs exposed. The thin aluminum spars held it gently, as if fragility demanded. Farther forward, less obvious components were spaced randomly, high and low. Destruction and preservation knew no logical pattern. Here, an unblemished panel or a cargo door in near perfect condition. There, seemingly unrecognizable metal shards, tagged and fitted nonetheless into their proper place.

The security guard sat at the rear of the hanger. A rent-a-cop. The workspace was arranged behind him, two rows of six-drawer file cabinets, back to back, flanked by government-issue conference tables, desks, a collection of mismatched chairs and a tangle of wires connecting to telephones and desktop computers.

Silverstein flashed his badge. "NYPD Special Investigations. I gotta look at the files."

"Can't you do that shit durin' the day? We open from nine to five."

"That's why I'm special, chief. I work five to nine."

The guard frowned. "Lemme see the ID one more time."

Silverstein flipped open his shield.

The guard made a pretense of examining it from five feet away, then straightened laboriously. He opened a ledger. Silverstein scrawled a name, adding a fictitious police serial number.

"He'p yourself." The guard gestured.

Silverstein walked to the filing cabinets. He squatted, reading the entries on the drawers. An impenetrable code. Flt Cert Form 299. Eng Maint-Periodic. Throughflights Inspec. Airframe Inspec/Repair. QC Checkouts. He was supposed to look for the flight logs. The records would be there, somewhere, DiGenero said. Where the aircraft had been, when, and how often. The investigators assembled the operating and maintenance files as their starting point, DiGenero had explained. They would sift through them, reconstructing the airplane's behavior—not just the travels and turnarounds, but the incidents, breakdowns, unscheduled maintenance, even the operating quirks and foibles. They reviewed the pilots' write-ups and the mechanics' corrective actions. It was methodical and took months, and it was only part of the story, one investigation among many that examined the pilots' past, the air traffic controller's performance, the safety of the airline itself. No one ever said so, but it was both the least and the most they could do. For safety's sake. And as requiem.

Silverstein opened the first file cabinet and browsed. Engine records. Inspections, tests, malfunctions, scheduled parts changes. He closed the bottom drawer and proceeded down the line. The next held airframes. Structural Integrity. Flight Controls. Landing Gear. He moved on. Avionics. Communications. Navigation. Autopilot. The order was clearer now. Maintenance came first. He walked to the other side and began with the second row of cabinets. Aircraft Op Rec. He pulled the top drawer wide open. He held up the first folder and smiled. "Operational Records-1988." Right church, right pew.

He took out a pad and wrote. The 747 was five years old, delivered by Boeing in June 1988 and assigned to London base. He skipped forward. The folders for 1989 through 1992 held the flight logs, recording flight numbers, times, takeoffs and landings, flying hours, and destinations. Silverstein opened the file for 1992, copying the acronyms. LHR/BAH/

BOM. BOM/ATH/LHR. LHR/AUH/DEL. DEL/DHA/LHR. London's Heathrow Airport to somewhere and back, with an intermediate stop. But where? He opened another drawer, two down. "Fuel Logs." He extracted 1992. The acronyms were the same, but numbers followed each entry. Kiloliters. "LHR-100,395,988. BAH-692,733,293. BOM-588,904,143." Then, Silverstein spotted the signatures opposite the quantities. "Certified Quantity Check." A name and title, attesting to the delivery of the amount stated. "Jahlwar Singh, Bombay Fleet Service Ltd." BOM. Silverstein's finger traced to the next stop. "A. Kahlil, Bahrain Fuel Pty." BAH. London, Bahrain, Bombay. He flipped back and forth through the fuel records for 1989–1992. Except for a brief interval in 1990 when it had temporarily serviced Tokyo and Seoul, the 747 had flown the airline's Middle East routes.

He found the folders for 1993. There were two. The first held the fuel forms for January through August. All Middle East and South Asian flights. He flipped forward. The forms for September were missing. Silverstein returned to the flight records. There were only three notations on the September flight log, each a one-hour flight. LHR/LHR. Heathrow to Heathrow.

He walked back to the maintenance files. The folder for September was full, a record of work done. Engines, avionics, airframe. Each entry was stamped, rather than handwritten. "Periodic Inspect & Repair." September was down-time. A major overhaul. Silverstein returned to the flight logs.

The second folder for 1993 was thin. The flight log began with another stamped entry, recorded in early October. "Returned To Service." Silverstein didn't need to cross-reference the acronyms that followed. LHR/BOS/LHR. LHR/JFK/LHR. Heathrow, Boston, Heathrow. Heathrow, Kennedy, Heathrow. He noted the dates on his pad. Since its overhaul, the 747 had flown only the Atlantic routes, overnighting in both Boston and New York.

Outside the rain was still falling. Silverstein double-timed to the car and slipped into the driver's seat. The engine ground to a start. He backed up and put the car in gear.

At the end of the row of hangers, Silverstein turned onto the tarmac and sped up. Ahead, yellow stripes led across the taxiway to Kennedy's perimeter fence. DiGenero was right about the paperwork. The files had narrowed the possibilities. In the month before its transatlantic flights began, BA 121 had been fully overhauled. All systems repaired and inspected. If anyone screwed around with the plane, it had to have been since October. And if it was done here, it could only have been done in two places. Boston. Or New York.

CHAPTER
17

THE WING DIPPED as the 727 straightened its line, correcting course on final approach. They bumped through the overcast. DiGenero looked out. The streets were gray, off-color. New York's rain was Boston's snow, blowing at an angle and sticking. The intricacies of the outer harbor slid beneath them, old docks and wharfs, tumbled-down sheds, alleyways leading to sidestreets that fed into East Boston's grid. Like LaGuardia, Logan Airport hung on the edge of the water. Zebra-striped land, its overrun, flashed below. The 727 flared and hit hard. Six across, heads bent over morning newspapers, memos, and legal briefs snapped up. The crescendo of the engines' reverse thrust died away, replaced by audible mutterings about ham hands and truck driver's landings.

Foley was waiting at the gate. In double-breasted camel topcoat, crystalline white shirt, and conservative tie, he wore the armor of success. A head taller, his smile beamed above DiGenero like a small sun. "Frank, meboy! Let's go." He steered DiGenero away from the shuttle gate. Pedestrians eddied around a Boston policeman, who touched his cap and snapped open an emergency exit. They descended a stairway.

"Are you the cardinal, the mayor, or what?" DiGenero asked.

Foley hustled him downward. "Bless you for thinking well of me, my son. Just a work-a-day lawyer with a friend here and there."

"Tell me about it," DiGenero said. Born in South Boston, the Irish ghetto, Michael Foley had worked himself out and up. First, a Triple Eagle: Boston College High, Boston College, Boston College Law. Then, the FBI. The Boston Field Office was his choice and theirs. Needless to say, Foley had been a natural and when he left the FBI for private practice, what followed was natural as well. In a city of castes and classes, Foley was a conduit among them. A lawyer with connections. Or, as the Southies said as they looked north across Fort Point Channel to Boston proper, "Michael Foley had climbed the hill."

At ground level, Foley pushed open the firedoor. Another patrolman directed traffic around the black Lincoln parked at the curb. "Get in," Foley said.

They pulled away. Leaving the terminal, Foley bulled his way into the traffic, swinging onto the expressway. The snow fell steadily, large flakes disappearing into the pavement. A sign passed above them. "To City Center." The cars and trucks bore off, obeying its generic direction.

DiGenero had phoned Foley late the night before, after Silverstein had given him the details from BA 121's flight records. He'd told a half-truth: he needed background on Johnny Scarlese, and for reasons he couldn't go into on the phone, he said to Foley, he needed it now.

Foley touched DiGenero's arm. His voice sounded strained. "I kept it short last night—when you called. If we'd talked, the pain in my heart about what happened to your wife would have made me start cryin'."

If anything was true about Michael Foley, DiGenero knew, it was that he did everything—loved and hated, argued and communed, worked and played, gossiped and kept the secrets, told the truth and lied—with identical passion. They had first met sixteen years before, when Scarlese sent DiGenero to mediate a local Mafia dispute. Although Foley had worked as his inside guy in Boston for only a few weeks, their friendship had remained, undiminished.

Foley listened to DiGenero's recitation of events since the bombing. Finally, as he finished, they merged into a thoroughfare. Congress Street. The snow temporized. A route sign passed. Dorchester.

"We're going to South Boston?" DiGenero asked.

"And why not? After all, it's guineas not the Irishmen that want to kill ya." Foley smiled. "Besides, my cholesterol count's getting low. We're going to the Harborside. The lobsters come on leashes." He cleared his throat portentously. "A friend of mine's meeting us there."

The traffic had seized again. Brake lights and exhaust plumes stretched ahead on Summer Avenue. They crawled between the Federal Reserve Bank and South Station.

"Who?" DiGenero asked skeptically.

"A cop."

"Wonderful," DiGenero said.

"Relax. I told him you're alright. In trouble, and unfairly so."

"That's all there is to it, huh?"

"For Jimmy McBain it is."

"How come you're so confident?" DiGenero asked, obviously unconvinced.

"Confidence has nothin' to do with it, meboy. Jimmy and I, we grew up in Southie. Next door. He worked his way up in the Boston PD, just as I did in the Bureau. We both knew the rules then. We do now. They don't change."

"What does that mean?" DiGenero asked.

"It means what happens on the south side of the bridge"—Foley motioned with his chin—"stays on the south side of the bridge. It's Southie's business, no one else's. Do ya follow? The police are the police as long as they don't get in the way. You know what they say about South Boston?"

"What's that?"

Foley smiled broadly. " 'Southie's safe because it's so fuckin' dangerous.' "

The Lincoln inched over the Summer Street Bridge into South Boston. Foley turned left and sped up, leaving the congestion behind. The signs announced the World Trade Center and Commonwealth Pier. DiGenero saw the water. "We're here," Foley said.

The Harborside was a magnet for tourists who came for the sights. Commercial rather than quaint, it offered the intimacy of a banquet hall. They deposited their coats with a bored hatcheck girl and climbed the stairs to the main dining room, an expanse of tables. At Foley's request, the maître d' had put them by the window, a half room away from the nearest diners.

Jimmy McBain waited. He rose and shook hands without smiling. McBain had the look of an aging middleweight, worn sinewy with no fat to cover past disfigurements. A hatchwork of veins decorated a near-flattened nose.

Foley seated himself between them. His Bloody Mary was waiting. McBain was drinking a whiskey, neat. DiGenero ordered beer. A *pro forma* toast dispensed with the pleasantries.

Foley began, putting his hand on DiGenero's shoulder but addressing McBain. "It's a sign of our sad times that a man whose given his life to the cause should be treated so badly." He described DiGenero's career undercover, Scarlese's vendetta, and only briefly, Erin's murder. McBain listened in silence. He studied his glass. His expression revealed no trace of sympathy. DiGenero sensed that Foley's narrative was a reprise, a story he had already told, presumably accompanied by a preliminary discussion about what should be done for his benefit.

When Foley finished, McBain looked up. "What can I do for you?"

"Some background," DiGenero said.

There was no reply to encourage or dissuade.

DiGenero continued. "Scarlese and the IRA. Johnny Scarlese."

"Yeah," McBain said.

"Does a hookup between Scarlese and the IRA make any sense?"

McBain shrugged.

Foley looked uneasily from one to the other. He prompted, "Now, Jimmy, tell the man."

McBain took a deep breath. "Scarlese went to school in Medford. You know that?"

"Tufts, right?" DiGenero said.

McBain nodded. "Graduate school in international somethin' or other."

"Politics," DiGenero interjected.

"Whatever. We kept an eye on him. We had nothing to go on—he was clean then, just a kid—but the son of a Mafia don deserved some attention, so we gave him loose surveillance. Not fancy. Just enough to know his patterns. We didn't expect anything funny, except maybe a drop-in from time to time by the Pasquales. Just keeping an eye. For the sake of old times."

"Dino Pasquale, right?" DiGenero asked. He recalled the face. Round, bald, and permanently penetrated with a cigar.

Foley broke in. "You remember Dino. The old don of the North End. He died two years ago. He was the one who called Scarlese for help when you came to arrange the sitdown with the Amatuccis from Providence back in 1976. Or was it 1977?"

"It was 1977," DiGenero answered. He looked at McBain. "And?"

"Johnny Junior didn't have anything to do with Pasquale," McBain said. "I mean Pasquale got him a broad now and again. But other than that, he spent his first year with the lefties on campus. The pro-Nicaragua, aid the Sandinistas, free Guatamala, stop the war in El Salvador crowd. Then—I think it was his second year—he changed flavors. The liberation theologians were active at BC—Boston College—and he hung around with them. Teach-ins, lectures, marches, that sort of thing. That fell off, too, after a while. Finally, in his third year, he switched again. This time, to Noraid."

"Noraid?" DiGenero asked.

Foley spoke. "The Irish Northern Aid Committee. The Provisional IRA's front. Their committee for fundraising, gunrunning, publicity in the States." He raised his glass. "Up the Irish." McBain did the same.

DiGenero lifted his beer perfunctorily. "Why?" he asked.

"Why what?" McBain stared at him.

"Why should Scarlese get involved with them?"

"Why any of them?" McBain looked away. He fell silent.

"Any speculation?" DiGenero asked.

"Not really. I had the PD intelligence unit check on him once or twice with their sources," McBain said.

"And?"

"Each time Johnny moved on, he left on good terms. He still wrote checks to keep the Sandinistas in rice and beans, gave donations to the flaming fathers who preached the word of holy mother Marx, subscribed to their magazines. Even screwed a few of their stringy-haired broads. It was like he was making the rounds, establishing connections. Other than that, who knows?" He yawned. "Go figure."

"And Noraid?" DiGenero asked.

McBain finished his whiskey and looked up. "What about it?"

"What about his connection with them?" DiGenero persisted.

McBain glanced at Foley in obvious ill-humor. He waved the glass over his head. In the distance, a waiter began to walk toward the table. The maître d' stopped him. The waiter diverted course to the bar and picked up a bottle. McBain looked at DiGenero with a palpable disinterest. "What was the question?"

"The reason for Scarlese's lash-up with Noraid," DiGenero repeated.

"'Bout the same."

The waiter arrived and filled McBain's glass. Foley ordered himself another Bloody Mary and a beer for DiGenero and asked for the menus. As the waiter departed, he cleared his throat genteelly. "I seem to recall you said Johnny had quite an interest in the Irish cause," Foley reminded.

"Did I?" McBain stared at the harbor. At the end of the Fish Pier, a trawler maneuvered, avoiding the others already moored. Angled half into its slip, the boat backed and pivoted, struggling with the opposing wind and current.

Foley patted McBain's back gently. "Give the lad a hand, Jimmy."

McBain's gaze remained fixed on the harbor. "It's different, Mike. I told you this morning. There's some things we don't speak of. You know that."

Foley nodded. He spoke, conciliating. "That's a fact, but we're not dealing with a simple situation, are we? The man's wife—a good man's wife—was killed in cold blood and he's getting no justice. Not from those he works for who owe him. Not from his own kind. We know what that's like, don't we? Now, tell me. What's the difference between his rights and those of ours who've been wronged? I can vouch for Frank. He means us no harm and he's deserving of our help."

The maître d' approached. The waiter accompanied with their drinks. DiGenero took his beer and poured. The maître d' began a monologue, the daily specials.

Foley held up his hand, interrupting. "There's only one choice. Lobsters." Foley collected the menus, handed them over his shoulder, and gestured. The maître d' bowed at the signal. He took the waiter's elbow, promptly ushering him away.

McBain watched them depart, then looked at DiGenero. "Do you know where you are?"

"Where? South Boston," DiGenero answered.

"No." McBain shook his head. "You're in the only place on earth—outside Ulster, that is—where people care that the Brits are still trying to crush the life out of the Irish cause. Sad to say, this is all there is. In this great nation we're it. Once you cross the bridge, things matter here that matter nowhere else. And that means, other things don't. If you catch my drift."

"Such as?" DiGenero asked.

"Such as whether federal agents score against Mafia dons. Or guns get run across the Atlantic. Or banks get robbed to pay for them." McBain took a long swallow of Bushmill's. "Or British airliners fall into the fucking sea." He put down the glass. "You may be lookin' for your wife's killers, or you may not, Mr. DiGenero. If Mike chooses to say you are, that's fine. For him. But in Southie, we have our own agenda and we deal with those who can serve it. Like a Chinaman once said, we don't care whether the cat is black or white—or a guinea, or a polack, or a Jew—as long as he catches mice."

"And Johnny Scarlese?" DiGenero asked.

"On that I can't help you."

Foley patted McBain's shoulder. "Now, Jimmy."

McBain shrugged hard, dislodging Foley's hand. "Don't 'Now, Jimmy' me, Mike! This man wants something I can't give. The facts are I don't know the answer to his question. But if I did, I'll tell you straight away, no matter my pity for him, I wouldn't say. It's not a secret of mine to tell and even if it was, you should know better than to ask that I do. This isn't one of your fancy political deals with the State House or the Beacon Hill crowd, or plea bargaining to get some guinea wiseguy short time from the judge. You've been over the river too long, I think. You need to come back here and find out how it is. As for you, Mr. DiGenero, my sympathies. But I've told you all I will. I've done what I said I would for Mike here. You can take as a fact that Johnny Scarlese and the Irish cause go back a long way. That's a not-inconsiderable bit of information I'm givin' you. Beyond that, you're on your own."

McBain rose. "Thanks for the drink, Mike. But don't do this to me again."

Foley looked up, discomfited. "For goodness sake, Jimmy, stay. The lobster's comin'."

"No."

"It'll just go to waste."

McBain bent down, this time putting his hand on Foley's shoulder. "As far as I'm concerned, it won't. Not if you shove it up your ass."

McBain stumbled into a chair, kicking it sideways as he strode away. A few heads turned, watching. Foley colored, embarrassed. "I'm sorry."

"You tried," DiGenero said.

"Not hard enough, it seems. He's right, you know. I've been making deals for too long. After a while you believe that everything's negotiable. You forget that there's always some who never bargain." Foley held up his Bloody Mary and made a face. He waved. "I believe we're ready for Jimmy's Bushmill's." The waiter made a round-trip in double-time, returning with two glasses and the bottle of Irish whiskey. Foley set aside DiGenero's beer with theatrical disdain and poured two stiff drinks. He raised his glass. "Salut."

DiGenero smiled. "Erin go bragh."

They drank doubles until the lobsters arrived. They were too large for the platters and steaming. The Bushmill's had an immediate effect on DiGenero's dexterity. The lobster's claws defied him, twisting and slipping as he maneuvered his tools. Foley worked away with considerably more success, ignoring his problems. The cracking and hammering occupied several minutes before DiGenero broke the silence. Persistence finally rewarded him with a fractured claw. He chipped away, exposing its innards. "About Logan," he said.

Foley looked up, "You don't have to go already, do you? The shuttle runs every hour. We've got plenty of time."

"No. I mean, who's got a lock on the place?" DiGenero asked.

Foley licked his fingers and picked up a cocktail fork. He poked expertly, dislodging the white flesh from inside the lobster's oversized tail. "The Amatuccis did for a time. Geography mattered then and it all fit together. The North End was their territory and East Boston—Logan— was just across the harbor."

"They don't anymore?" DiGenero asked.

"No. The feds got 'em. Amatucci was too fat and happy. Labor racketeering and air freight scams did 'em in." Foley wiped the veneer of melted butter from his chin. "For every strength, there's a weakness. In Amatucci's case, it was his organization. It was too good. I defended two of his boys. A losin' fight. Once they got one guy in the freight handlers' union to roll over, he gave up the next. It was only a matter of time after that before old man Amatucci went down."

"What happened?" DiGenero asked.

"At Logan? The Somerville gang took over. Timmy O'Shea's bunch." Foley cracked a leg and examined the halves, calculating whether its tiny morsel of flesh was worth the effort. "They haven't done nearly as well as the dagos. A much smaller take"—Foley looked up—"or so I'm told. From time to time, they have their problems. They get confused about who's in charge and have to shoot each other to figure it out." He tossed a leg aside and returned to the tail. "This is not New York, you know."

"Whaddyamean?"

"I mean, your average Irishman's no Machiavelli. He couldn't organize a conspiracy of one. That's his weakness." Foley waved his fork and smiled. "But it's also his strength. Take Logan, for instance. The feds and the cops bust a scam here, or a ripoff there, but never O'Shea's whole organization. They can't because it's not there, at least not in the form our one-foot-in-front-of-the-other law enforcers are out to find. For the Irish, things are more personal, like a network. 'Distributed management,' the business-school types might say." Foley chewed the last of the tail. He leaned back and burped. "That's why, I think, the IRA came lookin' for Scarlese. By Irish standards, the Mafia's a veritable model of efficiency. If I was after a partner for the long term, that's where I'd go."

"What about the cause?" DiGenero asked.

"Northern Ireland?" He gestured with a nod toward McBain's vacant place at the table. "Well, you saw firsthand what it does to people. The hoods are no different. There's plenty of those boys who do what they can individually, to be sure, but that's different from the mob. They've kept their distance. Let's face facts, it just isn't worth it and the IRA knows that's how the likes of O'Shea feels. It's the same for others at the top. If you're tryin' to make yourself a dishonest livin', you got enough to worry about right here at home. Why in the world do you want to bring every weird lawman down on your neck? Send money and you got the IRS and the Treasury combin' through your checkstubs. Run guns and its ATF—Alcohol, Tobacco and Firearms—and Customs come to do you grief. Bust a bank to help the Provos and it's the Bureau, God bless 'em. Causes are one thing, meboy, but there's mouths to feed."

"I see what you mean," DiGenero said. He reached into his jacket pocket and extracted a sheet of paper, proffering it.

Foley wiped his hands carefully and took the sheet, unfolding it. "What's this?"

"Another favor," DiGenero said.

Foley laughed. "I'm surprised your askin'. I haven't done so well today." He read, then looked up. "These are times and dates. Of what?"

"BA 121's arrivals and departures from Boston," DiGenero said. "All of them since it began flying to and from the States a month ago."

Foley furrowed his brow. "So?"

"I need to know who had access to the airplane when it was on the ground at Logan."

"Access? You mean maintenance crews, cleaners, that sort of thing?" Foley asked.

"Yes."

"I suppose that's easy enough. A look at the work schedules should . . . ," Foley began, thinking out loud.

DiGenero interrupted. "It's more than that. I need to know if anyone with ties to the IRA had access."

Foley pursed his lips. "I see. That's tougher, isn't it?"

"And I need to know soon."

"When?" Foley asked.

"Like now. My hotel phone number is on the bottom."

Foley folded the piece of paper and put it on the table. He slumped back in the chair. "It would have been so much easier if Jimmy McBain had stayed for his lobster."

DiGenero felt a sinking sensation in his stomach. "In other words, you can't."

Foley was quiet for several moments. "Did I say that?" He pointed at the harbor. The rain had stopped. "The wind's changing. I think the afternoon may clear up for a time," he said. Foley looked at DiGenero's half-eaten lobster. "Shame on you. Children in China are starvin'."

"So will anybody else who gets one of these without a sledgehammer on the side."

"I forgot. You come from a long line of pasta eaters. Next time, after things settle down, we'll try the North End."

"About the airplane," DiGenero said.

"Timmy O'Shea—from Somerville—had a hell of a time with the taxman last year. The green-eyeshade types were skeptical that he could live on nine thousand dollars a year. By chance, the head of the IRS office here used to be one of our sterling FBI accountants. I had a talk with him. I think Timmy owes me one, as they say."

"Thanks, Mike," DiGenero said.

"Don't thank me. I haven't done anything for you." Foley raised his glass. "Yet."

CHAPTER
18

THE NEXT DAY in New York brought winter's cold.

DiGenero's hotel room looked out on Gramercy Park. From his third-floor window, he watched its morning routine. The nannies had keys. Each used the same technique, unlocking the high iron gate with one hand while maneuvering their charges into the park's private sanctum with the other. Once safely inside, the gate closed behind them, the small bundles of parkas, corduroys, caps, and mittens found liberation. They ran ahead, ricocheting from bench to curb and back again. Wrapped in greatcoats and mufflers like soldiers on the eastern front, the nannies followed, pushing blanketed strollers or carrying bags of provisions. A few circulated, keeping warm, but most stood or found seats, prepared to wait out the daily release of childhood kinetic energy.

DiGenero had dozed late, hoping the call from Foley would wake him. When none came, he had showered, shaved, and ordered room service. Breakfast and a newspaper. He read all four sections thoroughly without interest. The economy either was or wasn't recovering. A long feature story described the United Nations' failures and promise. A half-page editorial vigorously praised the value of good ideas. He randomly sampled the want ads, scanning the *S*'s. They sought systems integrators and sales representatives over sheet metal workers and stockmen, five to one. The service sector over calluses, hands down.

Shortly after two o'clock, DiGenero went out. He walked south toward 14th Street. Within a block, the wind pursued, funneling between the buildings to encourage his pace. DiGenero found the surplus store at 14th and Third, where he remembered it. The clientele had changed, but not the decor. Hand-lettered signs in English and Spanish decorated the interior. Boxes served as shelves, tops torn off and sides cut down. The contents were imported and ersatz. Designer knockoffs, cheap seconds, and bogus military issue. He bought a parka, jeans, and a sweater. Back at the hotel, his room had been made up. Breakfast's residue was gone and the newspaper folded neatly on the bedside table. DiGenero looked out the window as he changed. The park was empty save for a few old men, some with their day care, a contrast to morning. They sat on the benches, unmoving. Immobile figures under trembling boughs.

At three-thirty, DiGenero went out again. He checked at the desk. A congenial clerk confirmed there were no messages. He walked west to Fifth Avenue, then followed its Christmas decorations uptown. People rushed, emulating the season, itself hurried to arrive before its time. He paused at Rockefeller Center to watch the skaters. They circled, balancing carefully as if husbanding a limited resource. One spun and danced, a teenager in tights designed to reveal rather than warm. She moved in and out, ostensibly ignoring the spectators. A collection of boys in oversized leather jackets and high-top sneakers tested her resolve. They leaned on the rink's barrier rail, their catcalls following her counterclockwise rotation.

DiGenero found a vacant pay phone at 50th and Second Avenue and dialed another five blocks away. Across from the United Nations, Silverstein answered on the first ring. "I'm freezin'. What took you so long?"

"Where is she?" DiGenero asked.

"Waitin' in the park at the north end. Where I said." The minor vibrato in Silverstein's voice registered the cold.

DiGenero glanced around. A bicycle messenger waited behind him, already impatient for his turn. "Anybody else?" he asked.

"Nah."

"No surveillance?"

"Nope," Silverstein confirmed.

"You sure?"

"You think we got a world of people walkin' around the UN gardens when its forty fuckin' below?" Silverstein sounded peeved.

"Okay, I'll be there in ten minutes." DiGenero hung up. He had left the message to meet on Jilian's answering machine. Silverstein was unhappy with the location, but had cased the surroundings nonetheless. Too public, he said, like hanging out bare-assed on Times Square. DiGenero had the opposite view. The UN grounds were a leveler. With a single guarded entrance, they offered no easy escape for either predator or prey.

He double-timed to First Avenue and turned south. Silverstein waited at the corner of 46th Street. DiGenero crossed First and followed the edge of the UN compound to the main gate. The flags snapped, a whip's report. He entered. Silverstein would watch and warn. Necessary but insufficient protection if things went bad.

DiGenero strode purposefully toward the auditorium's entrance. Just inside, he could see tour groups forming up, high school students and a clutch of senior citizens. He proceeded toward the main doors as if accompanying the stragglers, then bore off on his own. Behind the General Assembly building, the garden stretched to the river side. It was easy to find her. Jilian walked slowly down the path ahead of him, a solitary figure between the rows of bare trees.

She turned at the sound of his footsteps. An unqualified smile accompanied her greeting.

DiGenero stopped between her and the wind. "I'm sorry you waited. I had to be sure," he said.

"Of what?" Her question had a genuine innocence.

"That you'd be alone." His answer sounded suddenly stupid.

Jilian laughed. "Who did you expect me to bring? The King's Fusiliers?"

"Are they in town?" He took her arm. They walked toward the river.

The touch on his cheek surprised him. She turned his face gently toward her. "Are you alright? The bump on the forehead, I mean."

"Nothing but an occasional seizure."

"No, I mean seriously," she said.

"I'm okay."

Her hands sunk into coat pockets. He took her arm. They moved in step. "I worried. After you left the other morning."

He laughed. "About what? That you really should have gotten off a shot?" The words came too quickly. DiGenero knew at once it was the wrong thing to say.

"You really are a wiseass, you know?" She dropped his arm.

He reclaimed hers. "I'm sorry." They continued in silence. DiGenero felt clumsy, inept. He began anew. "I'm also sorry for what I said the other morning."

"Another apology?" Sarcasm emerged from its scabbard. "Isn't this getting a little monotonous?" She stared straight ahead. A gust swirled around them, carrying the smell of the river. Jilian reached up, gathering her hair. The motion reminded him of Erin. A sense of loneliness and guilt, as if he was cheating, came over him.

"I didn't get it right then," he said.

"You didn't get what right when?"

"Why you saved my life. I've thought about what you told me. About what happened to your fiancé. I wanted to tell you that."

"Did you now? I thought you had it all figured out. As I recall, you presented quite a comprehensive analysis. What I did was in service to the cause. All part of the operation. Wasn't that it?"

DiGenero shook his head. "Everyone looks at the world through their own navel. When all this started for me twenty years ago, it was a wire act. Me, all by myself, out there, alone. I walked or I fell. That's how I saw it. That's how I thought everybody saw it. But I realize that isn't where you began." DiGenero stopped on the path and faced her. "It isn't you."

"No, it's not," she said.

"And it isn't where I am today."

Her expression seemed to soften. "Oh? And just where are you?" She repeated his words without mocking this time.

"For openers, still a free man." He smiled.

"Yes, no mean feat, that." Jilian seemed momentarily embarrassed. "Thanks to me."

He shrugged. "Don't worry about it. The newspaper stories haven't helped, but DiGenero's law of organizations still applies. Whenever two or more gather together, incompetence rises geometrically. Same for the FBI and the cops as for the wiseguys. I operate on its corollary. I'm safe unless I screw up."

They resumed their walk. A story above in the conference building, the dining room windows looked out on the garden. The help cleared the tables. A few diplomats and international civil servants finished long luncheons. None seemed interested in the solitary couple strolling beneath them.

DiGenero spoke. "Once upon a time I had a friend. A born salesman. The type who could peddle iceboxes to Eskimos."

"He must have been quite successful," she said.

DiGenero nodded. "Too successful, actually. Sometimes his wife would come home and find nothing in the house. I mean, wall-to-wall empty. When it first happened, they were just married. She called the cops. She thought it was a robbery, one of those moving-van jobs where they pull up and strip the whole place. It wasn't. Her husband was in the furniture business. He'd met a guy who wanted stuff fast. After the third or fourth time she got home to find bare walls and dust balls, she stopped fighting the problem. Why bother? Not your typical homemaker's routine, but what the hell? They always came out better in the deal. New sofas, chairs, rugs, appliances. I learned a lesson from that."

"Let me see." Jilian considered. "Don't marry a furniture salesman?"

DiGenero shook his head. "He wasn't my type."

She smiled.

"No," he said. "Don't hang onto things for their own sake."

She turned toward him. "And are there things you're holding onto? For their own sake?" she asked.

They stopped by the river. In the channel, the tide and current contended. Halfway across, on the tip of Roosevelt Island, the afternoon's premature darkness had triggered the streetlights.

"I can help you. You can help me," he said.

"Really? From your vantage point, I'd have thought we'd 'helped' each other enough recently."

"I know how they brought the airliner down."

Her stare fixed him.

DiGenero continued. "You've got part of the story, but not all. Scarlese is more than the IRA's bagman. He set up their operation and he runs it. Without him, it can't work."

Jilian eyed him skeptically. "What do you mean, 'can't'?"

"I mean, they need to get to the aircraft as well as have somebody inside the FAA. Penetrating the air traffic control system isn't enough. They have to have access to the airplanes as well."

Jilian frowned, as if considering a dubious proposition. "In other words, without going into the technical details, you're telling me Scarlese's the linchpin."

"In a word, yes."

She nodded noncommittally, then turned away. She put both hands on the rail and studied the Brooklyn shore. Even from a distance, the buildings appeared grimy, neglected. "That's very interesting, but—how shall I put it—the implication is, well, rather self-serving."

"What's 'self-serving'?" DiGenero asked.

Jilian turned back to face him. "Scarlese being at the center of things."

"I don't understand," he said.

"Come now. It's where we began, you and I. Scarlese's important. On that we agree. It's just that I need to use him and you want to kill him. That still puts us at odds, don't you think?"

"Look, you asked me the other morning whether I was willing to see another four hundred people die."

"That's right."

"I'm not," DiGenero said.

"I believe you. But I also know what you want and how badly you want it and for that reason I can't trust you. It's that simple," she said.

"No, it's not. The fact is, you don't have time to put the pieces together by yourself, and you know it. You need help."

"Do I? What makes you so sure?"

"For one thing, you're here, talking to me. Aren't you?"

"Don't jump to any conclusions. You telephoned, remember?" she said.

"Did Scarlese take the bait?" DiGenero asked. He watched, gauging her reaction.

"The bait?" Jilian feigned momentary puzzlement.

He prompted. "The story about me in the papers. Your call for a sitdown. A meeting," he explained.

She didn't reply.

DiGenero pressed. "Have you seen him?"

She paused, as if deciding whether to answer. "Yes. We met."

"And?"

Jilian stared back without speaking.

"Scarlese didn't roll over, did he?" he asked.

She folded her arms self-protectively. "Look, it's none of your affair how I . . ."

He didn't let her finish. "What did you think he was going to do? Stand up and salute because you wave an IRA membership card? He's not going to let you in the door unless you bring the key. He didn't hook up with them yesterday."

"What are you talking about?"

"I'm talking about Boston, and Noraid. Scarlese has a relationship with the IRA that goes back ten years."

Jilian's expression betrayed her surprise. "Where did you get that?"

"You didn't know?" DiGenero took note of the unintended revelation.

"That's not what we have," she said defensively.

He shrugged.

She challenged him. "I know what's in the files. It's simply not there."

DiGenero agreed. "I believe you. Odds are it isn't in the FBI's files on Scarlese either. The only place you'll find it is in the Boston Police Department's archives. And in the heads of a few cops who did the surveillance on Junior. After all, who would have cared about that kind of trivia years back? Even on a Scarlese." DiGenero's gaze met hers. "Like I said, you need help."

Jilian tugged at her collar. She turned her back to the wind, half facing away from him. "Such as?"

"Such as first making sure another BA 121 doesn't happen while you're trying to discover whoever's planted on the inside."

"That's brilliant," she said sarcastically. "And how would you propose we do that?"

"How? By finding out what other planes on the London-New York route have just finished a major inspection."

"What does that . . ."

DiGenero broke in. "BA 121 was in for a complete look-see a month before it started flying to the States. It was regularly scheduled work. Routine. Whoever reprogrammed the onboard computer did it after that inspection."

"So?"

"So they could be confident the maintenance types wouldn't be poking around, running checks that might uncover what they'd done."

"Are you suggesting the IRA has someone inside British Air?" she asked, incredulous.

He shook his head. "That's not what I'm getting at."

Jilian glanced sideways at DiGenero, obviously confused. "Then how would they know when the inspection occurred?"

"Get on the airplane and look at the aircraft forms."

"They're carried aboard?" she asked.

"Copies are," he said.

She nodded, as if acknowledging the point.

"How many BA flights come into New York each day?" he asked.

"Three," she said.

"Okay. That means more than three airplanes. With equipment rotations for inspection and maintenance, I bet five, maybe six fly the route. You want to play it safe? Find out which ones just went through a major inspection and have the pilots break them. You know, one at a time, not so there's an epidemic. Have them write up a phony problem with the ILS—the instrument landing system—or inertial navigation, or the autopilot, whatever lashes together. Then, when the plane's in the shop for troubleshooting, change the hardware. Most of the computer gear—the black boxes—are 'remove-and-replace' items. Pull out the old unit, put in a new one. Who knows how well hidden the software changes are. Maybe they'll be easy to find, maybe not. But if you pull the boxes, at least you know you've bought some time." DiGenero paused. "What do you have to lose?"

Jilian didn't reply. She seemed to be examining DiGenero in a new light.

"Look," he said quietly. "I need help. Just like you."

"I know," she said.

"All I want is one thing."

"Scarlese," she said.

"Yeah."

"That's all." The ironic smile became her.

DiGenero nodded. "That's all."

"What makes you think I could deliver him, even if I promised?"

"Nothing," he said.

"Then . . . ," she began quizzically.

DiGenero interrupted. "Delivering isn't the issue. Knowing is."

"Knowing what?"

"How to get to him. I can't do it alone either. You don't have to set him up. When this is over, I just want my chance."

"When it's over? Why should I bother? Why should you trust me?" Jilian asked.

"Because you understand."

"Do I?" The sarcasm had disappeared from her voice.

DiGenero knew she was looking at him but seeing someone else.

"You must have loved her very much," she said.

He nodded.

Jilian took a deep breath. "I need to think. You don't mind, do you?"

"No," he said.

"Where can I find you?" she asked.

DiGenero smiled. "I'm between addresses right now."

"A phone number?"

He shook his head. "I'll find you."

"When?"

"Tomorrow morning, seven A.M. Schurz Park."

"You expect an answer by then?" she asked.

"Uh huh."

"That's not much time."

"I don't have much," he said. "And neither do you."

Ian Barry read Jilian's cable from beginning to end twice before he looked up. "Let me get this straight. You want me to send this 'Immediate' precedence?"

"That's right." Jilian stood over the table. The bubble was chilled, almost cold. The building lowered the heat after six P.M. By eight, even the residual warmth was gone.

"It's nine o'clock here. That means when this arrives and all the bells and whistles go off, you're going to wake up the worthies in Belfast at two in the morning?"

"Very good. You're right again."

Barry eyed her over the top of his half-glasses. "All because of this cockamamy theory about BA 121's scheduled maintenance that you heard this afternoon?"

Jilian ignored the question. "My recollection is quite specific on our arrangement. I prepare my messages. You send them. That's all there is to it. No clearances, coordination, editing. No required MI5 chops on my work. Just transmission. Nothing more."

"Jilian, do you understand what you're doing?"

"Perfectly," she said.

Barry leaned back. He slid his glasses upward, lodging them like goggles on his forehead, and rubbed the bridge of his nose. "May I offer some advice?"

"I don't think my permission has anything to do with whether or not you're going to."

Barry showed a tight smile. "If you send this, you're putting Belfast—Stormont Castle as well as the RUC—in an untenable position."

"Come on. I'm only doing my job, Ian."

His smile disappeared. He spoke with a tired resignation. "We're *all* only doing our jobs, Jilian."

"Then let the bureaucrats in Stormont and the RUC do the same," she snapped back. "They can make up their own minds what to do with the report."

Barry's voice rose. "That's exactly the point! They can't! Transmitting this kind of thing is going to raise holy hell."

"I don't understand why . . . ," she began.

Barry cut her off. "That's right, you don't. Let me make it simple. When this message is sent, it's the same as crying 'fire' in a crowded theater. They can't ignore it. Period. For Christ's sake, if one of those 747s falls out of the sky for any reason and they haven't disseminated your report, you can bet your pension this nonsense will leak. Between the press and the opposition, not to mention the self-righteous in the government who should know better, they'll hang every minister's ass whose ever even ridden on an airplane! Don't you see? Once we put this on the wire, Stormont and the RUC will have no choice but to go to the CAA—the Civil Aviation Administration—and to BA straight away, no matter what they think of it. And CAA and BA will have no choice but to pull the aircraft." Barry sat bolt upright and slapped his hand down on the cable draft. "All on the basis of what? Some dotty FBI agent who almost got you killed once and is still out there—you're not quite sure where—wandering around, looking for blood revenge?"

Jilian barely disguised her contempt. "Correct me if I'm wrong, Ian. But in a nutshell, you seem to suggest that the message could prove an embarrassment. Is that it?"

Barry slumped back into his chair. He rubbed his eyes. "Oh, Christ. Why am I wasting my breath?"

"Good question."

He tried again. "Look. From your perspective alone, this isn't a good idea."

"Oh? Why not?"

"Let's just say this FBI agent is onto something," he began.

"Alright." She sat and folded her arms.

"What will happen when BA starts to pull the aircraft out of service?"

Jilian shrugged. "If it's done properly, Bellflower and Scarlese, the IRA—whoever—will have to regroup. If DiGenero is right, they'll have to get access to some other airplane. We'll have bought some time."

Barry shook his head. "That's the optimistic scenario. But try this one. What if you don't pull the right plane? Let's say there are several that have been in for"—he picked up the cable and read—"this 'scheduled maintenance' you mention. What if they pick one that hasn't been tampered with and the PIRAs react? What if they conclude—correctly— that we're onto them, despite all the best efforts to make it look like unanticipated repairs? What if you push the bastards to act sooner rather than later and another airplane goes down? Have you thought of that?"

Jilian shifted uncomfortably. "And what if the PIRAs don't figure it out? Honestly, Ian, we can't play every act of Hamlet all the way through tonight, can we?"

"Openminded to suggestion as usual, I see." Barry sighed.

Jilian stood. "Openmindedness has nothing to do with it. Send the message."

Barry leaned forward, his tone conciliating. "The ground's slippery, Jilian. Rocchi and Ferringa were one thing. You were making progress, a step at a time. Now you're in trouble. You're not in control. The only wise course is to stand down. Take a few days. Rethink where you are."

"I know where I am." Jilian unlatched the bubble's door.

He spoke to her back. "Take my advice. Don't push," he said. "That's when mistakes happen."

"Just send the message, Ian." Jilian went out.

Barry listened to her footsteps recede. The door to the suite opened and closed. He stared at the cable draft without reading the words. "Why I try to save you from yourself is beyond me." Barry walked to his office. He switched on the desktop copier and waited for it to warm up. He ran one copy, penning a note in the corner, "Sent this date, IB." He slipped it into Jilian's folder. Barry walked down the hall to the communications room, extracting his keys. He unlocked the door and turned on the light. The standby indicators on the high-frequency radio transceiver

A Brother to Dragons

and the secure fax glowed. Barry removed the dustcover from the machine just below them and threw its switch. The "Ready" light came on at once. He fed in Jilian's cable. With a soft hum and a small shower of confetti inside the shredder's plastic bag, the paper was gone.

19

THE TELEPHONE RANG as Tony Benedetto crossed the threshold of his office. He stopped and leaned wearily against the doorjamb. The lighted extension blinked, a beat behind the sound. He could tell from a distance that it was the general number, from the FBI switchboard, not one of the direct lines they gave out for operational calls. By definition a low priority. He glanced over his shoulder. The squad room was empty. The same light blinked, unanswered on all the extensions. At nine in the evening, the call was his to take or ignore. Nothing or something, either ending or extending his fourteen-hour day. Benedetto waited, hoping it would quit, then sighed. The habit was too deeply ingrained. He retraced his steps. Who knows? Maybe it was his fairy godmother. A rich uncle just died and left him a million dollars. Better yet, he won the lottery.

He picked up the phone. "Hello."

The voice was vaguely familiar. "I'm callin' for Special Agent Tony Benedetto. Is he around?"

"Speakin'," Benedetto said.

"Tony, it's Mike Foley. From Boston. You remember?"

The voice and image snapped into focus. Benedetto pictured Foley a long time ago. "Do I remember? Sure. Howareya?"

"Couldn't be better. What's it been since you were up here chasin' the bad guys with us?"

Benedetto lowered himself into his chair and scratched his head. "I dunno. Fifteen years? But who's counting?"

"Like yesterday. You're not exactly workin' banker's hours either. Like yesterday, too, eh?" Foley asked sympathetically.

Benedetto propped his feet up. "What can I say? I got a squad."

"Good on ya," Foley interjected, congratulating.

"You know how that goes. Den mother, bookkeeper, chief cook and bottlewasher. It all takes time. Everything goes with the job except real money." Benedetto forced a laugh.

Foley commiserated. "Things don't get any lighter the higher you climb. It's always more weight you're pullin' behind you."

Benedetto vaguely recalled Foley's early retirement. "You're not still in the Bureau, are you?" he asked.

"No. I've got my own law practice. A little criminal hustle, the usual business stuff. It's a living, but I miss the excitement."

"Yeah, right." Benedetto looked at his watch. The hour did little to kindle his interest in reminiscing. He nudged the conversation. "Well, to what do I owe the pleasure? Are ya comin' to New York? Can I set somethin' up?"

"Actually, I'm callin' for some help. For a friend of ours—someone who just mentioned your name the other day."

"Oh yeah?"

"We need to talk confidentially." Foley cleared his throat. "Can I count on you?"

Benedetto yawned. He fastened on the obvious. Foley must have a federal case coming up in New York. Not unusual to run the trap lines, to look for the angles. Who's who in the prosecutor's office. Which one to see. Who might roll on a bargain. Why not help out? One hand washes the other. Benedetto rubbed his eyes, feeling the dull fatigue return. "Consider this never happened. Who we talkin' about?"

"Frank DiGenero," Foley said.

His feet came off the desk. "What about him?"

Foley heard the edge in Benedetto's voice and hesitated. "I know this isn't exactly low profile. I don't want to put you in a bad position. Are you sure it's okay? Us having this conversation?"

Benedetto struggled to collect himself. "Yeah, sure. I'm worried sick about Frank, that's all. He's in real trouble. You know the story?"

"Frank told me."

Benedetto's mouth went dry. The fatigue was gone, replaced by a flush of perspiration. "You talked to Frank?"

"Yesterday," Foley answered.

"Where?"

"Here. In Boston. What I'm gonna tell you is privileged, attorney-client, so I'm keepin' this to the bare minimum. To protect Frank." Foley paused. "And you, of course. Whatever happens, nothing gets repeated. You got that?"

Benedetto's mind raced. Why was DiGenero in Boston? He broke into Foley's preamble. "How did Frank happen to mention my name?"

"How? He said he saw you in New York. That's all. Good thing that he did, too. If he hadn't, I wouldn't have had a clue how to get hold of him. I've been callin' his hotel all afternoon but he hasn't been in. I don't want to leave a message. It's too sensitive, if you know what I mean. But if you're willin' to do the favor, you can get to him for me."

"Yeah."

"After all, there aren't many people you can trust. You and Frank go way back. Like brothers, right? From the old days."

"Sure," Benedetto said. "What's Frank's phone number?"

Foley sounded momentarily puzzled. "You don't have it?"

Benedetto dissembled. "I got it someplace, but he's moved around. I think maybe I got the one he had last week. Give it to me again."

"The Gramercy Park Hotel." Foley repeated the number.

"Okay." Benedetto wrote it down.

Foley spoke. "Tell Frank that I checked with Timmy O'Shea from Somerville. Timmy talked with the union boys at Logan."

"Logan?" Benedetto's stomach turned over.

"Yeah. The airliner that came and went last month?" Paper rustled. Foley continued. "BA 121. Tony, you with me?"

Benedetto sat silently. Sweat beaded on his forehead.

"Tony? You there? You got this so far?" Foley asked.

"Yeah," Benedetto said.

"O'Shea said nobody with sympathies for the cause—active sympathies, this is—got near the airliner."

"The cause?" Benedetto asked perfunctorily.

Foley lowered his voice, "The IRA, man. What else in this town? Just tell Frank that whoever got into the plane didn't do it in Boston."

"Not in Boston," Benedetto repeated by rote.

"Do you think you can get this to Frank right away?"

"Yeah. No problem."

"That's great. I gotta fly to the coast first thing in the morning and I didn't want to miss him." Foley seemed relieved. "Hey, when are we gonna get together? You ever come up to Boston?"

Benedetto barely heard the question. The silence persisted awkwardly until he realized he owed Foley an answer. "No, I don't. I mean, I haven't in a long time."

"It's a great town. Tell you what. We'll plan a reunion. When Frank gets outa this mess. Whaddyasay?"

"Absolutely. We gotta get together. With Frank." Benedetto stared at the phone for several minutes after Foley said his farewell. It was DiGenero again. The star attraction. The fuckin' world at his beck and call.

Benedetto put his head in his hands. He couldn't help counting. All the years until now he'd never done it. Now it was all he could do. Like a song that stuck in your head, playing over and over again. He added up the time. Fourteen hours a day, five days a week. Eight hours on Saturday. If you were lucky on Sunday, maybe the phone didn't ring. Usually it did and there were two or three more hours after that. Seventy-hour weeks, fifty-one-week years. Twenty years to a GS-15. And the cases. How many? They blurred. Maybe he remembered how they ended more often than how they began because he could count the days in court, waiting to testify, to play the dutiful reciter of facts, the interpreter of the minutiae, first led through the paces by a prosecutor half your age, then when their turn came, attacked by defense lawyers who made five times as much as you could ever hope to take home. He could see the perps, the defendants staring back, watching the play, smirking at the "yes, sir, no sir" routine. You remembered the ones that didn't go down, rather than those who did. The ones who walked, laughing at you, taking with them the days of your life you'd spent at twenty-two dollars and fifty cents an hour, frozen in front seats on all-night surveillances, knocking on doors in buildings where rats wouldn't go, sleeping in the office because you didn't have time to go home before you had to do it all again. For twenty-two dollars and fifty cents an hour. For twenty years. In the cheap seats. Opposite the Rolexes, the limousines, and the wiseguys that walked, laughing at you, in thousand-dollar suits. Benedetto sat up slowly. He rubbed his right wrist, an old man's worrying motion. Finally, the bus was leaving. His bus. It was time to get out. To get even. To get his. And DiGenero was in the way, fucking it up. He punched one of the unlisted extensions, lifted the receiver, and dialed.

Johnny Scarlese answered on the second ring. "What is it?"

Benedetto's voice wavered, telegraphing his tension. "I gotta see you."

"Is this necessary?" The implication was obvious.

He exploded. "You bet your ass it is! I said we gotta talk!" Benedetto breathed heavily, like a man who had just exerted himself. His was the only sound that broke the silence.

Scarlese spoke, obviously irritated. "An hour, the usual place."

Benedetto hung up. He rose. This time Benedetto walked much more slowly toward the door.

The tour boat passed astern, accompanied by its own reflection. Through the brightly lit windows, Benedetto could see several couples. From a distance, they appeared to be dancing mechanically, tiny figures joined together, circling a predetermined course. He could see the others seated at tables around them. None looked out, presumably tired of peering into windows that only revealed their own images.

The deck of Scarlese's offshore cruiser rose gently, displaced by the tour boat's wake. Benedetto put his hand on the rail, steadying himself. Enclosed by the arms of the Fulton Street piers, the mooring was thoroughly protected. The East River's swell passed along the deep V-hull's sixty-foot length. The lines groaned as the wake rebounded off the concrete and steel bulkhead and returned toward the channel, a shallower encore. A nonswimmer, Benedetto hated the water. He remained planted defensively at the stern, waiting for the modest rocking to subside.

Footsteps echoed on the gangway from the pier. They came closer, making their way toward the stern. He waited. Scarlese crossed the deck without speaking. He unlocked the door to the master cabin and went inside, flipping on the lights. Benedetto followed. Scarlese continued forward, slipping through a narrow passageway and descending a short set of stairs that led toward the bow.

In the center of the main cabin, a sectional sofa half circled a coffee table made from a refurbished hatchcover, the only furnishings. Benedetto took a seat. At the front of the cabin, a step up, just behind the windshield's rakishly angled glass, the captain's station filled one corner. A display of seagoing, high-technology accoutrements clustered around the wheel. Twin throttles, a bank of engine instruments, radios with dangling microphones and telephone handsets, two radar scopes, compasses and satellite navigational gear. Otherwise, the cabin's space was barely nautical. Without the deck's occasional motion, it could have been a den in the suburbs or a place in the mountains. Wood paneling, curtains, and deep pile carpet, wall to wall.

Scarlese returned with a bottle and two glasses. Canadian Club, a leftover from the boat's last Great Lakes foray. He put them on the table and stepped to the captain's station, touching a button on its control panel. Somewhere below, a blower moaned, winding up. Benedetto felt, then smelled a cold, dank draft. It rose from the vents behind him, followed abruptly by a dry, ozone-tinged aroma and warmth.

Scarlese took off his jacket and tossed it on the sofa. He poured two whiskeys. A half glass for Benedetto, barely a finger for himself. He handed Benedetto his drink and sat. "Okay, Tony. I'm here."

Benedetto took a deep breath. "Trouble," he said.

Scarlese eyed him, waiting for elaboration.

Benedetto drank, a healthy swallow. "I got a call tonight. From Boston. A lawyer. Used to be an agent. We worked with him once, a long time ago. DiGenero was there yesterday, talkin' about the airplane."

Scarlese's jaw set at the mention of DiGenero's name.

"The guy wanted me to pass DiGenero a message. He couldn't get ahold of him. He wanted me to tell him that nobody with IRA connections was involved with the plane when it stopped in Boston." Benedetto ran his hand through his hair. "You know what that means?" he asked.

"No." Scarlese stared.

"DiGenero's got it figured out. At least a big piece of it. He knows."

"Knows what?" Scarlese asked.

"Whaddya think?" Benedetto snapped back. "He knows how the operation is put together."

"From that one question, you conclude that DiGenero has got the handle on the whole operation? Is that what you're saying?"

"Yeah! No! For Christ's sake!" Benedetto hung his head. "I don't know."

"I gather as much," Scarlese said.

Benedetto spoke to the floor. "Look, I got no problem handlin' my part—I can control what we're doing to investigate. It's my case. You know what I mean? I run it. My squad has the action. I deal with the Brits. I'm the one in charge. But if DiGenero goes to somebody else—if he starts the fuckin' ball rollin' downhill someplace else in the Bureau—I got problems." Benedetto looked up. "*We* got problems. You understand?"

Scarlese nodded. "When did you see DiGenero? Last week?" he asked.

"Last week?" Benedetto chewed on his lip, distracted. "Yeah. I saw him then." He stopped chewing suddenly and stared at Scarlese. "Why you askin'?"

Scarlese shrugged.

Benedetto's eyes shifted back and forth, scanning Scarlese's expression as if looking for the answer. "Whaddya drivin' at?"

Scarlese smiled diffidently. "Just a question."

"I told you I saw him. Right away I called you. You know that. I mean, whaddyawant? DiGenero comes to New York, I give him to you on a platter. I tell you when he came over. I tell you where he's meetin' me for breakfast. All you had to do was follow him, pick 'em up, and whack him. Jesus Christ, is it my fault Ferringa and his fuckin' clowns can't get the job done? I can't do everything!"

Scarlese leaned forward. He patted Benedetto's knee. "Why would DiGenero be asking about an airplane? You didn't tell DiGenero anything about what we're up to, did you? I mean, not even a cute little hint, here or there, just to show you were on top of things? Something that was a little too close to the bone. Huh?"

"No!" Benedetto lied. "What the fuck would I do that for?"

"You're sure?" Scarlese spoke barely above a whisper.

"What am I, stupid? At my house, I tell him nothin'! At the restaurant on 86th, I tell him nothin'!" Benedetto waved, splashing his whiskey. "What? You don't trust me?"

Scarlese sat back and raised both hands, palms up. "Did I say that?"

Benedetto was breathing hard again. "You know who talked? I'll tell you who talked! That asshole, Ferringa! Or maybe his broad. What's her name? McCray. That's who!"

"Okay, Tony. Calm down."

"Yeah." Benedetto reached for the bottle and topped up his drink. He stood and began to pace, agitated into random motion. "You know, I don't like to bring this up. It's not my style. But I'm the guy who keeps the wolves from your door." He pointed indeterminately. "Not those fuckin' Irishmen." Benedetto stopped and drank. The tremor in his right hand, a minor palsy, agitated the whiskey. "If somethin' goes to hell, I take the fall. You know that, too. The Irishmen? They go home. You? You got a billion dollars worth of lawyers. Me? I go to fuckin' jail. For a thousand years."

Scarlese watched him pace.

"Yeah." Benedetto was talking to himself. "I gotta be in control of this. If I say we got a problem with DiGenero, we got a problem. I'm the one that's running the investigation. So I'm the one that knows what's goin' right for us and what's going wrong." He turned, facing Scarlese. "You understand?"

Scarlese spoke soothingly. "Absolutely. We're partners, remember?"

Benedetto grunted an acknowledgment, listening this time.

Scarlese beckoned. "Sit down."

Benedetto returned to the couch. He drank.

"That's better," Scarlese said. He poured another inch in Benedetto's glass. "You know what a partnership is, don't you? A relationship. Share and share alike. The risks and the benefits."

"You're talkin' risks?" Benedetto asked. "I'm lookin' at risks twenty-four hours a day, seven days a week."

Scarlese glared. "What do you think the five thousand dollars a month is for?"

Benedetto continued, oblivious to Scarlese's stare. He tapped his chest with his finger, a hollow drumming sound. "Me. I'm the guy with the risks."

"Is that so?"

Scarlese's tone finally penetrated. Benedetto looked up, sensing the makings of a transgression. "I don't mean . . ."

"That's right," Scarlese cut him off. "You don't mean anything, do you?"

Benedetto tried to recoup, to soften the impression of his disaffection. "Don't get me wrong. I'm was only sayin' . . ."

Scarlese interrupted again. "You weren't saying anything, Tony." Benedetto fell silent. Scarlese stood and walked to the captain's station. He stepped up a level, then turned, facing Benedetto. "Because if you were, we'd have a problem. A real problem."

Benedetto looked away sullenly. "Don't worry about it."

"What did you say?" Scarlese asked.

Benedetto took a deep breath. He spoke, without emotion this time. "I'm not sayin' nothin' at all."

"Good." Scarlese folded his arms and leaned back against the captain's chair. "Because we got a week to go. Maybe less. Then we're finished. When it comes to anybody asking questions here, like happened in Boston, don't worry. I'll take care of that problem. But I'm counting on you to make sure nothing else goes wrong. Not with the Bureau. Not with the Brits." Scarlese paused. "Not with DiGenero."

Benedetto's head snapped up. "Whaddya mean, 'DiGenero'?"

Scarlese continued. "You were right, Tony. Ferringa wasn't the man for the job. That was too bad. But I've got the one I need right here."

"Wait a minute!" Benedetto raised his voice.

Scarlese's eyes hardened like a killing frost. "You wait a minute. You've been banking five thousand dollars a month for the last three years. For what? Sitting on your ass and making sure your fucking squad doesn't stumble across us by accident? What do you think I'm paying you for? Now you earn your money. This is business, you understand? I'm talking about win or lose. We got one more airplane, then Bellflower is out of here."

Benedetto looked desperate. "DiGenero wasn't part of the deal."

"Too fucking bad. You're part of the deal. And that means you protect what we've got going—you make sure nobody gets to Bellflower. As far as DiGenero is concerned, I couldn't be happier it's you."

"I'm not gonna do it." Benedetto's adamancy had transformed to petulance.

Scarlese walked to the couch and sat down. He put his arm on Benedetto's shoulder. "How old are you, Tony?"

Benedetto looked as if he didn't understand the question. "Forty-five," he said.

"You lived here your whole life. Brooklyn, Staten Island?"

He nodded.

"And you joined the FBI. When? In your twenties?"

Benedetto stared.

"That's okay. I mean, it's an honorable profession, law enforcement. Twenty years-plus altogether. A career in your hometown. And you know what I respect in you? You weren't like DiGenero. You worked with him, but people knew who you were. You didn't lie. You didn't betray. You did your job, right, Tony?" Scarlese patted his shoulder. "Now, you've made an arrangement with us. For perfectly understandable reasons. In difficult times, you have to think of the future. To have something more than a pension set aside." Scarlese stood and looked down. "So what do I conclude from all this? You know how things are. You know the rules. And you know the answer to the question, the one DiGenero should have asked." He stepped to the captain's station and pushed a button. Below, the blower died. Scarlese put on his jacket and walked to the rear of the cabin.

Benedetto rose slowly. "What question?"

Scarlese opened the door. The warmth of the cabin dissipated at once, replaced by the damp chill of the river. "Just where do you think you can hide?"

CHAPTER
20

KNEELING AT THE DOOR of the Aircraft Machinists and Maintenance Workers Union, Local 301, DiGenero stared at the lock's burnished faceplate. The Butler Lock Company set the industry standard, a testimony to the enduring value of forged steel even in the era of high-tech security.

DiGenero glanced up at the building's facade. Save for the door, it was blank. Without features. The union office occupied a garagelike space, the last unit at the end of a one-story cinderblock warehouse, one of three in a nondescript, if eclectic industrial park that also hosted a body-builder's gym, cosmetic distributor, furniture refinisher, plumbing supply outlet, and a health food wholesaler. Whatever its aesthetic deficiencies, the location presumably suited its members. On the ragged edge of Queens, the local was only a few miles from Kennedy Airport. With luck in avoiding rush hours, its members from LaGuardia with union business had a twenty-minute drive due south on the Van Wyck and Grand Central.

The cold of the concrete stoop penetrated, instigating a dull ache in DiGenero's knees. He shifted stiffly into a squat. He opened the canvas satchel beside him. Silverstein had the usual assortment of burglar tools common to the trade. Claw hammer, pry and jimmy bars, medium and small, bolt and glass cutters, putty knives, assorted, for sticky windows, and cold chisels, graduated, for recalcitrant nuts. DiGenero rummaged. The wire needles had filtered to the bottom of the sack. He found one and felt for another.

Twenty years before, the new-agent class had offered a sampler from the black-bag curriculum—bugs, breaking and entering, clandestine photos. Locks and picks had not been his forte. Officially, if pretentiously titled "Introduction to Surreptitious Entry," the course had used the Butler for its final exam. He still remembered the old workshop at Quantico. Aligned in two rows, each bench had its set of Liliputian

doors with locks graduated in difficulty. They learned one a day: auxiliary rim, mortise, tubular, and cylindrical, including dead bolt. From
credit card slipped between jamb and door to the dummied master key.
A primer on the felonious in less than a week.

Frustrated, DiGenero pulled a flashlight from his pocket and snapped
it on. The beam glinted on the second pick, six inches of surgical stainless steel. The Butler lock, he remembered, had a master and a slave
tumbler. A proper key first displaced the interlocking wheel, rotating
master and slave together. The movement engaged their cylinders, allowing them to fall into place.

He faced the door and blew on his hands. His surplus-store purchases
earlier in the day had not included gloves. DiGenero inserted the needles
in the keyhole, poking and manipulating. He visualized the lock's innards, although after several minutes the mental image did little to
sharpen his technique.

A car door opened and slammed. Silverstein had parked in the last
space, nose-in, blocking the view from the street. Added to the surroundings, the unmarked car was sufficiently battered to complement
the pre-existing scene. Silverstein stood behind DiGenero, eyeing him
with obvious skepticism. "We havin' fun yet?" he asked.

"Pipe down." DiGenero concentrated.

Silverstein lit a cigarette. "Who's gonna hear? The only ones wit'in a
quarter mile is other geeks breakin' in."

DiGenero jiggled the needles, feeling the tumblers roll and fall back.
The picks slipped, then slipped again. He cursed under his breath.

Silverstein bent down, examining his lack of progress more closely.
"We ain't got all night, ya know." His smoke created miniature clouds, a
personal nimbus. He straightened up. "I'll be back." His footsteps receded.

The car's trunk opened and closed. DiGenero turned around, distracted. Silverstein was walking out of the light and into the shadow with
something in his hand. He called out, a stage whisper, "Hey!" Silverstein ignored him. He rounded the corner, out of sight.

DiGenero looked at the door, then back again, where Silverstein had
disappeared. He thought of retrieving him, but discarded the idea. He
was probably taking a piss. He concentrated on the lock, gingerly exploring its insides. With the picks, he could feel the master tumbler roll. But
each time the tumbler reached its apogee, the needles slipped, allowing it
to fall away. He was doing something wrong.

He extracted the needles and played with them as a child would with
pick-up-sticks, thinking. Then, he remembered. The crutch. DiGenero
inserted the needles and crossed their tips. Inside the Butler, he visual-

ized a tiny V. It helped. The V found the master tumbler's counter-weight. He pressed. It turned, rising. DiGenero smiled to himself. The crutch was perfect to raise the tumbler. He pressed upward with the crossed needles ever so slightly. It was working. He angled the picks, a miniscule motion. The crutch was pushing. The master was moving, its cylinders ready to fall as they passed the highest point on its roll. He held his breath. They were almost there, balanced like feathers and ready, when the glass shattered. DiGenero jerked reflexively. The lock slipped back, secured. He froze. Nothing moved. He heard another sound, distant and indistinct. Not glass, but a shuffling, muffled movement. He turned his head, listening. It was closer, approaching. He tensed. Suddenly the door opened. The picks, still inserted in the lock, jerked out of his hand. On his knees, DiGenero looked up, startled.

Silverstein beckoned with a tire iron. "Come on. Whaddya waitin' for?"

DiGenero stood. "What the hell did you do?"

Silverstein shrugged. "Broke a window."

"Are you nuts? What if the place is alarmed?"

Silverstein gripped his elbow. He raised DiGenero up and ushered him inside. He shut the door. "Frankie, think about it. If you was the Scarleses, would you waste good money on alarms? I mean, the Mafia controls this local for thirty years and everybody knows it, right? Now, I ask ya? Who's gonna be crazy enough to break in?"

Silverstein closed the blinds and turned on the lights, bathing the room in monochrome fluorescent white. DiGenero squinted. The floor, walls, and ceiling had once been a color. In the corners, the linoleum curled. Two secretary's desks stood side by side, each facing two straight-backed chairs. Visitors, it seemed, came in pairs. DiGenero strolled down the hall toward the rear. A toilet, broom closet, and storage room were on the left, a single office on the right. He pushed open the office door. Inside, a tastelessly oversized mahogany desk with the nameplate, "President, Local 301," had been planted in a field of green shag carpet, along with an executive's high-backed leather chair. A console television, unplugged, faced the desk, as did a matching credenza. He opened its doors and then looked through the desk. Both were empty.

DiGenero retraced his steps. Silverstein was already at work in the corner. "Over here," he said.

Three filing cabinets lined the wall. Silverstein stood in front of the third cabinet, a drawer open. A piece of paper lay on top of the file. "The first one's got the records from LaGuardia. Mine's got Kennedy." Silverstein pointed to the middle cabinet. "So does that one."

DiGenero glanced at the paper. Handwritten, it listed BA 121's ground times at Kennedy over the last month, extracted by Silverstein from the aircraft's records. He opened the middle cabinet.

The files in the first two drawers were arranged by specialty, then name. DiGenero combed through the subdivisions. Airframe, Avionics, Auxiliary Systems, Engine, Hydraulics . . . He scanned the names. Anderson, Arnold, Ascension, Azara, Bechtold, Burton . . . Under each, the records covered employment history, training, medical data. The paperwork told everything and nothing. All you didn't want to know and never would have bothered to ask. Altogether, there were three hundred names, maybe more, not counting the cleaners and baggage handlers. Nothing was in chronological order. DiGenero felt dispirited. A good idea gone bad.

Beside him, Silverstein riffled back and forth, pulling out, then replacing files. He muttered. "I got union dues, emergency locator cards, participation in community service activities. Here's one." He opened a file. "Kevin Rohan spends ten hours a month drivin' old ladies to daycare centers. Hey, you think that's a cover?" Silverstein pushed the file back into place. "How the hell we supposed to make somethin' outa this? Maybe I shouldn'ta been in no hurry to have you pick the lock."

"Keep trying." DiGenero looked at his watch. Nearly two A.M. He opened another drawer. The personnel files continued. He stared, discouraged. With time and resources—the kind of down-in-the-weeds investigation the instructors loved to hype as the Bureau's strength in their classroom lectures on criminology—you could collect all the pieces. The paper would have it, man by man. Who was working where and when at Kennedy. It might take a few weeks, but it was there. Not an impossible task. Time cards, shift rosters, vacation schedules, aircraft forms—who signed off what maintenance on the airplane. Theoretically, they could build the story inductively. Theoretically. But the Federal Bureau of Investigation wasn't doing the investigation. They were. Two of them. And they had days, maybe hours, not weeks.

DiGenero resumed scanning the drawer. Halfway back, his eye caught a tab, partially bent. It protruded from a heavy cardboard divider that separated the folders. He straightened it and read aloud, "Team Leaders/Work Schedules."

"Huh?" Silverstein looked up.

"Wait a minute," DiGenero said to himself. He yanked the drawer full out and shuffled through the files. There were thirty folders, more or less, subdivided into four categories. Flight Service, Engine, Avionics, Airframe. Arranged alphabetically, each folder had a single name and title. "Dunleavy–Flight Service Team Chief. Echaverria–Engine Team Chief. Golden–Avionics Team Chief. Lagomarsino–Airframe Team

Chief." Thirty—no thirty-two—team chiefs to cover all the maintenance areas on three shifts, seven days a week.

DiGenero pulled a folder. Inside, its sheets provided a record of the team chief's work schedule, subdivided by workweek, workday, and hours. The first presented the plan for the quarter—when the team was scheduled to work over each three-month period. DiGenero opened two other files. They were all the same. The normal rotation from one week to the next was *A-B-C*. First week, eight A.M. to four P.M., days, the *A* shift. Second week, four P.M. to twelve midnight, swings, *B* shift. Next week, midnight to eight A.M., *C* shift. Graveyard. For each chief and his team, days off rotated as well. Weekend coverage required that each team took its two days as they fit into the scheme of things. Saturdays and Sundays one week, then Sundays and Mondays, Mondays and Tuesdays, and so on.

DiGenero flipped through the other paperwork. In each file, it recorded the team's schedule as actually worked, accounting for the team chief's time and that of his crew. Extra days off, holidays, sick leave, and special requests, such as permission to switch temporarily to another shift.

Silverstein peered over DiGenero's shoulder. He yawned. "You got this figured out so I can go home now?" he asked.

"Gimme that." DiGenero gestured toward the listing of BA 121's ground time at Kennedy. Silverstein handed it over. Between its scheduled maintenance and crash, BA 121 had flown the transatlantic route for a month and a half, overnighting at JFK six times.

DiGenero spoke, thinking out loud. "Let's play the odds. We got thirty-two files here, but we don't care who was working at Kennedy in all the shops—engines, instruments, airframe, right?"

"We don't?" Silverstein asked.

"Most of the time, the airplane isn't broken. These guys aren't gonna even see it. No engine problems, no need for an engine specialist. No hydraulic or mechanical problems, no need for the airframe guy. Right?"

"If you say so," Silverstein nodded agreeably.

"Okay. So if you want to have access to the plane, who does that leave? Who could get on the plane any time without someone asking why he was screwing around?" DiGenero leaned on the filing cabinet. "Only one team," he said.

"Which one?"

DiGenero looked into the drawer, flipping through the folders. "Not Airframe. Not Avionics. Not Engines." He reached in and pulled out a handful of files. "Flight Services. They're the ones that turn the airplane around," he said.

"Whaddyamean?" Silverstein asked.

DiGenero took the files to the closest secretary's desk and sat. "The plane comes in. They park it, they check it, they fuel it, they get it set to go again. If it's broke, the pilot tells 'em. They see to it that it's fixed. They call the specialists—whoever they need. If Flight Services doesn't say so, there's no reason for anybody else to get on the plane." DiGenero counted the folders as he talked. He looked at Silverstein. "Nine flight service team chiefs. All we want to know is who worked on the days 121 was on the ground."

DiGenero opened the files. He glanced back and forth, comparing BA 121's dates at Kennedy and the schedules in the folders. He made two stacks and counted again.

Silverstein watched. "So?"

DiGenero sat back. "Okay. Five of the nine flight service chiefs worked at least one of the shifts—days, evenings, or graveyards—during BA 121's layovers." In the desk drawer, he found a pad and pencil.

"Now what?" Silverstein said.

"The number of shifts each chief worked when BA 121 was on the ground should all be about the same, right? I mean, this is a rotating schedule. For everybody. The pattern is the pattern. BA 121 or no BA 121." DiGenero drew a matrix on the pad. He listed the names of the flight service team chiefs down the left side and the dates for BA 121's ground times across the top.

He pushed the folders across the desk to Silverstein. "I'll give you the chief's name and the dates. You tell me what shift he worked. Call 'em off." DiGenero began with the first of the five names and BA 121's first overnight. Silverstein read out the shifts as DiGenero proceeded down and across the page, filling in the blanks.

When they finished, DiGenero put down the pencil. Silverstein circled behind him and examined the matrix. "Everybody worked two or three swings or midnight shifts. Except this guy," Silverstein said. He reached over DiGenero's shoulder and tapped the page. "Funny thing. He worked every four to twelve. Six outa six."

"Gimme his folder." DiGenero motioned. Silverstein handed him the file.

DiGenero scanned through the papers. "Two shifts were his—I mean regularly scheduled." He looked at Silverstein. "The other four?"

"Lemme guess," Silverstein said. "Special requests."

DiGenero nodded. "Which one of those cabinets did you say had the emergency locator cards?"

"I'll get it." Silverstein opened the top drawer of the last filing cabinet and searched. He withdrew a slim folder. "Here."

DiGenero opened it. The single form provided a summary of the union member's vital data: name, age, family status, employer, supervisor, health insurance, next of kin in case of emergency, and local address. "Why am I not surprised?" DiGenero said.

"What?" Silverstein asked.

"Flight Service Team Chief Peter Pagano lives at 2233 Harnett Parkway."

Silverstein furrowed his brow. "That's Howard Beach."

DiGenero nodded.

"Ain't no big coincidence. That's about ninety-nine percent Italian, right?"

"Right," DiGenero said.

"Wait a minute. This Pagano guy lives where?"

"Harnett Parkway," DiGenero repeated. "2233."

Silverstein paused. "Isn't that where the don lived? When you was . . ."

"Inside the family?" DiGenero completed the question.

"Yeah," Silverstein said.

"The same." DiGenero smiled. "Johnny Junior grew up at 2228. Three doors down the street."

CHAPTER
21

THIS TIME, it was his turn to wait. Rising unseen, a weak sun backlit the clouds, promising day but delivering only gray morning. Schurz Park was empty save for the joggers who monopolized the promenade along the East River. One approached, a woman veneered in a rainbow running suit. DiGenero stared, too tired to modulate his curiosity. Compared to his drab parka and jeans, she was magnificent. She eyed him warily, accelerating and giving wide berth. Maneuver as well as speed, it appeared, provided security for species in full plumage.

He looked at his watch. It was past seven. Jilian would come. About that he was sure. A few minutes early or late didn't matter. He relaxed, relishing the sensation, however unwarranted. Fatigue was a friend, husbanding the body's remaining resources and teaching lessons. Patience was one. As capabilities diminished, it grew in proportion.

They had returned to Silverstein's apartment at four in the morning, leaving the union office much as they found it, except for the broken window. Silverstein had gone to bed, asleep instantly, fully clothed. DiGenero had decided against returning to the hotel downtown just to come back again a few hours later. He'd called the desk. An obviously groggy operator told him Foley had left no message. He had showered and shaved, then searched the cupboards. There was no coffee. In the refrigerator, beside slowly culturing leftovers, he found only a bag of petrified bagels, too hard to cut, much less eat, and left, hungry. Walking east on 86th Street, he'd bought coffee and doughnuts. In the half darkness, he made his way to the park. Silverstein would pick him up at eight, when they would drive back to Queens in search of Pagano.

He sipped from an oversized Styrofoam cup. The coffee warmed him. In the river working its way north, a tug bulled a fuel barge against the current. He watched the mated pair. The tug's captain stood alone in the wheelhouse. A solitary figure, he seemed too small to control the forces of the river and the unwieldly mass of the barge. DiGenero felt a vague kinship. The captain sipped nonchalantly from his own Styrofoam. The mark of the fraternity of early risers. He turned back toward the promenade. A woman in a blonde fur with matching wolfhound passed. She walked briskly, carrying a plastic bag and scooper like a designer's accoutrement. The wolfhound ambled behind, obviously not a morning creature. She tugged the leash and commanded the dog ambiguously, encouraging either its pace or bodily functions.

He was about to survey the river again when Jilian appeared. In long leather coat and heels, she came toward him from 83rd Street, climbing the steps to the promenade. An outsized satchel hung from her shoulder —her purse or briefcase, he couldn't tell which. She had Erin's long stride, a naturally sensual rhythm. As the distance closed between them, she sensed his attention and smiled. Like sunlight, it reflected momentarily, illuminating him.

"First the UN, now here. You have a thing for gardens and parks." Jilian caught her breath. She had walked quickly. They stood face-to-face. In heels, she was almost as tall as he.

"I like wide open spaces," he said.

"Because of living out west?" Jilian took the Styrofoam cup from his hand and sipped. "That's good." She handed it back.

"No," he said. DiGenero finished the last of the coffee and pitched the cup in a nearby container. "Because nobody's gonna tap you on the shoulder and say, 'Guess who?,' when you've got your back to the river."

Running in tandem, a pair of joggers peeled off, passing them on either side, and returned to formation. "Let's walk," Jilian said. She took his arm. They stepped off briskly. She seemed to know where she wanted to go. At first, DiGenero wanted to slow down, but then decided to let her set the pace and direction. They headed north along the promenade toward Gracie Mansion, the mayor's official residence.

"I read about you in the newspaper yesterday. After we talked," Jilian said.

"Really?" DiGenero didn't remember any coverage in the editions he saw last night. "That story falls into the 'Ayatollah Khomeini is still dead' category, doesn't it?" he asked.

"Pardon me?"

"I mean, it's getting a little old." He glanced at her. "Unless you've given them a sequel."

Jilian acted as if she hadn't heard the last remark. "Not that, I mean I read about *you*. I went to the *Times*. After we talked yesterday afternoon. The newspaper morgue stays open late."

"The *Times*? You don't work for them. How come they let you in?"

"Professional courtesy," she said.

"Among reporters? Like sharks not eating lawyers when they fall overboard?"

"Something like that." Jilian smiled. "I looked you up." She spoke guilelessly, almost excited, like a little girl with a secret to tell. "You've quite a dossier—well, I mean your Scarlese case does. I read until almost ten last night. It was fascinating."

"I'm flattered," he said. "Or am I?"

"Well, it's a good deal more interesting than what I got from your fingerprints. That FBI stuff is really quite dull." She made a face. "So's ours, truth be known."

"I've lost track of the last 201 file that won a Pulitzer."

"For someone whose spent his career undercover, you're no stranger to celebrity," she said.

DiGenero nodded. "Funny you should mention it. Headquarters makes that point from time to time. When they do, though, I usually hear the word 'career' after the phrase 'end of.' "

"The background pieces that were done when Scarlese went to trial said that you grew up in his neighborhood."

"I grew up in New York. It was all Scarlese's neighborhood," he said.

She continued. "Dashing fighter pilot, who went to law school, then on to the FBI."

DiGenero winced. "Is that what the Bureau's flacks peddled?" he asked.

"Not true?" Jilian seemed disappointed. "It sounded quite appealing."

He held up his hands as if framing a picture. "In the neighborhood pantheon of the time, I would have been somewhere below Louie the 'Greased Pig' Salerno, here"—he pointed—"and to the right of Marty Verna, there. Louie ran the lead crew that broke arms for the don. Marty could deliver any car you wanted in six hours. Twelve if you wanted it in parts. Fighter pilots, lawyers? So what? You've gotta give recognition to those who truly serve the community's needs." DiGenero shook his head. He took Jilian's arm again. "It just so happened I didn't have a record when Vietnam rolled around. Back then, everybody was somebody to the local draft board. You were either *1A,* eligible to go, or *4F,* ineligible, or *2S,* a student, deferred until you finished school. Our neighborhood was special. We had our own category, something we called the *3–5F.* That was three-to-five for a felony count. It got you a different kind of uniform and an automatic deferment. I was unlucky. I didn't have a rap sheet—no record. I had to go to college to keep from getting drafted. When that was over, they handed me a *1A* along with the degree. I still had twenty-twenty vision and was smart enough to know flying beat the hell out of sitting in the mud. Voila! Career choice number two came when they wanted to send me back to 'Nam for a third tour. I drew the conclusion somebody in the Pentagon was trying to kill me and got out. The GI Bill paid my way through law school. Different, yeah. Hero? No."

"One story talked about your grandfather." Jilian looked at him. "Is he still alive?"

"Yeah," DiGenero said. He didn't want to talk about that story.

"To have left the Mafia, he must be quite something. I read that you were close to him. After your father died."

DiGenero didn't answer.

Jilian paused, watching him as they walked. "What did he say?"

"Who?"

"Your grandfather. About what you did? Afterward, that is. About bringing down Scarlese."

"I didn't discuss it with him," he said.

"Why not?" she seemed surprised.

"Obvious, isn't it? I was top of the hit parade. It was a connection they —Scarlese's boys—were watching to find me. Conversations with my grandfather—even if he'd wanted to talk—weren't good for my health."

"So you didn't see him?" she asked.

"No," DiGenero said.

"At all?"

DiGenero shook his head. "Nope." He lied.

"Was it hard when they all went to trial?" Jilian asked.

He had not expected the excursion into his past. "What are we talking about?"

"Any qualms, I mean . . ."

DiGenero broke in, "About Scarlese? The family? Look, these are guys who settled disagreements over bookie chits with piano wire necklaces. They cut bodies into bit sized chunks with chain saws to avoid the legal liabilities of *corpus delicti*. If you're asking whether I felt guilty for putting them away, the answer is no."

"No second thoughts." She persisted.

"Yeah, second, third, fourth thoughts. But couch time? Not on your life."

"How about for giving up part of who you are. For not being able to go home." Jilian pressed.

There was, he thought, no reason to confess sins already expiated. "Look," DiGenero said. "It was the cost of doing business. It had to be done that way."

"But that's the point, isn't it? Why *did* you do it?"

"Why did I do what?" he asked. For the first time he noticed the circles under Jilian's eyes. Her expression suggested a struggle somewhere deep inside.

She gestured. "Go back, of course. Become part of them. You didn't have to."

He stopped. They faced each other. "I didn't have the reason you did, if that's what you mean," DiGenero said. "Not until now. Besides, after a while, why you start something doesn't matter anymore. Either you take responsibility for it, or you don't. I only figured it out—really figured it out—when they killed Erin. She didn't die because of what I did or didn't do. She died because of me. Who I am. I'm not the same as the guy with the badge, the mortgage, the station wagon, the wife and kids, the one who can drive off to the suburbs at six o'clock every day and leave it all behind. When you go under, when you go inside, they define you, who you are. Forever. You can't walk away. Once I thought you could. I thought somebody else could take care of what happened next. Wrong, huh? My mistake. Big mistake." DiGenero let her arm fall. He put his hands in his pockets. "You began this where I ended. Because of somebody who mattered. The point is, for whatever reasons, we're here. And we need each other."

Jilian didn't move. She seemed to be studying him. DiGenero took her arm again. They began walking. The promenade was filling with the morning rush. Singly or in pairs, they came toward them, walking to work. Young mostly, with youth's sought-after sameness. They hurried, struggling to look purposeful. Identical expressions, haircuts, coats, ties, skirts, running shoes, papers-under-arms, sports bags, briefcases, ambitions. Going downtown in order to move up.

He spoke without preface. "Scarlese has a guy on the flight services crew at Kennedy. That's how they got at the hardware on the airplane."

"Informed speculation or something else?" she asked.

"Something else."

"You're certain?"

"I've got a name," DiGenero said. "Peter Pagano."

"Do you know what else they've gotten to? Beside 121, I mean. What other planes?"

"No. Not yet." He paused. DiGenero fished in his pocket and handed her a slip of paper. "Here's my number. The Gramercy Park Hotel. About Pagano," he said. "If you give him to the Bureau—for a trace, like you did with me—don't count on much. Everything on Scarlese's case is buttoned up tight. That much I do know." DiGenero looked at his watch. It was almost eight. Silverstein would be waiting. "I'd better go. I'll be in touch."

Jilian held the slip of paper with his number. "Yesterday, you wouldn't give me this. Now you will. Why?"

DiGenero smiled. "Hey, I've only been in New York a week. How many beautiful women do you think I've run into who want to give me a call?"

"Early to get back at it, aren't we?" Ian Barry bent down, dogging the door to the bubble behind them. "Is this a reprise of last night?"

"Did you send the message?" she asked. Jilian had come straight from the meeting with DiGenero. Barry was already in his office. She shivered. She'd left her coat at her desk a floor below. As usual, the blower had instantly turned the secure conference room in Barry's small suite ice cold.

"Of course. Copy's in your file," Barry answered.

"Any response?"

"It's only been a few hours. Give the poor bastards a break." Barry's mug steamed on the small café table. He made a motion as if prepared to unlock the door. "Tea?"

"No thank you."

"Alright then." He sat.

"I want an FBI trace on this man." She slid a piece of paper across the table.

Barry read her handwriting aloud. "Peter Pagano." He sipped the tea noisily. "What's it all about?"

Jilian ignored the question. "What I don't want is to have the FBI involved with him."

"That's simple enough, isn't it?" Barry said sarcastically.

"I mean, I don't want the Bureau nosing around because of the request."

"Well then, I'll just tell them we want the file, but after that they can butt out. I'm sure my liaison friends would welcome my guidance in their otherwise unstructured lives. After all, they took our discovery of this DiGenero fellow with such equanimity. I thought I was going to have the whole New York Field Office jump down my throat. Thank God I'm an accomplished professional prevaricator. That we'd stumbled across him following one of our IRA leads into a Mafia bar was strictly *ad lib.*" Barry blew on his tea. "No thanks to your tight lips when you gave me his prints, my dear."

Jilian tried to break their conversation's usual downward spiral, attempting conciliation. "I don't mean to suggest what you should say, Ian. I'm asking, that's all. I realize their antennas are up. All I'm after is how we can make this seem routine. What do we tell them to avoid drawing attention?"

"Before deciding what to tell them, why not begin by telling me?" Barry suggested.

Jilian sat back. Conciliation, it appeared, demanded substance as well as form. Barry sipped more quietly this time, obviously prepared to wait for an answer. Patience and obduracy were two sides of the same coin. Despite the morning hour, Jilian's voice had a day's end, weary tone. "Does this never end? Whose territory is whose. Who knows what. Who's in charge. MI5, RUC. Marylebone and Stormont. You and I. It's like dogs pissing on trees. Is it so difficult for us just to get on with it?"

"Those sound like questions for the ages." Barry smiled benignly. "Or are they specifically directed at me?"

Jilian took a deep breath. It was clear this morning there would be no victories on points. "Pagano is the chief of a flight service team at Kennedy. They take care of the BA aircraft. I'm told he's the one who provided access to the computers on board 121."

Barry's smile disappeared. "You're told by whom?"

She hesitated. "DiGenero."

The name caused no reaction. A reaction in itself. Barry put down his mug. He rubbed his face with both hands, as if physically changing his visage. "We're reaching a point where we need to iron things out, you and I."

"Please." Jilian rolled her eyes. "A name trace, Ian. *That's* all we're talking about."

He continued, obviously committed to his course. "Stormont sent you to do a difficult job. We all know that, and you've done well. Better than we . . ."

Jilian interrupted. "MI5's royal 'we?'"

Barry corrected. "Better than *I* expected." He folded his hands on the table, adopting a reasonable posture to match a reasonable tone. "From the beginning you were going to work your way inside, a step at a time. Carefully. That was the plan. To your credit, you did it admirably with Rocchi, then Sallie Ferringa. The fact that things went to hell isn't your fault. I don't consider it such. Neither would Marylebone. Neither does Stormont, I'm sure. And, I hope, neither do you." Barry paused, clearing his throat. "But I'm concerned that's not the case."

"You're concerned what's not the case, Ian?" she asked.

"I'm concerned you're overreacting. How shall I put it? Trying too hard. Overachieving, as it were. With Scarlese—now with this DiGenero chap—you're skating perilously close to the edge. If you fall, you'll take more than yourself with you." He leaned forward. "You can't get between Scarlese and DiGenero. With Scarlese, of course, you don't have a choice but to stay the course. The key is care. To exercise caution. To find another route through him to the PIRAs. To Bellflower. I can help with that. With DiGenero, it's different. He's dangerous, pure and simple. The Bureau wants him. The New York police want him. Scarlese wants him. If they—any of them—find you with him the risks are enormous. To you. To us. You're putting yourself in a bottle with two scorpions. You can't control them. Either one."

Jilian stared coldly.

Barry sat straighter, gaining height. "I also have to warn you that if you're discovered, I can't protect you."

"I wouldn't expect you to," she said.

"You don't understand. I'm not threatening you. The point is, you're putting me at risk. If things go bad, I won't even be able to protect myself. What do you suppose the Bureau would do if they learned we—you—were operating here unilaterally, even as I work with them on the same case? How many phones do you think would ring in London if they found that out? I'm sure you can see the equities here go beyond the RUC's. They go beyond this case, 121 that is. I think even Stormont would recognize the fact."

Jilian assumed her full posture. "All very good points, Ian. And well put, too, I must say."

He nodded, accepting the unexpected compliment. "I simply want to get our situation across," he said cooperatively.

She smoothed her skirt demurely. "May I ask one question?"

"Certainly."

"Are you requesting a trace on Peter Pagano or not?"

Barry's anger boiled over. "Have you heard anything I've said?"

She shot back. "Have I? Oh yes. I heard last night that you didn't want to wake Belfast or London with an 'Immediate' message on the chance it might prove embarrassing. Now I've heard that you think I'm skating 'perilously close to the edge'—whatever that means. Let me guess. You're trying to tell me this is all too risky, aren't you? Or maybe it's that anything's too risky when it's outside MI5's control. Or maybe you really and truly are concerned about stepping on the Bureau's toes. Let's see, if worse came to worst, just what would that mean? A polite request for a new MI5 man for New York and your ticket home? What a shame! Back to commuting to Marylebone from a little East Epping flat rather than a pleasant walk to the office from a three-bedroom-with-view on Manhattan's East side?"

Barry glared. "You don't believe I'm the only one who thinks you're a disaster waiting to happen, do you?"

Jilian rose. She undogged the door with two hard slaps. "Among your rummy little group? Probably not. But if that's the case, perhaps—just perhaps—one of the others would have the balls to do their job, risks and all, in order to have the pleasure of seeing me go down in flames."

A floor below, Jilian slammed her chair against the partition. Around her, heads rose, glancing about.

The pinch-faced stringer for the European business weekly stuck his head around the corner, "Is everything alright?"

Jilian nodded without turning. "Fine."

"Oh." She heard his chair scrape. He was gone, back in his cubicle as intended.

She folded her arms, looking out the window, trying not to think about the consequences of having gone too far, of needing to repair things at some point with Barry. Across the alley in the neighboring building, the office on her floor was already at work. A repertory theater. Curtain up, act one, scene one. Stage left, three women, two white, one black, sat before screens, hands moving at keyboards. Stage center, two men, both white, shuffled papers, rising periodically to retrieve the women's work. Stage right, a larger office adjoining, one desk, one man, white, received their offerings, dispatching those who attended him with a wave. A benediction or a command? Who knew? Maybe, Jilian thought, they were one and the same. To be told what to do was a blessing. Not having to decide, not needing to choose what came next.

Jilian glanced down. Her inbox was full. A temporary excuse to put things out of her mind. She sat and sorted through the stack, perusing and tossing aside. Press releases. The *Times, Journal,* and *Post.* Several flimsy airmail envelopes, the newspaper accounting department's queries about her expense vouchers.

The fax was half buried. She glanced at the cover sheet. It was odd, no letterhead or instructions for delivery. Only today's date, her name, and number.

Jilian turned the page and read.

ARRANGE A MEETING WITH OUR FRIEND THIS AFTER-NOON. HIS HOTEL ROOM. 888-3445. RM. 342. BE THERE.

She flipped back to the cover page. The stamp recorded the fax's receipt an hour ago. This afternoon obviously meant today. She furrowed her brow. Jilian punched the buttons on her phone, dialing. Listening as the call connected, she dug in her purse. Where was the note? She found it at the bottom of the bag as the phone clicked, its ringing interrupted. Even before the operator spoke, Jilian had a sinking feeling.

"Gramercy Park Hotel. May I help you?"

"Room 342, please," she said.

"With whom do you wish to speak?" the operator asked, double-checking.

"Mr. DiGenero," Jilian answered impatiently.

"I'm sorry, but no one by that name is registered in Room 342."

Her mind raced. Of course not. DiGenero's alias. "I mean, Mr. Falcone."

"Thank you." The operator went off instantly, followed by another tone, ringing. No answer. The operator came back on the line. "I'm afraid Mr. Falcone isn't in. May I take a message?"

"No. I'll call back." Jilian hung up. She looked out. Across the way, the man in the office waved, dispatching one of his subordinates. A benediction or a command? Who knew?

She glanced down at the desk. Crumpled from her purse, DiGenero's note lay atop Scarlese's fax. Jilian put her head in her hands and spoke, too soft for the hearing. "What now? What now?"

C H A P T E R
22

THEY STRUGGLED, prisoners of the traffic, until Silverstein had enough. "That's it! That's fuckin' it!"

Dozing, DiGenero woke with a start. "What?" He sat up and looked at his watch. It was after nine-thirty in the morning. Around them, three lanes barely moved.

Silverstein hit the brakes. They lurched, rolling more slowly. He bent down, ignoring the road, and groped under the seat.

DiGenero rubbed his eyes. He'd been dreaming, running down a jetway, trying to reach an airplane, to stop it from taking off. Ahead of him, Erin and Jilian were about to board, but no matter how hard he tried he couldn't catch them. DiGenero looked out. Cars, trucks, vans, and Queens surrounded them. "Where are we?" he asked.

"Jamaica Avenue and the Van Wyck. Where we shoulda been a half hour ago." Silverstein spoke, head down in the footwell. "We'd do better on our fuckin' hands and knees." Under the front seat beneath DiGenero, mysterious objects clanked and thudded as the search continued. "I got it," Silverstein said. He straightened, displaying his prize. A portable gumball light trailing an umbilical of wires.

DiGenero yawned. "Whose gonna make the siren noise, you or me?"

"You wanna retire on this fuckin' highway, I'll get 'em to send your papers. Don't be a smartass." Silverstein rolled down his window.

They'd left the city an hour before, taking false hope from their surprisingly easy escape, unencumbered almost to LaGuardia. Passing the airport, the Grand Central Parkway had snarled, previewing the tie-up that ensnared them southbound on the Van Wyck Expressway. Above the road, the sign reminded them of their plight. "JFK 8 Miles."

Silverstein planted the gumball light on the roof with the clank of magnet on metal. On either side, drivers stared, diverted from the traffic jam's boredom. He fumbled with the wires, finding the end, then yanked out the cigarette lighter and jammed in the plug. Around them, windows and windshields suddenly reflected a rotating red hue. Heads turned. "At least somethin' works," Silverstein muttered. On DiGenero's side, a garbage truck, a traveling partner in their slow progress, kept pace, its airbrakes squealing with each application. The driver looked down at Silverstein's now obvious plan of escape and smiled appreciatively. He raised both hands, a clear salute, and applauded.

Light flashing, Silverstein blew the horn. One note sounded, discordant and off key. He edged from the far left lane toward the right shoulder, his intrusion greeted diffidently by others as he crossed their files. Faced with their recalcitrance, Silverstein leaned out of the window and encouraged cooperation. "Get outa the fuckin' way!"

They bisected the lanes, reaching the shoulder. Silverstein hit passing gear. Gravel spewed. They accelerated south, horn blowing.

"Take Liberty Avenue through Ozone Park, then turn on Cross Bay Boulevard. Harnett's south of the Shore Parkway five blocks, then a left," DiGenero said. The directions came back like it was yesterday.

They veered off the expressway and merged into another morning file, this one a steady westbound stream. Silverstein removed the gumball light from the roof and dropped it on the seat between them. He stayed in the left lane, moving at a purposeful pace. They turned south on Cross Bay Boulevard and headed toward Howard Beach.

DiGenero leaned back. Howard Beach was a colony, one of the remaining that marked where Little Italy's progeny had gradually ventured from lower Manhattan, first to Brooklyn, then from Brooklyn to Queens. For the first generation, and even some of the second, it was a high-water mark, an Italian middle-class enclave, before the diaspora— "the mixing" as his grandmother used to say distastefully—when marriages outside the clan scattered their offspring in the hybrid suburbs of Nassau and Suffolk counties farther east.

He pictured Harnett Parkway. In a neighborhood fixed in time, the houses were legacies not possessions, meant to be maintained and handed down, not changed. Modest, from the forties, they stood in disciplined rows, each with porches, overlooking their own maples or oaks, aligned between sidewalk and curb, shading small grass plots and the street. Two and three stories, mostly frame or aluminum siding, some stuccoes. Empty driveways separated them, too narrow for the vans and sedans now parked in the street. At 2228, the old don was gone, but his widow remained. In the same house, with the same neighbors. Even today, DiGenero knew it would be no different from the others, or from the time almost twenty years ago when he came twice a week and more.

He told Silverstein to slow as they approached. Number 2233 was four houses from the end of the block. They drove by once. Pagano's family van was wedged in the driveway. A new sedan with a JFK parking sticker sat at the curb.

"Two cars. Looks like everybody's home," DiGenero said.

"No lights, nothing happenin'," Silverstein said. He fidgeted, shifting back and forth in the seat. He eyed the rearview mirror as they reached the end of the block. The street was empty and no one followed. A light rain began, a prelude to more.

As they rounded the corner, an old man balanced on his front walk, managing a three-point stance with his cane. He watched the car pass. DiGenero turned his face away as he spoke. "The kitchen's in the back. If Pagano just worked the four to twelve or graveyard shift, they'll either be having breakfast late or he'll be in bed." He pointed to the next corner. "Go right again, then come back."

They circled the block and returned. The street was still empty.

"Leave some space when you pull up. In case we've gotta beat it outa here," DiGenero said.

Silverstein stopped a car length behind the van. He opened the glove compartment and took out a cardboard sign, propping it in on the dashboard.

DiGenero bent it back and read. Long Island Gas Company. "Whaddya tell 'em when somebody says, 'what's the gas problem?' " he asked.

"I tell 'em we got a report of a major leak and the whole street could go up any minute, but if they wanna hang around that's okay." Silverstein shrugged. "Usually works." He sat, one hand on the wheel, the other on the butt of his automatic, holstered inside his jacket. His eyes moved restlessly, searching around them. "You got a plan, Sherlock?" he asked.

"Stay here. Keep the motor running. Anybody comes you don't like, beep the horn once," DiGenero said.

"Anybody comes I don't like, you listen for the sound of squeelin' tires. Don't stay for lunch. Neighborhood's like this, they don't like you, they don't take no prisoners. Especially if you're a nice Jewish boy, like me."

DiGenero got out. Up and down the street, the curtains were drawn, houses quiet. He walked to the front of Pagano's parked sedan and touched the hood. The metal was cold. In the driveway, the hood of the van was the same. If Pagano had worked at Kennedy the night before it was the *B* shift. He'd come home in time for the car to cool.

He climbed the front steps and knocked on the storm door. The chain rattled anemically against the aluminum. DiGenero pushed the doorbell. Inside, an electronic chime replicated a familiar scale. DiGenero recognized it but couldn't remember the tune. He waited. No one came. Alone on the stoop, he glanced around self-consciously. Only Silverstein watched from behind the wheel. DiGenero shrugged, then pantomimed that he was going to the rear. He glanced up at Pagano's house. The windows were shut, blinds pulled.

In the driveway, a child's wagon and tricycle blocked his way. He stepped over them. DiGenero knew the odds were against it, but he hoped only Pagano was home. He had one card. With Catholics, it played best alone. The confessional. The badge, revelation, admission, catharsis, forgiveness. His was not unlike the priest's ritual, albeit in the secular case an incomplete sacrament, lacking the true penitent's sought-after final step. At best, DiGenero thought, he could fake it. A mock absolution.

He checked the backyard. Compulsive neatness persisted. Plastic sheeting covered the outdoor paraphernalia. A lawnmower, rake, hoe, and garden furniture each had its place against the rear of the house. A wading pool was deflated and neatly folded, its porpoises and seahorses lying lifeless, forlorn after their season.

DiGenero knocked again, this time on the side door. Silence greeted him. He stood on the step and looked in. The door opened into a small utility room. On the left, shelving held canned goods. On the right, a built-in closet rack held assorted garments. They bulked outward into the space, blocking his field of view. He spotted Pagano's parka. DiGenero remembered the reflective tape and lettering from the fatigues of the Air Force ground crews. The parka covered several coats, obviously hung last. Just beyond the utility room, he saw kitchen cabinets. The lights were off, but below them DiGenero could make out a small section of counter. Surrounded by several glasses, a plastic container lay on its side.

He tried the door. It opened. He pushed it part way and called. "Hello?" There was no answer. DiGenero's mouth was dry. He touched the weight in his pocket reflexively. The .38 seemed heavy. Obtrusive. He stepped back into the driveway and walked toward the street, considering. Silverstein motioned. He looked worried. DiGenero waved off the invitation to come to the car. He signaled wordlessly that he was going in.

He let the side door close behind him and stood in the utility room. The smell was clean but seasoned—waxes and soaps, the hint of deodorizer, a lingering aroma of last night's cooking. Sweet and pungent. Familiar. A tomato sauce *Bolognese*. From somewhere in a front room a clock ticked. Farther still, upstairs he suspected, a radio played. He rationalized. Easy-listening music, the kind that could be left on all day. He called again, louder.

DiGenero stepped into the kitchen. The juice container lay on its side, the contents creating a small pool, puddling on the counter and floor. Beside the refrigerator, the toaster had unloaded two slices, both medium brown. A milk carton and cereal boxes, open and upright, stood next to the sink. He touched the milk. The carton was damp and soft. Lukewarm. He stepped around the corner.

The dining room was formal, undersized, and overfilled. A breakfront bracketed by side chairs and two heavy oil paintings—generic seascapes and sunrises—filled the two blank walls. The heavy mahogany table was arranged for breakfast, three placemats, silverware, jam and butter, cups and plates. One setting, a size smaller than the others, had clowns and balloons and a spoon with its handle shaped into a mouse, smiling. Two chairs were positioned square to the table. One was angled, as if someone had arisen, called away and yet to return. DiGenero stepped around them, moving toward the living room, then stopped.

Under the archway between the two rooms, the slipper protruded. It splayed outward naturally, as if accommodating someone in a prone position. Above it, the edges of a pink nightgown and burgundy housecoat fell decorously, turned up to expose a bare ankle but little other skin. He drew his gun and let it hang by his side. Neither protection, nor comfort, nor a sign of resolve. Simply an action, something to do.

He stepped to the threshold. The woman lay on her stomach, stretched out, her face turned to the left. Unlike the natural position of her legs, her arms were bent oddly, trapped beneath her as if she had attempted to rise, then collapsed, giving up. Her eyes stared, examining the room from ground level. The stain spread beneath her chest, but no further. Under his feet, DiGenero could feel the carpet's heavy pad. It had absorbed most of the blood, although a heart shot also had stopped the organ before its pumping action extended the mess.

Pagano crouched on the floor beyond his wife in the small front foyer. DiGenero walked toward him, then stopped at the boundary of his stains. Not nearly so neat. The story was relatively easy to tell. Pagano had taken issue with the instructions of whoever had caused him to rise from the breakfast table. His departure had neither been sudden or easy. Behind and around him, the holes in the wall suggested he had run, or tried to. From his final position, it appeared he died from several shots in the back and head when he stopped to open the door. DiGenero surmised the woman came behind, from the kitchen. Whoever followed Pagano had turned and silenced her quickly. From the looks of how she fell, she was probably dead before she hit the floor.

He would have missed the child if it hadn't been for the bear at the foot of the stairs. When he saw it, he didn't want to look up, to follow the line it had taken as it fell. The stairway rose from the foyer along the outer wall of the house. Finally, DiGenero walked to it. She was curled as if asleep, her head resting on the top step, one arm a pillow, the other extended where the toy had slipped from her grasp. He started to cry. On her pajamas, the same mouse smiled.

He didn't know how long he'd been standing there when Silverstein came in. He took DiGenero's gun gently out of his hand and slipped it in his own pocket. Silverstein looked around like a man who had witnessed an accident and decided against offering his account. "Come on. Pagano ain't in the mood to tell secrets today."

"Who would kill a child?" DiGenero asked.

Silverstein took his arm and nudged.

"Why?"

"Let's get outa here," Silverstein said, more insistently this time.

"I wanna look around." DiGenero pulled back half heartedly.

"Bullshit! Some babushka across the street's probably already made the fuckin' car. You wanna give 'em a snapshot, too?" Silverstein glanced around the room. "What did you touch besides the door?" he asked.

"Nothing."

"Good. Then, let's get the door wiped and get movin'. They already got a DiGenero fan club started at Manhattan Homicide. They're gonna have chapters in every borough if you keep showin' up in places like this."

DiGenero looked at the bodies, then at the living room. Things were all in their place. Except for Pagano's attempted escape and his wife's terrified reaction, there had been no struggle. Someone Pagano knew had shot him. He'd let them in—there was no sign it had been otherwise. But still, there was no logic to it. No reason that what DiGenero knew—what they'd learned only a few hours before—should have been compromised so quickly. "How did Scarlese find out?" DiGenero spoke to himself, thinking aloud.

"Find out what?" Silverstein asked.

"That we knew about this." He gestured toward the body.

"Well, Pagano's not gonna tell ya." Silverstein held him by the elbow.

"How?" DiGenero repeated.

"Come on, for Christ's sake!" Silverstein tugged hard on his arm.

He took a few steps slowly, then stopped. Silverstein groaned. He glared, exasperated. DiGenero looked down at the woman. Only inches away, she stared at his shoes. "We just found out about Pagano last night. It's not possible." His voice trailed away to a whisper. "Not possible. How in the hell did they know?"

The limousine slid into the underground garage like an animal returning to its lair. It spiraled downward, a continuous left turn. The private elevators serviced the private floors from private parking, the third and lowest level. The chauffeur flashed his lights, alerting the attendant, who opened the security gate. He accelerated. The car crossed the half-empty space, then swung in a long U-turn around the pillars, bringing its right rear door to a stop precisely beside the elevator bank.

Scarlese was out of the limousine before the chauffeur could reach the rear door handle. He paused to button his double-breasted suitjacket and smooth his tie, offering the driver another opportunity. The chauffeur changed course. He opened the door to the glass-enclosed elevator bank. Scarlese entered the small waiting area. A third man dressed in a blazer and slacks had climbed from the front seat. He followed. Without looking back, Scarlese pointed to a spot on the floor. "Here. Nobody goes to the penthouse. Got it?" he said.

"Yeah." He planted himself where directed, back to the elevator. He folded his arms, straining the blazer's material across his shoulders and biceps.

Scarlese inserted a key. The elevator door opened at once. Inside, there were only four choices. He inserted the key again. The door closed. Alone, he ascended.

Fifty-six floors above, the door opened at Scarlese's first knock. "Well. And to what do I owe this unexpected pleasure?" She smiled.

"And it will be one, too." Scarlese enfolded her in his arms, gently at first, then with force, pulling her hard against him.

"Take your clothes off," he said. Her tongue darted into his mouth, interrupting. The motion of her hands matched his, reaching down to explore. A mutual stroking.

He began again. "Once a month isn't enough."

She pushed back. Her laugh was full, a challenge. "You're not going to tell me you spend your evenings with leprechauns and fairy queens? Don't give me that!" She undid his arms and turned, leading the way. "Come on. Business first." Scarlese followed.

The hall divided the office suite. Two rooms on either side and at the end, an open bay. Unexceptional space save for the view through the solid bank of windows. To the north, the East side's grid organized the boxes, squares and rectangles, all heights and sizes. To the east, the river carved the island. Across it, the industrial maze of Hunts Point, Long

Island City, Astoria and Queens. The blue line of Flushing Bay created the far horizon. Above it, an invisible tether drew airplanes from the sky, one after another, toward LaGuardia.

Save for a desk, computer hardware, and several office chairs, the open bay was empty. She walked to the desk and turned, leaning against it. Scarlese stood.

Her tone changed, adding authority. "First things first. We had an understanding that with Ferringa gone, we'd minimize risks. Why the unscheduled meeting?"

Scarlese cleared his throat, "We have to talk about your next step."

" 'We'?" She folded her arms. "Do we now? And why is that?"

Scarlese walked to the window. "A problem. Minor and manageable, but one we want to take care of."

Sarcasm tinged her response. She drew out his name. "Johnny. Don't bullshit me with your management doubletalk. That's okay for your crushers. They're suitably impressed, I'm sure. But don't forget I went to college, too. I said, what's the problem?"

Scarlese turned, obviously displeased. "The problem is someone knows that we've got a connection at JFK. That means we need to step back and assess whether it does any damage. I'm not suggesting you change plans, but it might be wise to defer things, alter the schedule until we can figure this out."

"How much do they know about JFK?"

Scarlese waved peremptorily, dismissing the question. "Don't worry about that. Whatever they know, they can't learn any more. We've taken care of that aspect of the problem."

"And what does that mean?" she asked skeptically.

"We whacked Pagano," he said.

"Oh, that's fine. That does us a goddamn lot of good."

Scarlese reacted, defensive. "There was no point in temporizing. He knew. Whaddyawant? He had to know or we couldn't have gotten our hands on the airplanes. That was the fact of the matter. So what were our choices? Tell him to keep his mouth shut? Gimme a break. Move him? Where? Whack him. It was best." Scarlese shrugged. "So what? The Paganos of the world are not exactly a commodity in short supply. I've got a lock on Kennedy. We'll replace him. Don't worry about it."

"When did you kill him?" she asked.

"This morning, early. I guarantee you, nobody got to him."

The reassurances appeared an irritation. She frowned. "You killed him based on what information?"

"Based on what Benedetto told us," he answered.

"Ahh." She nodded slowly. "So we're worried about the FBI, are we? They're the ones who know . . ."

"No," Scarlese shook his head. "They're not it. Look, why don't you let me take care of this." He tried to change the subject. "With Pagano gone, we've got to talk about . . ."

She exploded. "Goddamn it! Don't tell me what we have to talk about! If it's not the FBI, who is it?"

Scarlese hesitated. Finally, he spoke. "DiGenero."

"DiGenero," she repeated the name. She examined him coldly. "The one Ferringa didn't get."

He nodded almost imperceptibly.

"The one whose wife Rocchi killed in Salt Lake City."

Scarlese's stare turned baleful.

"After I told you not to send him," she said.

He didn't answer.

"After I said we're not to cross wires. No compromising our arrangement with your personal vendettas." The words were clipped with serrated edges.

Scarlese spoke, low and malevolent. "Don't tell me how to run my fucking business. Not now. Not ever."

The silence lasted between them. Finally, she stood and walked to the window. Scarlese followed her with his eyes. When she spoke, her voice was matter-of-fact. "I think you're right, Johnny." She turned to face him and smiled benignly. "I think we do need to reassess. You and I."

Scarlese returned the smile. He seemed to relax, vindicated by her behavior. He walked closer and stood, then touched her cheek, caressing. "We're a partnership," he said. "The two of us are the microcosm. What you believe matters to me. If it didn't we never would have met in Boston. But what distinguishes us, what makes us strong, is how far we can see. Take this." He spread his arms, encompassing the office. "You've carried the cause beyond its old limits and look what you've been able to achieve. You could shoot a thousand more Brits on patrol in Ulster, dynamite half of London, blow away a cabinet minister—what would it get you? A story on the six o'clock news in New York. Beyond that?" Scarlese shrugged. "You'd be back at it with nothing gained the next day. Am I right?" he asked.

She returned the question. "Are you?"

"Of course. To understand that, you've got to understand history. What happened to other causes when they only operated at home? Who cared about the Palestinians or the Iranians until they started operating on western turf? Frankfurt, Paris, even Munich in 1972. Were the acts achievements by themselves? No, obviously not. But they changed the world, didn't they? It's the same for you. All politics is local. You want to put leverage on London. Do it here." He pointed to the computer. "With this, you're not on their turf. They're on yours. When Washington starts to scream, the Brits will have to listen. What choice do they have? All you need is patience. Who knows? Another airplane may not even be necessary. The question isn't *if* you'll get what you want. It's *when.*"

"And can you be patient?" she asked. She stepped away again. Scarlese watched her walk to the desk.

"That's the key. Your gain is mine. 'Ours,' " he corrected.

"Oh? How's that?" She sat.

"Forty years ago my family was at the cutting edge. In a generation, from the twenties to the fifties, they went from bootlegging to the union rackets, to war work contracts—keeping peace in the factories—to investment in legitimate businesses. Now it's time for another change." Scarlese faced the windows and pointed. "In five years I want what I have here to be in place in Europe." He turned toward her. "In other words, in the EC, I want my market share. Legitimate business as well as our"—he smiled—"more traditional product lines. For that I need an entrée. With your help, I'll make that happen before Europe pulls itself together. Before the new world order knows what it is."

"So it's a long-term strategy I'm hearing you describe," she said.

"That's it."

"And that's the reason we're to have patience. As are you. Do I have this right?"

"Right on the money." Scarlese smiled.

She nodded. "That's good. Because when I hear you talking about patience and about reassessing things"—she looked directly at Scarlese, eyes wide—"now, I know you don't mean this, but it could make a person wonder whether Johnny Scarlese is backing out of a deal." She folded her hands primly. "That certainly wouldn't be the way *I'm* hearing you. But there's others we've got to consider who might not have the sophistication to understand things your way. Those in Belfast I'm speaking of might believe that a man who counseled delaying the next step—someone who's talking about reassessing things—was getting cold feet because of the risks he'd suddenly come to run. They might be especially prone to draw that conclusion if we were being asked to reassess because of something unfortunate, such as DiGenero—something wholly extraneous to our cause. And if that was the case, my darling— and I'm sayin' this as someone who cares for you—I'd worry, if I were you. I'd worry a good deal."

Scarlese walked to the desk and stood over her. His lips were pressed white, a fury barely contained. "Listen, cunt! Don't think you can threaten me."

She smiled and looked up. "Of course not, my darling. But I do need to tell you, if you want our help, 'long-term' for us—and for *you*—means 'today.' We're not having any delays or reassessments. That's that."

"Go fuck yourself!" Scarlese spun on his heel.

"Oh. I thought you had some interest in that. But I can manage by myself, if I must, thank you." She laughed aloud. "And one more thing," she called out. Her voice followed Scarlese down the hall. "Speaking of being fucked, you'd best take care of your problem with DiGenero—*now*—before he does it to you again."

CHAPTER
23

THE SMILING MOUSE stayed with him. They drove to Manhattan through the rain. DiGenero sat silently, thinking about the little girl. Silverstein was hungry. They stopped for lunch at a diner, a silver-sided replica of the fifties. DiGenero ordered, but couldn't eat. Silverstein finished a platter of hamburgers and fries, then DiGenero's. A belch recorded the accomplishment.

"Whaddya wanna do?" Silverstein asked. He twisted a straw into a dental implement, deftly policing the gaps in his teeth.

"Sleep," he said. "Then, regroup. Later."

Silverstein drained his cola. He crunched a mouthful of ice. "I'll drop ya at the hotel, then do a background check on Pagano. See if he's connected to anybody with a file who works Kennedy, okay?"

He nodded.

"I also got a cousin with the Port Authority Police, the ones responsible for airport security. Sometimes they got info on who's who they don't put in the hopper, their own files, ya know what I mean? I'll give him a ring. I'll call ya later at the hotel."

Driving through Brooklyn, they stopped in Williamsburg, near the Bridge. Silverstein got out to telephone a Queens homicide detective he knew, tipping him off about the hit. DiGenero didn't object. A local investigation was random motion, but even indiscriminate activity might help. Like beaters in the bush, the villagers turned out to flush game.

DiGenero waited in the car, motor running. The street was well kept, residential. On either sides, apartment buildings, brick blocks as tall as they were wide, sandwiched once-elegant rowhouses now transformed into pricey walk-up flats. The rain fell harder. On the windshield it refracted the light, creating a kaleidoscope of shapes and motion. Competing trucks and cars, a bicycle messenger, crouched and dripping, a woman with a grocery cart navigating the passages between puddles in the street.

Tired beyond redeeming, DiGenero let his mind drift, entertained. He snapped on the wipers. They swept intermittantly across his field of vision, providing a survey of artistic schools. A pass across the glass, clarity: the realists. The first drops, precise distinctions blurring: impressionism. More rain, all objects created from the same constituent elements: the pointillists. Water accumulating, rain transubstantiated, the perceived ascendant over the objective: the abstract.

Silverstein returned. They wormed their way onto the Williamsburg Bridge, inching into lower Manhattan. Traffic was worse in the city. They crossed town on Delancey Street, found Bowery, turned north to Third Avenue, then west on 21st Street to his hotel.

DiGenero walked past the desk. He thought of calling Foley in Boston to find out what he'd learned about BA 121, but decided against it. He was too tired to listen, much less talk. Beside the elevators, the lights on the display panel showed both cars at the top floor and holding. He took the stairs. He counted each step, concentrating to be sure he didn't trip. His room was at the end of the hall. He walked, floating in his own medium.

When he opened the door, Benedetto was sitting in the chair by the window. DiGenero stared dumbly. The room was as he'd left it, still made up from the day before. Benedetto was posed stiffly, with both feet on the floor, as if part of the furnishings. His raincoat was folded in his lap.

"Shut the door and sit down, Frank," he said.

DiGenero obeyed. Benedetto watched him with policeman's eyes. He eased down on the edge of the bed. "This is sweet of you, Tony, but you could have left a message. I'd love to come to Sunday dinner. Can I bring something? A casserole?"

"You shoulda taken my advice last week. You know that?" Benedetto said.

DiGenero could feel his body working, the message going out from the brain along the circuits, trying to tap a reservoir of energy not already depleted. He was awake again, wide awake, but still running slowly, in second gear. Adrenaline struggling to overcome exhaustion. Stimulus but only limited response. He nodded. "I thought about going back, like you said. But you know Quantico this time of year. The society season's over and what's a boy to do? All the beautiful people are in New York."

Benedetto stared, flat-eyed. "You think you're so fuckin' cute."

DiGenero held up his right hand like an oathtaker. "Alright. You got me. Good lookin', maybe, but I swear I never said 'cute.'"

"The Ferringa thing was no good. No good," he repeated.

"I wasn't the shooter, Tony. There's more to this than you know."

Benedetto gave no sign DiGenero's words even registered. "You shoulda left well enough alone."

DiGenero shifted uneasily on the edge of the bed. People generally talked to you, with you, or at you, but in this case there was not even a pretense of such social forms. Benedetto spoke like a judge delivering an opinion, coherent if crude. A decision already made, to be handed down, made public via statement not dialogue. The authoritative presentation of a construction of facts and rules to support a judgment that followed.

"I get it," DiGenero said. "This is the 'come on, we're goin' downtown' speech, right? Okay, you can relax. I'm not gonna start a fight. I'm not that crazy. I'll go peacefully. I understand I'm in deep shit, but at least let's have a conversation first. You and me. You gotta listen. Our boy's up to his eyeballs in . . ."

"There's nothin' to listen to," Benedetto said.

He contradicted. "Yeah, there is. Scarlese himself is tied up with the IRA bunch that brought down that airliner. He . . ."

Benedetto shook his head. "Shut up, Frank."

DiGenero reacted, irritated. "Whaddyamean, 'shut up'? The case—Scarlese and the Irish—is yours. I know that. You got a lock on it, every piece of paper. You know Rocchi and Ferringa were part of the story. Now there's an airline mechanic, his wife and kid dead out in Queens. He was the one who . . ."

Benedetto's color rose like the sun. "I said, shut up!" He yanked the raincoat off his lap and raised the automatic.

DiGenero stared at the silencer. He felt queasy, unsteady for the first time. The 9mm trembled in Benedetto's hand. He was breathing unevenly, short, heavy respirations. As he labored, Benedetto's face mottled. His lips moved soundlessly like an old man's, animated by the obvious effort at self-control.

DiGenero leaned back on the bed, propping himself on his hands. "How much, Tony?"

"How much what?" Benedetto sounded genuinely obtuse.

"How much is Scarlese payin' you? Five thousand a month? I got it right, don't I?"

Benedetto ignored the question. "You came back and made your own bed. Now you gotta lie in it. You did this, not me, you asshole."

"Sure," DiGenero said sarcastically. "I sent Scarlese an engraved invitation to kill my wife. I . . ."

Benedetto wasn't listening. "I finally had a way outa this. After all these years of grubbin', I got my ticket paid. And you know for what? For just lookin' the other fuckin' way." Benedetto had the doleful eyes of the permanently misunderstood. "I don't have to do a goddamn thing that leaves fingerprints. Nothin'. I got it all arranged to get a piece of the action. Down the road. Profit-sharing. I don't gotta do more after this IRA operation goes down." He shook his head. "I perform, they perform. That's it. When Scarlese sets up in Europe the checks start comin' in regular. Payment for services received. I don't even have to break a sweat, you understand? All I do is handle the investigation, make sure it moves the right way. That's all." Benedetto stared. "I mean that *was* all. Until you came back. Until you did what you always fuckin' do. Just like before. Nobody else matters, do they? Not to the goddamn star, the prima donna. I told you in Salt Lake City I'd take care of this, but that didn't mean shit to you. When I saw you, you didn't think even for a minute that I was askin' you for somethin', askin' you to stay out of the way. You didn't think that for once you was supposed to be the giver, not the taker, huh? And whaddya do? You gotta have it your way. You walk all over my life again. You walk all over me."

"What life did I walk all over, Tony? Your fuckin' sellout to Scarlese? I'm so sorry that isn't gonna work out. But you see Scarlese caused me a little heartache . . ."

Benedetto interrupted, shouting. "I was gonna take care of it! I told you! But you didn't even give me a chance! You think I can't operate one-on-one with these fuckin' wiseguys? You think you're the only one that's got the balls? You never even thought that I could do it, did ya? The fuckin' idea never even crossed your mind! You! It hadta be you! You hadta come back here. Nobody else could handle this, right?" Benedetto lifted his head, chin out. "Me! I deal with Scarlese. Equals."

DiGenero sat, silent.

Benedetto leaned forward, poking a finger at DiGenero. "Scarlese don't own me. We got a deal—one deal. That's all. He's got his business. I got my job. He knows that. He knows." Benedetto sat back, nodding, agreeing with himself. "When I was ready, when the time was right, I was gonna take down Scarlese for you. Me! That's who. I bet you never even figured on that, did ya?" Benedetto ran one hand through his hair. "I got one arrangement with him, that's all. The rest? He's just another fuckin' greaseball. Nothing else. He can't push me around." Benedetto looked away. His voice faded. "He knows."

DiGenero stared, cold-eyed. "I got only one question, Tony? Why didn't you give me a call?"

Benedetto looked every way except at DiGenero.

"Why didn't you warn me? Tell me that, old buddy?"

Benedetto collected himself. "I don't have to tell you squat."

"You're right," DiGenero said. "I've already got the answer. You didn't know Scarlese was gonna kill my wife."

Benedetto stared.

"As a matter of fact, you don't have a clue about what Scarlese's up to. And you know what? You're figuring that out right now. Listening to me, it's getting through, right, goombah? You've been set up. You got a deal with Scarlese? Lemme tell you the deal. Scarlese's told you that if you want to get your checks when you're an old man, you gotta kill me."

Benedetto started to speak but the knock on the door silenced him. He trained the automatic on DiGenero and rose, stepping to one side, outside a newcomer's field of vision. "Come in."

The door opened. Jilian entered. "Frank, that didn't sound like you. I . . ." She followed DiGenero's eyes toward Benedetto.

Benedetto pushed the door closed behind her and extended his hand. "The purse."

Jilian hesitated, then handed him her bag.

"Sit down. Beside him." He pointed to the bed. Benedetto remained in the corner.

"You see what can happen when you get in the habit of visiting men's hotel rooms," DiGenero said.

Jilian looked back and forth between the two. "You left a message at the desk that said come up straight away."

DiGenero motioned toward Benedetto. "Not me. Meet Tony Benedetto, FBI."

She eyed Benedetto, then DiGenero. "And did he also send the fax?"

"What fax?" DiGenero asked.

"This morning. It came to my office, telling me to arrange a meeting with you, here, this afternoon. I tried to call but you were . . ."

"Out," he said.

"I thought Scarlese sent it and . . ." she began.

Benedetto broke in. "You're so fuckin' smart, Frank, I bet you got this one figured, too, huh?"

"Why don't you help me, Tony."

"I'll give you the condensed version. Sallie Ferringa's distraught sweetheart finds his killer, shoots him, then turns the gun on herself." Benedetto was perspiring, his pupils contracted. He wet his lips. "I didn't give a shit who came first. You or her. Whoever showed up, we'd wait for the other one."

You think you can walk out of here? It won't work," DiGenero said.

"I don't have to walk outa here, asshole. When it's over, I just pick up the phone. I'm the one that's investigating the case, remember? I come lookin' for you. I find you and her. Dead. My squad's got jurisdiction.

You don't think I can handle that?" Benedetto took a step forward. He motioned. "Just lie back, Frank. This won't hurt a bit."

DiGenero looked at Jilian. Her eyes were dark with fear. "For Christ's sake, wait a minute!" DiGenero slipped one hand into the pocket of his parka. Then, he remembered. At Pagano's house, Silverstein had taken his gun. He felt weak, sinking into helplessness. "I'm not the only one that knows, Tony."

Benedetto shook his head. "It won't work. Lie back, like I said."

This time the knock boomed. Benedetto's eyes darted toward the door, then back. Confusion contorted his features.

"Who is it?" DiGenero called out quickly. His voice sounded strange, high pitched.

"Shaddap!" Benedetto hissed.

"Jilian? Are you in there?"

She answered at once. "Yes!"

The handle rattled hard. "It's locked." The voice came clearly through the door.

Benedetto held his ground. His eyes caged right and left, his face a mask of perspiration.

A fist struck the door, drumbeats. "Hello? You'll need to give me some help here!"

DiGenero spoke quietly. "Okay, Tony. Whaddya gonna do now? Kill me? Kill her? Kill whoever's knocking? Come on."

The pounding was louder, heavier. "Jilian? Are you opening this?"

Benedetto looked sick.

DiGenero pressed. "We can put this back together, right? Whaddya done for Scarlese, anyway? You said it yourself. It's what you haven't done. Maybe you don't have problem number one. You can't prove a negative, right? What can anybody say about what's not happened on a case, about what hasn't gone down? Who knows how things have been up to now? Only you and me, right? So it's what happens from here out that matters. We can make that right. You and me. Together. Okay?"

Benedetto didn't answer. He held the automatic with both hands, staring vacantly at DiGenero, then the door, mouth open, swaying on his feet.

DiGenero stood. Benedetto's eyes offered an opening inward, a vision into a lost soul. The 9mm drooped. DiGenero shook his head in disgust. "You can't even say yes or no, can you, Tony?" He walked past Benedetto and opened the door.

Jilian looked up. "Ian!"

Ian Barry entered the room. "Hello there."

Barry's right hand was in his car coat pocket, the outline of the gun barely concealed in his fist. For an instant, when their eyes met, DiGenero saw that Barry knew.

Barry turned toward Benedetto. "What have we here, Tony?"

Benedetto seemed uncomprehending.

Jilian rose and slipped behind Barry. She took DiGenero's arm and edged him toward the door.

Benedetto's eyes shifted from face to face, a man trying to come to grips with events moving too quickly, beyond his control. He gestured weakly toward DiGenero with the automatic. "Wait a minute."

Barry reached deftly for the 9mm, removing it from Benedetto's hand as he spoke. "Ah yes. We must be discussing the merits of the Glock automatic." He kept up a constant patter as he hefted the gun. Barry unscrewed the silencer from the barrel. "I'm not a fan of plastic weapons —doesn't seem quite right, does it?—but it is light. Decent performer, they say, although if it was mine, I'd be nervous about a safety built into the trigger. Makes it touchy, or so I'm told." He pressed the release on the grip, ejecting the magazine. "Loaded guns are such dangerous things." Barry dropped the silencer and magazine in his pocket, then handed the automatic back to Benedetto. He smiled. "If you're not careful, quite easy to shoot yourself in the foot."

Benedetto was pale. "What are you doin' here?"

Barry glanced behind him. Jilian and DiGenero were gone. When Barry turned back, so was his smile. "I think you know."

"This is none of your fuckin' business." Benedetto squared himself to Barry, legs apart. His voice wavered, contradicting the bully's stance.

"I think it is," Barry said quietly.

"That broad"—Benedetto gestured spastically toward the door—"if she's one of yours, not declared, I mean, we got a major problem. You know that?" Benedetto sounded more petulant than threatening.

"Really?" Barry folded his arms.

Benedetto spoke louder, trying ineffectually to regain the initiative. "You bet your ass. You don't even think about operatin' here without our say-so." He leaned toward Barry. "You don't get in the middle of our shit." Benedetto stabbed the air with his finger, this time pointing toward the absent DiGenero. "He's domestic. Ours. Period!"

Barry nodded noncommittally.

"You understand?" Benedetto leaned forward, as if physically pushing for an affirmation.

Barry didn't reply. He stepped away. Barry walked slowly about the room, casually inspecting its contents. Benedetto's eyes followed him, examining his every move, looking for clues and finding none, growing more anxious.

"You understand?" Benedetto repeated querulously.

At the window, Barry held the curtain aside. He looked out at the park. Below, Jilian and DiGenero were getting into a cab. When he turned back to face Benedetto he held the stubby tube of the silencer in his hand. "If there'd been a dead British subject in this hotel room, you'd have had a bigger problem. Don't you agree?"

"Gimme that," Benedetto commanded weakly.

"This?" Barry asked. He held up the silencer as if discovering it for the first time. "Of course." Barry flipped it to Benedetto, who bobbled the catch. Barry walked toward the door. "I'll give you something else as well. A piece of advice." He paused. "When we meet again for our regular liaison session, one-on-one, it would be wise—wise, that is, for you—to fill me in on all the details about Scarlese and the PIRAs that you have. Including what you've got on DiGenero. What he knows about Scarlese's connection."

"Wait a minute . . ." Benedetto was perspiring again.

Barry continued. "And I wouldn't mention the woman who was here to anyone at the Bureau. I think it would raise far more questions for you —about what you were doing here—than it would for me."

Benedetto stared, mouth open.

"I must admit, as a friend, this little hotel-room scene doesn't look terribly good. I mean, what conclusions would you draw?" He smiled sympathetically at Benedetto. "Seems like a difficult situation to put in a good light. You. One of your old partners, a fugitive from justice, wanted for three murders here in New York. A surreptitious meeting in his hotel. A silenced weapon. Illegal here even for lawmen, isn't it? I'm sure some of the hotel staff saw your arrival. And there are fingerprints— yours, too, I'm sure—in the room. Hard to get them all wiped, eh?" He shrugged. "Of course, as you say, it's none of my business. But if I was in your shoes, I'd think very hard about how to explain it." Barry's smile disappeared. "Just in case word got out and you had to try."

CHAPTER

24

JILIAN AND BARRY had argued for almost an hour. DiGenero sat by the window. He closed his eyes. In the darkness, the fatigue settled on him like a blanket, insulating him from their voices.

After leaving the hotel, the cab had taken them to Times Square. They rode the subway shuttle to Grand Central, walked a pattern through the station, doubling back to be sure no one had followed. Satisfied, they climbed to the street and walked to Jilian's apartment. She had listened, collecting things in an overnight bag while he told her about Benedetto. They were in the hall, about to close the door, when Barry called. They took another cab, then the subway to the Bronx. Barry was waiting when they arrived.

DiGenero let his mind drift. He knew the neighborhood. Two stories below, the yellow pools under the streetlights led east to the Grand Concourse. Kingsbridge Road hosted solid apartments, fifty-year-old fine-finished brick and stone. Once they were permanence for a second generation that had moved uptown, leaving behind the first generation's temporary lives. A few of the originals remained, pockets of poorer elderly, Jewish, Italian, and Irish. Their children, too, had moved, but they clung to the Bronx neighborhood, much as their parents had clung to the harsh but known certainties of lower Manhattan's immigrant ghettos.

In law school, DiGenero had rented a room five blocks away, finding the ad in the Irish *Echo*. When the landlords first opened the door, he was surprised to find an old Italian couple. He learned later that the *Echo* was an open secret, the place to advertise for whites who could sustain a building's last stand against the next wave, blacks and Puerto Ricans. The Irish had replenished themselves with a small, but steady flow, singles and young families, mostly poor and escaping Ulster. They and the Puerto Ricans created a volatile chemistry, temporarily stable on Friday nights, Sunday mass, and holidays at the parish, but otherwise a fulminate, erupting into legendary fights in buildings they shared.

DiGenero resisted the urge to slip away, to sleep. The argument had begun almost as soon as they had arrived, neither including nor excluding him, but apparently resuming where the two had last left it. He concentrated, trying to follow.

Barry glanced at him, then away. The hostility was vague but palpable. DiGenero's renewed interest seemed clearly unwelcome. Seated opposite Jilian, he leaned forward, elbows on knees. Barry lowered his voice, its volume inversely proportional to his insistence. "Think of it this way. If I hadn't found the fax on your desk and decided to check on you this afternoon, where would you be?"

Jilian leaned back, reintroducing the space between them. "I really don't know, Ian."

"I don't expect the King's Cross, but you might consider that you and he would be quite dead." Barry nodded toward DiGenero without looking his way.

"I think he wants you to say 'thank you' again for saving our lives." DiGenero smiled helpfully.

Barry examined him with an expression reserved for intrusive children. His attention returned to Jilian. "We need to talk about today. It's a turning point. That's all."

"At least we can agree on that, can't we?" she said.

Barry ignored her sarcasm. "Given his circumstances, Benedetto's not going to run to the Bureau. It's Scarlese I'm worried about. If Benedetto goes to him . . ."

Jilian interrupted. "I don't know."

Barry glanced at DiGenero, obviously wishing they were alone. DiGenero watched, his expression neutral, that of the stranger who had seated himself inadvertently amidst a family argument.

"The facts are these, like them or not," Barry said. "Scarlese was either prepared to use you to kill DiGenero or to eliminate you along with him. One way or another, you're expendable. If Benedetto was acting on Scarlese's instructions—not pulling this plan out of his hat—your usefulness here is finished. I don't think there's any argument about that." Barry paused.

Jilian neither agreed nor disagreed.

He continued. "But even if Scarlese used you only as a means to set him up"—he nodded again toward DiGenero—"it's the same."

"How so?" she asked.

Barry reacted as if she'd missed the obvious. "Don't you get it? You're not important. Not someone who's going to be let into his confidence.

Despite what you've told him—about your orders from the IRA command and all that—Scarlese hasn't bought it. He's using you. That's all."

DiGenero had stretched out in the chair, extending himself toward them. He crossed his hands on his chest. "Maybe not," he said.

Barry regarded him with irritation. "I don't think there's any 'maybe' about it." He turned back to Jilian. "As I was saying . . ."

DiGenero interrupted. "That's all logical, okay? But it's not Scarlese."

"If you don't mind . . ."

DiGenero ignored him. "Let's put this together from day one. Johnny sent Vito Rocchi to kill my wife. Rocchi was his main mule, the guy who traveled back and forth to Ireland. When Benedetto tipped him that I was in New York, he used Ferringa to get me that night on Ward's Island. Main man number two for the IRA operation. When that didn't work, who got the job next? Benedetto himself, a real prize for Scarlese, his mole in the Bureau and his means of control over the FBI investigation into BA 121. What does that tell you?"

Barry sat silent, his jaw set.

DiGenero answered his own question. "It tells you that when it comes to me, Johnny Junior's not logical. Not a rational man. He wants me dead—bad—and he'll pay the price, even if it screws up his deal with the IRA."

Barry smiled condescendingly. "Interesting speculation, but frankly it strikes me as a narrow point of view. Understandable, given your position in Scarlese's bull's-eye. But I don't think it accounts for what we know, the intelligence we have in this case."

DiGenero laughed. "Intelligence? You just had a fucking building fall on you. This isn't too tough to figure out. Scarlese's wired into the Bureau—Benedetto's squad, the one you're working with, right? That means—logically—the IRA is, too. Whatever you do, they know."

Barry stared.

DiGenero continued. "What I'd conclude is that your intelligence on this case, at least what you've gotten from the FBI, isn't worth shit. How do you know what Scarlese and the IRA have fed you through Benedetto? You can't be sure now what's reliable and what isn't. That's the bad news. But the good news is, you learned something. If Scarlese is willing to go for me twice—to risk his IRA connection twice—odds are he'll do it again. That makes him vulnerable. And it makes the IRA vulnerable, too."

"Given who's tried to kill whom, I find your analysis a little odd, to say the least," Barry said.

"Whaddyamean?" DiGenero asked.

"Obvious, isn't it? I'd say you're the one who's vulnerable, not Scarlese. But more to the point, who's trying to kill you is *your* problem, not ours. *Our* problem is to keep the PIRAs from bringing down more airliners. For that, we don't need to get into the middle of a Mafia blood feud."

"I think Frank's right," Jilian said.

Barry rolled his eyes, exasperated. "Oh, for Christ's sake."

She spoke. "Look, Scarlese's failed twice to kill him. What's changed? Today, tonight, tomorrow, Scarlese will know that he's still alive, if he doesn't already. And he'll know that I'm still available to help him try again. He can reach me. He did this morning. Scarlese needs me." She smiled. "When it comes to getting DiGenero, I'm all he has."

"By George, I think she's got it," DiGenero said.

Barry shook his head. "Do you honestly believe it makes sense to get involved in this vendetta?"

Jilian shrugged, "I don't think we have a choice, Ian."

DiGenero stood. "Where's the bathroom?"

Barry gestured. He disappeared down the hall.

"Listen to me." Barry leaned forward, speaking softly. "You're making a mistake. One that could hurt us all." He glanced in the direction DiGenero had taken. "You're undeclared, operating illegally in this country. Since you've arrived, I've tried to protect you, to advise you, to help you. Whether you choose to believe me or not, I'm on your side. Right now, depending on whether I've put the fear of God in Benedetto, his superiors may or may not know about you. If they do, there'll be hell to pay. But it will be nothing if they find you in the midst of a purely domestic case"—he jabbed toward DiGenero's chair with his finger—"this one, involving a Bureau agent no less." Barry's voice dropped to a whisper. "You read his file. He's a cowboy. A loner. What do you think you can do at this point? Direct him? Don't be silly. Under the best of circumstances, DiGenero would have been difficult to control. Now?" Barry shook his head. "The man is after revenge." He glanced down the hall again, then sat back. "DiGenero is someone—a problem—you should leave to me."

"What do you mean?"

He leaned forward again. "I mean, we have to solve this, but we can't break every piece of crockery in the shop to do it. Knowing how the PIRAs operate here—their connections to Scarlese, to others—is invaluable. It's an investment. The cruel fact is, there'll be other 121s, even if we stop this cold. We can't make this the Holy Grail." Barry spoke deliberately, enunciating one word at a time. "It just can't be done." He leaned back in his chair. "As for DiGenero, our interests simply are not his. I grant you, he could give us access to Scarlese. If we're lucky. Very lucky. But the price of failing—of your being caught up along with him by the Bureau—would be enormous. Too great to contemplate."

"And?" Jilian asked. She waited.

"We 'inadvertently' stumbled across him once, didn't we? When I requested his file for you. I think we can 'inadvertently' stumble across him again. A call to the Bureau with a tip as to his whereabouts—say, his new hotel for this evening?"

Jilian listened. "And that would take care of it?"

"I don't follow," Barry said.

"I mean you paint a picture of DiGenero the wild man and then propose we eliminate the risk by turning him in to the FBI? I don't follow," she said.

Barry pursed his lips. "There are other more permanent choices." He paused, searching for her reaction. Jilian returned his stare. Barry continued. "Of course, if we turned DiGenero in, we couldn't be sure what he'd say."

Jilian furrowed her brow. "About?"

"Anything. But I'm thinking of you, in particular. In fact, even now we don't know what he's said or who he's talked to, do we?"

"No, we don't," she said.

Barry glanced down the hall. "Has he mentioned anyone else to you? I mean, anyone who may be helping him. Who may know about Scarlese, the IRA connection?"

"No."

"But we couldn't be sure once the Bureau had him. Prudence would dictate another step."

"And what would prudence say?"

Barry cleared his throat. "We should fold your operation. Not right away, but the point is, DiGenero's unpredictability could affect us all."

"I see what you mean, now."

"About prudence? I'd hoped you would." Barry returned her smile.

"No. About turning things over to you."

He looked hurt. "Not at all. You don't think . . . Look, I'm simply asking you to follow the logic of a difficult situation." He looked down the hall, staring this time. "Even if we take the prudent step—let the Bureau pick him up—you're still at risk. Striking the tent would be no reflection on you. None." Barry half rose, peering toward the bathroom door. He spoke, irritated. "What the hell did he do in there? Fall in?" He eyed the nearby armchair. "Where's his coat?"

"His what?" Jilian asked.

"His parka. Whatever he wore when he arrived with you."

"I don't know," she said.

"Didn't he put it there"—he pointed—"when he came in?"

Barry rose and checked the closet. Then he walked tentatively down the hall. He knocked on the bathroom door. "Hello?"

There was no answer. He stepped past the door and opened another. The bedroom. It was empty.

"DiGenero?" He knocked again on the bathroom, then tried the handle. The door opened. Jilian watched Barry lean inside. The exclamation echoed. "He's gone!"

Barry returned double-time to the front window and looked out. "The window in the lou's open. Son of a bitch went down the bloody fire escape!"

Jilian laughed out loud.

"What the hell are you laughing about?"

"I can't imagine." She couldn't help herself.

Barry seemed momentarily perplexed. "What did he do that for?"

"Perhaps he didn't feel you had his best interests at heart, Ian." Jilian burst out laughing again, louder this time, obscuring the sound of the key unlocking the apartment's front door.

"Well, a high time here, I must say!" Groceries in arm, key in hand, Chris Barry stood in the doorway. "First I find you two alone in Daddy's office. Now, I discover just the two of you in my little nook." She put down the grocery bag and folded her arms. "Is there something you want to tell me?"

"Is this your flat?" Jilian looked over her shoulder, genuinely surprised. "I thought . . ."

Barry broke in quickly. "Jilian and I had to catch up on some insider gossip from Dublin and London. Sensitive stuff. You know, rumors and political chitchat of the highest order. We don't want to have the whole New York press corps know the Economic Development Council rep leaks like a sieve. Anyway, Belfast was ringing my phone off the hook at the apartment as well as the office. I'm sorry, love, but I was going to stop up and see you this evening anyway, so I just took the liberty of inviting Jilian here. Much more private. I suppose we could have gone to her place, but if you're shocked at this, imagine how that would have looked if you'd found out." Barry laughed. "Whatever you do, let me be the one to tell your mother."

"Well, I suppose if you're going to talk of things Irish, what better place to do it than here among us exiles. The least you could do is let me in on your secrets. But as for my real suspicions"—she frowned in mock reproof and wagged her finger—"just don't let me catch you at it again."

CHAPTER

25

THE RESTAURANT HAD nearly emptied when Silverstein drove up. Ruggiero's was a storefront, plate-glass windows showcasing booths, tables, the obligatory red-and-white-checked cloths and Chianti-bottle candles, decor that obviated the need for signs. DiGenero was watching a family finish its meal, enough pasta and bread for eight served to four. On the floor, twins on the verge of walking, each speckled and moustached in red sauce, played with spoons. They crawled itinerantly, testing the waiter's dexterity in avoiding moving obstacles. Without looking, their father reached down and shooed them between his feet, a herding instinct obviously not lost in evolution for either parent or child.

Silverstein found him. He slipped into the booth, looking both worried and relieved. "You mind tellin' me what you're doin' in the fuckin' Bronx at nine o'clock at night when I been tryin' to get you at your hotel since three?"

"Finishing my tortellini. You want some?" DiGenero pushed the plate across the table.

Silverstein made a face. "Never touch the stuff. Dago food makes your hair fall out. Where the hell ya been?"

DiGenero told him about what happened earlier in his hotel room and later with Jilian and Barry.

Silverstein listened without comment until DiGenero finished the story. "Lemme get this straight. This Barry guy saves your ass. You and them got a place that's warm and dry to talk things over. You're all wearin' white hats, on the same side. Tell me somethin'. Why'd you go out the window?"

"A feeling."

"About what?"

"That Barry was gonna roll over on me," DiGenero said.

"Turn you in? To who?" Silverstein asked.

251

"The Bureau."

Silverstein stared for a moment, obviously thinking, before he spoke. "I don't get it. He turns you in, then you'd talk. You're not gonna take a fall for Ferringa gettin' whacked. You're not the shooter. And even if he don't know that, he's gotta figure you'll tell your Feebee pals what's happening. Then, the broad—Jilian—goes down." Silverstein paused, considering, then sought clarification. "She works for him, right?"

"Nope. Barry's British intelligence and internal security. He's the liaison guy with the Bureau—the contact with Benedetto's squad."

"Yeah, okay, but she's . . ."

"She's from the Northern Ireland Police, working here undercover. Except they haven't told the Bureau. Bad form. Breaks the rules. Ruins Barry's day."

Silverstein looked perplexed. "Jesus, I thought we was complicated with the PD, the state police, the feds. Anybody else involved in this I should know about? Monty Python? Elvis?"

DiGenero explained. "For Barry, I'm a major-league complication. If he delivers me, it solves two problems. It forces Jilian to roll it up—to go home, to get out of his hair—for the reasons you say. He—and she— have to assume I'm not going to do thirty-to-life for putting Sallie away, right? So Barry counts on the fact Jilian will realize that and throw in the towel. Plus, handing me over is money in the bank for him. Let's say Benedetto reports on Jilian, tells the Bureau that the Brits are running an operation here without saying 'please and thank you'—asking permission first. Unilaterally. All by themselves. Turning me in is good karma in heaven for Barry when Washington comes for a piece of his ass. He's covered, short and long. He wins both ways."

"Or at least he don't lose," Silverstein said.

"I went out the window because I can find Barry whenever I want. Same's not true for him finding me, thank goodness. He's got to have me to deliver me up. That's why I walked."

"That explains something else."

"What?" DiGenero drained the last of his coffee. The waiter looked their way. He waved, signaling for the check.

Silverstein eyed DiGenero's plate, having second thoughts. He leaned over, taking a spoon from the closest table, and scooped a sample of tortellini. Silverstein talked with his mouth full. "The new bulletin. On you and the Ferringa shooting. I saw it today. At the precinct." He scooped again. "Before they wanted you for questioning. Now you got better billing. It says you're armed and dangerous and a suspect in the case."

DiGenero groaned. "Benedetto."

Silverstein nodded. "He's gotta be the one. Your old partner musta upped the ante."

The waiter appeared with the check.

"You got ice cream?" Silverstein asked.

"Spumoni," the waiter said.

"I thought he pitched for the Giants." Silverstein stared, deadpan. The waiter stared. DiGenero said something in Italian. The waiter nodded and walked away.

Silverstein watched him leave. "No sensahumor. Whaddya say?" he asked.

"I told him I had to have you back on the locked ward by ten," DiGenero said. Across the room, the family departed, the twins, giggling packages, dangled one each from their father's arms. They reminded DiGenero of the little girl in Howard Beach. The smiling mouse. "What's happening with Pagano?" he asked.

"They're started. I talked to my buddy in Queens homicide tonight. They got basics only. It was a .38. There's no prints in the house. Nothin' stolen. No sign of forced entry. Nobody seen nothin' in the neighborhood."

"A half block from Johnny Senior's old homestead? Surprise," DiGenero said.

Silverstein continued. "No priors or mob ties for Pagano on record. Debts okay. Wife's background clean. The Queens guy's gonna call—keep me posted—if they find anything."

"Why does he think you're interested?"

"He don't give a shit. He knows I work undercover and don't talk about a lot. It's an 'I-owe-ya-one.' That's all." Silverstein's expression rendered his judgment. "You know how it goes. Queens homicide ain't gonna get no place from the bottom up."

The spoon scraped the plate. Silverstein finished DiGenero's tortellini and spoke. "By the way, we're also not outa business at Kennedy. While you was talking about old times with Benedetto, I learned a few things."

"Like what?" DiGenero asked, interested.

Silverstein pawed in the breadbasket and found the last slice. He tore it in half and wiped the plate. "Like it ain't so easy to get a job workin' for the airlines these days. Times is tough. A few years ago, everybody's growin'. We got new airlines all over the place. They're buyin' planes left and right. The world's fulla jobs. Today? Different story. Everybody's losin' money, airlines goin' broke, consolidatin'. The whole business takes it in the ear. Look at the company Pagano worked for. The maintenance-services company that handles BA's work at JFK. They hired next to nobody in the last year."

The waiter returned with the spumoni. Silverstein dug in. "Anyway, that's what my cousin—the one in the Port Authority Police—tells me this afternoon on the phone. So I says, 'Stevie'—that's my cousin's name, Stevie—'how do I find out somethin' about who works for this company? You know, who they are, when they work, what they do.' He says, 'when they work, what they do, I can't tell ya. The company or the union's got the records. But who they are, that we got.' Stevie says, 'wait a minute, I'll pull the file.' I says, 'what file?' He says, 'the security file.' I says, 'holy shit! That's right. All these people gotta be checked out.' Security is very important, right? I mean, they don't want no ragheads with attitudes bendin' wrenches or puttin' somethin' beside gas in these planes."

DiGenero leaned forward. "So?"

Silverstein ladled a large spoonful of spumoni and popped it in his mouth. "So Stevie comes back with five names. The only ones who's been hired in the last year." He swallowed the ice cream, wincing at the cold. The waiter lingered nearby. They were the last in the restaurant. DiGenero beckoned. He handed the waiter twenty dollars and the check. Silverstein continued. "Stevie looks through the files while we're talkin' —each one's got background sheets and a security questionnaire, so the Port Authority cops can issue 'em a badge. Each badge is for a certain area in the airport, so there's also a sheet from the company, tellin' where they're gonna work." Silverstein scooped again, finishing the dish. "All five are workin' in Flight Services—they didn't hire no new special- ists—and they're all on rotatin' shifts, just like Pagano. So, some of 'em musta worked with him. I asked Stevie, 'can I check 'em out?' He says, 'sure.' "

DiGenero leaned back. "Why not? But it's a long shot."

Silverstein swallowed the final spoonful. "What else ya got? We can try to check out the rest of the flight-services types, but you remember the size of those files? We're up against a lot of names. Whaddyathink? Maybe seventy or eighty out of the three hundred folders?"

DiGenero nodded. "Probably."

"If my buddy in Queens turns somethin' up—people Pagano was close to, like other guys at work—that might help. Could be there's another Scarlese connection, but findin' out will depend on how quick they work. Queens ain't exactly known for bein' on fast forward. I'm gonna go out to Kennedy tomorrow morning, first thing. Stevie's got copies of the files for me. And pictures."

"Pictures?" DiGenero asked.

"Yeah. For the airport badges. They shoot extras, just in case a badge gets lost."

DiGenero nodded.

I'll run the traces downtown. Maybe we'll turn something up.''

DiGenero saw one of the waiters standing by a box on the far wall, throwing switches. Ruggiero's neon sign went off. Outside the sidewalk changed color. Wet from the rain, the cars transformed, reflected red to monochrome black and white. In the rear of the restaurant, tables fell into shadow. From the kitchen, garbage cans banged. A finale.

"I forgot." Silverstein dug in the pocket of his carcoat. "You also got this."

DiGenero recognized the Gramercy Park stationery. A front desk message form. He tore open the envelope as Silverstein talked. "When your room didn't answer, I went to the hotel. They got helpful real fast when I showed 'em the badge." DiGenero unfolded a sheet of paper. Silverstein tried to peer over the top. "Whazzat?"

"A fax," DiGenero said. "From Foley in Boston, the guy I went to see a couple days ago. He sent it this afternoon."

DiGenero read. "Oh shit," he muttered. "No wonder I didn't hear anything from him about 121."

"What's the problem?"

DiGenero looked up. "When Foley couldn't get in touch with me, he called Benedetto to pass on what he had—what he'd learned about who had access to the airplane in Boston. He must have thought Tony was working with us. You know, for old-times' sake."

"Great. At least it explains how Benedetto found out where you were stayin'."

DiGenero read on. Silverstein watched his expression. When he finished reading, DiGenero sat, contemplating the paper.

"You don't look too happy," Silverstein said.

"I've been better."

"Whazzitsay?"

DiGenero sighed. "When Foley talked to his Irish wiseguy buddies—the ones who have the lock on the rackets at Logan—he did the usual gumshoe thing. He said to get back to him if they found out anything more. You know what that usually gets you?" DiGenero said.

"Nothin'," Silverstein confirmed.

He nodded. "Whaddyaknow? They got back to him." DiGenero tapped the fax. "This is Foley getting back to me. It didn't take a rocket scientist to figure out why somebody was asking about 121. The union guys at Logan—whoever Foley's wiseguy contacts asked—explained that since September, the date I told Foley to start the check, two other airplanes have flown London–New York–Boston. Besides 121, that is.

One of them is about to go into scheduled maintenance and to be re-placed by a 747 from European and Middle East routes."

"How do they know that in Boston?" Silverstein asked.

"They probably get the tail numbers—the aircraft serial numbers. Some piece of paper, a schedule or whatever that tells them about equip-ment changes coming up. You know, a roster of which aircraft are going to fly where."

"You said there were two. What about the other airplane?"

"It came out of major inspection and overhaul in September. Just like 121."

"In other words," Silverstein said, "it's flyin' right now."

He winced. "I wish you hadn't put it that way. This says it's on a Monday-Wednesday-Friday schedule." DiGenero looked down at the page, then up again at Silverstein. "It arrives in New York again two nights from now."

CHAPTER
26

He left Silverstein's apartment for the subway before first light. Nearly empty, the Lexington Avenue Express careened south to 14th Street passing local stops, vacant save for the perpetual wanderers, the shapes only, homeless and abandoned.

DiGenero waited on the platform for the train to Brooklyn, watching the arrivals. At that hour they came and went singly, attracted like particles to their predetermined place in the nucleus. Work clothes, uniforms, scarred shoes, tired eyes. Night auditors, bellmen, cleaners, security guards, pulled to the center hours before. Now spent, they gave way to the next wave, backroom clerks, secretaries, delivery boys, salesgirls. A few coats and ties, the white-collar precursors, intermingled. He recognized the types. Young, aggressive, subordinate before superior, ambitious before established. A part of the molecular structure, equally impelled by the physics of the city.

DiGenero took the train for Carnasie/Brooklyn. At Grand Street, a transit cop passed. Disinterested, he made his rounds through the cars with a sailor's rolling gait. DiGenero took no chances. He buried his face in his parka, feigning sleep. His story was still in the tabloids, now page three. Benedetto's hand. An FBI backgrounder for the local crime-beat reporters had tipped them to the change in his status. Subject to suspect.

He got off at Bushwick Avenue and walked east toward the new morning. In the street, cars and trucks moved toward the bridges and tunnels. At the lights they waited, their exhaust rising in the morning cold. Approaching the neighborhood, he decided against the shortest route. He went south an additional two blocks and looped wide, leaving the avenue to avoid the early risers, the shopkeepers and long-time residents who knew the foot traffic. Who might see him, a stranger, and remember.

The side streets were quiet, almost deserted. The rowhouses marched beside him, proletarian, flat fronts with vestigal porches, cared for but austere in their sameness. DiGenero kept his distance from the house until he neared the street. Any surveillance would cover the front. He passed the intersection, a block over, then turned left. He could hear the hoe's scraping as soon as he entered the alley. He walked toward the sound. Steel on soil. On either side, the high board fences echoed, a hard chunking, steady and purposeful. It seemed out of place in Brooklyn, like a foghorn in Iowa, or the growl of traffic in mountain wilderness. He knew the source. It had traveled a great distance.

The gate was unlatched. He pushed. The hinge protested. His grandfather looked up.

"An early start for the day," DiGenero said in Italian. He closed the gate behind him.

His grandfather stood, both hands on the hoe. He was dressed in gum boots, heavy wool pants, and a sweater. Under his familiar snap-brimmed hat, his face had ruddy patches. He had been at work for some time.

He examined DiGenero, then looked back at the garden. "No. A late end for the season. The tomatoes and zucchini bore well. Good fortune always creates unrealistic hopes. It was almost October when I took the last fruits. I thought to myself, 'perhaps there could be more.' So I waited. It's human nature, never knowing when to decide things are at their end. To finish and prepare for another season."

His grandfather turned to the garden. He worked the hoe with a practiced chopping motion, reestablishing his pattern—from the rear of the plot to its outer margin. He spoke. "In this garden I have only a few square meters. It matters little. I chop up the vines and turn them under. The sun helps. Even late in the fall, it strikes here in the afternoon. But you remember, don't you?"

DiGenero nodded, although his grandfather wasn't looking his way.

"Without the warmth of October, the vines will decay more slowly." The old man shrugged without breaking rhythm. "No matter. By next season, when we plant again, they will be part of new soil." He straightened and gazed at something distant. "If I made this mistake in the old country, it would be another matter. To prepare the soil for winter is very important. In the south of Italy and Sicily, what rains we have come early in the spring." He looked at DiGenero. "You know that."

"I know," he said.

His grandfather nodded. "When they begin, the plants must be in the ground. You must be ready. Here"—he gestured dismissively—"a small corner in a backyard? A month more or less?" He smiled. "An old man finding something to do? There is no loss. The price I pay is only to work on a cold morning."

"What will you plant here next year?" DiGenero asked.

"The same. Tomatoes, zucchini, some peppers. No reasons to change things." His grandfather returned to his hoeing. He was quiet as he concentrated again, working methodically. "You didn't come to the front door."

"No," DiGenero said.

"If you had, your grandmother would have been happy to see you."

"Tell her I'm sorry, but these days"—DiGenero searched for the right word in Italian—"prudence dictates the servant's entrance."

His grandfather chuckled. "The servant's entrance? I like that. A nice ring. That's the first time anyone has ever said that about our rear gate." He chopped the vines, steadily moving toward DiGenero. "I have not seen anyone watching," he said.

"If they don't get their hands on me pretty soon, I imagine they'll get around to it. One day. Between Scarlese, the Bureau, and the cops, I didn't know if maybe I'd find them triple parked already."

"Of course, one never knows," his grandfather said. "I remember years ago. We used to send Christmas gifts to all the old women—the widows. We had at least one on every block in Little Italy. We gave each useful things. Fine olive oil. A ham. They were appreciated. We asked nothing except, from time to time, to talk with us when we called. To say what they saw when they sat looking out their windows. It was a good investment. When the police"—he smiled slightly—"or federal agents tried to watch us, we'd know."

"Not a bad idea," DiGenero said. "My guess is Johnny Junior has cut out the hams and olive oil." He thrust his hands in his pockets and hunched his shoulders against the chill. "The way he figures things, throwing one of the old ladies out her window would be all the encouragement the others would need."

"You're still in the newspapers," the old man said, glancing at him as he hoed.

"Funny, huh? After a career trying to conceal who I am, I should be everybody's headline story for breakfast."

His grandfather stopped and turned, looking directly at him. His expression had hardened. "Is that what you were doing? Spending a career trying to conceal who you were?"

DiGenero felt suddenly defensive. "In a matter of speaking, I guess. I mean, that was part of it."

"I thought you were doing what you thought was right. What had to be done."

A pale sun broke through the overcast in the east. Its light spilled over the fence, a pallid reminder of a warmer season. DiGenero hesitated. "I don't know any longer, grandfather. I simply don't know."

The old man contemplated him for several moments. He stepped slowly out of the garden and propped the hoe against the fence. "Let's sit and talk."

DiGenero followed him to the bench. Supported by two logs from a long-dead elm, the wooden plank stretched beside the garage. Weathered and cracked, it had been there as long as he remembered, a seat as well as a place beneath which to store the season's necessities: the clay pots that held his grandmother's summer herbs, planting boxes for spring seedlings, stakes to hold the tomatoes in August when they were too heavy to stand. As a small boy, the bench had been his spot. He'd sat impatiently watching his grandfather work, nagging him usually with some success to stop and entertain. Years later, on summer evenings, it was the same. They would pass the time, talking about the old man's past, DiGenero's future, and the present, then a facade shielding his secret, or so he thought. He remembered that his grandfather never questioned him, never asked for more than DiGenero would volunteer. He wondered if that was his way, or if he had a reason. If he suspected and had decided that it was better only to listen and not to know.

His grandfather gripped his knees for leverage as he eased himself onto the bench. DiGenero sat beside him. The garage provided their backrest, hardly comfortable, but familiar. They leaned against it. DiGenero surveyed the work in progress from the new vantage point. The old man must have begun early, in darkness. Even though he had interrupted him not long after sunrise, the garden was half done.

"What did you expect?" his grandfather asked.

"What do you mean?" he said.

"When you came here to find Scarlese, what did you think would happen?"

"To tell the truth, I didn't know and I didn't care. I only wanted to kill Scarlese. Whatever it took was alright."

"And what has happened?"

"I'm still going to kill him, but . . ." DiGenero couldn't complete the sentence. He looked down, as if searching for the final clause on the ground. But how? But when? But what?

"You are beginning to know the price, Francesco."

"What do you mean?" DiGenero asked.

"What you will pay for revenge. An eye for an eye? It will not stop there, believe me. Revenge may be just, but it is not justice. It is not the result of a judgment, something final, understood. It is personal. It does not write in a book, close it, and put it away. Revenge becomes vendetta.

It adds a chapter and leaves the page open, for more to be written. An eye for an eye for an eye. That is its tragedy and it is your responsibility to understand. If you do this thing—if you succeed—it will not end with Scarlese's death."

"I know."

"Do you?" his grandfather asked skeptically. "I don't mean that the law will punish you. I mean that somehow, somewhere, sometime in the future, the Scarleses will come for you again. Or for someone you love. That's what happened in Salt Lake City, is it not? He had your wife killed. To make you pay. And it will happen again. It will go on. It will be no different if you kill him. This thing will not stop. You must understand that. Whatever happens will be because of you, not because of what happened a few weeks ago. If you do this, there will be no end to it."

DiGenero lifted his head and looked at his grandfather. "You're telling me to drop it."

"I'm telling you nothing. I'm describing what you must understand."

DiGenero shook his head. "I have no one, grandfather. If they kill me, I lose. That's it."

"Perhaps that's true today. At this moment. But are you saying you will never have anyone again? Never care for anyone again? Never love anyone again?"

The questions struck him like physical blows. He shut his eyes. He could picture the bathroom, the bedroom, the hallway, hear her footsteps, the front door closing, opening again, her voice, asking about her keys. He could see it all, hear the sounds, feel the textures. All except Erin. She was gone and his mind wouldn't bring her back. She had been torn away, ripped out of his life, taking part of him with it. He had bits and pieces, but nothing he could reassemble into the whole. Not even in memory. And he would never have her. Not in this world. Not ever again. The sob came from somewhere deep inside him.

DiGenero stared at his grandfather but couldn't see him. He put his head in his hands. The tears felt cold on his face. They sat in silence. Finally, he spoke. "I don't know."

"Not now perhaps, but someday you will know. If the answer is no, that you will never love again, even if you wake and breathe every day, Scarlese will have killed you," his grandfather said.

The old man put his hand on DiGenero's shoulder. In Italian, the words sounded soft, like a sad melody. "But if the answer is yes, then you must think about the consequences of your actions—not just because of those you loved, but for those you may love. Those you don't know now, but one day you'll touch. Or who'll touch you. That's all I'm telling you."

DiGenero nodded.

"For the living, there is always a future, Francesco. The dead are the ones who only have a past."

He sat up and rubbed his eyes. "I understand, but I can't stop this now."

"Can't? What you begin, you can stop," the old man said.

DiGenero explained what he knew of Scarlese's alliance with the IRA, about the airliner's crash, about Jilian and Ferringa's shooting, about Benedetto, and finally about Pagano's death.

It was the last point that his grandfather questioned first. "You have proof that it was Scarlese who killed"—he corrected himself—"who had this Pagano killed?"

"I have no proof of anything," DiGenero said.

"I'm not talking about lawyers and courts."

"In that case, there isn't a doubt in my mind."

"And his wife and child?" his grandfather asked. He mentioned them with obvious reluctance as if their recollection even in the abstract as victims unknown to him brought a personal pain. "Why would he have them killed? This is something I don't understand. Even today, there are rules."

"You really think so?" DiGenero retorted too harshly.

He shrugged. "The old live in the world as they know it. But families are not soldiers. There are rules," he repeated.

DiGenero stretched his legs out and crossed them. "I think it fits together. For a mind like Scarlese's, that is. Start with Pagano's death. The circumstances are enough to make a case. The timing—my trip to Boston, Benedetto learning of what I'd asked from my friend who called him because he couldn't reach me, then the shooting. One, two, three. Then, look at Pagano's job, not to mention his work schedule. They needed someone to get them on airplanes at Kennedy. The chief of the flight services crew could do that. No one would question if he unbuttoned—opened up—the aircraft and went aboard. And on the four to twelve and graveyard shifts? A plane that parked someplace out of the way, not scheduled to fly until the next day? How many would be there to see? To know?"

"But why the wife and child?" his grandfather asked. DiGenero realized that it was the innocent not the guilty that concerned him. His grandfather seemed unable to comprehend why they died, what could have motivated the murderer's act.

"I'll give you another unsubstantiated conclusion," DiGenero offered. "They were killed because Pagano was the only one on the inside at Kennedy working this operation for Scarlese. This is the logic. Scarlese killed the whole family. If there were more people involved, he might have done it anyway. Who knows? Maybe there are others we haven't found yet someplace, dead. But I don't think so. The killings make the most sense if Pagano was the only guy. Then, eliminating him—and his wife—is insurance. Ironclad, as Scarlese would see it. Odds are the wife knew. Besides Pagano himself, she was the only one who could talk."

His grandfather stared at the fence, as if its blank boards were a work of art to be contemplated. He shook his head slowly, speaking to himself. "But the child. The child." The old man was silent for a moment. "Why is Scarlese doing this with the Irish?" he asked. DiGenero looked at him. The old man's hands held his knees, his back straight against the garage. A don's formal pose. Or a peasant's.

"I don't know for sure," DiGenero said.

"I understand what Scarlese is doing for them. But what are they doing in return? Are they paying him? Is that it?"

"I doubt it. I don't think it would be worth his while."

"Then what?"

DiGenero shrugged. "I'm guessing."

"Guess," his grandfather ordered.

"My guess is Scarlese wants the same thing from them that he's providing. A means to do business without being discovered. Cover and access to new territory. Not through the IRA itself, but through its network. Its supporters. Businessmen, bankers, lawyers, politicians, whoever can help him over there."

"Why would they help him?"

"Every cause has its backers. The faithful as well as the ones just covering their bets. I'm sure they're no different. Some listen to speeches and sign petitions. Some go to meetings and drop money in the hat. Others do more, including what their told. *Quid pro quo*. One hand washes the other. Scarlese runs an operation for them here. They make arrangements for him there. Let's say Johnny wants to open up shop in Ireland. To make an investment, start a business. Given the attention we'd pay, the Irish cops would have a hard time ignoring him if he popped up in Dublin, even if they wanted to. We'd know. They'd know. But if a guy with a name like O'Shaunessey fronts—sets up on his behalf? Who's going to get wise? Scarlese doesn't need them as permanent partners. Just long enough to get established, to put his own people in place. To recruit qualified help, establish some bank accounts and customers, if it's a legitimate game. To find his retailers and buyers, if he's into business as usual. Say, drugs."

The old man glanced dubiously at DiGenero. "But Ireland is not America. Small, poor, what does it offer?"

"My guess again?" he asked.

His grandfather nodded.

"Opportunity. It opens the door. Ireland's part of the European Community. The EC. For Scarlese, it's a jumping-off point. First, into Britain, then the continent. The walls are coming down. Free trade, no border restrictions, in the future, the same currency. Scarlese probably is banking on that, and on the fact that law will have to play catch-up. With no borders, what are they watching? More than that, who's in charge? Who rings the bell and says, 'follow that guy'? How do the French know who shows up from Dublin when the gate at the airport says, 'EC passport holders, go right through'? Johnny knows if he gets off the plane from the States, he'll be noticed. But not if his boys are Europeans who come from London or Bonn. That's where he wants to wind up, I think. I'm sure the cops will sort this out, but it's going to take time. Johnny just wants a running start, to be in on the ground floor. My guess is that's what this deal gives him. A chance to be there."

"Do you know any of this for a fact?" his grandfather asked.

DiGenero looked at him. "I know none of this for a fact."

"Surely if he attempts to do this, others will discover him eventually. Your people, the Europeans . . ."

"Eventually? Maybe, but I wouldn't bet on it. You find what you're looking for. No one is looking for an Irish banker fronting for the American mob, much less for Scarlese's money laundered into a legitimate business that some Irishman starts up in Frankfurt."

The sun's brief cameo had given way to overcast, dark clouds that promised a reprise of the rain or perhaps with the temperatures, snow. His grandfather clapped his hands together, warming them. He folded his arms. "In 1940, I was sent back to Palermo with Don Carlo Vinnizzi. Did I ever tell you this story?"

"No," DiGenero said.

"Don Carlo was not the boss of bosses, but the New York families had empowered him to negotiate on their behalf. He was their emissary. Each family supported his mission—and protected its interests—with a lieutenant. Me? A young man, I carried his bag, nothing more." His grandfather glanced over and smiled. "Permit me. Ancient history, eh?"

"Please."

"The war was coming. We all knew. Italians had once again deluded themselves into believing they were Romans. Mussolini was Il Duce. People knew in their heart of hearts that their fate was irreversible. That is the definition of tragedy, is it not? After all, the Germans were not

Italians. They took their mission seriously. Hitler had swallowed Europe —whether Il Duce liked it or not—in the Axis's name. At any rate, those were the times when we got off the boat in Palermo. It, too, was the beginning of a new era. Or perhaps, better said, the end of the old.

"There were several in our party. We stayed at the Hotel des Palmes. Do you know it?" his grandfather asked.

DiGenero shook his head.

He continued. "It was magnificent then. A mansion. Wonderful gardens, sitting rooms gilded from floor to ceiling, and all filled with the finest antiques. A place for leaders to meet. They gave us a private meeting room, a suite overlooking the city. Windows on three sides so that we only needed to keep the unwanted away from the door. We took turns, the young men, on watch. When they were off duty, the others would look for women. I would sit behind Vinnizzi's place at the table. To listen and learn." His grandfather paused, watching DiGenero. "His host was Santo Buscetta."

"Ah." DiGenero's eyes widened in recognition. "The old don of dons."

"The same," his grandfather confirmed. "Then, Buscetta was the leader of Sicily's families. Until he died in 1952, even since, the longest-sitting *capo di tutti capi* among the Sicilians. At the time I saw him he was in his prime. In charge."

"It sounds like a serious sitdown," DiGenero said.

It was more than that. It was the forging of a pact." The old man smiled wryly. "A pact, I might add, that none of Europe's 'statesmen' " —he spoke the word contemptuously—"could manage, then, to keep themselves out of war.

"We agreed on several things. First, we decided—mutually—that we would protect each other's interests. If there were families that had relatives who needed help—prisoners in the war, for example—ways would be found to assist them. Blood was thicker than water. That was not a difficult point. Second, we agreed to remain neutral. In a war that we did not start, for whom were we dying? Obviously, we did not expect Buscetta to challenge Mussolini, nor did he expect us to sabotage Franklin Roosevelt. But we would do the minimum necessary to maintain our respective positions so as to make certain, when the war ended, that no new blood feuds emerged from something not our cause.

"And finally—and most important—we agreed to a certain division of roles. When peace came again, we each would manage our own territory. The Sicilian families obviously in Italy, but also in Europe. Our families in the United States, Canada, South America. This was not an agreement to monopolize. No one was so foolish as to think we could predict the future, where our businesses might take us, or even because of the war, how our interests might change. Each of us retained the right to operate in the other's areas. To protect old enterprises and to begin new ones. But"—his grandfather shook his finger in the air—"only with permission. Only after consultation and discussion. Only with the explicit approval from whomever's territory was at stake. As you might imagine, the debate over who got what was serious—the Sicilians didn't like the idea of ceding South America and many of the families in America wanted to have access to their old Sicilian regions as well. But on one point—that we should deal with each other by seeking permission—there was no dissent at all."

"Has it worked?" DiGenero asked.

"Of me you must ask, 'did it work?' It's been a long time."

"Did it?" he rephrased the question.

"Nothing is perfect, but on the whole, yes. Then." The old man rose stiffly. He bent his arms and knees, limbering. "The cold I can feel now in every bone."

DiGenero stood. "You left the life a long time ago, grandfather. Things change," DiGenero said.

"Do they? I suppose." He put his hand on DiGenero's arm. "How old was the little girl?"

"Two, maybe three," DiGenero said.

"And this airplane business. Will it happen again?"

"I don't know."

His grandfather walked to the fence and took his hoe. He stepped back into the garden. "I don't recognize Johnny Scarlese in what you tell me. We had our differences when I left the life, but some things—the rules—we understood. I hear the Scarlese name—the name his son carries—when you speak, but I recognize nothing of the family I knew in what you say." He began to hoe, breaking the soil and chopping the vines where he had left off. "I recognize nothing," his grandfather repeated. "Nothing at all."

C H A P T E R

27

SILVERSTEIN LEANED on the counter and fidgeted. Documents and Records —DNR—occupied the precinct's third floor, once a storage room, later converted to files, and finally to computer equipment. Desks and hardware coexisted, mismatched but mated nonetheless by cables that snaked along the walls. In the reorganization *du jour,* the latest bureaucratic flourish dictated by the series of short-lived police commissioners who had served at the pleasure of the mayor, a headquarters notice had decreed that henceforth DNR would be known as the DC. The Data Center. A rectification of names. The notice was posted on the door. Nothing changed, except a month later, the commissioner.

Silverstein watched the clerks. The scene combined freeze-frame and half-speed. In Documents and Records Section, day shift was preferred. Seniority dictated. Three sat—two with telephones, heads down, virtually motionless—engaged in indeterminate activity. One walked, a shuffle from desk to computer terminal to printer and back again. The answer to his request accumulated, pale green and white paper, perforated and folded accordian-style, a layer per cycle, emulating geological time.

"Marion, sweetheart, watching you walk like that, I'm startin' to lose control of myself." Silverstein leaned forward, extending his arms in a lover's supplication. "You do things to me. You gotta get me my stuff soon or I'm gonna come over this counter and take you right here."

The printer beeped, announcing another emission. Outbound, Marion Grolkowski reversed course like a large vessel at sea. A three-hundred-pound body in motion demanded attention to maintain a dynamic equilibrium. She chanced a brief glance at Silverstein, a hint of suggestiveness, then concentrated on completing her turn. Her hands touched the nearby desks as if wirewalking. "You getta holda yershelf, honey. Or whatever ya gotta geta holda over there. I'll be witcha when I'm witcha."

Marion docked. She held the printer for a moment, steadying, then reached for the paper that had unscrolled. She read, head back, the farsighted's corrective posture. "This is it. The last part."

"I love ya." Silverstein moaned in gratitude.

She ripped the printout and swung out of port, with cargo and back on course. At her desk, Marion scooped up Silverstein's request under both arms and carried it to the counter. "Dat's all, honey. We got ya whatcha want on four outa the five. The fifth one's not a hit."

"Nothin' on the name?" Silverstein asked.

Marion was already backing, full astern. She spoke, swinging to starboard. "That's what I'm tellin' ya. We got nothin'." The turn was stately. She spoke to the assembled. "I'm goin' to lunch." She moved toward the rear exit, this time full ahead.

Silverstein took the stairs to the squad room, a floor below. It was empty except for two detectives investigating a collection of Chinese carryout cartons. Each settled down with a preferred choice, ignoring him. Silverstein's desk was in the corner. A week's accumulation spilled from his inbox, comingling with the litter of yellow telephone messages. He put the printouts on his chair and opened the desk's bottom drawer. He bundled the paper into a rough stack and dropped it in, garnishing with the yellow slips, then kicked the drawer closed.

Silverstein separated the printouts by name, re-creating four piles on the desk. Beckwith, Catalia, Keyser, Wozniak. The new hires in the flight services team at JFK. He settled into the chair. Each printout listed all the possible hits—first and last names that matched the one requested. Silverstein arranged all in the same order. First, the Department of Taxation printout. Then, Motor Vehicle License, Motor Vehicle Registration, and Professional License. He slipped the last printout, Criminal Records, at the bottom of the stack, maintaining the symmetry. On that, the computer had answered the same for each: "No Entries."

Silverstein groped in his jacket pocket, removing a folder, dog-eared and bent double. The Port Authority Police background files on the five new hires in Flight Services. He smoothed the five sheets and put them to one side. Requesting the traces using social security numbers had simplified DNR's task. He eyed the first printout, then the others. On each, the first name matched the social security number he'd provided. Those following—others with the same, then similar names—allowed him to identify whether anyone had requested duplicate documents using false social security numbers or addresses.

Silverstein compared the background sheet from the Port Authority Police against the details of the printouts. He spread each pile across his desk, looking first for the basics—same name, same spelling, same social security number, same address. Then, moving down a level, he examined a finer grain, cross-checking. State and city tax records showed when someone began and left a job, bought and sold a house and car. Automobile registration also listed changes of addresses. Finally, professional licensing, in this case, the Federal Aviation Administration's certification as a qualified "A and E"—aircraft and engine—mechanic, recorded education and work experience, another reference for two of the four.

It took him almost two hours to work through the lists. Finished, Silverstein picked up the phone and dialed. Upstairs, Marion answered. "DNR."

"Doll, it's Arnie. That pile of paper you gave me? I loved every word, but I didn't find what I want."

"Whaddyatalkin?" she asked.

"I mean, all these names check out. Solid citizens. I need to know somethin' about number five," he said.

"Number five what?" she asked.

"I give you five names. You give me four traces. You said you didn't get no hits on number five."

"So?"

"So, sweetie, I'm crazy about ya, but gimme your advice. Where now?"

"Ya got no hits, ya got no hits," she said. Silverstein heard a snap and crunch. Marion was chewing. A candy bar with nuts? "Whazzaname?" she asked.

He pawed through the paper. The sheets from the Port Authority Police were buried. He found it. Silverstein read. "Coleen Murphy."

Lips smacked. "I don't think you'll get nothin', but you could try INS. Only other place that might do good on short notice. Otherwise we gotta send to Washington. It won't come back till tomorrow. Maybe next day," Marion said.

"Can't wait. INS? Immigration and Naturalization?" Silverstein asked.

"But ya better move. It's two o'clock. They close at three." A wrapper tore, followed by another snap and crunch.

"Where?" he asked.

"Federal Building. Second floor."

Silverstein shoved Coleen Murphy's background sheet in his pocket and stood. "I'm outa here, but ya gotta promise."

"Wha?" Marion chewed.

"Whaddya think, sweetheart? Someday you'll save a piece for me."

* * *

The phone was ringing. DiGenero woke. Silverstein's apartment had a twilight hue. The ringing stopped. He lay still for a moment and wondered about the phone. Silverstein trying to reach him? He could have picked up, but it was wiser not to. The Gramercy Park was blown, as was his alias. At least this was one place he was sure no one could find him.

DiGenero sat up. When he returned from his grandfather's, Silverstein's note had been taped to the bathroom mirror. He had gone to Kennedy to pick up the files on the new hires from his cousin, then on to the precinct to run the traces. He had waited for Silverstein to return, then fallen asleep. He looked at this watch. It was after three, almost three-thirty. Silverstein wasn't back yet.

He walked to the bedroom window and looked out. The rain had stopped. Above the street, the sky was gray and clearing, a cold steel strip. He glanced around the bedroom. Silverstein had a real-time system for laundry. Darks piled in one corner, lights in the other. He opened his closet. A collection of white shirts, never worn, hung at one end. DiGenero pondered their purpose. An emergency supply. Wear in case overcome by decorum? He selected a shirt and tore off the plastic bag. One size too small, it would do. DiGenero searched the closet shelf, then the dresser. He found sweaters in the bottom drawer. Silverstein's casual collection consisted of three. He selected a navy blue and held it up. It seemed stretched nearly to his proportions. Given the likelihood that Benedetto had updated his description, the changes were smart, if inconsequential.

He put on the shirt and sweater, then sat and reached for the phone. He had tried Jilian's apartment twice, then her office. In both cases a machine had answered. He didn't leave a message. He started to dial again, then stopped. What was the point? Other than himself as the sacrificial lamb, what did he have to offer? Pagano was gone. If Silverstein got a hit from the traces, maybe there would be another angle. Without one? He was the bait. It was the best he could do. Her ante for the pot to draw out Scarlese.

In his hand, the telephone receiver whined, the automatic warning of a broken connection. He hung up. Then it struck him. *That* was the point. Their connection was broken. When he left her in the Bronx, he hadn't meant that to happen. He had to reconnect. She couldn't. He picked up the phone and dialed.

It rang once, twice, then clicked. His heart fell. The office answering machine again. Her voice. "I'm not here right now . . ."

He started to hang up when the recording clicked again. A new message. It was Jilian's voice. "Meet me at four this afternoon where we talked at first light." The machine snapped off, finished. She'd changed the recording sometime since he'd called this morning. It was for him. A message only he would understand. DiGenero looked at his watch. Schurz Park was five blocks away. He had ten minutes.

CHAPTER

28

JILIAN WAS ALONE on the bench. She wore the same coat as the day before, its upturned collar pillowing her hair. DiGenero sat beside her.

She looked relieved to see him. "I hoped you'd get my message." In the failing afternoon, her eyes were dark, pupils wide, as if anticipating the night.

"I called your office this morning. And the apartment," he said. "I figured I owed you some sort of explanation for bailing out last night."

"The bathroom window? I thought it was obvious." She threw her head back and laughed. "Too bad you didn't see Ian's expression. It was priceless."

"Oh yeah? In that case, maybe I owe him the explanation."

She laughed again. "That's kind of you, but somehow, I think Ian has probably figured it out by now."

"Was he bent out of shape or just dented?" he asked.

"All but broken, I'd say. He'll get over it." Her smile persisted, illuminating him.

"Does he know where you are?" he asked.

"No. When I left him last night, I said I'd be back in touch. He wasn't happy."

"I can imagine. Is he a friend of yours?" DiGenero asked.

"A friend?" She answered a different question. "He's MI5."

"That's not what I mean. Is he . . ." DiGenero felt inexplicably awkward, as if venturing onto long-untrod ground.

"Oh. Are you asking about the two of us? You mean, are we lovers?"

He blushed despite himself. "Yeah."

"No." She shook her head. "The truth is I can't stand him."

His expression betrayed more than he intended. More than he thought it would. "Just asking. I didn't know," he said.

"No, I suppose you wouldn't," she said.

272

"Do you trust him?"

Jilian pushed her hands into her pockets and thought for a moment, staring at the pavement. Finally, she looked at him. "I've never thought about it, not in a 'yes, I do' or 'no, I don't' sense, I mean. Ian's always been so predictable. There never was any need. Interesting question, though." She nibbled her lip like a student standing before the class, on the spot, stumped by the teacher. "I suppose it depends on how you define trust. If you mean, can I count on Ian to be Ian, no matter what?" She smiled wryly. "The answer is yes. He doesn't want me here, doesn't like what I do, tries to control me, exacts his pound of flesh, shred by shred for everything I need, each bit of help I have to have." She pursed her lips. "In that sense, I suppose"—she drew out the word, as if deliberating on a final verdict—"yes, he's been a consistent enough pain in the ass to make me say I trust him."

She leaned back against the bench. Looking east, the clouds domed over Long Island, silver at their pinnacle, transforming to gray as they descended to the horizon. Behind them, unseen, the sun dimmed, disappearing into a low line of black cumulus, another front moving out of the west. The river's current ran smoothly, joining the tide at ebb. Between weather fronts, the wind, too, had stilled. Intermission. A temporary truce among the forces of nature.

She looked at DiGenero. "But now, when we've reached a fork in the road, I don't know. I mean, we've all got our Ians, don't we? For him, it's ripples but no waves, please. That's why I'm such a problem. So are you." Her expression simplified to an unambiguous sincerity. "I accept that about him. Really, I do. After all, under the circumstances, what would you expect from a sniveling, penny-ante little bureaucrat?"

It was DiGenero's turn to laugh aloud.

Jilian's eyes sparkled, enjoying his reaction. She held his gaze. "And the FBI agent. What about him?"

"Benedetto?"

"What will he do?" she asked.

"I don't know," DiGenero said.

"After what happened in the hotel, how can he go on as before—just seeing all this through?"

"It depends on whether Tony's nerve holds."

"What about Ian? Benedetto has to assume he knows. That we've told Ian about his tie to Scarlese," she said.

"What good is that? What you and I said. Your story? From someone Barry can't surface in person to the Bureau without singeing his own ass? And mine? Corroboration from an alleged perpetrator in question?" DiGenero shook his head. "I don't think Barry's going to be eager to blow the whistle on Benedetto. If Tony keeps his head, he could gut it out. *If.* But he's gotta stay cool."

"You're right about one thing," she said.

"What's that?"

" 'Blowing the whistle on Benedetto'—as you put it—wasn't Ian's choice. Not last night anyway."

"He said so?" DiGenero asked.

Jilian nodded. "After a fashion. Actually, he intended to blow the whistle on you. He wanted me to go along—to agree that it was the best way."

"He wanted you to go public?" DiGenero asked skeptically.

"No, no. Just to be a good girl and pull out, to go home and leave things to him. For Ian, that would be two for one: get rid of you, get rid of me. But that can't be any surprise. I assumed you'd already come to that conclusion about Ian when you romped down the fire escape last night."

DiGenero nodded. "Barry was one reason."

"Oh?" She raised her eyebrows. "What was the other?"

"You."

"Me?" Jilian looked surprised. "What do you mean?"

Watching the river, he didn't see her expression change. "I mean, I wasn't sure whether you were part of the set-up," he said offhand.

He glanced over. Her eyes brimmed with tears.

"What's the matter?" he asked.

"You son of a bitch!"

Her anger took him aback. "Wait a minute." He struggled, confused.

"After all this, did you think . . ." She broke off and began again. "Do you honestly think . . . ?"

DiGenero looked left and right, as if the answer was somewhere around them, something obvious that he'd missed. He began ineptly. "It's just that I wasn't sure. Yesterday morning, I gave you Pagano's name, my hotel. A few hours later, Pagano's dead, Benedetto's in my hotel room. Then, you walk in. 'How did this happen?' I'm thinking to myself. How did Scarlese find out? What can I say? I didn't know who'd tipped who, that Benedetto had gotten my address from Foley in Boston, that . . ." He stopped.

Jilian wasn't listening. She stared at the river. He felt as if it was between them, as if he had thrown her into the current and she had struggled out on the opposite shore. When she spoke again, her voice was cold, far away. "I don't understand you."

He wanted to say something, to apologize, to explain, to cast over a line, even a thread, anything that could reach her, but no words came.

"What do you think I am? Do you think I'd take three lives just to deliver you up to be killed?"

He shook his head. "No. Not now." Despite its contempt, he held her gaze, afraid to look away, afraid that if he did, she'd be gone, lost forever.

"'Not now'?" She twisted the words. Her anger was her anchor, her grip on the shore just achieved. "Well, thank you very much. But I want to know about 'then'?"

"I mean, I didn't . . ."

She interrupted. "'Then.' What did you think 'then'? What in God's name? That I was some sort of hired killer? That I shot Sallie and the other two as part of the plan? That it was all my subterfuge? That I intended to sit there and watch Benedetto kill you in cold blood? Jesus! Is that how your mind works?" She paused. "Is that you? Is that what I saved?"

"No," he said quietly.

"She caught her breath. "Do you think I don't see that night, hear it, smell it, over and over again? The three of them? Do you think I don't lie awake, wondering what I've done? And 'now'? Yes, let's talk about 'now.' Now, because of you, because of what I did, has this all been a waste? Two years gone for nothing. And now, will four hundred more people die?" She looked away. Her eyes overflowed. "Now, what do I do? What in the bloody hell do I do?"

"Trust me," he said softly.

Jilian turned. "Trust you?" She repeated the question harshly, but without sarcasm.

DiGenero held his breath. Anger and hope warred in her eyes. He wanted to hold her, touch her cheeks, wipe away her tears. "The way I trust you," he said quietly.

She examined him, seeming to still, not all at once, but slowly, like a storm dying. He watched the calm come over her.

Behind them, a couple passed on the promenade, arm in arm, laughing. They glanced over their shoulders at the two of them, incorrectly diagnosing the scene. A lovers' quarrel. DiGenero waited. Jilian wiped her eyes. Her tears had traced the curve of her cheek, the only evidence of their falling. Her hand trembled.

"You must have loved him very much," he said.

Jilian looked at him without expression. He wondered who she saw. DiGenero was afraid to move, afraid even a gesture would be the make-weight in her decision.

They sat without speaking for a long time. Finally, she rose. "Come with me."

He looked up hopefully. "Your place?" he asked.

She was businesslike. "No. It's not safe." She paused. "For either of us. I have a hotel room."

"Who knows?" he asked.

"No one."

"Good," DiGenero said. He stood. "Let's go."

The reservoir was opaque, under the lowering clouds like slate, without reflection. Invisible, the bordering trees diced headlights into strobes. Each flashed briefly, then disappeared, demarcating Central Park's far perimeter.

The hotel was on 93rd Street and Madison, small, ambitiously renovated, but ten blocks too far north to claim the East side's cachet. They had waited in the lobby, watching the elevator's electronic display record its halting descent. Around them, a tour group clustered, Eastern Europeans in mismatched prints and plaids, heavy-soled shoes, and cheap sweaters, speaking an unrecognizable language, alternately guttural and melodious. They flocked together, jostling, as if outlyers were at risk.

Jilian took him to the twenty-fifth floor. The room was in the northwest corner. The windows made a right angle, with deep sills, almost seats, and oversized proportions designed for an earlier time when ventilation meant outdoor breezes rather than central air-conditioning. DiGenero stood, looking at the park and beyond. Across its dark interlude, distant habitation glittered, the lights of the upper West side. He watched, raised above the city's details and dangers, for a moment at least, liberated by the perspective.

They ordered room service. Two steaks, a salad, wine. When it arrived, DiGenero pushed the small table into the corner. Jilian tied back both sets of drapes with their pull cords, giving each a view. As they began to eat, they made small talk. Then, she asked him about Erin, tentatively at first, but later forthrightly, with a genuine curiosity. He explained how they'd met—his assignment in Montana ten years before in an undercover operation to identify dealers who illegally trapped and sold peregrine falcons, Erin's relationship with an old friend he discovered in the business, the tangled plot that ultimately led to his friend's death, and finally, their life together afterward in Salt Lake City, where they'd married and stayed on. Near the finish he was crying, not from sorrow, but from the remembering, the recognition that he could bring it all back. That it wasn't lost. That Erin wasn't lost. That he wasn't lost. That he could still feel something again.

Silence came with the last two glasses of wine.

"May I ask you something?" Jilian's question was her first in some time. It struck him that she had drawn the past from him with her presence rather than words.

"Sure."

Despite his assent, she hesitated. Compared to the duration of the delay, the brevity of the question surprised him. "Is it too soon?"

DiGenero didn't understand. "For what?" he asked.

She looked out the window, discomfited by the need to clarify things, then met his eyes. "For you to make love to another woman?" Her stare was simultaneously bold and embarrassed.

"I . . . ," DiGenero stammered. "I don't know," he said honestly.

She leaned across the table and touched his hand lightly with her fingertips, no more than brushing, as if testing a delicate physical connection. The feeling was electric, a current not a shock. "Could we see?"

He didn't move.

She rose and took one step, standing beside him. This time she touched his cheek. He stood as if commanded. Before he could move further, she held his arms to his side gently and kissed his lips. Eyes closed, he felt her hands tugging his sweater. He let her slip it over his head. Her fingers unbuttoned his shirt, then caressed his chest. Her lips brushed his cheek and neck, then moved down his body. She straightened, nestling against him, then released his arms. Her hands slipped lower. Her voice was a whisper. "I'll stop only if you want. Only if you tell me."

He pulled her to him and then to the bed but as before she controlled him, undressing, exploring, touching, probing, light and hard, rising up to reveal herself, then slipping beneath the covers to hold and kiss and excite him. She was lean, defined by long lines rather than curves, making her breasts as they brushed across him more tantalizing, the softness of her thighs more inviting. When it was time, she pulled him on top of her and guided him inside, relinquishing herself without hesitation. And after her body arched and gripped and arched again, her legs locking to imprison him, she held on, keeping him inside. When they finished, he was exhausted, not just spent, but he fought the urge to sleep, and he held her. It was his turn to listen, first to the steady rhythm of her breathing, then as she touched his cheek, thinking he had slipped away, to her crying.

CHAPTER
29

THE RAIN RATTLED against the window, at once constant and uneven. In the darkness, he listened to its tattoo and to her. Resting against him, using his length for comfort, she seemed part of him, legs intertwined, her breathing his, their skin indistinguishable, her flank, his palm, each equally warm to the touch. She was awake, but he lay still purposely, trying to banish any doubt she might have that she could remain as long as she wanted, as close as she wanted, just as she was. Without plan or words, they conspired, holding themselves in suspended animation. Hiding. Stopping time.

DiGenero whispered. "How long has it been?"

"How long has what been?" Breathing alone carried her words.

"Since he died. You told me once," he reminded.

"Ten years. Ten years this fall. We were getting married in September, then leaving."

"For Hong Kong," he said.

"You remember."

"Can you picture him? Still?" he asked.

"Not like a photograph, no," she said. "I have snapshots and class pictures and holiday portraits—those kinds of things—but they're all stored away. So is he, in my mind. The image of him, I mean." Her hand moved lightly on his chest, finding a new position. It was different than Erin's—tentative, rather than assured, polite rather than possessing. "But that doesn't matter. I remember him in other ways. As part of my life. Part of me. Not as someone by himself, framed on the mantel. I think that's better. Do you know what I mean?"

"I'm not sure," he said.

"It's like the stories people tell, over and over again. The ones about who they are. The couple who ate beans and greens for the entire Depression, with enough money for meat only one meal a month. The little old lady who reminisces about what it was like in the bomb shelter during the worst night of the Blitz. The story that tells the whole tale of her war. The cottage-at-the-lake story. You know the one. The family's holiday place, idyllic memories, children growing up, falling in the water with their clothes on, getting lost in the woods, dramas relived and repeated summer after summer. I have those, or my version of them. For the two of us, I remember him that way. I remember us. Not just him."

"Are you Catholic?"

"No." Jilian raised her head, looking at him. "Why do you ask?" She paused, then answered her own question. "Oh. The crucifix around my neck." She moved. For a moment, he felt anxious, worried that she was rising, going away. She lay on the pillow beside DiGenero, watching him. He turned toward her, on his side. In the darkness she seemed a vision. Something revealed to him. A spirit come to be queried for answers that otherwise would be forever unknown. "It was his," she said. "He was Catholic." The crucifix lay against her breast. She raised it in her hand by the chain. The cross dangled for a moment between them, swinging as if in silent benediction. She let it fall. "It helps, even now. Part of the cover. That's crass, isn't it, but what the hell? After all, what would a soldier in the cause be other than one of the faithful?"

"You do what you've got to do," he said.

She traced the line of DiGenero's lips, as if her fingertips were recording their contours in memory. She spoke. "Ironic, isn't it? Not only that he should have died a senseless death, but that they should have killed one of their own. Stupid." She repeated the word. "Stupid. Causes always kill their own."

"When this is over . . . ," he began.

"You are a typical American optimist, aren't you? When what's over? Do you honestly believe this will ever be over?" She laughed. "I should have seen this before, I really should. We are so much alike, you and I. Not who we are, but the godawful messes we're in."

He began again. "When this is over, Scarlese's a dead man. But I won't kill him until you either have what you want, or you tell me you've gone as far as you can. I promise."

She smiled impishly. "What a rich fantasy life you must have." Her hand reached beneath the sheets. She stroked upward along his thigh, then held him. "On behalf of Her Majesty's Government, I accept your promise," she said. The smile disappeared. She moved closer, onto him, and rising up. Her hair covered him, entrapping the moisture of her breath against his neck and face, enclosing them with her aroma. She melted into him, fusing to his body. DiGenero moaned. He closed his eyes, not thinking—not wanting to think—only feeling her surround

him. In motion, she whispered. The last words incarnated in her breathing. "When this is over, I only hope we're both alive to tell each other
anything at all."

Beside him, Jilian rested on one elbow, watching as he dialed Silverstein.

"He knows?" she asked skeptically.

"Silverstein? Everything," DiGenero said. He glanced at her. "Except
about you."

"Do you trust him?"

"Yes." DiGenero looked at his watch on the night table. It was after
ten-thirty. Closer to eleven.

Silverstein answered on the first ring.

"Arnie, it's me," DiGenero said.

"Well, where the fuck you been?" Silverstein was wide awake. He
sounded worried.

"Believe me, that choice of vocabulary's more appropriate than you
know."

"You okay?" he said.

"Yeah, I'm fine," DiGenero said.

"That's good 'cause they got the heat turned way up on you. You seen
tomorrow's papers?"

"No," he said.

"You're back on page one. They're playin' a different game. I swear,
the old guys in the mob must be rototillin' the cemeteries, rollin' over in
their goddamn graves."

"Whaddyamean? I saw the newspaper stories today. Benedetto, I figured, trying to pump up some attention," DiGenero said.

Silverstein snorted. "That ain't nothin'! Johnny Junior's gone public
with an interview. In the *Times* and the *Daily News*. Whadda piece a
work! I gotta hand it to Scarlese. He's got those puppies eatin' outa his
hand. They're treatin' him like the aggrieved party. Basically, he's sayin'
that the Bureau, the cops—everybody who's got a badge—ain't doin'
shit. They got a wacko FBI guy—you—on the loose, tryin' to get him,
and they're suckin' their thumbs. It's beautiful! Here's a big picture of
Johnny in some fuckin' library—looks like a college professor—and all
kinds of words wrapped around that say he's the new generation who's
left his past behind, a sophisticated young man of the world. We got a
couple do-gooder foundation presidents and some dago congressmen he
gives money to all singing his praises in the story and wonderin' what the
fuck taxpayers like Johnny are gettin' from the deadbeat feds beside the
shaft. I mean, it's all there. You come to town, start shootin', warmin' up

on these two-bit wiseguys like Ferringa, lookin' for the kid who's gone straight. What can I tell ya? Read this and it's obvious he's bein' persecuted by a crazy knuckle-draggin' agent who put away his old man and then had one of the bad guys from the old days come back for revenge. I mean, your wife gets one line. On top of that, your buddies in Washington are stainin' their drawers. Their statement, where's the statement?" Paper ripped. "Here! The FBI barely mentions Salt Lake City. They're sayin' the Bureau's lookin' high and low for you, and that you wasn't— well, normal. Not a Sears and Roebuck, find-'em-on-any-streetcorner-with-the-same-haircut-and-suit, all-American, FBI kinda guy. I gotta tell ya. After I read this shit, even I got my doubts about you, DiGenero. Compared to you, Johnny Junior looks like a real mensch."

DiGenero groaned. "From this I draw the conclusion I should not have brunch at the '21' Club tomorrow."

"The '21' Club? I wouldn't have an Orange Julius on the fuckin' corner, if I was you. You know what the undertakers call their business prospects? With this kinda publicity, I think you're already in the category: predeceased."

"How about . . ." DiGenero began.

The newspapers rustled over the telephone. "Wait a minute! There's one more thing. Let me find it." Silverstein turned pages. "Here! It's in tomorrow's *News*. The latest story on the Ferringa shoot. They got the name of Sallie's squeeze. It says—I'm readin' now—'investigation sources have identified Jilian McCray, a reporter for a Dublin, Ireland, newspaper and romantically involved with Ferringa, as having been with DiGenero on the night of the Ward's Island murders. New York police are looking for McCray, although federal sources said they have no evidence on whether she has any ties to the fugitive FBI agent.' That's you."

"Thanks for reminding me." DiGenero cupped his hand over the mouthpiece and turned to Jilian. "Congratulations. You're in the newspapers. Linked to me and Ward's Island."

She sat up. "What?"

DiGenero put his finger to his lips. "Shhh." He couldn't take his eyes off her breasts. "What else?" he asked into the phone.

"Who you with?" Silverstein asked suspiciously.

"Nobody. Come on. What about . . ." He started to ask about the names from the Port Authority Police at Kennedy, but Silverstein interrupted.

"Don't hyperventilate already. I got a hit," Silverstein said.

"On which traces?" DiGenero asked.

"Only one of 'em. It's just a lead, but at least it's somethin'. Four out of the five new hires in Flight Services checked out. Solid citizens. But on one—a Coleen Murphy—DNR gave me nothin'. Zip. All the details on her security sheet from the Port Authority cops was bad. Licenses, address, social security, taxes. Nothin' checked out. If she's workin' out there, makes you wonder what the fuckin' airport cops are doin' for a livin', don't it? I took a flyer and went to Immigration—INS—and whaddyaknow? The name turns up with a different address and with somethin' else. This Murphy broad, or whoever she is, is applyin' to be a"—Silverstein paused, reading from notes—" 'permanent resident alien.' The sweet young thing at INS tells me this is like an E.T. who never goes home. Anyway, to do that, she's gotta have bank references."

"A green card," DiGenero interjected. "It lets her live here as long as she wants, even though she isn't a citizen."

"Green, blue, whatever you say. I checked out the address on the West side she gave INS. It's a phony, too. But I still got the bank references." Silverstein read again. "Credit International Bank. Up on 72nd Street. The branch, the main bank, I dunno. I never heard of it. I'm gonna scope 'em out in the morning."

"What name?" DiGenero broke in.

"Credit International. Why? You know somethin' about 'em?"

DiGenero remembered the Saturday morning meeting with Vergilio, Scarlese's Fulton Street accountant. According to Louie, the cashier's checks brought back by Rocchi and Ferringa from Ireland were all drawn on a Credit International Bank.

Jilian watched him, leaning forward, listening intently to his half of the conversation. Her form was a figure study, one leg crooked over the other. Sharp angles leading to curves, recesses and shadows, flowing lines that drew him from one element of her composition to the other.

"You still there? What's goin' on?" Silverstein asked.

He answered. "That all you got?"

"Whaddyawant, Jimmy Hoffa?"

DiGenero interrupted. "I'll call you in the morning before you go to the bank, okay?"

"Waitaminute!" Silverstein protested.

He hung up. Jilian waited to hear. He told her what Silverstein had said. She listened without comment, then leaned back against the headboard.

"We're getting closer," he said.

She drew the sheets around her as if needing their protection. "But so are they." He didn't reply. They sat, quiet for a moment. "I'm not sure how much time we have anymore," she said.

"Were you ever sure?" he asked.

She thought and shook her head. "No."

"Then what's changed?"

Jilian looked at him. She smiled and touched his hand. "You remember your promise?"

"Of course," he said.

"That's what's changed." She leaned forward and kissed him. Her grip loosened on the sheet. DiGenero took it away. He pulled her toward him. Her fingers dug into his back, holding on. Jilian followed rather than guided his motion as she slid beneath him, this time letting him cover her, control her, carry her away.

She reached across him, taking the phone.

DiGenero woke. He rubbed his eyes. He fumbled on the tabletop and took his watch. "I don't want to pry, but its after midnight. Who you gonna call?"

"Myself." Jilian dialed. "I just remembered. I'd best check. My answering machine at the office is remote control. I can call in and dial the code. It plays back the messages waiting. You can also change anything you've put on the machine." She touched the tip of his nose playfully, pressing it like a button. "That's how I arranged this assignation, remember?"

"Vaguely," he said.

Jilian listened. The machine clicked once, playing through her message. She touched the phone's keypad. The answering machine clicked again twice. At full volume in playback, even DiGenero could hear the voice. "Call this number in the morning before ten A.M. You'll need to be available for an afternoon meeting. 516-324-9831." The machine snapped off. She put the phone down.

"Who was that?" DiGenero asked.

"I don't recognize him," she said.

Even in the darkness, DiGenero could see her expression had changed. "What's wrong?" He sat up.

"I do know the number."

He pulled himself up. "Oh yeah? What is it?"

"Westhampton. Johnny Scarlese's house."

Ian Barry watched the tiny red light on the answering machine extinguish. The playback had completed. Inside the small box, the tape cycled, resetting itself for the next call. The ready light illuminated. Barry pressed the eject button and removed the microcassette, replacing it with another. He snapped off Jilian's desk lamp and sat for a moment, contemplating the darkness. Across the alley, blank windows stared back. At midnight, the office bay was quiet. He'd already listened once to the tape. A coincidence that Jilian had played back her messages from wherever she was while he was there, checking on her.

Barry turned the cassette over in his hand like a found object. Best he keep this secure in the event someone comes looking. At least she'd called, still sound and well. No matter what she was up to—or thought she was up to—he could still contact her via the machine, even if she tried to avoid him. Whether she listened to any messages he might leave, much less chose to obey them was another matter. He made a face. But he could "communicate"—as the Americans liked to say in their horrible jargon. From Marylebone's perspective, it was the most at this point they could reasonably expect him to do.

He tossed the tape in his hand. The messages were hardly difficult to decipher. The first—hers, arranging a meeting earlier this morning—only confirmed what he already suspected: Jilian and DiGenero were still in touch. Two days ago, after talking with DiGenero, Jilian had badgered him to send the immediate message about pulling aircraft from the New York–London run. Then, the next morning first thing, because of him again, she demanded a trace on the mechanic at Kennedy. He smiled. Poor Jilian. Amateur, really. Hardly a difficult surmise who would be meeting her "at first light."

The second message was more problematic. The 516 area code was Suffolk County, Long Island, the local exchange Westhampton. Another invitation? With Scarlese, her plan had been step by step, a little at a time. Despite her enthusiasms, he'd been able to tolerate that, even to help her, to assist in small ways. Despite misgivings, Marylebone found it useful for him to do so, encouraging his limited support of the venture for the sake of broader cooperation with the RUC—other fish to fry, so to speak. Her messages to Stormont recorded that they were working together, collaborating. His advice and opinions frankly given and rejected also were a matter of record. In the event things went badly, the cables made clear how far he'd been willing to go and the reservations he'd maintained—Marylebone's as well as his own.

Now, however, things had changed. He had warned her in no uncertain terms about the risks. Scarlese was dangerous by himself, but with DiGenero on the loose, too many were watching—there was altogether too much attention. For himself as well as her. To find one self exposed to the Americans as abetting a unilateral operation by a sister service? And if something happened to her? If Jilian was killed? In that case, he knew the question Marylebone would ask: why did he let this happen? It was one others in London would share, BA 121 notwithstanding. Yes, control was the key—control of Jilian, control of Scarlese, control of the process. That was foremost, even with 121 hanging over their heads. Jilian had to be controlled for her own good. For all their "goods." If something befell her, the consequences would be unpredictable. For more than just him.

Barry stood. He had offered her an "out" only yesterday. All would accept the fact that she had done her best. She could retire from the field with honor. At least without disgrace. Too bad she hadn't listened. Only she believed that she could press on. Too bad. Ah well. If she failed to make the proper choice, faced with the publicity he had arranged, Stormont would do it for her. The oily little reporter he'd called over from the *News* had asked all the right questions. What could he say? A correspondent for the Dublin *Register* was well within her rights to have a drink now and again in what had once been New York's West side Irish bastion. "Could she have met others—not of the same extraction, so to speak—and could a relationship have developed?" the little Jewboy had asked. "Off the record," he'd answered, "you might check with the bars in the neighborhood, like the one on the corner of Tenth and 45th. By all accounts, it was a popular place."

Barry looked at his watch. After midnight. He'd draft the cable to Marylebone in the morning. There was ample time. The papers wouldn't be out on the street with the mention of Jilian until daybreak. No reason he should be expected to know about the unfortunate disclosure or to convey the worrisome news until then. He would have to word his message to London carefully. A shame that the publicity risked her cover and threatened to spoil so much good work. Perhaps, he might suggest respectfully, given the dangers if Jilian's now limited exposure went further, Marylebone might find it in its wisdom to counsel with Stormont on withdrawing her before a dicey situation got out of hand.

Barry walked to the elevator. He pressed the down button. Even if Marylebone ignored him, it would put him on record. The elevator arrived. He stepped aboard. In this case, such counsel could serve equally well however things went. If Marylebone and Stormont took it, Jilian departed. If they didn't and she stayed, who's to say what else might find its way into the newspapers? After all, now that the cat already had one paw out of the bag, no telling when the rest would emerge?

The elevator doors opened. Barry stepped into the darkened lobby. To keep control. That was the thing. For just a few days longer. He was best positioned to do that. On behalf of all concerned.

C H A P T E R

30

JILIAN ASKED for the phone. The clerk's welcoming smile faded. She pointed wordlessly and turned away, obviously uninterested in all but the drugstore's paying customers. Jilian angled between the displays. Cosmetics, cold pills, panty hose, cleaning supplies. In the rear, the pharmacist's head bobbed, a bald pate behind a high glass partition. The wooden booth stood in the corner opposite "Prescriptions."

She sat and closed the door, collecting herself. Better here than the hotel, where a trace on Scarlese's phone could also reveal her. It was almost ten. Time was running out. She picked up the telephone and dialed. Through the glass in the door, she could see a drug company calendar hung high above the pharmacist's counter. It was Friday. By the end of the day, the week would be over. The question was: what else would be, too?

Ascending the stairs, the maid balanced the tray with a practised finesse, a learned skill. As a little girl, she had imitated her mother's swaying motion when she carried, the rocking equilibrium of her hips. By the time she was ten, she could manage the steep mountain trails, bearing the daily water supply from the high spring to their Guatemalan village as if the pottery on her head was fine china, not rough fired clay. After that anything was easy, including a black laquered tray with white dishes.

She crested the stairs and stepped to the small table. She had set the tray precisely: dry toast, juice, coffee, no cream, margarine not butter, knife and spoon wrapped in white linen. She adjusted the newspapers and portable telephone and angled the chair before stepping back. Ten o'clock exactly. She smoothed her apron and skirt and walked quickly to the end of the second-floor hall.

She knocked and opened the master bedroom's door. She bowed, her eyes on the floor. "Your breakfast, señor."

Naked, Johnny Scarlese finished his sit-ups. "Okay." He acknowledged and dismissed her without a glance. He rose and put on his robe. On the bed, the morning *Times* was open to the latest story of Ferringa's shooting and the companion piece, his own profile on the facing page. His father and the others like him had invested in things—businesses, stocks and bonds, real estate—diversifying to blur the lines between illegal and not. But in the final analysis they had failed, remaining in their persons the connections they had tried to obscure. The living link between means and ends. He had invested in himself, reinventing and redefining who and what he was. Scarlese examined his picture in the paper and smiled. This was the return, the best of both worlds. The benefits of a family name that still inspired fear and respect in one world, but also his own unique identity in others. The chairman of the city's prestigious Council on International Relations singing his praises. Brooklyn's congressman describing his civic role. The state's junior United States senator decrying the government's effort to visit the sins of the father on the son. His father had once had such support as well, but privately, behind the scenes. His came openly, not with late-night telephone calls or secret handshakes, but on the front page of the New York *Times*.

Scarlese walked to the dining room. The maid waited. She adjusted his chair as he sat, then poured coffee. Through the window, ocean and sky blended, a gray mist obscuring their distinctions. Scarlese waved her away and reached for the *News*. He thumbed open the tabloid, finding his story and beginning to read just as the portable telephone beside him rang.

Scarlese lifted the handset. "Yeah?"

Jilian spoke without introduction. "You asked me to call."

He put down the newspaper. "We have some unfinished business."

"That's something of an understatement. What did you think you were trying to do in that hotel room?"

Scarlese ignored the question. "We need to talk."

"Go ahead," she said.

"In our last conversation, you made a proposal regarding how we— how should I put this?—'manage' things here. For the sake of ensuring your project's continuing success. You follow?"

"I do," Jilian said. Taking over Bellflower's handling because of the risks posed by DiGenero's vendetta had been her gambit in their first— and last—conversation.

"I've reconsidered."

"Oh?" Jilian cursed herself for allowing the note of surprise into her voice. She hadn't expected Scarlese to capitulate.

"Provided," he said.

"Provided what?"

"Provided you can deliver what I want."

"Which is?" she asked.

"Don't bullshit me, sweetheart! Given the way the meeting concluded the other day in the hotel room, I'm assuming that's still possible. If it's not, say so," Scarlese said.

The booth felt warm, overheated. Outside, a woman with little boy in her arms—how old, eight months, maybe ten—stood before the pharmacist who talked, pointing at a bottle of medicine in his hand, then at the child. A sick baby. An image through the phone booth door, but immediately recognizable for what it was. Something real, understood without words or explanation. She envied the woman. In the glass, Jilian could see a partial reflection, her own coat but nothing else. The dark, but not the light. Not her face, not her hands. She closed her eyes. Was she there or was all this just a figment of her imagination. Oh God, what was real and what was not?

"Well?" Scarlese asked.

Her lips moved, but another voice spoke. Not hers. "It is."

"Good," he said.

"When?" Jilian asked.

"Today."

She felt weak, the victim of something poisonous and powerful suddenly injected. This wasn't how she thought would happen. Not this fast. Not today. "It may take some time to . . ."

Scarlese interrupted. "Today."

Her mind leapt ahead, trying to shape things, to impose a structure. She spoke too quickly, too loud. "Look. If we're going to meet today, the best I can do is tell you . . ."

Scarlese interrupted. "No. There's no 'if' and no 'telling,' got that? For you, it's 'show and tell.' You deliver."

She stumbled backward, too quickly again. "I don't know if I can."

He ignored her. "Village Tavern. Westhampton. Three o'clock. You have what I want. I'll have what you want."

Jilian started to speak, but the phone was dead. She hung up. Outside, the pharmacist continued to talk, the woman to listen. Hoisted over his mother's shoulder, the baby saw Jilian, her motion attracting. The baby's eyes widened, watching. From the front of the store, voices rose. The baby glanced toward them, then back, watching Jilian again. Her face didn't move. She was an image behind glass without sound. Only a face.

A cash register bell rang, then laughter. Distracted, the baby looked away. What was real and what was not?

In Westhampton, Scarlese put down the phone and snapped his fingers. The Latina appeared. He pointed. She refilled his coffee. He sipped. His personality profile in the *News* lay before him. He scanned it, satisfied. All investments had value. Some, like property, plant, and equipment, were tangible; others, like an entry for goodwill on the company's books, not. Scarlese lifted the phone again and dialed. He spoke without identifying himself. "It's on. Where I said. Today. Tell them." Then, without waiting for a reply, he hung up.

Special Agent Larry Maloy watched the extension light blink. From nine to noon on Fridays, Maloy did his stint of general line duty, fielding the tips, questions, and cranks referred to the Organized Crime Squad in the New York Field Office by the FBI switchboard. So far, the morning had been light.

Maloy lifted the phone. "Organized Crime. Maloy. Can I help you?"

The voice was muffled but clear. "I have the time and place when you can pick up Frank DiGenero."

The name didn't register at first. "Who?" Maloy asked.

"I take it you don't read the newspapers? Frank DiGenero, the FBI agent who killed the three on Ward's Island."

Maloy sat up straight. He noted the time—11:16 A.M.—and the name —"DiGenero"—on his legal pad. Behind the operators' station two floors below, the bank of recorders routinely taped all general line calls. He raised one hand high and waved. Across two rows of desks, a pair of agents looked over simultaneously. Maloy gestured, signaling them to pick up the extension. Both reached for their phones.

"Who's calling?" Maloy said.

"Don't be silly. Now, have you had enough time to get others on the line and get the recorders going?" The sarcasm was chiding, not impolite.

"It would help if you could tell us . . ." Maloy began.

The voice interrupted. "The Village Tavern. Westhampton, Long Island. Three o'clock. Today." The pause lasted long enough for Maloy to scrawl the details. He glanced up. Phones trapped between head and shoulder, the other two agents were writing as well. "Got that?"

"That's very helpful, but where can we . . ."

"Don't be greedy. DiGenero will be there. You be, too." The line went dead.

Silverstein and Jilian examined each other across the delicatessen booth with the eyes of skeptical appraisers. Silverstein played with the salt and pepper shakers. Jilian sat. Both looked up as DiGenero entered the front door, pocketing rental car keys. They watched him approach, obviously welcoming the chance to focus their attention on his arrival. DiGenero joined Jilian on her side. She shifted toward the wall. He shimmied sideways, positioning himself across from Silverstein.

The waiter shuffled over, an old man no less than eighty, wizened but preserved somewhere inside an oversized white jacket. "Wha?" He greeted them and solicited their orders. An economy of words.

Silverstein raised his chin, looking around the waiter toward the deli case. "Howzepastrami?"

"Whaddyat'ink? The place's been here fifty years. You see anybody dead on the floor?"

"Rye," Silverstein said. "No pickle."

The waiter waved dismissively, rejecting the instructions. "Ya don't want, don't eat." He looked at Jilian and DiGenero.

DiGenero ordered. "Two coffees. Bagels, plain."

"That's all?"

"Yeah," he said.

The waiter gestured. "For her, too?"

Jilian smiled. "Yes."

"Wha? Ya outawork?" The old man shook his head reprovingly. He shuffled away.

Silverstein watched the waiter until he reached the deli case. Without looking, he tore their order from his pad and impaled the sheet of paper on the counterman's long steel spike, moving on a well-worn track toward the table with tea and three of his vintage coworkers at the rear. Jilian gazed over the top of the booth at the second floor of the building across the street, the truncated perspective through the deli's front window. Silverstein looked at DiGenero. "Lemme offer a humble opinion. You're fuckin' crazy."

DiGenero smiled diplomatically. "Jilian, meet Arnie. Arnie, meet Jilian."

Jilian looked mistrustfully at Silverstein, who pointedly ignored her.

"I got nothin' but warm feelin's for this kinda cooperation. So help me, I do," Silverstein continued. "But I got an itsybitsy worry." He held up a thumb and finger, only millimeters apart, illustrating the ostensible magnitude.

"Which is?" DiGenero asked.

"She and you go different places if this don't work, you know what I mean? She goes home and you go six feet underground."

"Wait a minute," DiGenero said.

Silverstein leaned forward. "Ain't no reason she can't drive out to the Island and talk to Scarlese. I mean, we got big road signs. It's easy to find. You speak English, right?" He looked at Jilian, but didn't wait for an answer. "If she don't wanna go alone, I can drive her. It don't make no sense for you to go. No fuckin' sense."

DiGenero shook his head. "It doesn't make sense for me not to. Scarlese's not gonna go after me in Westhampton, for Christ's sake. He doesn't want a goddamn murder rap on his million-dollar doorstep. Besides, I'm too hot to be on the streets and there's things you gotta do in the city."

Silverstein extended both hands, palms up on the table, this time supplicating. "Have her go talk." He addressed Jilian in the third person. "If Scarlese's gonna deal, he's gonna deal, right? If you ain't there, he ain't gonna tell her to buzz off."

DiGenero nodded. "That's exactly the drill. She pitches Junior for what he's got. When he says—'Where's DiGenero?'—she lets him call me on the phone. I'm in the neighborhood, a local number. That's all. We see if he comes through."

"That's all?" Silverstein asked skeptically.

"If he's by himself, who knows?" DiGenero shrugged. "Maybe we meet."

Silverstein rolled his eyes. "I'm not hearin' this. Whadda you know about who he's got out there? In Westhampton? What if there's a car fulla bozos around the fuckin' corner? What if it's a setup and they blow her away? What if . . ."

DiGenero interrupted. "What if, what if . . ." He frowned, irritated. "Gimme a break, Arnie. I've made a few meetings before. We're leaving here and driving out to Westhampton early. We'll have plenty of time to case the neighborhood."

"That ain't the point, Frank. What I'm sayin' is, 'who do ya trust?' "

Jilian stared, cold-eyed. "What is that supposed to mean?"

Silverstein glared. "Whadda you think?"

DiGenero held up both hands like a referee. "Okay, okay."

An approaching shuffle announced the waiter's return. Pastrami on one arm balanced by two bagels and two coffees on the other. The sandwich plate with pickle banged on the formica in front of Silverstein, an indecent portion only notionly covered by rye. The old man dealt the bagels and coffee in front of Jilian and DiGenero. "Okay?"—an announcement, not a question—then he was gone.

DiGenero changed the subject. "What about the bank? The Credit International account. You go this morning?" he asked.

Silverstein glanced at Jilian uncomfortably.

DiGenero saw him. "She knows."

Silverstein's first bite barely dented the mound of pastrami. He chewed. "I tried once already. The asshole assistant manager won't give me nothin'. The manager will when he comes in." He swallowed. "After lunch." Silverstein probed between his molars with his tongue, searching to dislodge something snagged. He glanced at Jilian again, then spoke to DiGenero. "I called the airline like you said."

Jilian looked up from her coffee. She turned toward DiGenero. "What about the airline?"

"You told me last night you'd cabled your people. About pulling the planes on the London–New York route. Like I suggested," DiGenero said.

"I did." Jilian confirmed. "The other day."

"When you were out this morning I called Arnie and asked him to check. To see if they had."

Silverstein looked from DiGenero to Jilian and back again. "They didn't," he said.

"That can't be!" Jilian exclaimed.

Silverstein shrugged. "That's what they told me."

She shook her head. "Ian said they'd have no choice. I mean, how could they ignore the warning." She looked at DiGenero, worried, then at Silverstein, suspicious. "Are you sure?"

Silverstein dropped his sandwich, angry. "Hey! I called 'em and said I lost important papers on their fuckin' airplane, but I don't know which one. Shoved down in a seat pocket. 'I gotta find 'em,' I said, 'can you check?' They said, 'sure.' I said it was a week ago, maybe more—you know, I gave 'em some bullshit story about flyin' on business, back and forth a couple times a week, big-shot stuff. I said, 'maybe you gotta look around. Maybe these planes ain't flyin' to New York, but are goin' different places now.' They said, 'nope, we got the same planes on the route. Nothin's changed.'" He eyed Jilian, presenting an expression of minor victory. "That's what they said."

DiGenero looked away, distracted. "I wonder."

Silverstein bit into the sandwich. "Wonder what?"

"Why Scarlese changed his mind," he said.

"He wants your ass."

"No." DiGenero shook his head. "I mean, I wonder about the timing, that's all." He looked across the table at Silverstein. "That fax from Foley said one of the airplanes—the one that came out of major inspection a month ago, just like 121—flew when?"

"Yeah. When was that?" Silverstein looked at the ceiling.

DiGenero remembered first. "Monday-Wednesday-Friday."

Silverstein extracted a generous slice of pastrami from the sandwich, reducing its dimensions. He popped it in his mouth and nodded as he chewed.

"That means . . ." DiGenero began.

Jilian looked pale. This time she interrupted. "That means it arrives tonight."

The three women sat on a raised dais, each attempting to outshout the other. Waving for attention, they bounced in their swivel chairs. A man with a microphone, the talk show host, walked in and out of the scene, laughing, declaiming, questioning, goading. The three competed, interrupting and disagreeing as they praised the quality of sex with one species of animal over another. Off-camera, an audience hooted, equally animated by their antics and the host's provocations.

Benedetto turned down the volume. The knock was louder this time. He rose from the bed and walked to the window, pulling back the edge of the drape. The motel's parking lot held the usual assortment of cars at midday. In the street, a small collection of black kids kicked a hubcap. It rolled and skittered from the pavement to the unkempt grass. Benedetto looked left and right, checking. No cops, no unmarked cars from the Field Office. He glanced farther afield. The cul de sac was virtually self-contained, cordoned by chain link with a barbed wire fringe. A block from the motel, Kennedy Airport's security fence demarcated the dead-end. Across the street, another protected the rows of cheap sedans in the adjoining rental car lot. Beside the security fence, two stripped chassis were parallel parked, resting on rims and the curb. Skeletons of the breed that failed to reach sanctuary.

Benedetto stood to one side of the door. "Yeah? Who's there?"

"We're ready to go." The voice wasn't familiar.

"Whaddyatalkin' about?" Benedetto challenged.

"Johnny sent me."

He looked through the peephole. One guy. It was time. Not too soon. He'd told the office one story: annual leave. He'd told his wife another: a stakeout, two, maybe three days. A day and a half holed up was enough, pressing his luck. He opened the door.

The caller, in a leather jacket and jeans, stepped in. "Howyadoin'?" There was no smile. He pushed the door closed behind him. "You're leavin' in two hours. You're supposed to get your stuff together now. Then we go."

Benedetto stared. "You got the tickets?"

"Yeah, sure." He looked around the room. "Pretty fuckin' seedy place they put you in."

"Lemme see 'em." Benedetto extended his hand.

"Yeah, sure." He reached inside his jacket and fished out an airline folio.

Benedetto checked tickets. Business class for Paris, then a commuter line to London City Airport. From London, another flight to Dublin. "Where's the passport? And the money?"

"Yeah, sure." He fished again, handing over an envelope this time. Benedetto opened it. The passport was in alias. The travelers checks were blank, unsigned. He counted.

Benedetto looked up. "Five thousand. That all?"

"The money? There's more at the other end. They're gonna meet ya. Don't worry."

Benedetto counted the travelers checks again. "Okay." He let himself relax. "Gimme a minute. I gotta get a few things."

"Yeah, sure. Johnny always takes care of people. Like he says."

Benedetto entered the bathroom, collecting his toiletries. He spoke over his shoulder. "I knew he would."

"Yeah, sure." The leather jacket walked around the room. "Johnny said he's sorry the DiGenero thing went bad."

Benedetto's head emerged from the bathroom door. "You know about that? What else he say?"

"Nothin'. Why?"

Benedetto shrugged. "Forget it." He felt a momentary relief. He had debated telling Scarlese about Jilian, but decided against it. It had been his job to keep the law away from Scarlese's IRA connection. The Brits as well as the Bureau. If he told Scarlese about her, it would be another admission of failure. Too risky. Too dangerous when there was only one way out and Scarlese had the key.

The leather jacket made a circuit of the room. "You got everything in the bag, right? You ain't forgettin' nothin'?"

"Just this." Benedetto came out with shaving cream and razor in hand. He dropped them in the suitcase, then bent down, arranging the contents. He busied himself with small items, tucking and retucking them into corners and crevices. His hands moved nervously, redoing what was just done. "It's good to get me outa here for a while. I'm a little wound up. I mean, if the DiGenero thing had worked that woulda been alright. But I can't take the chance by stickin' around to see what happens next." Benedetto straightened up and turned, anxious. "You sure somebody's gonna meet me in London? I mean, five thousand ain't gonna go very far. I gotta stay gone for a while. You sure it's all set?"

"Yeah, sure. Johnny told me to tell you he's gonna take care of it. Not to worry." He gestured. "You got everything out of the bathroom? You ain't leavin' nothin' behind? You wan' me to check?"

Benedetto nodded. He made a slow, uncertain circle, then turned back to the bag. "I got it all. Gimme one more second." He bent down, opening his toiletries kit. "I wanna see if I brought my toothpaste. I don't know what kind they got." He laughed nervously. "I ain't never been over there before, you know what I mean?"

The leather jacket stepped behind him, looking down into the bag. "Yeah, sure. Take all the time in the world."

The shot at the base of the skull dropped Benedetto like an animal expertly felled, facedown, killing instantly, an effect ludicrously disproportionate to the cause's small pop. The caller backed up, putting his ear to the door. In the hall, there were no sounds. He stepped to the bathroom and took a towel, dropping it for the moment on the bed, then lifted Benedetto by the arm, raising his chest. He had collapsed, half on the suitcase, half off. He extracted the bag, tossing the tickets, money, and passport inside, then emptying Benedetto's pockets of wallet, keys, and identification, adding those as well before zipping the suitcase and setting it beside the door.

Circumnavigating the room for a final check, he gripped the silencer screwed into the barrel of the 9mm automatic and twisted, tightening, then returned to his position behind the body. He nuzzled the barrel against Benedetto's temple, decorously covering the automatic with the towel.

"Like I said, Johnny told me to take care of you." Three pops followed. With each, under the towel, Benedetto seemed to be nodding in assent.

CHAPTER

31

THE TRAIN RAN backward. Alone on the platform, they stood silently, watching the last car approach first, air hoses and couplings dangling like torn ligaments from its blunt end. In the next car, the conductor had opened the door. He leaned out, holding his hand before him, a half salute to the rain.

"Speonk is eight minutes from Westhampton Station, the next stop. The cab will be waiting." DiGenero repeated what she already knew for something to say. They had called from the station's pay phone fifteen minutes before. The cab dispatcher in Westhampton had promised they would have someone there, on time.

Jilian watched the train. It was covered with grime. Rain streaked diagonally, rear to front, as if the cars had been racing before the wind and winning.

"You know the drill," he said, asking for confirmation.

She nodded.

Behind them, in the parking lot, he had left the rental car idling. Drops peppered the hood, a tinny sound. The engine purred, exhaust rose, the wipers swept the windshield. A ghostly animation.

"You're going to call me at 3:20 sharp, right?"

"Yes," she said without looking at him.

"I'll be across the street."

She nodded again.

"If you say 'Hi,' things are fine. 'Hello' means you're in trouble."

"Hi and hello," she repeated mechanically.

After leaving Silverstein at the deli, they had spoken little on the drive east. DiGenero had taken the Long Island Expressway, detouring to Islip, where they rented a second car at the airport. Jilian had followed him south from Islip to Sunrise Highway. Turning east again, the signs for the Hamptons and Montauk took them past the suburban shopping strips and summer tourist kitsch, now dark and closed, then finally, beyond Shirley, into open space, fields and rolling dunes. Save for local traffic and the occasional off-season traveler, the road was empty. All theirs, as if someone had prepared the way.

The brakes squealed. The three cars of the midday commuter slowed. DiGenero glanced up as the train reached them. The windows passed one after the other, each reflecting identical pictures. The small station. Vacant. The platform. Deserted. The two of them. Together. Or alone. Inside, the seats faced backward, empty. No one prepared to get off.

They had pulled off the road at Westhampton, a two-car caravan stopped just beyond the exit. She had listened to his instructions and examined the map. DiGenero had pointed out her route, then followed her for a mile, stopping to wait at the first gas station. Jilian had driven by the restaurant once, then circled back, returning to change coats and cars and to put up her hair. A new profile in case there was surveillance already in place. She'd driven by a second time. The restaurant was small, standing alone. Across the street, a local food market, once a family store, now retrofitted with a well-known New York name, anchored a nondescript mall. She had parked and gone into the market, finding the phone and copying its number, then walked a cart down the aisles to the rear. Through the double doors to the storeroom, she could see the loading dock. Beyond, framed by two dumpsters, an exit to a back street offered another way in and out.

The train's squeals ascended the scale, accompanied by grinding, the final throes, metal on metal. The cars jerked to a halt. Jilian turned to go.

DiGenero held her arm. "Remember, your call is 3:20 sharp."

"I remember." She looked at him for the first time in a long time. Composed, her face was a mask. "Why did you make your promise?"

The question surprised him. "Hell of a time to ask that," he said.

She searched his expression for clues that might clarify the evasion. "Why?" she asked again.

The conductor watched them, one foot on the step of the car, whistle in hand. Six months from now on a Friday afternoon the platform would be crowded. The male migration, white shirts with ties undone and suitcoats over shoulders, climbing down, greeted by the season's female settlement, tennis whites and children in technicolor tee shirts and swimsuits. A ritual summer joining with tribal costumes and customs. DiGenero wished it was six months from now and that the conductor's whistle had already blown.

Jilian's gaze held him, its intensity demanding an answer. "I don't know," he said.

"I don't believe you."

He shook his head.

"You doubted, didn't you?" She challenged him.

It was a different Jilian. She had composed herself, already preparing for Scarlese. Confidence filled her like a vessel. Her voice had changed, direct, in control. Beside him, she stood straighter, taller somehow. He saw the woman he remembered that morning after Ward's Island. Beautiful, self-possessed.

"Doubted what?" he asked.

"That you could kill him."

The conductor intervened. "'Board!"

"No." He felt suddenly defensive.

Nothing suggested she accepted the answer. She kissed him once, brushing his cheek with her lips. Jilian stepped away before he could react. She climbed on board. He saw her in the car, a solitary shadow moving along the aisle. She took a seat just above him, looking down. The train jerked, then pulled away. Behind the glass, her image disappeared into reflection. The diesel passed, barely straining, gathering speed.

He watched until the train was gone, then walked to the car and sat. The question from behind the mask came back. Why had he promised? Was she right? Did he doubt that he could do it, walk in and kill Scarlese? If he did, what was the doubt? Not the right and wrong of it. About that there was no question. Scarlese deserved to die. DiGenero rested his head on the steering wheel. What was it? Fear of what would happen to him if he pulled the trigger? Being killed? Arrested? Tried and jailed? No. He sat up and put the car in gear. He angled across the parking spaces and out of the lot. The short section of station road ended. He turned left at Montauk Highway, heading east. DiGenero lifted his foot from the accelerator, slowing to the speed limit. In his jacket, he felt the automatic, heavy against his leg. Silverstein had given it back. It weighted him like her question. The highway wound past side streets with picturesque names—Warner's Neck, Little Bay Lane. Hints of the water views beyond. Trees bordered the road, mostly low scrub, a few old, spreading and enduring. The sign, "Westhampton Town Limits," flashed by, half hidden in the shrubbery. What was it? Why did he promise? For Jilian? For himself? For both of them? Maybe there weren't answers, only questions. What did you owe the living? What did you owe the dead?

Only Scarlese's limousine occupied the restaurant's parking lot. A hostess was waiting for her at the entrance when the taxi pulled up. She led the way to the corner booth, menu in hand, and announced Jilian, as if there might be some question about her destination.

"Your guest, Mr. Scarlese." She bowed herself away.

Scarlese made a pretense of rising, then beckoned to the space beside him. A busboy appeared, filling her water glass. A basket of bread, a wine bottle, and salad plates were already placed. Scarlese poured the Beaujolais.

"The last of the nouveau," he said. "It should be drunk this year. A wine with no patience."

"A good choice." Jilian smiled cooly.

Scarlese wore a black cashmere jacket and an open-necked shirt. A watch with a custom gold band was the only adornment above understatement. He raised his glass. "Salute."

Jilian raised hers, "Cheers." She gestured toward the room. "One of your favorite places?" The question bore its sarcasm embedded. A collection of ship models, buoys, sports trophies, team photographs, and commemorative plaques suggested a long-term as well as eclectic investment in bad taste.

"Off-season in Westhampton doesn't offer a great deal to choose from." He shrugged. "I simply thought you'd be more comfortable in a public place."

"Did you?"

"In light of what happened the other day." Scarlese sipped, examining her over the edge of the wine glass.

"Yes, tell me, what did happen the other day?" The intricacy of the answer, Jilian knew, bore no relationship to the simplicity of the question.

"Let's not talk about it here." Scarlese smiled. He glanced around nervously.

"Why not? I don't like being threatened." She smiled back. "You didn't think that killing me would solve your problems with us, did you?"

This time, Scarlese looked genuinely discomfited. He spoke through clenched teeth, a man not used to having his directions ignored. "I said, *not here.*"

"Alright, not here."

On either side of the dining room's entrance, the busboy who had filled her water glass and the hostess who had led her to the booth busied themselves with minor chores. Straightening menus, filling sugar bowls, arranging trays.

A waiter approached. Tall, well built, clean shaven. Like the busboy. "Would you like to order?" he asked.

"No. This is fine," she said.

Scarlese waved him away. "Let's get down to business, shall we?" he said.

Two booths away, the waiter had deposited his tray on a serving cart. He begun to reset tables, adjusting knives and forks and refolding napkins. "Why not?" Jilian said.

"I told you to bring him. Where is he?" Scarlese asked.

"Do you expect me . . . ," Jilian began.

"I said, where is he?" Scarlese hissed.

"We trusted you to help us for one reason and one reason only." Jilian spoke, keeping watch on Scarlese's eyes. They burned, her words their fuel. Too little and the flame would fail to catalyze the reaction she wanted. Too much and it would flare, hatred consuming him—and her. "Once you could protect Bellflower in a way we couldn't. That's no longer true. It's time you . . ."

Scarlese gripped her wrist. "Forget the fairy tale. I know who you are and what you want."

"What are you talking about?" She tried to pull away.

Scarlese twisted harder. He smiled, enjoying the effect. "Do you want me to spell things out?" He lowered his voice in mock conspiracy. "Try R-U-C. Sound familiar?" Scarlese yanked hard, pulling her toward him. He bent closer, his lips near her ear. "And something else." His voice dropped to a whisper only she could hear. "Even if I told you where Bellflower was, it's too late for you to do anything about it. Tonight it's over."

Jilian felt suddenly cold. Her eyes darted toward the door. Neither the waiter nearby nor the busboy and hostess had looked up. Her purse was beside her. She groped with her right hand, pulling it closer and felt for the top, a leather drawstring.

"Let go of me," she said.

"I told you to bring him." Scarlese tightened his grasp. His voice was animal, a predator's snarl. "Once more. Where's DiGenero?"

She looked around. The waiter was one booth closer, unmindful, continuing his chores. Scarlese had pulled her hand below the table. He contorted her wrist. The pain ran deep into the bone. She opened her bag. The automatic was in the inside pocket, butt-end up. "You're hurting me!" The waiter's head came up.

"Where is he?" Scarlese twisted.

Her left hand was numb, no longer a part of her. She felt blindly with her right, touching the pistol butt. Jilian looked around. The waiter was beside her. He reached into the booth, snatching away her bag, then stepped back.

"That's enough," the waiter said.

Scarlese ignored him. "Where is he?" He twisted harder.

"Knock it off!" The waiter's voice rose. He stepped forward. Across the deep table, Scarlese was out of reach. Others moved toward them. Scarlese was bending her sideways. She followed his torque, trying to undo the twisting by repositioning her shoulder.

Jilian cried out. "Let go!"

The waiter spoke. "I said, that's enough!"

Scarlese snapped back. "Shutup!" He twisted. "Where's DiGenero?"

The booth trapped her, limiting her contortions. Pain radiated. The waiter lunged over the table, upsetting the wine. Jilian felt herself blacking out. She gasped. "Stop, please! I'll get him."

Scarlese twisted.

In her wrist something tore. The room was starting to swim, to change shape and color. She whispered. "A phone."

Scarlese released her. Jilian slumped. Her eyes filled with tears.

"Keep your hands off her!" The waiter grabbed for Scarlese's lapel, but missed.

Scarlese batted away his hand. "Just get the fuckin' phone." He glared.

The busboy put an extension in front of Jilian. She reached, but the waiter shook his head. "I'll dial," he said. "What the number?"

Backlit by the front door, several other silhouettes filled the dining room's entrance. Her wrist throbbed, already swelling. Jilian wiggled her fingers. Pain shot through her arm but they moved. At least the bone wasn't broken. She glanced at her watch. It was nearly 3:20.

"Come on!" Scarlese ordered. "Give him the fuckin' number! And it better be local!"

Jilian spoke. "326-1182."

The waiter dialed.

Scarlese stared at her. "And you tell him, *here!* I want to see the son of a bitch *here! Right here!*"

She took the phone.

DiGenero came on the line even before the first ringing tone ended. "Are you okay?"

Jilian forgot the code. "Frank, it's tonight's flight! Stop it! This is a trap!"

The back of Scarlese's hand hit her full force across the face, dislodging the phone and slamming Jilian's head against the wall. Like a man possessed, Scarlese lunged, grabbing the skittering receiver. Glasses and plates skittered across the table. His scream echoed. "DiGenero, you fucker! You're dead! You hear me? You're a dead man!"

The waiter pulled Jilian away. Hands closed on her arms, protecting and restraining. Jilian tasted blood. A tooth felt loose, maybe two. Her ears rang. The busboy and two others reached, half lifting her from the booth.

The waiter shoved Scarlese back.

"You'd better fuckin' find him!" Scarlese pointed at Jilian. "She knows!" He slid out the opposite end of the banquette and moved toward her, menacing, but the waiter stood in the way. Scarlese stalked out. At the dining room entrance, the silhouettes parted as he passed, reforming behind him. Jilian heard car doors slam.

The waiter reached into his jacket, extracting a small leather case and flipped it open. Jilian saw a badge mated with an identification card.

"FBI, Ms. McCray." Agent or waiter, he spoke, a monotone. "We'd like to talk to you about Frank DiGenero. All of us." He nodded at the busboy and hostess. Behind them, Jilian saw four more in suits and ties, apparitions materialized from somewhere. "Is he here, in Westhampton?"

She shook her head. "I need to speak with your counterterrorism people. It's urgent." Jilian touched her lip. It was swollen, making words thick. Her arm hurt from fingers to shoulder.

He nodded noncommittally. He gestured toward the phone. "Can you reach him again?"

Jilian ignored the question. The waiter-turned-agent seemed to regard their dialogue as utterly matter-of-fact, certainly not meriting undue emotion.

"You don't have anything you want to tell us about DiGenero?" he asked.

The throbbing in arm and shoulder overtook her, a heartbeat's rhythm making her sway. She marshaled her energy, focusing. "Did you hear what I said?"

"Perfectly." He motioned.

Jilian felt hands close on her again. The hostess stood before her. She patted her from head to toe, running her hands up and down her thighs, then turned to the waiter and spoke. "Clean."

The waiter turned toward the busboy. "That all?"

The busboy held up her automatic and purse. "In here, that's it."

"Wait," Jilian said. They paused, obliging. "You're taking me into custody and Scarlese goes free. I don't understand."

"We want Frank DiGenero and Scarlese," the waiter said. "But we only have a federal warrant for one of them. We had a tip DiGenero would be here, looking for Scarlese. Believe me, if I could pick the people in this country we'd protect, Johnny Scarlese wouldn't be on the list."

The waiter motioned. The hands that held Jilian guided her toward the door. "The counterterrorism people," she repeated.

The waiter-turned-agent spoke, following behind. "This is a conversation we need to continue. In New York."

DiGenero swung onto the Long Island Expressway at the Brookhaven National Laboratory and melded into the westbound traffic. He accelerated around a tractor trailer, then merged into the right lane again. Approaching, the stream of cars already had headlamps on in the early darkness. A lighted chain, it flowed unbroken, bright and alive against the clouds lying sullen and low in the west. He tuned the radio through the dial, finding an all-talk station. Sports, business, ads, coming features, finally weather and traffic. The announcer read each with the same mechanical enthusiasm. Fog, rain, poor visibility, another front moving in to spoil the weekend. He cautioned to expect delays in air traffic, then peremptorily switched to sports.

DiGenero turned on his lights. He had recognized the vans when they first drove by the restaurant, just before Jilian's call. The Bureau's favorite. Customized, recreational, garish, with smoked bubbles, running lights and antennas to disguise cameras, eavesdropping equipment, and radio communication gear. Trojan horses with room in back for a surveillance team or as much of a squad as could squeeze in for a bust.

The Bureau. After him? Yes. But with Scarlese? Why? And how? How did they connect? Was it Scarlese and Benedetto? Did they know Scarlese had turned him? Scarlese and the IRA? Were they onto the bargain, Scarlese's deal? Or Scarlese and the Bureau, another link altogether, something direct? DiGenero pressed down on the accelerator. His speed climbed, past seventy, eighty. And why now? At this place and time? Waiting for who? For Jilian? For him? Taillights flashed ahead. He slowed. A state trooper's car sat by the road, blue strobe illuminating a hapless Winnebago. DiGenero watched the pair recede in his rearview mirror. He picked up the pace. Nothing he saw an hour ago made sense, only what he heard. Only Jilian's voice, first on the train platform, then on the phone. Now he had the answer to her question. He had promised because of what she had said, but before she ever spoke the words, the first of her few on the phone. DiGenero looked at his watch. It was almost five. The flight arrived at nine. He pulled out and accelerated around a string of cars. The road ahead was clear. He stayed in the passing lane this time.

CHAPTER

32

IN A BUILDING of windows, the interrogation room had none. Aside from the furnishings—a table, some chairs—there was only a door and an electric outlet high on the wall, power for a clock that no longer hung. Symbols by their presence and absence. A suggestion to those questioned that there was only one way out and no reprieve from the passage of time.

They'd been at it for more than two hours, Jilian seated at the table with one or two others, the rest in chairs along the wall. The room had filled and emptied several times, not all at once, but one by one, a person going or coming, here and there. All but the waiter. He had stayed with her from the beginning. Until a moment ago. Jilian heard the latch opening. She looked over her shoulder, turning carefully to avoid antagonizing the bruises Scarlese had inflicted somewhere inside.

The waiter entered and shut the door. He spoke before he'd taken his place across the table. "I talked to Barry."

"Good," she said.

"He said he knows you."

Jilian nodded. "Now we're getting somewhere."

"Yeah, right back where we started." The waiter sat. He rubbed his eyes wearily. "Mr. Barry knows you're Jilian McCray, the correspondent for the Dublin *Register*. An acquaintance"—he spoke the word like an epithet—"not an undercover officer of the Royal Ulster Constabulary."

"That's nonsense," Jilian shot back.

"That's what he said."

"Look," Jilian said. "He's MI5. He knows that . . ."

"No, you look!" the waiter broke in, exasperated. "I don't know where you got the story about Barry being British intelligence. I'm not here to tell you that's right or wrong, God's truth or bullshit, understand? I'm not an intel type. They're down the hall. I'll let them worry

304

about that. I'm tellin' you he doesn't corroborate your story. This RUC thing. So we're back to square one."

The waiter leaned back, balancing the chair on two legs. "Now, I won't say this hasn't been entertaining. A wonderful adventure about Irish terrorists inside the FAA. About a deal between Johnny Scarlese and the IRA and his plan to take over the world. A hair-raising tale about why that airplane crashed a week or so ago. Even a truly creative explanation of how come DiGenero blew away Sallie Ferringa and his two buddies."

"*I* shot them, *I* said." Jilian glared. "For God's sake? Why don't you check out my gun? I told you what happened. They were going to kill DiGenero."

"Yeah, right." The waiter wearily waved off the protest. "We'll check it out. But I gotta tell you, this room full of guys"—he gestured encompassing the audience—"all does organized crime for a living. We don't do terrorists, or Irish crazies, or little green men invading from Mars. We're just hometown boys, one-foot-in-front-of-the-other, simple, work-a-day stiffs. And to us, what you've been sayin' doesn't make a goddamn bit of sense. I mean, maybe there's somebody over in counterintelligence or counterterrorism who'd love to listen, but you're going to have to do better than that right here."

"Counterintelligence?" Jilian looked up. "And maybe I could call Belfast and get the IRA's General Command on the phone, too. I'm sure they'd love to talk with you," she said sarcastically. "Let me repeat myself. Your counterintelligence unit is compromised. Benedetto is part of it!"

Behind Jilian someone moaned. The waiter's face darkened. "And I told you not to give me that shit! I know Tony. We all know Tony. We've all worked with Tony. He's a stand-up guy. The best. I haven't the faintest idea why DiGenero wants to smear him, but you'd be smart not to play along. Not in this room. You wanna throw mud? For your own good, you'd better find somebody else."

Jilian leaned forward. "Alright. You don't want to hear the truth. Let's just deal with facts. Benedetto runs one of your counterintelligence units, am I correct?" Jilian asked.

"I'm not the one who answers the questions. You are." The waiter stared.

"If you're responsible for organized crime and he's responsible for counterintelligence, ask him why he met with DiGenero—why he was going to kill DiGenero and me—two days ago. At the Gramercy Park Hotel. All you need to do is have someone go by the hotel with his picture. Question the staff if they saw him there. Surely that kind of investigation isn't beyond the capabilities of the FBI."

"Don't give me more bullshit."

Jilian persisted. "Too hard? Why not look at Benedetto's bank accounts? To provide personal banking records isn't an unusual request, not for one of your officers with all of the fancy security clearances someone in counterintelligence must carry. When you do, ask Benedetto about the entries you'll find, the payments of five thousand dollars a month. Ask him what that little stipend from Scarlese is for."

Dermott took a deep breath. "Stop playin' games."

"Oh? Fine. I'll give you the easiest suggestion yet. Ask him why he ran traces on DiGenero week before last."

The waiter shook his head, disgusted. "Traces on an FBI agent? That's wonderful. Nobody would notice that. Gimme a break. Why don't you . . ."

From behind Jilian, a voice interceded. "She's right, Terry. Benedetto did."

Jilian turned. Seated along the wall, one of the audience stared back, nodding in assent.

She glanced at the waiter and then at the agent behind her. The waiter spoke. "Whaddyatalkin' about?"

"She's right. Tony came in and asked for a trace. He had prints. The make on the prints came back with a security hold—you know, because DiGenero's still undercover. We got Tony the clearance for access and then DiGenero's personnel file—or at least parts of it. I gotta admit I was surprised. I mean, the only reason I knew about it at all was because Tony had to go through us for clearance to get the file, so it really was none of my business. But I asked him anyway—'what's goin' on with tracin' agents?' Tony said it was nothin'. An old case that Justice was cleanin' up. One he and DiGenero had been involved in a long time ago. He'd been called to help reconcile some evidence and background information. That was all."

The waiter exploded. "We're chasin' our tail to find DiGenero and I don't hear about this! Why the fuck didn't you tell me?"

The agent shrugged. "Hey, Tony said it was history. Not current. No big thing. How many traces do we do in a month? A couple hundred? Sorry, Terry. What can I say?"

Jilian spoke quietly. "The prints came from me. DiGenero approached me in the bar on the West side, as I told you. I wanted a check on him. I got his prints on an umbrella, gave it to Ian Barry, who went to Benedetto to have the traces done. That was two weeks ago. The file that came back had DiGenero's personal history, the details on his falcon-smuggling undercover operation—including on the man, the Iranian, he shot years ago."

The waiter looked over her head at the agent who had spoken. "Is that right? What she says about the file? What was in it?"

The agent answered. "Right on."

The waiter nodded toward the door. "Give Tony a call. See if he can come in and talk."

Jilian heard the door open and close.

"You need to have Barry here as well," Jilian said. "He can corroborate why we need to get word to the airline. About the nine P.M. flight."

The waiter raised both hands, palms up. "Hey, let's do one thing at a time. Now that we've all fallen down the rabbit hole, my job right now is to sort out this Alice in Wonderland story. Before we start chasing airplanes, I wanna get that out of the way."

Jilian interrupted. "There isn't time! You don't have to prove me right or wrong. Just get word to the airline to divert the plane. Warn them. That's all."

"Just 'warn' them? That's 'all?' " He shook his head. "What do you think happens when the FBI warns an airline? Two or three people sneak around, quiet as church mice, and whisper to the pilot to fly someplace else, rather than land where he's supposed to, just this once, and nobody knows? Jesus Christ, it'll be all over the eleven o'clock news! Then, when I start answering telephone calls that ask why, what am I gonna say? 'Well, this woman walked in and told me to do it?' Come on! They'll laugh me all the way up the river to Albany! Right now, we've got something to check out. Barry says he doesn't know you. Let's talk to Tony. Maybe he can . . ."

Behind Jilian the door opened. The agent returned. "Something's funny," he said. "Tony's signed out for annual leave for two days. Time off. I called his wife. She says he told her he's at work. On a stakeout. One, maybe two days. That's what he said. His squad hasn't seen him in two days. They thought Tony was off and he'd be back in the office today. He didn't show."

"So where is he?" the waiter asked.

"Nobody knows."

The waiter furrowed his brow. "And where does that leave us?" He looked at Jilian. "You still don't have anybody to back up the story. And I'm still spinnin' my wheels with you on DiGenero."

"If you can't find Benedetto, find Barry!" You've got to talk to him! For God's sake, that won't embarrass the Bureau! Bring him in!"

The waiter stared, considering, then finally nodded. "Okay. Let's take a break. I'll go call Barry again." He left. Behind him, others filed out.

Jilian slumped in the chair. The interrogation had changed direction, she knew, however subtle and tenuous the shift. She put her head in her hands. Her wrist throbbed along with her shoulder. How long had they been at it? She looked at her watch. After six. Less than three hours left.

They had returned her to the city in style, a journey obviously prepared for DiGenero. First, a van from the restaurant to the Westhampton airport. Then a helicopter to a landing pad on the lower East side. Then, an unmarked car to the depths of a basement garage in the Federal Building, where they ascended to the windowless room on the twenty-fourth floor. There, a doctor had ministered to her briefly, wrapping her wrist, testing her arm's motion, and offering a sling, which she politely refused. When he had finished, the waiter and the others had entered and begun.

At first, the waiter was reasonableness incarnate. Still in his white shirt and cummerbund, he sat opposite, hands folded on the table. He had introduced himself precisely. "Special Agent Terrance Dermott, Deputy Chief of the Organized Crime Squad for the New York Field Office, FBI." Jilian had acknowledged the courtesy, nodding as if making his acquaintance for the first time. Locating Frank DiGenero, Dermott had explained, was his responsibility. She knew where DiGenero was and could help, he had asserted blandly. They knew of her relationship with Vito Rocchi and Sallie Ferringa and that she'd met Johnny Scarlese several times. They surmised that somehow DiGenero had learned as well. DiGenero had used her—perhaps, Dermott allowed without undue criticism, taking advantage of someone unwitting—to learn what he needed, even to arrange the murder of those he thought responsible for his wife's death. Witting or not, he had said, she appeared to be an accessory, possibly guilty of abetting a crime. In peroration, Dermott's tone plumbed new depths of sincerity. The tragedy that befell one of their own pained them all. But DiGenero's vendetta also reflected a man—an FBI agent—who had never conformed. DiGenero had stepped beyond the bounds, he said, taking matters in his own hands, perhaps even denying the Bureau—the government—its opportunity to bring the real killers to justice, not under the laws of the jungle, but under the law of the land.

Dermott had paused for effect, pleased with himself, then proceeded from preamble to text. They had questions about Ferringa and Rocchi and about others she might know, he said. But her help was needed most to find DiGenero. Where he was, who had helped him, what he planned.

Jilian had listened to Dermott enumerate his questions without interrupting, allowing him to hold forth and have his say. She had waited until he finished before she spoke. When she said he was dead wrong about everything, including DiGenero, he looked as if she had hit him with a bat.

After months alone in New York with her secrets, the audience intended to overwhelm and intimidate her had, perversely, the opposite effect. Listening to Dermott, she had come to her own conclusion about what to do. Unlike Barry, she had no relationships to tend nor battles to fight another day. There was, in short, only one answer to Dermott's questions. The truth. She had held forth, describing her role, the RUC's operation, and DiGenero, from their first encounter on the West side to the night on Ward's Island and finally, his promise. When she was done, she sat back and looked at their faces. It was only then that it struck her: they were organized crime, not counterterrorism. They had listened, observed, taken notes, but hadn't believed a word. She might as well have spoken Greek. At least that was so until a minute ago, when the voice behind her piped up.

The door opened. Dermott, the waiter, was back. Alone. "Barry's gone. Not at his office. Not at his apartment." He sat heavily, obviously fatigued himself. His eyes seemed to offer a flicker of sympathy. "Now what do we do?" he said.

Jilian turned, wincing at the effort. Behind her, the room was empty, the door closed. She faced Dermott, speaking quietly. "We have to get word out about the nine o'clock flight. I'm telling you the truth."

"The same goes for me. Without something—someone—to back you up, I can't ring that bell."

In remission for only a moment, desperation again welled up. "Don't you have files? Barry's been in touch about this case with your people. I know that. He's worked with Benedetto. There must be something on paper."

Dermott sighed. "I've checked already. Like I said—for the record—I can't confirm one way or the other who Barry is. But I can tell you that what Benedetto's doing is compartmented. Do you know what I mean? Highly classified. Segregated. Benedetto's the one who's got control of the paper. Not his deputy, not his squad, nobody else. He's it. I can't go rooting around. He can approve who has access or not and you heard where he is—who knows where?"

"You can't call Washington? Your headquarters? Isn't there someone?"

"It's Friday night. I'd be lucky to get through to somebody at the right paygrade, much less a warm body who knew what the hell to do."

"Christ!" Jilian covered her eyes. "You mean to tell me that's all? There's nothing you can do?"

Dermott shrugged. "Well, there is one other possibility—I mean, it's stretching."

Jilian looked up. "What?"

"If you could get a call to DiGenero . . ." He paused. "Maybe he and I could talk. Who knows? I'm willing to listen. I know Frank. Or at least I knew him. Maybe if he can fill me in on what you've said—his side of the story—we could put the pieces together in time to get a message out to the airline. To put your mind at ease. It might be worth a call."

"I told you the truth. About what I did. About what he didn't do."

Dermott held up one hand as if to forestall movement down an unwanted road. "I understand what you told us," he said, conciliating. "But if I could talk to him, I'd be happier. Look, you're asking me to go public with a front-page story on your word alone. Wouldn't you feel the same in my shoes?"

Jilian looked away, thinking. She met Dermott's gaze. "I want to talk to him privately. Alone."

"Sure."

"And, this would be his decision. Whether he talked to you."

"Absolutely." Dermott nodded emphatically. "We'll get you an office. All yours."

"And if Frank . . ."

Dermott interrupted. "If Frank confirms what you say, we get a warning to the airlines. Pronto. My word."

Jilian spoke. "Go ahead."

Dermott stepped to the door and went out. Jilian smiled, amused at the metamorphosis.

From the twenty-fourth floor, the windows of the corner office faced south on Broadway, a clear cut corridor running straight between the old granite and stone growth and the newer, taller glass-and-steel seedings, lower Manhattan's next generation. The first buildings, once sunlit, were now covered, once the heights, now the undergrowth in the shadows of the second canopy. Jilian sat, looking out. At the buildings' peaks, the clouds met, as if joining to rest temporarily before pressing down. The view offered a relevant perspective, she thought. Narrow and increasingly constrained.

There was, Jilian knew, no question what would happen when she picked up the phone. Dermott's ploy was transparent. She would call, they would trace. She knew that. But without Benedetto or Barry, what choices did she have? She had described, reasoned, argued, pleaded for almost three hours. She looked at her watch again. Six-thirty. Two and a half hours to go. She needed someone to help her, someone who could get through to them. There were no guarantees, but also no choices.

DiGenero had given her the number, the place to reach him just in case. Jilian put her hand on the phone. The words came to her like a prayer. Please, let the right one be there. Not him. Please. Not him.

She picked up the receiver and dialed.

Silverstein answered on the second ring. "Yeah?"

Jilian talked nonstop, allowing no interruption. "Frank, you've got to help me. I'm trying to get them to believe me, but they don't. I've told them everything. Now they want to hear it from you."

Silverstein tried to break in. "Waitaminute! This ain't . . ."

"You've got to consider this carefully, I know. They just want to talk to you. That's all. But I want you to make the decision. I need your help."

"Hey!" Silverstein tried again unsuccessfully.

"Think it over. Please. For me. I'll ring you back in a few minutes. It's important, Frank. But it's your choice."

Jilian hung up. Outside the clouds were lowering. She closed her eyes. Now, finally, there were no more choices. Now, she could only wait. Hope. And pray.

Two floors below, in the small communications room behind the telephone operators' console, Dermott stood beside the technician, who was seated, watching the video display terminal.

Dermott bent down, peering at the letters as they printed across the screen.

CALL NOW PROCESSING.

A voice rose, one of the agents behind him. "Attaboy, Terry. She fell for it!"

Dermott stared at the screen, stonefaced.

The technician spoke. "Got it!"

"Where's the phone she's calling?" Dermott asked.

"Wait a minute," the technician tapped the keys. The video screen lit, orange on black. Across the top, the area code and telephone number. The technician talked as he worked, typing commands. "QTT—Quick Trace Technology—picks up the number and localizes on the phone as soon as the caller presses each digit. From area code, to exchange, right down to a local extension. It's brand new. All traced in real time. As a matter of fact, we tap into the line being called before the call even goes through." He looked up, beaming. "Ain't high-speed microprocessors great?"

"Wonderful," Dermott said. He pointed impatiently at the screen. "But where is he?"

"Hang in there," the technician said. "The data base search only takes a second." As he spoke the screen lit again. Silverstein's name, address, and apartment number printed orange on black.

"East 87th Street," another voice behind them, one of the audience, read aloud. "Christ! On Friday night with bad weather, in the traffic that'll take us thirty minutes from here. That is, if we're lucky. Do we want to call the local precinct to pick him up?"

"Hell no!" Dermott shook his head. "This goddamn case has gotten goofy enough. I don't want the cops fuckin' it up as well. He's ours."

"Who's Silverstein?" The voice behind Dermott asked.

"Who cares? That's where DiGenero is," Dermott said. He turned. "Whaddyawaitin' for? A fuckin' invitation? Go get him!"

Ninety-six blocks north of the Federal Building, DiGenero barged into Silverstein's apartment as soon as he opened the door.

"Well, did you have a nice time at the beach?" Silverstein asked.

DiGenero caught his breath. "The Bureau's got Jilian. It was a trap."

"Oh yeah? Is that where she is?" Silverstein's face brightened with understanding. "Not ten minutes ago, I got the weirdest call from her. She's talkin' nonstop to me like it's you—I mean, it's Frank, this, Frank, that. She needs you to back up her story, whatever that is. She says it's your decision, but doesn't let me get a word in edgewise that I'm the one on the phone, not you. Then, she hangs up. You figure."

DiGenero looked worried. "Was she on long enough for a trace?"

"I dunno." Silverstein shrugged. "Maybe, maybe not. It was quick."

DiGenero stared, thinking. "When she called from the restaurant—to warn me—she said the nine o'clock flight's in trouble."

"How does she know?" Silverstein asked.

"Beats the shit outa me."

"So call the airline," Silverstein said.

DiGenero made a face. "And tell 'em what? 'Hi, this is Frank DiGenero. You may have seen my picture in the paper. I'm wanted by everybody with a fuckin' badge in this town for a triple hit. I called because it occurred to me you might be interested that the IRA is gonna make your nine o'clock flight crash.' Come on, Arnie! They screen threats. Grade *A, B, C, D.* I got less credibility than a supermarket tabloid. Even if you call, whaddya gonna tell 'em? About IRA moles inside the FAA. Tomorrow's flight will have landed by the time you finish that story. All they're gonna hear is a crank."

Silverstein shrugged. "Okay, whadda we gonna do?"

DiGenero paced. "Did you find anything at the bank? The new hire with the phony addresses? Anything at all?"

"Only this." Silverstein walked to his reclining chair. He picked up his car coat, hung on the back, and dug in the pocket. A dog-eared notepad emerged. "This honey's got an account there alright. But the only address the bank's got is a commercial post office—one of those 'pack and send' places that rents mailboxes." He flipped the pages of the pad. "It's a couple blocks from here." Silverstein squinted at his own handwriting. "First Avenue and 81st. The bank sends the statements there. The manager says that's all they know."

"We're down to the nub, huh? Come on. I'm double-parked downstairs." DiGenero waved. He opened the door. "Let's go!"

The hardware store, turned dry cleaner, turned "Pack and Post, Inc.," occupied the corner. In the affluent upper East side neighborhood, a good location for something, although the site's commercial fortunes had yet to determine what. In the back room, the clerk had just turned out the lights when the car swerved and then wheeled into the bus stop zone fronting the store, jumping one tire over the curb. He walked to the counter and looked out to investigate the commotion as the two men ran across the sidewalk and burst through the door.

Silverstein flashed his badge. "Police, we got an emergency situation here and gotta see your records, okay?"

"Oh my!" The clerk's hands fluttered to his throat. "Certainly, may I help you?"

Silverstein showed him the entry on his pad. "This name, this post office box. Whaddyagot on your records for the boxholder?"

"Let me see." The clerk opened a drawer and extracted a metal card file. He opened it and thumbed to the *M*'s. "Yes, Coleen Murphy. Here it is." He pulled a card. "Oh dear, I'm sorry." He looked up apologetically.

"Sorry about what?" DiGenero asked.

"There's nothing here but her name and bank reference. We have a notation in the corner that she'll be back with a permanent address." He read. "It says, 'just arrived in the area, living with friends.'"

"Fuck!" DiGenero slammed the counter with his hand.

The clerk jumped.

"Let's open the box," Silverstein said to the clerk.

"Oh, I'm so sorry," the clerk waved his hands as if swatting away flies.

"Whaddya sorry about this time?" Silverstein asked.

"Well, I'd love to help, I really would, but you see we're required by federal law to operate just like the post office. The rules say that we have to have a court order to open mailboxes to anyone but the owner or their written designee. And, of course, this card doesn't have you recorded as a written designee. So, you see, I'd be breaking a federal law if I allowed you. . . ."

Silverstein leaned across the counter and smiled. "What's your name?"

The clerk smiled back. "Martin. My friends call me Marty." His hands fluttered again.

Silverstein grasped his shoulder and patted. "Marty. I gotta admit we're lookin' at a legal question here. Constitutional even. The right to privacy, huh? What can I say? But we got a practical problem. We gotta get in that box as soon as we can. So I'll tell you what. I'll give you two choices."

"You will?" The clerk brightened. He nodded vigorously, eager to cooperate. "Alright."

"You open the box with your key or we'll open it. Whaddyasay?"

The clerk's eyes widened. "You can't . . ."

Silverstein reached inside his jacket and withdrew his revolver. The clerk paled. He held the snub-nosed .38 Smith and Wesson by the barrel, displaying the butt. "With this." He patted the clerk's cheek. "Now it's up to you."

The clerk unhooked a key ring from his belt. Trembling, his hand made the collection rattle as he passed it to Silverstein and pointed. "That's the one."

DiGenero had bent down to peer in the small window of the box. "There's something in there."

Silverstein opened the door and extracted the letter. "It's a phone bill."

DiGenero took it and tore open the envelope. The clerk gasped. DiGenero spoke. "This is for a company. Her name above it. 'Digicom International.' No address but this post office box and the record of calls and charges for Digicom's phone, wherever that is."

"Come on, bring it!" Silverstein said. He made for the door.

"Where you goin'?" DiGenero looked up from the bill.

"I got a crisscross directory back at the apartment. That's the closest place to look the number up."

It took DiGenero ten minutes to go four blocks. At Silverstein's corner, a van angled, blocking the way into the street. Silverstein opened the car door. "You wait. By the time you get around the fuckin' corner I can have this looked up. Stay with the car. I'll be back." He got out and slammed the door. DiGenero watched Silverstein disappear down the sidewalk. The van maneuvered, backing and turning, attempting to negotiate around double-parked cars. Five minutes later, finally freed amidst a chorus of horns, the van pulled ahead.

DiGenero angled around the double-parked cars. Silverstein's apartment was in the middle of the block. Three buildings away, he jammed on the brakes and pulled over. A pair of black four-door Fords were parked at the curb, motors running, in front of Silverstein's door. DiGenero groaned. From the positioning of the antennas on the left front corner of the trunk lid, he recognized the trademark. The compulsive by-the-manual approach for installation of two-way radios drilled into every FBI communications technician.

He started to look behind him for room to back up when the door to the apartment opened and Silverstein emerged. Four surrounded him, one on each arm, the other two leading and trailing. The trailer held something to the side of his head. A cloth or a handkerchief. Even in the dim light and rain, the stain on his trenchcoat was visible. DiGenero couldn't help smiling. The minder on Silverstein's left arm walked with an odd gait, as if favoring a groin injury. DiGenero slunk down in the seat. They bracketed Silverstein in the backseat of the first car. The jostling suggested that even then, handcuffed, he was not a congenial traveler.

The first car pulled away. The other stayed. DiGenero looked beside him. On the seat, Silverstein had left the phone bill. He had the apartment's key, but obviously someone remained. Jilian's call. He should have counted on the trace, not just figured the possibility. DiGenero slipped the car in gear and pulled out, passing slowly by the car parked at the apartment's entrance. The digital clock on the rent-a-car dashboard changed, catching his eye, registering 7:30.

Two blocks east DiGenero pulled to the curb. The rain was falling steadily, harder than before. He got out and ran across the street. The restaurant marquee illuminated the phone. DiGenero hunched under the cover of the half booth, rain blackening his shoulders. He held the bill to the light and read, then deposited a quarter and dialed. The telephone rang. With each tone, he felt himself descending, lost, suffering for past wrongs, helpless like a soul traveling to the lowest circle of the inferno. Three rings, four, five. He looked away. Seven, eight, nine. He sagged hopelessly against the phone when the voice came on the line. "UN Towers operator, may I help you?"

"I . . . Who? . . . I was calling 655-9768," he said.

"That office is closed. This is the building's weekend answering service. May I take a message?"

"Where are you?" he asked. "First and what?"

"Forty-four and First, sir."

"Okay." He hung up.

DiGenero looked at his watch. The rain soaked his arm, wetting the dial. It was 7:40 P.M. He sprinted for the car. Forty blocks. An hour and twenty minutes to go.

CHAPTER

33

THE FBI AGENT took a deep breath, gulping air open-mouthed before he spoke, not unlike a diver preparing to take a plunge. The heel of Silverstein's palm had required the cotton wadding in each of his nostrils. Whether in statements or questions, D sounds predominated. "You know where he is. You know what he's up to. Don't waste our time."

"Oh? You don't wanna waste time? Then, go find a telephone." Darkening from apple to plum, the right side of Silverstein's jaw ached, a singular pulse transmitted with every word.

"Don't start on that again." On Silverstein's right, the other agent who had greeted him at his apartment stared with monocular intensity, one eye swollen shut.

"Okay, Cyclops. What say we start on somethin' else. Howzabout a different name for FBI? You keep the initials, we change the words. Maybe 'Fuckin' Bumblin' Idiots.' After tonight, gettin' that approved won't be no trouble at all. I know I'm not makin' contact, but shut your eye and listen real hard. Go find a phone—you know, one of those black things—dial 911, and tell 'em that there's a nine o'clock flight to Kennedy that's gonna crash. Be a nice boy and do that, huh?"

"Very funny." Behind Silverstein, Dermott leaned against the wall, arms folded. "Whaddya think this is gonna do for you? Or maybe you don't care. Is that it? Cops don't rat on cops. That's right, huh? You and DiGenero go back a long way. I understand that." Dermott pulled a chair from the table and sat. The interrogation room was small, enough space for five or six people. Dermott continued. "We all understand. But what's abetting a murder suspect gonna get you? Nobody here's cryin' about Ferringa and the other two. With what happened to Frank's wife, DiGenero did a righteous thing. But you can't hide him and he can't run forever. We're gonna pick him up. You aren't keepin' anything from happening. You're just slowin' it down."

317

Silverstein leaned forward. A pain ran from his kidneys to ribs, the result of the one-eyed agent's knuckle shots. "What time is it?"

Dermott looked at his watch. "8:10."

Silverstein nodded. "You got less than an hour to get your shit together. DiGenero's out there somewhere tryin' to keep that nine o'clock airplane from buyin' the farm. You got a woman—Jilian McCray—in here who knows all about why that's gonna happen. She's an undercover —a cop, a constable, whatever they fuckin' call it over there. She's the one who shot Ferringa, not DiGenero. She tell you about that?"

Dermott sat, mute.

Silverstein continued. "She tell ya about Scarlese and the IRA?"

Dermott rolled his eyes. "You gonna give me Alice in Wonderland, too?"

Silverstein spoke. "She knows what she's talkin' about. She tell you about Tony Benedetto?" Dermott didn't reply. "I'll lay you ten-to-one odds, he's parts unknown." Dermott's gaze flashed to the other two agents and back to Silverstein, who smiled. "I'm right, huh? He's gone 'cause his story's out. Shit, he told DiGenero—Scarlese's got him on the payroll as his insurance man. Tony makes sure his guys chase their own tails, not Scarlese's and his IRA buddies'."

"Uh huh." Dermott stared noncommittally.

"And last but not least, you got somebody out there who's gonna do a BA 121 all over again." Silverstein examined each for a reaction, one after the other. "In fifty minutes. That's who Frank's lookin' for. That's who we was lookin' for when Abbott and Costello here showed up at my place. We got one lead—a phone number in the city. 655-9768." Silverstein tapped his forehead. "All you gotta be is smart enough to look it up in the crisscross. Then, send somebody to scope it out. In the meantime, call the airline, or the FAA, or whoever and tell them to make that nine o'clock flight go someplace else." He sat back. "What's it worth to you? If I'm wrong, I look stupid. If I'm right and you don't do nothin', you're gonna look more than stupid. You're gonna have big trouble in your life real fast."

Dermott nodded to one of the agents. "Go look up the number." The one-eyed agent rose. "And tell 'em to bring McCray in." Dermott added.

The door opened and closed and opened again.

Jilian entered, accompanied by two more agents. She sat beside Silverstein. The two stood behind her, along the wall. She spoke to Silverstein. "I'm sorry about the call. They didn't believe me. Barry won't acknowledge who I am. Benedetto's disappeared."

Silverstein waved, dismissing the apology. "No big deal. They don't believe me either."

Jilian turned to Dermott. "Are you out of your mind?"

Dermott spoke to one of the agents, who had just entered. "What's in your files, Matt?"

Matt Einhorn, Deputy Chief of the Counterintelligence Squad, answered. "Tony's gonna have my ass, you know that."

"Yeah." Dermott nodded wearily. "I'm beginning to get the feeling everybody's gonna have somebody's ass before this is over. Just tell me, what did you find?"

"Nothin' about her," Einhorn said, gesturing toward Jilian. "If she's one of theirs, we woulda known. MI5 liaison knows the rules. We sign off on their unilaterals from time to time, but they know they're looking for heartache if they try to blow one by us without approval. Is it possible she's in that category?" Einhorn shrugged and answered his own question. "Anything's possible, I suppose. But the Brits have been straight with us in the past—Christ, we got one hundred and fifty CI guys in the city and they know the odds if they're not. I don't remember 'em ever trying to slip in anybody like RUC, a free-lance cop."

Dermott nodded. "What else?"

Einhorn shifted uncomfortably. "I went through Tony's compartmented file on Scarlese and on the PIRAs."

"The what?" Dermott furrowed his brow.

"The Provisional Wing of the IRA. The *bona fide* Irish bomb throwers. I didn't have time to read it all, but we got paper on Scarlese and the IRA, or at least on the family's relations with 'em."

"You do?" The surprise registered across Silverstein's face. He sat up. "Sayin' what?"

Einhorn addressed Dermott. "Sayin' the relationship is based on drugs. We've seen stuff like this before. I mean we had the zips—the Italian Mafia—workin' with the Medellin cartel in the eighties, right? That was one tie-in that moved stuff into Europe from Colombia. We had Libyans and IRA years ago. Raghead crazies givin' the Irishmen hardware. Small arms, explosives. So now, the wiseguys are gettin' into the act. They're figurin' out they can throw the druggies off the scent by using the IRA to move money and dope. For the IRA, it's an income stream on the side. It keeps 'em in bullets. Tony's onto this Scarlese-IRA lash up." Einhorn followed Dermott's gaze to Silverstein. "What the hell is he sayin' about him?"

Dermott regarded Silverstein malevolently. "You wouldn't believe me if I told you."

Silverstein glared. "If that's what you got in your files, that's the biggest crockashit I heard tonight. That's a fuckin' cover story! Can't you figure that out?''

"Speaking of crocks of shit, I think you filled your share already,'' Dermott said. He rose.

"Look, asshole.'' Silverstein stood. The FBI agent beside him grabbed his arm. Silverstein jerked it away. "Lay off! Whaddya think? I'm gonna smack him? I already busted up enough of you pussies tonight.'' He groped inside his coat. "I gave you a fuckin' phone number. I got a picture here someplace of who it belongs to. You wanna know who it is?'' Silverstein dug in another pocket. "It's a broad working at Kennedy on airplanes—right now!—including the one that crashed and the one that's coming in, in an hour. That's how they get their hands on the airplanes' computers. So they can reprogram 'em. And you know what? She don't exist! Every piece of paper on her is phony. Day before yesterday somebody blew away her boss—in Queens—'cause we was askin' questions. Where the hell is that picture?'' Silverstein tried another inside pocket. "Whaddya gotta have? More bodies fallin outa the sky before you get serious. Here it is!'' He tossed Coleen Murphy's photo on the table.

Jilian gasped. "Oh my God!''

"What?'' Silverstein asked.

Her color had drained. "That's Chris!''

"Chris who? Whaddyatalkin' about? That's supposed to be Coleen Murphy,'' Silverstein said.

"It's Ian's daughter. Chris Barry.''

Dermott laughed. "I love it. Now we're back to Barry. His daughter no less. Maybe we oughta give Bellevue a ring. Have 'em get a rubber room ready. No, better make that two.''

Einhorn spoke. "Barry does have a daughter here. He told me. I think her name is Chris.''

Dermott looked from Einhorn to Jilian, then at the picture.

Einhorn continued. "She works for some computer outfit. She's a software type.''

The door opened. One of the agents returned. He spoke. "We checked the crisscross directory. That phone number—655-9768—belongs to Digicom International.''

"Jesus, I coulda told you that!'' Silverstein said.

The agent continued. "It's a software company. We looked 'em up in the business directory. They're subcontractors on big computer projects. Their specialty is developing security systems for computer software. The kind that keeps hackers from breaking in. They've got contracts with telephone companies, credit card businesses, the government.''

"Who in the government?" Jilian asked.

The agent read from his notes. "NASA, Interior Department, FAA."

Dermott's lingering smile disappeared. "What are they doin' for FAA?" he asked anxiously.

"The business directory says they do the security software for the FAA's new air traffic control system. They're also . . ."

Dermott broke in. "Where's Digicom located?"

The agent answered. "They got offices at the job sites, but this phone's at 44th Street. UN Towers. We rang it to verify. Nobody answers."

Thinking, Dermott licked his lips, looking from one to the other. His eyes shifted from side to side. He pointed at the agent, then the door. "Call the PD. Have 'em meet us there. Get movin'!" He met Silverstein's gaze. "Come on. Let's go."

DiGenero stood in the lobby of the UN Towers, waiting. The night guard had called for the private elevator from his control panel. He watched DiGenero, glancing up repeatedly, obviously uncomfortable with the decision. Despite his FBI shield, the rain-soaked parka and jeans did little to add credibility to his story of urgent, after-hours federal business at Digicom's office.

The elevator arrived, its doors silently opening. DiGenero looked at his watch. 8:20 P.M. The doors closed and the car accelerated, a sudden rush. An oversized numeral flashed, then two, changing with the ascent. Rising, the numbers blurred, then reemerged as the elevator slowed, retarding their progression. He swallowed to clear his ears. 50, 53, 55, 56. The door opened, a soft whoosh. Digicom's name adorned the wall. Light wood on dark. The office suite was directly opposite. A single door. DiGenero knocked. If this didn't work, then what?

He recognized the face from the photograph Silverstein had shown him. The picture of Coleen Murphy was recent, a perfect likeness of the woman who opened the door and smiled. "Yes?"

DiGenero smiled back despite himself. "Ms. Murphy?"

"Yes?"

He produced his badge. "Frank DiGenero, FBI. May I come in?"

She nodded, as if expecting him, and stood aside. "Of course."

DiGenero entered. The vestibule was small, the hall leading away narrow. At its end, he could see them both, reflections in the glass. She left the door open.

"You have me at a loss. What can I do for you?" she asked. The accent was light, barely discernible.

"I'd like to talk with you about your work at Kennedy Airport."

"Kennedy?" She looked puzzled. "Oh!" Her face lit. "You must mean Digicom's contract with the FAA. You see, I design software. I think you want to speak with our contract administrators who handle the . . ."

DiGenero shook his head. "No, I mean *your* work at Kennedy."

She began again. "I'm afraid I don't . . ."

"Flight Services." DiGenero paused. "Am I making myself clear?"

She didn't reply, but closed the door slowly. The smile vanished, a casualty of the clarification. The recognition in her eyes belied her request. "You'll have to explain yourself."

DiGenero pointed toward the windows at the end of the hall. "Why don't we sit down and talk in there?"

She glanced away and back. "I'd prefer here."

"No." DiGenero contradicted.

She shifted, for the first time uncertainly. "If you're not able to explain to me why, Mr. DiGenero, or if there's no warrant, I'd prefer not."

"Let's talk in the other room," he repeated. "Or is there something you don't want me to see?"

"Of course not." She shook her head. "I'm here to finish a project—working late. It is Friday night. If this isn't urgent, I don't intend to spend my life here. If you'll excuse me." She started to open the door, to show him out.

DiGenero slammed it shut. "Let's go in there. Now."

Her eyes flashed. "I don't know who you think you are, but . . ."

"Now!" He gripped her arm and shoved.

Fear, lines quickly sketched, wrote itself across her face. She stepped ahead, walking slowly. He followed.

They entered the office bay. The floor-to-ceiling windows were dark, wet with rain, and at closer proximity, only imperfectly reflecting. DiGenero paused. At the desk a computer screen glowed. Beside it, a radio scanner crackled. The scanner's lights flickered, a regular cycle as the circuitry transversed each segment on the frequency spectrum. Periodically, the lights stopped and a voice—sometimes strong, sometimes weak—filled the room.

"New York Center, United 921. Through 12,000 to 10." An airliner called the air traffic control center on Long Island.

"Roger, United 921. Hold at 10." A controller replied, with instructions.

"Holding at 10, United 921." The pilot acknowledged.

She stood with her back to DiGenero. He drew his automatic. "Why Bellflower?" he asked. "I don't understand what it means."

She turned. Her voice was steeped in contempt. "That's the point, isn't it? There isn't supposed to be any. Code names are meant to conceal, not reveal."

"Turn off the computer," he said.

She glanced over her shoulder, for an instant, uncertain. "No need. It's done."

"Turn it off anyway." DiGenero motioned with the automatic.

"Don't you understand? It doesn't matter!" She crossed her arms defiantly. "On or off, you can't do a thing about what's going to happen."

"Oh yeah? I can blow the goddamn thing away!" DiGenero leveled the pistol.

In the room the sound of the shot deafened, an explosion. A blow struck him. DiGenero's ears rang. Bellflower stared, eyes wide. He could taste the smoke, a thin blue haze, acrid, cloying. DiGenero looked at his pistol. In his hand, it seemed an object just discovered. Dazed, he tried to remember pulling the trigger. Had he fired? He didn't think so. Then, he felt the wetness, like sweat, trickling down the convex of his back. His breath caught just as his legs gave way. On his knees, the trembling began. He turned. Before him, Ian Barry stared down. He lifted one foot and pushed hard on DiGenero's chest, toppling him over. DiGenero rolled onto his back. Barry stepped on his right wrist and bent toward him, wrenching away the automatic. He held his own loosely, its barrel still smoking.

DiGenero tried to breathe, but the gasps were shallow and fast. Anxiety overcame him, a wave, precursor of a groundswell building to panic. He looked left and right, then craned his neck, eying the windows.

"Don't trouble yourself with false hopes," Barry said. "We're the only office on this floor. The building empties by six on Friday nights, so no one's below us. The shot can't be heard outside. Not fifty-six stories up. We're alone. Period."

DiGenero nodded. Polite acknowledgement of a helpful explanation. He concentrated, trying to collect himself. He touched his chest. It was dry. No blood. Barry had only fired once. Therefore, whatever went in, hadn't come out. His back felt warm, sticky below his shoulder blades, the wetness spreading. He pressed his shoulders hard against the floor, trying to staunch the flow. He licked his lips. His mouth was cotton, not sweet. Barry must have aimed down, a trajectory that could have taken the bullet below the lung, missing, or at worst knicking it, but there was no telling yet. From a lung wound, the blood may not have had time to work its way upstream.

Concentrating on his self-diagnosis, DiGenero felt his breathing slow, a temporary calming. The two of them watched him. Barry turned toward Bellflower. "It's almost 8:30," he said.

She had paled, on the verge of sickness but obviously morbidly curious as well.

Barry persisted. "Hadn't you best get to work?"

She nodded, for a moment unsteady on her feet, then took her chair before the computer. She turned up the volume on the scanner. Her voice sounded weak. "I've got to locate him first. At the last call, they were on time, but still too far out. I need to wait until they reach Montauk."

"They know I'm here," DiGenero said. A chill suddenly shook him, a tremor running through his arms and legs.

" 'They'?" Barry asked, a mocking tone. "In the fix you're in, who in the world comprises your 'they'?"

"The Bureau," he said.

"Please." Barry shook his head, admonishing. "You're a wanted man, Mr. DiGenero, and not in the sense you're trying to suggest. If the Bureau knew where you were, they'd have you in a cell while they worked on the specifics of an indictment. We both know that. So let's not grasp for incredible diversions, shall we? I appreciate your effort to entertain, but it's really not necessary."

"And the New York police."

"Hmmm." Barry paused for a moment, thinking. "I doubt it." He smiled. "Don't strain yourself. Even your imagination. Not in your condition."

DiGenero turned his head. Bellflower was listening to the scanner. It crackled.

"Continental 1222, New York Center. Turn right, heading 340, descend to 6,000 and hold." Instructions to another incoming flight from the air traffic control center. Vector and altitude.

The confirmation came back from the aircraft. "Right to 340, 6,000 and hold. Continental 1222."

DiGenero looked at Barry. "I gotta admit, my imagination is deficient in one respect. I can't figure out how you could be a mass murderer."

"He's accusing us of mass murder, love." Barry spoke to Bellflower. "Should I enlighten him?" he asked.

"I don't think they understand, Daddy. Any of them."

"Daddy?" DiGenero's face mirrored a new confusion.

"Let me explain," Barry said.

The scanner crackled. New York's air traffic control center calling again. "United 921, New York Center. Hold 10,000 and turn left to heading 270. You will be on a TRACON Category 3 approach to Runway 13 Right."

The pilot acknowledged the instructions. "Holding 10, left turn to 270. On TRACON Cat 3 approach to Runway 13 Right. United 921. Roger."

The chills brought trembling. DiGenero felt his pulse speed. Shock expanding its effects. He tried to meter his breathing, to establish a rhythm.

Barry stepped closer and peered at him. "Your color's still good. Relax." He bent down and whispered. "I'd finish you, but I don't want to upset her"—he nodded toward Bellflower. "Besides you may be dead by the time we're through. If not, when she's left, I'll put you out of your misery." He straightened and resumed his monologue at normal volume. "As for your question, it's one that deserves to be answered from the beginning, although I'm afraid we don't have the time this evening to do it justice, do we? Perhaps more precisely"—he smiled—"you don't. You see, the British have been murdering the Irish *en masse* for five hundred years. Ulster is all that's left for them to work with, but they're soldiering on with the same dogged determination as ever. It's quite a commentary that their crimes go unremarked simply because the killing is spread over centuries. Eliminate four hundred souls in one fell swoop—a miniscule percentage of what's been done in the name of England's greater glory—and there's such an outcry. There must be some sort of mathematical equation that portrays it." Barry assumed a professorial tone. "Outrage is a function of the sympathy of the beholder as measured in inverse proportion to the extent of carnage over a given period of time." He chuckled. "What say? Does that explain it? Why genocide from Elizabeth I in the sixteenth century to the famine her worthy heirs engineered in the nineteenth, even to the British Army's vaunted hit teams, the ones that officially murder Republicans in the name of law and order, get so little notice today? I mean, you Americans do get excited over Somalis and Yugoslavs, but not the Irish. Strange, isn't it? With so many of them here? Why do you suppose?" He shrugged. "Or perhaps not so strange, if you understand the Americans' Mary Poppins view of things British.

"But I digress. What we're doing here is really quite simple. We've been at this war for some few years, but never with the ability to hurt them. I mean, even the bombings in London a few years ago—the ones in the City—only got their backs up. The fact is, vulnerability doesn't begin at home. Finally we've learned that." Barry pointed with his pistol at the ground, gesturing. "It begins here. Do we expect the Brits to deal with us because an airliner—no, sorry, two airliners—go down? Of course not. We want to change the terms of the game. When our story gets out—on your front pages—it will be remarkably different. Why? The building that burned down is not across town. It's in your neighborhood now. Makes the problem an American one—regrettably, with a few American lives lost. It's not some foreign correspondent reporting from darkest Belfast, but the local beat reporters exploring the 'cause'— whatever it may be—with that wonderfully born-yesterday quality your novitiates have. As if discovering each time for the first time that there's reason on both sides of some faraway, seemingly irrational issue. As if realizing that people bleed, no matter what they die for. After all, isn't that what the Palestinians finally understood in the eighties? The *Intifada*. The uprising on the West Bank? No more masked men on airliners. Just simple villagers with someone else's army on their streets. Brought the story home, didn't it? We don't have quite that opportunity since our uprising is old news. But we can borrow a leaf from the book, can't we? We can bring the story to you. We thought once the Irish here would do that. How wrong we were. Oh, they convinced each other that the cause was just, but as for the rest? After all, they came here, didn't they? The 'paddys' much preferred to put money in envelopes and send them home—to make it all go away with a donation—rather than to get involved."

DiGenero felt himself fading. He struggled to concentrate, like a man overboard amidst flotsam, to find something tangible that would bear his weight. To find anything to grasp and hold onto. He peered up at Barry. From the floor, he looked ten feet tall. "Fuck the politics," DiGenero said. "I mean you, you bastard. How the hell can you murder that many innocent people?"

"Oh. A personal statement is that what you want?" Barry pursed his lips. "How mundane." He stood over DiGenero. "Well, picture this. Father, Irish, emigrated to the north of England—the mines—looking for work after the war. Dead at forty-six. Mother, Irish, family already there, went into the same holes in the ground a generation before. A drunk with nothing to live for, dead five years later. And young Ian, plucky lad, what of him? Education? Private school—your public schools, that is. Decidedly second-class. Career? None at home, so into the army. Intelligence, posted to Ireland, then MI5, recruited for that oh-so-valuable experience. Ah! A future you say, rising above the family's rung on the ladder." Barry snorted derisively. "There's the rub. Not even as a traitor to the cause. I remember the interview after my training was done as if it was yesterday. I was told in no uncertain terms that I was to remain associated with 'the Irish problem'—my niche, a solid position on the 'middle track,' as they put it, for my 'career.'" Barry bent lower over DiGenero. "Have you been keeping score?" he asked. "Let me recapitulate. Second-class, second-tier, second-track. Have the tally?"

DiGenero felt tired and cold. He was breathing deeply, like someone who had run a distance. "A tough life. You're breakin' my heart. So what?" he asked.

Barry's eyes hardened. "Oh yes. I forgot the punchline. Then, they destroyed my son. I didn't mention that my wife is Irish. I met her when I was in the army, stationed in County Armagh. She's still there—across the line though in Dundalk, in the Republic. That's where she raised our children, when I was serving in Ulster." Barry paused. "That's where my son decided—like his sister—that neither intended to be second-class anymore. Special Branch caught him one night, on a crossing, going north from Dundalk. It was his second trip as a courier. I'd spent fifteen years with them at that point. They didn't inform me, or anyone else for that matter that they had him. They knew who he was, but they kept him. When he came home, he was broken. Oh, he can walk and talk, but he's a cripple. Inside. In his mind. He sits in his room and drinks. He's gone." Barry stared down at DiGenero. "You see now, don't you? That's what they did to one of their own. To me. My son hates me. That's what they did to him, even though I'd given my life to their side."

Barry straightened and gestured toward Bellflower. "Her? She was already with them. I'd surmised, even before they took him that night." He smiled. "It's a different generation, it is. What they did to her brother put her over the edge. From sympathy to soldiering. She's the one who made the connection for me. With the General Command."

"I don't get it," DiGenero said.

"Get what?"

"If you're Scarlese's connection to the IRA, why did you stop Benedetto in the hotel?" DiGenero shut his eyes, trying to concentrate. The room spun. "Why didn't you let him kill Jilian and me? Why didn't you get rid of her, even before I showed up, instead of stringing her along?"

Barry raised his eyebrows? "You don't know? An undercover officer like yourself?" He smiled condescendingly. "But then, after all, you are a policeman at heart, aren't you? I suppose I shouldn't jump to too many conclusions. Not for your type." He sighed. "The subtleties do escape. Look, Jilian's a wonderful girl. She truly is. A bit of a bitch, at times, to be sure, but quite competent. For an amateur. Truth be told, I gave her a chance to withdraw gracefully. The newspaper stories. Did you see them?"

"About her and Ferringa? The other day," DiGenero said.

"Precisely. It would have been preferable for all concerned. All she needed to do was recognize the obvious. She'd been blown. Much better for me, you understand, if the operation had folded because of natural causes. Compromised in the press. All impossible for her to foresee, much less forestall. Her chance presence at a Mafia hit or some such thing. If she'd just gone gracefully, it would have suited my interests. Sadly, she didn't exercise proper judgment."

"Amateurs," DiGenero said.

Barry continued. "You must see it from my vantage point. What purpose would have been served if I'd eliminated her? Certainly, she posed risks, but I controlled her communication with Belfast, knew her plans, understood her objectives." Barry smiled. "After all, what better position could I have been in? She was after me, but I knew her every move. If something unfortunate had happened to her, what would have come next? A stink for one thing. She was operating in my territory, MI5's that is. Christ, there would have been hell to pay. For yours truly. And it would have raised other risks."

DiGenero coughed. His blood tasted sugary. "Such as?"

"Such as Stormont—the RUC in Belfast—assigning a successor who just might have been more competent. More difficult to deal with. This shouldn't be too hard even for a policeman to grasp. The devil you know is preferable to one you don't. Makes sense, doesn't it?"

DiGenero nodded. "Okay, so you control Jilian. But what about . . ."

Barry shook his head. "No, no. Listen closely. You control *everything*. That's the point. Take Benedetto. Poor man. I made quite certain he never knew we were on the same side. Just as well, of course. Better for my security. Besides, he isn't a particularly bright chap. But even if he was, it was much more suitable for my purposes to have—well—a division of labor. Compartments, if you will."

"And Scarlese? What does he know?" DiGenero asked.

"Oh. He knows everything"—Barry smiled—"more or less."

"About Jilian? The RUC?" DiGenero pressed.

Barry nodded. "In the end, I told him about her. Not quite the whole truth, I admit. He called me about Jilian right after Sallie Ferringa died —the day she visited him for the first time in Westhampton. I put him off, told him I'd check. I admit, I did shade the truth. As he understands it, in my checking I 'discovered' Benedetto had been dealing with her on the side. I advised him that I'd learned—after much probing in London —that the RUC was running its own operation here, in New York, in touch with Benedetto independent of my 'office.' I told Johnny that I assumed Benedetto had apprised him."

"You son of a bitch," DiGenero said.

"Yes, I'm sure that's what Benedetto would say, too. Johnny wasn't pleased. But each of us has our secrets. After all, Scarlese didn't ask our permission when he used Vito Rocchi to kill your wife. If he hadn't done that, you wouldn't have become such a complication in our lives. We all have our sins to atone for."

"You killed Vito, didn't you?" DiGenero asked.

"Very good! A loose end. Not my preferred choice, but the game is to play on. Don't you see? We're here to do a chore—Bellflower is, I mean —and it's not over tonight. This operation will finish, but there'll be others. We have to protect ourselves. Me especially. After all, I'm quite valuable to the cause. From what better place to run the show than from inside MI5."

The scanner came alive.

"New York Center, BA 125 Heavy. Leaving 18,000 for 12."

Bellflower spoke. "There it t'is. The nine o'clock flight."

The air traffic controller responded. "BA 125 Heavy, hold 12,000 and your heading."

"Roger, will hold 12 and heading. BA 125 Heavy."

DiGenero floated as sensations bore him up from the floor. Above, the fluorescence warmed, no longer indoor lighting but a summer sky. "Where will you . . ." He started to speak, then stopped, choosing instead to abbreviate the thought. "They'll catch you."

Barry disagreed. "I doubt it. You see, this is it. We're finished in just a few minutes. We leave tonight. All they'll find is a computer, a radio, and you. At this point, I don't think you'll have much to say." He nodded toward Bellflower. " 'Coleen Murphy,' our paper creation, will be gone, as if she was ever here."

Bellflower inserted a small data disc and tapped on the keyboard. She spoke. "They're a little behind schedule. A few minutes, that's all."

The computer screen was reflected in the window. With the click of each key, a pinpoint bloomed, black on green, a thread moving left to right, stitch by stitch. The screen blossomed and went blank, then blossomed again. Green to orange to white to green again. The colors entertained him.

"BA 125 Heavy. Descent to 10,000. Turn right to heading 260."

"To 10. Right turn to 260, BA 125 Heavy," the pilot responded.

Fifty-six stories below on 44th Street, the first car in the caravan of the three black Ford four-doors jumped the curb. It bottomed on the sidewalk, then slammed down hard again, careening into the driveway for UN Towers. Lights flashing, the others followed. Jilian and Silverstein were in the third. Four New York police cars waited, scattered at odd angles at the front door. In the lobby, a gaggle of blue suits and plainclothes surrounded the desk. They turned as the FBI agents double-timed through the door.

One of the police motioned to Dermott, who pushed his way forward. "Fifty-sixth floor. The security guard says a guy in a parka and jeans went up fifteen, maybe twenty minutes ago. He showed an FBI badge."

"DiGenero," Silverstein and Jilian said simultaneously.

"The guard doesn't know who else is up there." The cop pointed. "Only that car goes to the floor."

Dermott ran toward the elevator. Jostling, cops, agents, Jilian, and Silverstein piled in.

"BA 125 Heavy. Descend to 8,000. Speed 300 knots. Hold 260. Now handing you over to TRACON for your Category 3 approach." The air traffic controller at New York Center signed off.

"To 8,000. Speed 300. Holding 260 and over to TRACON for a Category 3. BA 125 Heavy."

The keys rattled. Bellflower typed, a steady pace. The screen radiated, a brilliant blue. Words appeared before her. Once again, Bellflower was inside the air traffic control system.

THIS IS THE NEW YORK CENTER'S TRACON IV AIR TRAFFIC CONTROL SYSTEM. YOU NOW HAVE ACCESS TO THE ON-LINE, REAL-TIME FLIGHT MANAGEMENT FUNCTION. SPECIFY FLIGHT CALLSIGN FOR ENTRY OF COMMANDS TO CONTROL AIRCRAFT.

ENTER CALLSIGN:

Bellflower moved the cursor and typed:

BA 125 HEAVY.

TRACON IV responded instantly:

BA 125 HEAVY. STATUS: APPROACHING FINAL VECTOR, JFK RUNWAY 13 LEFT. BA 125 HEAVY FLIGHT PROGRAMMING NOW UNDER YOUR COMMAND.

At floor level, DiGenero saw the power cords running from the computer. One. Or were there two? He squinted, trying to focus. Yes, there was one. Sounds—the keys, the scanner, his own breathing—were distant now, disconnected and disembodied. If he was floating, he could move. If he could move, he could reach. If he could reach, he could grasp. The power cord. All he needed to do was pull. He rolled up on one shoulder and extended his arm.

Barry's shoe struck hard, jamming him back to the floor. "Don't be silly."

Anger welled up. Somewhere in his mind's recesses, DiGenero assessed himself. Odd. Anger at the indignity of being stepped on, while only seconds ago he had placidly accepted the idea that the same man was going to kill him a few minutes from now. "Get your foot off me, asshole." DiGenero grabbed Barry's shoe, trying feebling to wrestle it from his shoulder.

Barry pressed down. "I said, don't!"

The crash came first. The door splintered. Barry pivoted toward the hall. DiGenero held his shoe with both hands like a child playing a game. Barry wrenched, trying to pull away. DiGenero grinned idiotically. His arms wrapped Barry's leg as if the foot was his possession rather than an indignity.

Shouts filled the room. "Drop the weapon! Police!"

Barry twisted. He raised the automatic, trying to aim.

DiGenero could see the first blue suits crouch and fire. The blasts melded together, deafening. DiGenero looked up expectantly. Above him, Barry tipped, leaning backward at an odd angle, like a cartoon figure, standing but canted the wrong way in a stiff breeze. When he fell, DiGenero was disappointed. As if holding on hadn't been enough. As if his own small role couldn't keep Barry upright, no matter how hard he tried. As if he, personally, had let Barry down.

At the computer Bellflower had turned, her face a picture of horror. For an instant, the firing stopped. DiGenero could see the computer screen, its prompt blinking:

ENTER COMMAND:

Suddenly, it became a nova, a green explosion. Sparks and a shower of glass. A few feet away Silverstein, his pistol gripped in both hands, fired again at the smashed terminal. He stopped.

The room was silent save for the scanner.

"BA 125 Heavy, this is TRACON. Descend to 6,000 and turn right to 310. 310 will be your heading for final vector to Kennedy."

The confirmation came back, an English accent. "To 6,000 and right to 310. Will hold as final vector to Kennedy. BA 125 Heavy."

Bellflower stared, uncomprehending. She started to rise, but the first of three policemen wrenched her out of the chair. Limp, like a doll, she staggered. Two others pinioned her arms. She hung between them, quiet. The handcuffs snapped closed. Only then, looking down, did she see Barry. His front was torn open, unkempt and bloodied. Her moan built to a scream as they dragged her past her father's body.

DiGenero felt hands roll him up on one shoulder, then allow him to settle again.

Someone discussed him in the third person. "It's below the left shoulder blade. He's in shock. Lost a lot of blood. Gimme a coat. Cover him."

Walkie-talkies squalked. The world contracted. Feet shuffling. Voices conversed in a miniature stratosphere. He looked left and right. Silverstein swam into view. Or was it someone else? He slipped momentarily below the surface of the pool, then struggled back. Breaking the water, he opened his eyes. Now it was Jilian. Clear for an instant, then dissolving. He was losing buoyancy. He sank, floating down this time. The water interceded, dimming the light. He tried to rise, to break through. Her face shimmered, indistinct above the surface. It was her. He was sure. But was she smiling or crying?

CHAPTER

34

IN THE WEEK before Christmas, the immigration lines at Montreal's Mirabelle International Airport wound together, serpentine queues that expanded and contracted but rarely untangled, even at midnight or six A.M. It was then the charter flights came, filling otherwise vacant terminal gates. For holiday travelers, large families, many poor, however, an overnight journey and predawn arrival mattered little. Hardly an inconvenience if it allowed them to complete a family circle, broken save for a distant voice on the telephone eleven other months of the year.

Amidst the squalling babies and bleary eyes, two men—one elderly, one middle-aged—who had deplaned from the Alitalia charter waited, edging slowly closer to the immigration officers' booths. Well but modestly dressed, they carried the usual assortment of bags and paper satchels, luggage as well as gifts. At the immigration booth, the inspectors barely looked up. Both passports were new, unused, but at this time of year, it was not unusual. During holidays, many from the old country took their first trip to see relatives long since settled in the new world. Without a second glance, the inspectors handed back the documents and turned to the next in line.

After customs, the two men made their way through the throng to the rent-a-car desk. With limited English and no French, they advised that a reservation had been made. The clerk found the slip, printed their forms, examined their international drivers licenses, and handed over the keys and a map. He pointed, directing them to the shuttle bus for the rent-a-car lot.

A hour later, at four A.M., they drove south, following the signs to Route 15. The map and instructions advised it would merge with Interstate 87 at the border, taking them into the United States. In the early morning, a black sky covered them, a dome over a fresh dusting of snow.

Forty miles south of the St. Lawrence River, they turned off at the exit for Napierville. Just beyond the highway, a car waited. A man emerged, watching them pull over behind him. As their window lowered, he bowed respectfully. His breath surrounded them in a white crystal fog. He handed over an envelope, tipped his cap and departed. They opened the envelope, extracting two Canadian passports with the same names and pictures as their new Italian documents. Looking both ways, they made a U-turn and drove back onto the highway, heading for the American border.

Two hours later, forty miles inside the United States, they pulled over again at a gas station, still closed. Darkness shrouded the new morning, but a faint red line graced the eastern sky, hinting at the dawn of one of the year's shortest days. The phone booth stood with two vending machines. The instructions in the envelope had been clear. Call after crossing the border. Use a pay phone. Pay cash.

The older of the two men got out and made his way to the booth. In the foothills of New York State's Adirondack Mountains, the snow was heavier, but a way had been cleared. On his shoes, the powder rose and settled like dust. In the booth, he closed the door and stamped his feet, then picked up the phone, deposited three dollars in change, and dialed. It rang only twice before the voice came on the line.

"Yes?"

"Buongiorno, Vincenzo! We've arrived. I'm calling from the frozen north!" The old man in the booth laughed, his breath a cloud marking his mirth.

"Ah Mario! So good to hear you. I'm grateful you're here. A good trip?"

The man in the booth shrugged. "The most comfortable, no, but under the circumstances, all went well. We will arrive this afternoon?"

"Yes. It's a long drive, but the road is good all the way. You'll be tired, I'm sure. We can meet after you rest."

"No, we'll meet today. We're anxious to see you!" the caller said.

"Of course. If you wish. A late supper so you'll have time to refresh. The restaurant is Formaggi. In Little Italy. Your hotel will arrange a car for you. We have a private room. Is that alright?"

"Certainly." The cold radiated from the ground. The caller stamped his feet again. "At nine P.M.?" he asked.

"That's right. I'll see you then."

In the phone booth, Mario Giordano hung up. It had been over fifty years since he'd last seen Vincenzo DiGenero. Then, both were young men. Aides, assistants to their leaders, the representative of the New York families and Santo Buscetta, the Sicilian Mafia's don of dons, respectively, when they met in Palermo to discuss the uncertain future. To decide how they would manage in the difficult times ahead. Now, over fifty years later, Giordano had succeeded to Buscetta's role. He trudged back to the car and slipped into the passenger seat. Behind the wheel, Felipo Puma, his consigliere, looked at him. "Well?"

Giordano motioned. "I see my old friend Vincenzo at nine o'clock tonight. For supper." He motioned at the road. "Let's drive."

The rental car pulled back on the highway and accelerated, in the darkness, a solitary pair of taillights heading south.

As befitted the host, Vincenzo DiGenero was waiting when his guest arrived. On the first floor, Formaggi was a trattoria, all glass, tables overlooking the street, but on the second, it rose in formality, with two dining rooms, their privacy made more complete by two flights of stairs providing a rear as well as side entrance and exit to the street.

They embraced like friends, pausing only long enough to assess the effect of time on one another before taking their seats and beginning to reminisce. The waiter—the owner—came only when called, allowing them to digress, to wander, to remember without being pressed.

Finally, after an hour, Giordano spoke of his purpose.

"I wouldn't have come—personally, that is—if it wasn't for you, Vincenzo. If it wasn't for what you told us. For me, traveling is complicated. Better I send others." He smiled. "I'm an old man. I make too much work for my people, and accomplish too little when I go myself."

"You've read the newspapers, I trust," DiGenero said.

"With great interest. Your predictions are coming true, I see." Giordano inclined his head, paying wordless compliment.

The old man shrugged. "It's not a difficult future to foretell. For some in this business the publicity would be welcome. After all, as long as there are no penalties, it adds to the aura. The don is seen as powerful, ruthless, eh? For Scarlese, however, the publicity has a price."

"A loss of his hard-won respectability?" Giordano asked. The derision was barely hidden.

Vincenzo DiGenero nodded neutrally. "Still, he is a very smart young man. His position, while hurt by this, also insulates him. After all, there is nothing to tie him personally to this bizarre alliance with the Irish—at any rate, nothing that has fallen into the hands of the law. His men, the ones who were involved, are dead. The other side's are either dead or gone. Those who have evidence can't testify against him personally, but only on the basis of what others have said. Hearsay. And the government itself is reluctant to act. The stories from Washington make that clear."

Giordano raised his eyebrows quizzically. "Reluctant? Why?"

"Who likes to think that a few people with computers could make giant airplanes crash? Without ever literally raising a hand."

"Please. I have to fly home, remember?" Giordano sipped his wine. "We have choices, too."

DiGenero nodded. "You know why I left the life when I did."

"Indeed, I do," Giordano said.

"We had rules. When some decided we would deal in drugs, I chose to go my own way. Many wanted to make an example of me. Perhaps I lived because of my good fortune. But I know that Santa Buscetta's word—and yours—had its part to play. Now, I return the favor. If it was a question of my grandson's wife only, I would not trouble you. Her death at Scarlese's hands is a crime in its own right—and there are other innocents who have died as well—but that isn't my reason. Believe me."

Giordano nodded again. "I do."

"I'm returning the favor."

"I understand fully." Giordano poured more wine. "Our agreement . . ." He put down the bottle. "Maybe I should say, 'their' agreement since it was our superiors who forged it. Anyway, 'the' agreement has worked well. I can't speak for the families here, but on our side we believe there is value received for the taxes we pay. And a reason to maintain our peace. Fifty years ago we forged an understanding on where each of us would operate. We may argue over other things, but not over territory. It's one of the secrets of our success." Giordano leaned back. "We pay our taxes for doing business here. A percentage. The American families do the same in Europe. When times were good here, we were struggling. After the war. But we didn't ask to renegotiate. We made do. Now, we are all doing well"—he raised one hand, palm up —"perhaps some a little better than others, but we share. Under the rules. America for the Americans. Europe for"—he smiled—"the Italians. Anything else? We pay each other for the privilege." He paused. "That is one of our strengths, don't you think?"

"To be sure," DiGenero said.

"It's good to see you after all these years. I appreciate what you have told us. An old friend's counsel only becomes more valuable with time. My thanks." Giordano raised his glass in toast.

Vincenzo DiGenero did the same. "To the rules," he said.

Giordano met his gaze. "To the rules."

The two limousines snaked under Franklin D. Roosevelt Drive and into the narrow parking space abutting the East River Heliport. Rotors still, the charter Jet Ranger waited, a nearby gas turbine generator whining. The ground crew beat their arms against their sides, attempting to ward off the late afternoon chill.

In the first limousine, the driver opened his door and stood, motioning. One of the ground crew detached himself from the others and jogged toward him. The driver shouted over the noise of the auxiliary power unit. "Take Mr. Scarlese's bags and load 'em, willya? He'll be gettin' onboard in a minute." The driver pressed a button. The trunk popped up.

"Close the goddamn door! I'm freezin!" shouted Scarlese to the driver from the backseat. The door slammed shut. Felipo Puma nodded, "Grazie. This is too cold for a Sicilian."

Scarlese smiled. "It's never cold when you're here, Felipo. You bring the warmth of friendship. Please give Don Mario my regards. I know it's difficult for him to get away. Perhaps one day, when the time is right, I can visit him."

Puma smiled. "As his consigliere, I'll tell you that I've counseled him that any time is right when Johnny Scarlese wishes to visit. I know he would say his door is open." He gestured toward the helicopter. "An important man, with important business waiting. The holidays are here. You have obligations. Don't let me keep you."

Scarlese shook his head. "Nonsense. I'm just going to my house in Westhampton for the weekend."

"Well, I'll leave these with you then." Puma passed over two attaché cases. "They cover our annual payment at ten percent from our cocaine interests here and for the money laundering." He smiled. "At the end of the year, for everyone, it is always tax time. We're no exception. For the privilege of doing business on each other's territory, we all must pay. Under the rules." Puma reached into his pocket. "Both attaché cases are locked. Here are the keys."

Scarlese took them. "As always, Felipo. A pleasure. Arrivederci."

The two men climbed out and shook hands. The helicopter's rotors turned. Scarlese lifted the attaché cases and walked quickly to the doorway. Inside, a pair of hands reached out, taking them. Scarlese climbed aboard. The ground attendant slammed the helicopter's door shut. The turbines spun up, igniting with a rush and a whine.

Puma climbed in the second limousine. As in the helicopter, another man waited. "Where is this Westhampton?" Puma asked. He watched the helicopter rise. It backed slightly, the pilot testing the air currents, then turned left, dipping its nose to accelerate over the river.

His companion, an American, spoke. "Out at the end of Long Island. They'll fly down the harbor, then turn east over the south shore. It's over water, all the way."

In the helicopter, Scarlese looked out. Lower Manhattan slipped behind on the right. Heading south, the upper harbor rolled in a heavy chop. They angled past Governor's Island, then the Statue of Liberty. A ferry made for Staten Island. The helicopter gathered speed, pointing toward the Verrazano Narrows Bridge. Squat and sprawling, Brooklyn lay before them.

Scarlese handed the keys over his shoulder to his bodyguard. "Open 'em. Double-check."

Behind him, the bodyguard inserted one key, then the other into the first attaché case. Neither opened the lock. "Somethin's funny," he said.

"What?" Scarlese turned.

The bodyguard repeated the procedure on the second case. "Nothin' opens nothin'."

Scarlese spoke, irritated. "Whaddyatalkin' about? Gimme that!" He took one case and the keys. Scarlese inserted the first and turned to no effect. "What the fuck did that asshole do? Gimme the wrong keys?" He inserted the second. The helicopter bore southeast, following the shoreline. Ahead, the Verrazano Narrows Bridge approached, arching above the straits that divided New York's upper and lower harbor. On the span, headlights moved east and west, a necklace of diamonds.

Seven miles away, the limousine with Felipo Puma maneuvered, backing and turning out of the heliport's parking lot. The American beside him looked at his watch. In his hand, the small box had a single switch and a tiny antenna.

"Well?" Puma asked.

The American nodded. "Time." He flipped the switch.

Johnny Scarlese had just positioned the second attaché case in his lap when the helicopter vanished. From the Verrazano Narrows Bridge, the explosion appeared at first like a celestial decoration, the helicopter's instant incineration at two thousand degrees. A starburst on the eve of night. As it fell, however, the fuel billowed black and soiled. Shards, torn pieces, plummeted, on fire. They twisted and turned, end over end, recognizable for what they were. A tail assembly here. A door or landing skid there. A seatback. Luggage. For those who looked quickly, even parts of bodies, although not Johnny Scarlese's. At the source of the nova, he had completely disappeared.

CHAPTER

35

THE LAST HEAVY SNOW of spring came late in the Salt Lake valley, wet and impermanent under the April sun. It was gone well before midday in the city, although higher to the east in washes and on slopes, remnants clung. In the cemetery, shadows protected the whiteness, an epidermis covering the alien, imported grasses that in turn, hid the gravel and rock, the hillside's natural subcutaneous gray brown.

DiGenero picked his way among the markers. They were set flush in the soil and on their upturned faces the snow melted first. By late afternoon, nearly all had emerged, row after row, a muster of names and dates. He looked back, counting the ranks to orient himself. Where he had stepped the snow had vanished, replaced by grass or gravel. Despite the afternoon hour, his was the only track, a small blemish but conspicuous nonetheless. A random path across orderly files.

Erin's grave stood higher than most, near the edge of the field. When DiGenero reached it, he turned, sharing the view. In the city, the end-of-day exodus massed, arranging itself, block after block. Like an army, the cars advanced in formation, paused at the lights, then advanced again. Units combining, dividing, and recombining, soldiers with well-rehearsed missions, moving into the field. Behind him, where he couldn't see, he knew much the same was true, only in mirror image. A few thousand feet higher, beyond the next ridge line, the skiers descended in afternoon's gold light, albeit in their case all converging at the same point.

DiGenero looked at the small stone marker. His rehabilitation had been slow, a more complete recovery in some categories than others. Inside him the bullet had ricocheted. His shoulder blade and a rib had saved his life, deflecting it into muscle not organ. His therapy had taken nearly three months. To prevent a cripple's healing, they demanded that he twist and turn against the pattern of all natural motion. He knew it was necessary, but he woke every morning dreading the therapist's smile. A cheerful prelude to her necessary sadism.

Inside the Bureau, his administrative hearing came at the halfway point in the hospital's torture. The panel, gray suits and faces, listened for two days, tight-lipped. Coincidentally, their verdict came six weeks later, when the doctors finally declared him recovered. A reprimand, administrative probation, and a four-year review of his on-the-job performance. He didn't care, but at his age, he knew it was the kiss of death for any promotion. Silverstein, too, had been spared. Foley had come from Boston to argue his case before the New York police review board. He had taken creative advantage of the FBI's desire to keep things quiet to convince a Democratic city police commissioner that it was in his interest to follow the lead of a Democratic Attorney General in Washington—for all their sakes.

For a time, DiGenero had read the papers, looking for the story. To his modest surprise, the bureaucracy's hull held against leaks. Territorial claims by the counterintelligence division dictated that the hearing board's chairman throw a classified security blanket over his proceedings. A few of the Bureau's kept press got a background story, producing reasonably balanced, if vague Sunday supplement pieces in one New York and one Washington paper, both speculating about Scarlese's ambitions. Most reporters only bayed and snapped, leaving hungry. They repeated old stories of DiGenero's desire for revenge and speculation that internecine mob wars took Scarlese. The case died without embarrassment. Nothing revealed about either the IRA's penetration of MI5, or more thankfully for the Bureau's seventh floor, an FBI-Mafia connection.

DiGenero had testified twice, both bloodless affairs before special, secret grand juries. At the first session in Washington, he had waited in an anteroom with two British diplomats, who had pointedly ignored him. They came and went with averted eyes, as if it somehow rendered them invisible. The Justice Department attorney told DiGenero afterward that their appearance was a courtesy, not required under conditions of diplomatic immunity, but offered by the British government as "allied cooperation." The attorney suggested that London and Washington had common interests in disposing of Bellflower's case. Despite the claims of United States law, her trial as a terrorist under British statutes carried far heavier penalties as well as an all-but-guaranteed conviction. The two embassy officials had appeared "voluntarily," the attorney said, to explain those facts to the grand jury. As a secret, *in camera* proceeding in Britain, he added, the court could hear intelligence information, making for a considerably stronger case than was possible here. When DiGenero suggested that the secrecy of a British courtroom also kept the FBI, FAA, and others from looking like jackasses, the attorney only cleared his throat.

When he had talked to the second grand jury in New York, he had come early, hoping to find her. He had wandered the courthouse corridors and explored the vacant waiting rooms, irritating the guards who had sealed the floor for security reasons. Finally he had asked. One of the Assistant United States Attorneys told him that the Bureau had kept and questioned Jilian until the week before—a measure of its pique—then quietly sent her home. The phrase would have been "recalled by mutual consent," he said, if she had been a diplomat rather than an illegal. The grand jury proceedings were a formality. Referring to the institutions rather than their inhabitants, "the Justice Department and the White House," he explained pompously, had decided not to indict on the Ward's Island shootings. For diplomatic reasons.

DiGenero watched evening arrive. Lower now, the sun hung in the west, barely touching the horizon. Joining the earth, it cooled, offering only a reflection of itself, long, rose-colored rays shining upward out of the valley. Around Erin's marker the snow crystallized. DiGenero touched the surface with his toe. It was hardening, reverting from its spring afternoon softness to the night's icy crust. A temporary permanence. Spring snow wasn't meant to last, but here and there it still went slowly. Here and there, it took longer for the sun to touch the earth. Here and there, the past season remained, despite the warmth of new days.

DiGenero took the letter from his pocket. It had been addressed to him at the Bureau. Forwarded through his two phony addresses and the Bureau's antiquated cover office in Washington, it had reached him only yesterday. Airmail stationery opened and read several times, the paper was already dog-eared. He unfolded it again. Handwritten, Jilian's message was brief. An invitation to London. When the time was right, she said. She wanted to see him, but it was for him to decide. I trust you to make the right choice, she wrote. With her pen, she had underlined one word: trust.

DiGenero carefully refolded the letter and put it in his pocket. The light was almost gone. Transforming blue to black, the sky was cold but clear. He retraced his steps, descending the hill. Tomorrow, there would be sun again. A chill in the evening, but a little warmer the next day. When the time was right, he thought. When the time was right.